THE TEN THOUSAND

PAUL

KEARNEY

THE TEN THOUSAND

First published 2008 by Solaris
an imprint of BL Publishing
Games Workshop Ltd
Willow Road
Nottingham
NG7 2WS
UK

www.solarisbooks.com

ISBN-13: 978 1 84416 647 3
ISBN-10: 1 84416 647 3

10 9 8 7 6 5 4 3 2 1

A CIP catalogue record for this book is available from the British Library.

Designed & typeset by BL Publishing
Printed and bound in the UK.

For John McLaughlin and Charlotte Bruton

Grateful acknowledgements to:

Mark Newton, Christian Dunn, Patrick St Denis, Darren Turpin and James Kearney. And Marie of course, as always.

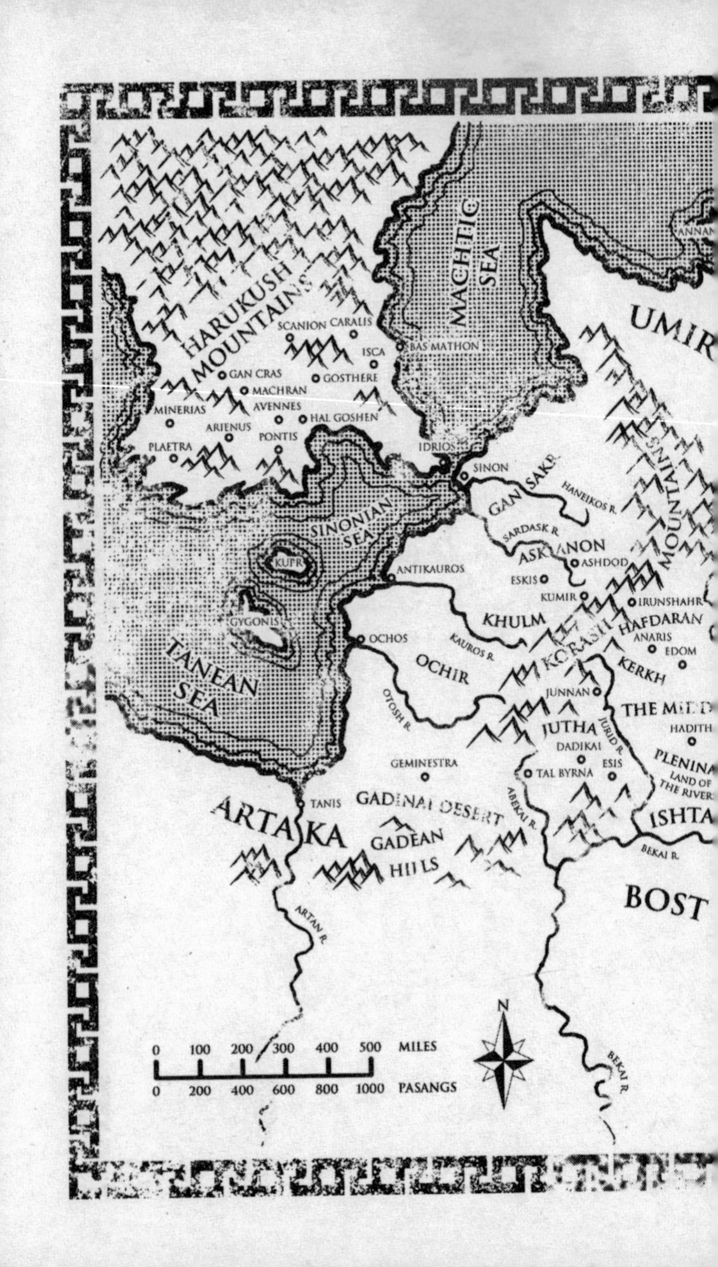
HARUKUSH MOUNTAINS
MACHTIC SEA
UMIR
SCANION
CARALIS
ISCA
BAS MATHON
GAN CRAS
GOSTHERE
MACHRAN
MINERIAS
AVENNES
HAL GOSHEN
ARIENUS
PONTIS
PLAETRA
IDRIOS
SINON
GAN SAKR
HANEIKOS R.
SINONIAN SEA
SARDASK R.
KUPR
ANTIKAUROS
ASHDOD
ESKIS
KUMIR
IRUNSHAHR
GYGONIS
KHULM
HAFDARAN
OCHOS
KAUROS R.
ANARIS
EDOM
TANEAN SEA
OCHIR
KERKH
OTOSH R.
JUNNAN
JUTHA
JURID R.
HADITH
DADIKAI
GEMINESTRA
TAL BYRNA
ESIS
LAND OF THE RIVERS
TANIS
ABEKAI R.
ARTAKA
GADEAN
BEKAI R.
BOST
ARTAN R.
N
0 100 200 300 400 500 MILES
0 200 400 600 800 1000 PASANGS
BEKAI R.

KUF
THE EV-MERIDACH
PADRAN
HONAN
PASTIR R.
ANAMIR MTS
BEKAI R.
UDRUK
CARCHANIS
KAIK
MOUNTAINS
HAMADAN
ASURIAN GATES
ASHUR
ASURIA
BOKOSA
ARAKOSIA
ADRANOS MTS
YUE
MAGRON
OSKUS R.
MEDIS
KOSAN
PANJIR R.
IRGUN
KANDASAR
VIDEHAN GULF

PART ONE

ANTIMONE'S PITY

ONE
THE MEANING OF DEFEAT

By the sea, Rictus had been born, and now it was by the sea that he would die.

He had thrown away his shield and sat on a tussock of yellow marram grass, with the cold grey sand between his toes and a blinding white lace of foam from the incoming tide blazing bright as snow in his eyes.

If he lifted his head there was real snow to be seen also, on the shoulders of Mount Panjaeos to the west. Eternal snow, in whose drifts the god Gaenion had his forge, and had hammered out the hearts of stars.

As good a place as any to make an end.

He felt the blood ooze from his side, a slow promise, a sneer. It made him smile. I know that, he thought. I know these things. The point has been made. A spearhead from Gan Burian has made it.

He still had his sword, such as it was, a cheap, soft-iron bargain he'd picked up more out of a sense of decorum than anything else. Like all men, he knew his real weapon was the spear. The sword was for defeat, for the black end when one could no longer deny it.

And he still had a spear. Eight feet tall, the old, dark wood of the shaft scored now with new scars of white. It had been his father's.

My father. Whose home, whose life I have now thrown onto the scales.

Again, he smiled under the heavy helmet of bronze. But it was not a smile. It was the final baring of teeth that the bayed animal must show.

And so they found him, three winded foot-soldiers of Gan Burian who had also cast aside their shields, but to aid pursuit, not flight. These too had their spears, every point bloodied, and in their eyes there was that glaze which comes to men from wine, and sex, and killing. They gave a shout as they sighted him, this bowed figure by the shore of the sea, his tunic bloody at the side. And now they darted a change of course as swiftly as fish in shoal, teeth bared. Happy. As happy as man can be. For what can make man happier than the annihilation of his enemy when all is at risk: his woman, his child, the place he calls a home? The men of Gan Burian had defended their city from attack in a wrenched, bowel-draining fight which had lasted all of the morning. They had won. They had won, and now, how bright the sky seemed, and how good did the fine salt air off the sea taste in their mouths. The sweetest of all dishes. And now, they would savour a little more of it.

* * *

Rictus saw them come, their feet raising little surfs of sand as they bounded across the dunes towards him. He stood up, ignoring the pain as he had been taught. He filled his lungs with that good, cold air, that salt, that slake of earth. Closing his eyes, he smiled a third time; for himself. For the memory of the sea, for the smell.

Lord, in thy glory and thy goodness, send worthy men to kill me.

He leaned on the spear a little, digging the spiked butt into the sand, sinking it past the gleam of the bronze. He waited, not even bothering to touch the leather scabbard wherein lay his contemptible little sword. Past his head there broke a black and white formation, a piping squadron of birds. Oyster catchers, frightened off the flats of sand by the men who approached. He was as aware of their wingbeats as he was of the slow pulse in his side. Death's abacus, the beads knocking home ever slower. A moment of strange bliss, of knowing that all things were the same, or at least could be the same. The drunken clarity of pain, and fearlessness. It was something—it truly was something—not to be afraid, at this moment.

And they were here, right before him. He was startled, as he had not been startled all day, not even when the shield-lines met. He had been prepared for that crash all his life, had expected it, had wanted it to be even grander than it had been. This was different. It was seeing other ordinary men with his murder in their eyes. Not anonymous, but as personal as could be. It shook him a little, and that uncertainty translated into a white-cold flood of adrenaline through each of his nerves. He stood, blinked, forgot the pain and pulse of his life-blood as it trickled out of him. He was the beast at bay, about to snarl at the hunters.

They spread about him; ordinary men who had killed their fellows and found it quite good. A sport almost. They had come uncertain and apprehensive to battle, and had prevailed. With the breaking of their enemy's line they had found themselves heroes, part of what might one day be history. Later they would reform into their phalanxes and would make the light-hearted march to the city of their foes, and would there become conquerors. This—this killing—was no more than a garnish on the dish.

Rictus knew this. He did not hate these men who had come to kill him, as he was quite certain they did not hate him. They did not know that he was an only son, that he loved his father with a fierce, never-to-be-spoken adulation. That he would die to save the least of his family's dogs. They did not know that he loved the sight and smell and sound of the sea as another man might love to let gold coin trickle through his fingers. Rictus was a bronze mask to them. He would die, and they would brag to their children of it.

This is life, the way things work. All these things, Rictus knew. But he had been taught well, so he took his father's spear in both fists and ignored the pain and started thinking about how to kill these smiling men who had come about him.

* * *

With a short, yipping yell, the first bounced in to attack, a high-coloured face with a black beard framing it, and eyes as bright as frosted stones. He held his spear at the midpoint of the shaft, and thrust it at Rictus's collarbone.

Rictus had grasped his own weapon at the balance-point, a short arm's length from the butt, and thus had a longer reach. Two-handed, he clapped aside the point of his attacker's spear and then reversed the grip of his own—all in a movement which was as beautiful and fluid as the steps of a dance. As his own spear spun, it made the other two men jump backwards, away from the wicked edge of the aichme, the spearhead. Two-handed again, he lunged with the sauroter, the lizard-sticker they called it, a four-sided spike of bronze which was the aichme's counterweight. It struck the black-bearded man to the left of his nose, punched through the thin bone there for the depth of a handspan before Rictus jerked it out. The man staggered backwards like a drunkard, blinking slowly. His hand came up to his face, and then he sat down hard on the sand as the blood came spurting from the square-sided hole in it, steam rising in the cold air.

Another of the three screamed at this, raised his spear over his shoulder and charged. Rictus had time only to throw himself aside and went sprawling, his spear levered out of his grasp as the aichme plunged in sand. As he got up the third man seemed to rouse himself also, and stumped into the fight unwillingly. He was older, a greybeard, but there was a black calm about his eyes. He moved in as though thinking about something else.

Rictus rolled as the second man's spear stabbed the sand at his side. He got his arm about it and clamped the spearhead against his injured ribs, the pain scarcely felt. Then he kicked up with both feet and one heel dunted his attacker in the groin. The man's cheeks filled. Rictus came up off the ground at him, climbing up the spear-shaft, and butted him in the face with all the strength left in his torso. The bronze of his helmet rang, and he was glad of it for the first time that day. The man fell full length on his back and coiled feebly in on himself and the red ruin of his face.

A moment of triumph, so brief it would not even be recalled later. Then something seized the horsehair crest of Rictus's helm from behind.

He had forgotten about the third man, had lost him in his brief, bloody map of things.

The crest-box grated against bronze, but the pins held. A foot thumped into the hollow of Rictus's knee. He tumbled backwards, his helm askew so that he was blinded. His feet furrowed the sand uselessly. Someone stood on his chest, and there was a grating noise, metal on metal, as a spearpoint lifted the chin of his helm, slicing open his lower lip as it did so.

The older man, the greybeard. He had hair like a sheep's pelt on his head and his eyes were dark as sloes. He wore the old-fashioned felt tunic of the inner mountains, sleeveless, ending above the knee. His limbs were brown and knotted with blue veins over the bunched muscles. One-handed, he raised the aichme of his spear until it rested on Rictus's throat and pricked blood there.

When Rictus swallowed the keen spearpoint etched fire on his throat. He felt the blood flowing more freely from his side now, darkening the sand under him. It was trickling down his chin also. He was leaking at the seams. He breathed out, relaxing. It was done. It was over, and he had done something to make them remember him by. He looked up at the washed-pale blue of the sky, the fading of the year's glory, and the oyster catchers came piping back into it to resume their places on the strand. He followed their flight as far as he could with his eyes.

The older man did also, the spear as steady in his fist as if it had been planted in stone. Behind him, his two companions were thrashing in the sand, struggling and hooting with sounds that seemed barely those made by men. He glanced at them, and there was naked contempt in his face. Then he stabbed his spear in the sand, bent, his foot pushing the air out of Rictus's lungs, and yanked the helm clear off the younger man's head. He looked at him, nodded, then tossed it aside. The sword followed, flicked through the air like a broken child's plaything.

"You lie there," he said. "You try to get up, and I finish you."

Rictus nodded, astonished.

The man poked his finger into the bloody lacerated hole in Rictus's side, and Rictus stiffened, baring blood-slimed teeth. The man grinned, his own teeth square and yellow, like those of a horse. "No air. No bubbles. You will live, maybe." His eyes sharpened, danced like black beads. "Maybe." He see-sawed his bloody hand in the air, then slapped Rictus across the face. A blunt forefinger with a filthy, over-long nail tapped Rictus on the forehead. "Stay here." Then he straightened, using his spear to ease upright again and grimacing, like a man who has been remonstrating with a child.

"Ogio! Demas! Are you men or women? You keen like girls." He spat.

The hooting noises subsided. The two other men helped each other to their feet and came staggering over, feet dragging in the sand. One of them drew a knife from his belt, a long, wicked, sliver of iron. "I take this one," he said in a gargled tone that was horrible to hear. He was the one with the hole in his face. It jetted blood with every word as if to lend them emphasis.

"You tried. You failed. He is mine now," the older man said coldly.

"Remion, you see what he has done to me? I am like to die now."

"You will not die, if you keep it clean and don't stick your fingers in it. I've seen men live with worse." Remion spat again. "Better men than you."

"Then kill him yourself!"

"I'll do as I please, you rat's cunt, whatever you say. Now see to Demas. He needs his nose straightened."

Some moment had passed, some kind of unspoken compact had been made. There would be no more fighting now. The time which had been—that time of license and slaughter and free-flowing violence—that had gone now, and the normal rules of life which men lived their lives by were slipping back into place. Rictus sat up, feeling it, but hardly able to put the knowledge into rational thought. They would not kill him now, and he would not hurt them either. They were all civilized men again.

The older man, Remion, was cutting strips off the hem of his tunic, but the felt frayed under his knife. He cursed, then swivelled to regard Rictus. "Off with that shirt, boy, I need something to plug this man's face."

Rictus hesitated, and in that second the eyes of all three of the other men fastened on him. He drew his tunic over his head, gasping at the pain in his side, and tossed it to Remion. All he had on now were his sandals and a linen breechclout. The wind raised gooseflesh off his limbs. He clamped his elbow to his injured side. The blood was slowing. He spat scarlet into the sand.

Remion ripped the tunic to strips, discarding the blood-soaked part under the armpit. His two companions uttered hoarse, low growling sounds as he saw to their hurts. There was a crack as he levered Demas's nose back into place, and the man screamed and clouted him on the side of the head. He took it in good part, shoving Demas on his back in the sand and laughing. He slapped Ogio's hand away from his punctured face and stared intently at the bloody hole, wiping around it.

"When you get back, have the physician stitch that hole closed. What's behind it will heal in time by itself. For now, let it bleed free; let it bleed the dirt out. A sauroter spike is a filthy thing to have had in you." He clapped Ogio on the arm, grinning his yellow grin, then rose and padded over to Rictus. In his hand were the rags of the tunic. He tossed them into Rictus's lap. "Bind yourself up. You're likely to bleed to death else."

Rictus looked into his dark eyes. "Why do you not kill me?"

Remion frowned. "Shut your mouth."

Rictus wondered if he were to die anyway. On the battlefield his wound had seemed a thing of little account. He could still move, run, thrust a spear and behave as a man ought. But now that the bloodied press of the phalanx had been left behind it all seemed so much worse. He looked at the men he had wounded and felt sick at their blood—he who had been around blood and killing all his life.

You want to eat; then something must have its throat wrung, his father had said. *Nothing can be had for nothing. When life gives you something, something else must be taken in return. That is the merest logic.*

"Why do you not kill me?" Rictus asked again. Bewildered.

The man called Remion glared at him and raised his spear as if to stab. Rictus did not flinch. He was past that, still in the place where his own life did not matter. He looked up with wide eyes. Curiosity, resignation. No fear.

"I had a son," Remion said at last, his face bunched as tight as his blue-veined bicep. His eyes were black.

They broke the fittings off his father's spear, leaving an arm's span of splintered wood, and with this they made a yoke, binding Rictus's hands before him and then sliding the shaft through that space between spine and elbows. Rictus did not resist. He had been brought up to believe in victory and death. He did not know quite what to make of defeat, and thus stood like a pole-axed ox as they bound him—not with spite—but like tired men who are keen to get home. Hurt men. The blood-smell rose even over the stink of shit on Broken-nose's thighs.

They picked up the aichme and sauroter. Remi stowed them in the hollow of his tunic. No doubt one day he would burn them out and reset them in virgin wood. Good spear fittings were more valuable than gold. They would see service again. The horsehair-crested helm was claimed by the man with the hole in his face, Ogio. Already, his face was swelling up like an apple, shiny and pink.

Finally, some of Rictus's numbness gnawed through.

"My father lives in the green glen past—"

"Your father is carrion now, boy," Remion said. And there was even a kind of pity in his face as he said it.

Rictus twisted, eyes wide, and Broken-nose beat the flat of his spear-shaft into his nape. A white detonation. Rictus fell to his knees, opening one up like liver. "Please," he said. "Please don't—"

Again, he was beaten. First the spear-shaft, and then a fist clumping again and again into the top of his spine. A childish punching, fuelled by rage more than the knowledge of where a fist does damage. He rode it out, forehead on the sand, blinking furiously and trying to make his thoughts come in some kind of order.

"The bastard begs!"

I didn't beg, he thought. At least, not for me. For my father, I will beg. For my father.

He twisted his head, still pounded, and caught Remion's eye.

"Please."

Remion understood perfectly. Rictus knew that. In these few, bloody minutes he had come to know the older man well.

No, Remion mouthed. His face was grey. In that instant, Rictus knew that he had seen all this before. Every permutation of this stupid little dance had already printed its steps in the older man's memory. The dance was as old as Hell itself.

Something else his father had said: *Do not believe that men reveal themselves only in defeat. Victory tugs the veil aside also.*

Goddess of the Veil; bitter, black Antimone, whose real name must never be spoken. Now she smiles. Now she hovers here about these dunes, dark wings flickering.

The black side to life. Pride, hate, fear. Not evil—that is something else. Antimone merely watches what we do to ourselves and each other. Her tears, it is said, water every battlefield, every sundered marriage-bed. She is un-luck, the ruin of life. But only because she is there when it happens.

The deeds, the atrocities—those we do to ourselves.

TWO
A LONG DAY'S TROUBLE

"We are late to the party, my friends," Remion said.

Dusk was coming on, and a bitter wind was beating around the pines on the hillsides. Rictus's arms were numb from the elbow down, and when he looked at his hands he saw they were swollen and blue. He sank to his knees, unable to look at the valley below.

Broken-nose yanked his head up by the hair. "Watch this, boy. See what happens when you go about starting wars. This is how it ends."

There was a city in the valley, a long, low cluster of stone-built houses with clay-tiled roofs. Rictus had made tiles like that on his father's farm. One shaped the mud upon the top of one's thigh.

For perhaps two pasangs, the streets ran in clumps and ribbons, with a scattering of pine-shadowed lots among them. Here and there the marble of a shrine blinked white. The theatre where Rictus had seen Sarenias performed rose inviolate, head and shoulders above the swallow's-nest alleyways. And surrounding all, the very symbol of the city's integrity, was an undulating stone wall two spear-lengths high. There were three gates visible from this direction alone, and into each ran the brown mud of a road. A hill rose up at one end of this sprawling metropolis, one flank a sheer crag. Upon this a citadel had been built with a pair of tall towers within. There was a gatehouse, black with age, and the gleam of bronze on the ramparts.

And people, people everywhere.

The sound of the city's agony carried up into the hills. A dull roar, a swallowing up of all individual voice, so that it seemed the sound was not made by men and women and children, but was the torment of the city itself. It rose with the smoke, which now began to smart Rictus's eyes. Plumes of black rose in ribands and banners within the circuit of the walls. Crowds clogged the streets, and in the midst of the roar one could now make out the clangour of metal on metal. At every gate, mobs of men were pressing inwards with spears held aloft, bearing the hollow-bowled shields of the Macht warrior class. There were devices on those shields, a city badge.

Rictus looked to his side in the gathering darkness, at Remion. His captors had retrieved their cached panoplies on the way here. White on scarlet, there was painted upon Remion's shield the sigil *gabios*, first letter of his city's name. Almost all the shields below had such devices.

"Isca dies at last," Remion said. "Well, it has been a long time coming, and you folk have been a long time asking for it."

"You thought you were better than us," Broken-nose sneered. "The mighty Iscans, peerless among all the Macht. Now we will fuck your women and slaughter your old and make slaves of your vaunted warriors. What have you to say to that, Iscan?" He punched Rictus in the side of the head.

Rictus staggered, straightened, and slowly rose to his feet. He stared at the death of his city, the red bloom of its fall now beginning to light the darkening sky. Such things happened perhaps once in a generation. He had merely been unlucky, he and all his comrades.

"I say," he said quietly, "that it took not one, nor two, but three cities in alliance to bring us to this. Without the men of Bas Mathon, and Caralis, you would have been chased clear off the field."

"*Bastard*!" and Broken-nose raised his spear. Remion took one step forward, so that he was between them. His eyes did not shift from the sights in the valley below. "The boy speaks the truth," he said. "The Iscans bested us. Had it not been for the arrival of our allies, it would be Gan Burian burning now."

Ogio, he of the swollen, punctured face, spoke up. "The Iscans began it. They reap what they have sown."

"Yes," Remion said. "They have earned this." He turned to regard Rictus squarely. "You Iscans put yourselves apart, drilled like mercenaries, made war in the same way others planted the vine and the olive. You made it your business, and became better at it than we. But you forgot something." Remion leaned closer, so that Rictus was washed by the garlic of his breath. "We are all the same, in the end, all of us. In this world, there are the Kufr, and the Macht. You and I are of the same blood, with the same iron in our veins. We are brothers in our flesh. But forgetting this, you chose to take war—which is a natural thing—to an unnatural end. You sought to enslave my city."

He straightened. "The extinction of a city is a sin in the eyes of God. A blasphemy. We will be forgiven for it only because it was forced upon us. Look upon Isca, boy. This is God's punishment for your crime. For seeking to make slaves of your own people."

Up into the sky the red light of the sack reached, vying with the sunset, merging with it so that it seemed to be all one, the burning city, the dying day, the loom of the white mountains all around, stark peaks blackening with shadow. The end of the world, it seemed. And for Rictus, it was. The end of the life he had known before. For a moment, he was a boy indeed, and he had to blink his stinging eyes to keep the tears from falling.

Broken-nose hoisted his shield up so that the hollow of it rested on his shoulder. "I'm off. If we don't shift ourselves the prettiest women will all be taken." He grinned, for a moment becoming almost a likeable man, someone who would stand by his friends, share his wine. "Come, Remion; leave that big ox harnessed here for the wolves. What say you to a scarlet night? We'll drink each cup to the lees, and rest our heads on something softer than this frozen ground."

Remion smiled. "You go on, you and Ogio. I will catch you up presently. I have one last business to attend to."

"You want help?" Ogio asked. His misshapen face leered with hatred as he peered at Rictus.

"Go get the carnifex to look at that hole," Remion said. "I can attend to this on my own."

The other two Burians looked at one another and shrugged. They set off, sandals pattering on the cold ground, Rictus's helm dangling from one of their belts. Down the hillside, following the hardened mud of the road, into the roar and glow of the valley below where they would find recompense for their long day's trouble.

With a sigh, Remion set down the heavy bronze-faced shield, then laid his spear on the ground. His helm, a light, leather bowl, he left dangling at his waist. From the look of it, he had eaten broth out of it that morning. He took his knife and thumbed the edge.

Rictus raised his head, exposing his throat.

"Don't be a damned fool," Remion snapped. He cut the bindings from Rictus's wrists, and slid the spear-shaft free of his elbows. Rictus gasped with pain. His hands flooded with fire. He sat back on the ground, air whistling through his teeth, white agony, a feeling to match the sights of the evening.

They sat side by side, the grizzled veteran and the

big-boned youth, and watched the dramas below.

"I remember Arienus, when it went up, twenty, twenty-five years ago," Remion said. "I was a fighting man then, selling my spear for a living, with mercenary scarlet on my back instead of farmer's felt. I got two women out of the sack and some coin, a horse, and a mule. I thought I had climbed the pig's back." He smiled. Isca's burning lit tiny yellow worms in his eyes.

"I married one of the girls; the other I gave to my brother. The horse bought me citizenship and a *taenon* of hill-land. I became a Burian, put aside the red cloak. I had—I had a son, daughters. The blessings of life. I had heart's desire."

He turned to Rictus, his face as hard and set as something hewn out of stone. "My son died at the Hienian River battle, four years back. You killed him, you Iscans." He looked back at Isca below. It seemed that the spread of the fires was being stymied. Beetled crowds packed the streets still, but now there were chains of men and women leading from the city wells, passing buckets and cauldrons from hand to hand, fighting the flames. Only up around the citadel did it seem that fighting went on. But still, from the houses in the untouched districts, the screams and shouts rose, wails of women outraged, children terrified, men dying in fury and fear that they might not see what was to become of those they loved.

"I fought today because if I had not I would have lost the right to be a citizen of Gan Burian," Remion said. "We are Macht, all of us. In the world beyond the mountains I have heard that the Kufr tell tales of our savagery, our prowess on the battlefield. But among ourselves, we are only men. And if we cannot treat one another as men, then we are no better than Kufr ourselves."

Rictus was clenching and unclenching his bulbous fists. He could not say why, but Remion made him feel ashamed, like a child admonished by a patient father.

"Am I your slave?" he asked.

Remion glared at him. "Are you cloth-eared, or merely stupid? Take yourself away from here. In a few days' time Isca will be no more. We will raze the walls and sow the ground with salt. You are *ostrakr*, boy; cityless. You must find yourself another way to get on in the world."

The wind picked up. It battered the pines about their heads and made the branches thrash like black wings grasping at the sunset. Remion looked up.

"Antimone is here," he said. "She has put aside her veil."

Rictus shivered. The cold from the ground ate into his buttocks. The wound in his side was a half-remembered throb. He thought of his father, of Vasio, the old steward who had helped them on the land. Zori, his wife, a nut-brown smiling woman whose breast Rictus had suckled at after his own mother had died having him. What were they now; carrion?

"There will be stragglers by the hundred out in the hills, looting every farmstead they come across," Remion said, as if he had caught the drift of the younger man's yearning. "And they will be the worst of us, the shirkers who kept to the rear of the battle line. They catch you, and you will not see morning. They'll rape you twice; once with their cocks, and once with an aichme. I've seen it. Do not go back north. Go south, to the capital. Once you're healed, that broad back of yours will earn your keep in Machran."

He rose to his feet with a low groan and hoisted shield and spear again. "There's weapons aplenty lying about the hills, in dead men's hands. Arm yourself, but take nothing heavy. No point one man alone lugging a battle line shield about. Look for javelins, a good knife." Remion paused, jaw working angrily. "Listen to me. I'm become someone's mother. Get yourself away, Iscan. Find yourself a life to live."

"It happened to you," Rictus said, through chattering teeth.

"What?"

"Your city was destroyed too. What was its name?"

"You're a persistent whelp, I'll give you that." Remion lifted his head, peered up at the first of the stars. "I was of Minerias once. They had a war with Plaetra, and lost. A bad slaughter. There were not enough men left to man the walls." He blinked rapidly, eyes fixed on something beyond the cold starlight.

"I was nine years old."

Without another word, he began to tramp down the hillside towards Isca, spear on one shoulder, shield on the other, the leather helmet butting against the shield rim with every step, like a dull and tired bell. Rictus watched him go, following the dogged shadow he became until he was lost in the press and mob of men about the gates.

Alone. Cityless. *Ostrakr*. Men who were exiled from their city for a crime sometimes chose suicide rather than wander the earth without citizenship. To the Macht, the city was light and life and humanity. Outside, there was only this: the black pines and the empty sky, the world of the Kufr. A world that was alien.

Rictus beat his fists on his frozen thighs and lurched to his feet. Searching the sky he found, as his father had taught him, the bright star that was Gaenion's Pointer. If he followed it, he would be going north. Back to his home.

That first night became an exercise in finding the dead and avoiding the living. As darkness drew on it became easier to stay clear of the marauding patrols which cast about the country like hounds on the scent of a hare. Most of them carried lit torches and were loud as partygoers. Their comings and goings were marked by the shriek of women, the bubbling death-cries of desperate men, cornered and finished off as part of the night's sport. The hills were full of these torch-bearing revellers, until it seemed to Rictus that there were more of them on the hunt amid the pine forests and crags around Isca than had faced him in line upon the battlefield.

The dead were less easily found. They were stumbled across in the lightless shadow below the trees. Rictus tripped over a bank of them, and for an instant set his hand on the cold mask of a man's face. He sprang away with a cry that set the wound in his side bleeding again. By and large the dead had been stripped of everything, sometimes even clothing. They lay pale and hardening in the cold. Out of the dark, packs of vorine had already begun to gather about them, the grey-maned scavengers of the hills.

A healthy man, on his feet, alert and rested, need not fear the vorine, but a man wounded and reeking of blood, staggering with tiredness—he drew their interest. When they circled him, green eyes blinking in the dark, they snarled their confidence at Rictus, and he snarled back at them, as much a beast as they. Stones, sticks, bravado—he beat them away with these until they went seeking less lively prey.

He stripped a corpse of a long-sleeved chiton, not minding the blood that stiffened it. The dead man lay on top of a broken spear, an aichme with some three feet of shaft still set in it. With these on his back and in his fist, Rictus shivered less. The vorine could smell the bronze, and left him alone. The torchlit patrols inspired anger now as well as fear, and in his head Rictus fantasised about surprising them at their barbarous work, the stump of spear working scarlet wonders in his hand. The fantasy hovered in his mind for pasangs, until he saw it for what it was; a glimmer from the far side of Antimone's Veil. He put it out of his head then, and concentrated on the track before him, that paleness under the stars that ran between the midnight dark of the trees.

One patrol passed him as he lay pressed into the fragrant pine-needles at the side of the track. A dozen men perhaps, they bore the light shields of second-line troops: wicker peltas faced with hide. The *mirian* sigil was splashed in yellow paint across them. These were men of the coastal city, Bas Mathon. Rictus had been there many times with his father; for all that it was eighty pasangs away to the east. He remembered now the gulls screaming over the wharves, the high-prowed fishing smacks, the baskets of silverfin and horrin, bright as spearheads as they were hauled up on the quays. Summer sunlight, a picture from another age. He silently thanked the goddess for granting him the memory.

The men were drinking barley-spirit from leather skins, pressing the bulging bags until the liquid squirted high in the air, and then fighting and laughing like children to have their mouth under as it descended. In their midst two women limped barefoot and naked, heads down and hands bound before them. From the bruises which marked them, they had been captured quite early in the day. One had blood painted all down her inner thighs, and breasts that had only begun to bud. Hardly a woman at all.

They passed by like some twisted revel of the wine-god, lacking only pipe-song to complete the image. Rictus lay a long time in the dark when they had gone, letting the shadow bleed back into his eyes after the dazzling torchlight, seeing beyond the darkness the hopeless face of the young girl, eyes blank as those of a slaughtered lamb. Her name was Edrin. She came from the farm next to his father's. He had played with her as a child, he five years older, carrying her on his back.

It was the middle part of the night before Rictus stood once more at the lip of his father's glen. *Andunnon*, this place was called; the quiet water. It was brighter now. Rictus looked up to see that both moons were rising above the trees. Great Phobos, the Moon of Fear, and fiery Haukos, Moon of Hope. He bowed to them, as all men must, and then set off down the hillside to where the river glittered amid the pastures in the bottom of the glen.

He could not so much as stub a toe on this track, even in the dark, so well did he know it. The smells of wild garlic from the edge of the woods, the thyme in the rocks, the good loam underfoot; all these were as familiar to him as the beat of his own heart. He allowed himself to hope for the first time since the battle line had broken that morning. Perhaps this place had been passed by. Perhaps his life was not yet shipwrecked beyond hope. Something could be salvaged. Something—

The smell told him. Acrid and strange, it drifted all through the valley bottom. There had been a burning here. It was not woodsmoke, but heavier, blacker. Rictus's pace slowed. He stopped altogether for a few seconds, then forced himself on. Above him the cold face of Phobos rose higher in the night sky, as if wishing to light his way.

Rictus had been a late child, his father already a grey-templed veteran when he had sired him—much like Remion, now he came to think of it. His mother had been a wild hill-girl from one of the goatherder tribes further north. She had been given to his father by a hill-chief in payment for service in war, and he had made of her not a slave, but a wife, because he had been that kind of man.

Perhaps the mountain-blood, the nomad-spirit, was too fine and bright to be chained to a life of the soil. There had been children—two girls—but both had died of the river-fever before they had so much as cut a tooth. Over the years, Rictus had wondered about these pair, these dead siblings who had not even had a chance to acquire personality. He would have liked sisters, company of his own age growing up.

But it was as well, now, that they had died when they did.

Rictus had come along a scant six months after their deaths, a brawny red-faced fighting child with a thick shock of bronze-coloured hair and his mother's grey eyes. He had not been born here at the farm. His father had taken his pregnant young wife to the coast, to one of the fishing villages south of Bas Mathon. He would have no more children carried off by river-fever. There, in the clean salt air, Rictus had entered the world with the waves of the Machtic Sea crashing fifty paces away.

Whatever strength his mother had given to him had been taken out of herself; she had delivered him squatting over a blanket with Zori clucking beside her, and then Rictus's father had carried her to his rented bed so she could bleed to death in comfort. Her ashes had been brought back from the shores of the sea and scattered in the woods overlooking the farm, as those of her dead babes had been before her. Rictus had never been told her name. He wondered if she watched him now. He wondered if his father walked beside her, his arms filled with his smiling daughters.

They had burned the farm, driven off the stock. The longhouse was a gutted, smoking ruin open to the sky. Rictus shuffled to the main door, and as he had expected, most of the bodies lay there. They had fought until the burning thatch came down around them. His father he recognised by the two missing fingers on his spear-hand. He used to call them war's dowry. Were it not for that old wound he would have been in the battle line today beside his son, fighting for his city as every free citizen must. The council had exempted him, because he had given such good service in the past. He had been a rimarch, a file-closer, in his younger days. In the phalanx the best men were placed at the front and the rear of the files, to keep the fainter hearts in the line and lead them into the *othismos*, the hand-to-hand cataclysm that was the heart of all civilized warfare.

Beside Rictus's father lay Vasio, his bald pate the only part of him which was not burnt black; he must have been wearing his old iron helm, but it was gone now. And Lorynx, his father's favourite hound; he lay at his master's feet with his flesh carved to ribbons and the fur seared from his skin. They had all died shoulder to shoulder. Scanning the ground about the house in the bright moonlight, Rictus counted eight separate gouts of blood that had blackened the beaten earth of the yard and now were beginning to glister with frost. A good accounting.

His eyes stung. The burning had kept the

vorine from the bodies, but they would soon regain their courage. Things must be done right; his father would have it no other way. Rictus dropped his broken spear and with one hand he ripped the neck of his looted chiton. Eyes open wide he stared up at Phobos and Haukos and began to croon the low, slow lament for the dead, the Paean, part of the ancient heritage of the Macht as a single people. Men sang it on the death of their kin and they sang it going into battle, the beat of it keeping their feet in step with one another. Rictus had sung it only that morning, heart bursting with pride as the Iscan phalanx had advanced to its doom.

He gathered the bodies together, fighting the urge to retch as the blackened flesh came off in his hands, the white bone laid bare as a carved joint. Zori he found beside the central hearth of the longhouse, beneath a pile of smouldering thatch. She had dressed in her best for the end, and had not been touched by the invaders. Asking her forgiveness, Rictus slipped her pride and joy, her sea-coral pendant, from about her neck before replacing what remained of her veil upon her face. He would have need of it, he told her. She had never denied him anything, and had been his mother in all things but blood.

There were enough red embers to light the pyre. Rictus piled up broken timber, hay, his father's favourite chair, all on top of the bodies of his family, and above them he laid the dog, that he might watch his master's door in the life to come. A flask of barley-spirit he broke over the pyre and it went up with a white flare of hungry flame. He sang the Paean again, louder this time, to be heard by his mother's spirit so that she might be there to welcome her husband. He stood by the bonfire of his past for a long time, not flinching as the flesh within it popped and shrank in the heat. He stood watching, dry-eyed, until the flames began to sink. Then he lay down beside it with his truncheon of a spear to hand. And, mercifully, he slept at last.

THREE
THE COMPANY OF THE ROAD

Gasca hitched his cloak higher about his shoulders and set one flap to cover his right ear so that the snow might not find so easy a passage. It was a good cloak, goat's leather rimmed with dogskin, but it had been his older brother's before this, and that big bastard had given it much hard wear. Besides which, there was no cloak made that would keep out the bitterness of this evening's wind. But a people who had made their home in the highland valleys of the Harukush had grown up with it. So Gasca shrugged off the discomfort, as a man ought, and kept his head up, using his spear as a staff to pick his way along the treacherous gravelled slush that was the road, his left arm fighting to keep his bronze-faced shield from flapping up like an old man's hat.

The Machran road was not busy, but those who had need to travel it at this time of year tended to draw together somewhat. In the evenings it made for an easier bivouac, and there were informal arrangements. Men gathered firewood, women fetched water. Children got under the feet of all, and were cuffed promiscuously by their elders. It was safer to sleep as part of a large camp, for the footpads and bandits in this part of the hills were renowned. As a fully armed soldier, Gasca had at first been avoided, then courted, and now was welcomed in the company of travellers. He had a fine voice, a pleasant manner, and if he was not the most comely of fellows, he had still the good-natured forbearance of youth to recommend him.

All Machran bound, the company was a varied lot. Two merchants led, with plodding donkeys laden with all manner of sacks and bags. Haughty fellows, they refused to divulge the contents, but it was easy enough to smell the juniper berries and half-cured hides once the fire began to warm them. A pair of young couples followed, the men as possessive as stags around their new wives, the girls flirtatious as only married women can be. Then came a grey-haired matron with the bark of a drillmaster, who herded round her skirts a half dozen ragged urchins, orphans running from some war in the far north. She was taking them to sell in the capital, and looked after them with the close attentiveness a man might show to a good hunting dog. One of the girls, she had already offered to Gasca, but he did not like his meat so tender, and besides, he had no money to spare for such indulgences. The children seemed to sense the essential charity in his nature, and when night fell one or two of them would invariably wriggle under his cloak and sleep curled against him. He did not mind, for they were good warmth, and if they were crawling with vermin, well, so was he.

Five days, this serried company had travelled in each other's ambit, and they had become comrades of the road, sharing food and stories and sometimes going so far as to venture a little personal history about the campfires. The two merchants had unbent somewhat, and over execrable wine had let slip brawny yarns of the battles they had fought in their youth. The young husbands, once they had torn themselves from their bedrolls and wiped the sweat from their brows, confided to the company that they were brothers, married to sisters, and apprenticed to a famous armourer in Machran, Ferrious of Afteni by name, who would teach them his secrets and make of them rich men, artists as much as artisans.

The pimping matron, while picking lice from the hair of one of her charges, extolled the virtues of a certain green-walled house in the Street of the Loom-Makers, where a man might indulge any craving his appetite could muster, and for a very reasonable fee.

"And you, soldier," one of the merchants said to Gasca over the fire. "What takes you to Machran? Are you to offer your spear for hire?"

Gasca squeezed himself some wine. It was black root-spirit he guessed, cut with goat's blood and honey. He had drunk worse, but could not quite remember when.

"I go to take up the red cloak," he admitted, wiping his mouth, and tossing the flaccid wineskin to one of the wan young husbands.

"I thought so. You bear a blank shield. So you'll paint some mercenary sigil on it and wear scarlet. Under what commander?"

Gasca smiled. "Whatever one will have me."

"You'll be a younger son, I'll bet."

"I have two elder brothers, the apples of my father's eyes. For me it was the red cloak or a goatkeeper's hut. And my fingers are too big to fit round a goat's tits."

The men around the fire laughed, but there was a furtiveness to their regard of him. Though young, Gasca was as broad as any two of them put together, and the glued linen cuirass he wore was stained with old blood. It had been his father's, as had the rest of the panoply he carried. Stealing them had been no easy thing, and one of his favoured elder brothers had taken a few knocks before Gasca had finally made it clear of his father's land. These weapons and armour he bore were all he owned in the world, an inheritance he had felt to be his due.

One of the young husbands spoke up. His wife had joined him at the fire, a lazy cat's-smile on her face. "I hear tell there's a great company being gathered," he said. "Not just in Machran, but in cities across all the mountains. There's a captain name of Phiron, comes from Idrios; he's hiring fighting men by the hundred. And he's a cursebearer, too."

"Where did you hear this?" his wife asked him.

"In a tavern in Arienus."

"And what tavern was this?"

Gasca's mind wandered as the squabble grew apace on the far side of the campfire. His own city, Gosthere, where he had the right to vote in assembly, was a mere stockaded town at the headwaters of the Gerionin River, two hundred and fifty pasangs back in the mountains. As much as anything else, he was going to Machran because he wanted to see a real city. Something built of stone, with paved streets that had no shit streaming down the middle of them. In his haversack he had a copy of Tynon's *Constitution*, which described the great cities of the Macht as if they were all set up in marble, peopled with statues and ruled by stately debate in well-conducted assemblies—not the knockabout mob-gatherings they had been back in Gosthere. That was something he wished to see, and if it did not exist in Machran, it likely never had anywhere.

To serve under a cursebearer—now that too would be something. Gasca had never so much as seen one before. Gosthere's nobility did not run to such glories. He wondered if the stories about the black armour were true.

I am young, Gasca thought. I have taken my man and my wolf. I have a full panoply. I do not want to own the world; I merely want to see it. I want to drink it by the bucketful and savour every swallow.

"And that bitch; that goatherder she-pig—she was there, wasn't she?"

"Woman, I tell you I was there for the turn of a water-clock, no more."

Gasca lay back in his cloak, tugging the folds about him and staring up at the stars. Scudding past the moons there were rags and glimmers of cloud. It would be very cold tonight. As children, he and his brothers had buried embers under their bedrolls on such nights, up in the high grazing. They would chaff each other for hours to the clink of the goat-bells, and Felix, their father's hound, would always lie next to Gasca. When he growled in the dark they would all be up on their feet in a moment, shuddering with cold, reaching for their boy's spears. Gasca had been thirteen when he had killed his first wolf. Like all the men of his city, he had chiselled out one of its teeth. As he lay now, far from home, he reached up to his neck and touched it, warm from his flesh. For a moment he felt a pang of loss, remembering his brothers when they had all been boys together, before the complications of manhood. Then he grunted, rolled himself tighter in his cloak, and closed his eyes.

When morning came he found that two of the urchin-children had wormed under his cloak in the night and were spliced to him like wasps to a honeycomb. In the warmth under the cloak all his vermin and theirs had come alive, and he itched damnably. Even so, he was reluctant to rise, for the cloak and the ground around it had a light skiff of snow upon it that had frozen hard, and the sunrise just topping the mountains had kindled from it a hundred million jagged points of rose-coloured light. Even the log-butts from the fire had frost on them. When Gasca blinked, he could feel his eyebrows crackle.

The children squealed as he threw aside the cloak and rose to his feet, stamping his sandals into the stone-hard ground and stretching his limbs to the mountains. He strode out to the roadside and pissed there, standing in an acrid cloud of his own making and blinking the sleep out of his eyes. Looking up and down, he saw the road was empty in both directions. To the south it disappeared between the shoulders of two steep white hills, on one of which there loomed the rocky ruins of a city. That was Memnos. They had hoped to see it this morning when they woke. Machran now lay a mere thirty pasangs away, an easy day's march. Tonight they would sleep under a roof, those who could afford it. Gasca had promised himself a good meal, and wine worthy of the name. He spat the taste of last night's out onto the road, grimacing.

Something moved in the treeline. The original builders of the road had hewn back the woods on either side for a bowshot, and though those who maintained it now had not done so well, there were still a good hundred paces of open ground before the tangled scrub and dwarf-pine of the thickets began. In the dawn-light Gasca's piss-stream dried up as he saw the pale blur of a face move in there. He turned at once and dashed back to the campsite, booting aside one of the yawning urchins. His spear was slick with frost and he cursed as it slipped in his fingers.

By the time he had turned back to the woods the figure was visible. A man walking towards the road with his arms held out from his sides, and in one fist a single-headed spear. The man thrust this point-first into the ground for lack of a sauroter, and then came on with both palms open in the universal gesture. *I mean no harm.* Gasca's breathing steadied. He strode forward. Others from the company were blinking their way out of their bedrolls, throwing aside furs and trying to make sense of the morning. One of the younger children was crying hopelessly, blue with cold.

Gasca stood between the approaching figure and the waking camp, and planted the sauroter of his own spear in the roadside. He wished now he had clapped on his father's helm.

"What's your business? State it quickly. I have good men at my back," he said loudly, hoping those good men were out of their blankets. He scanned the treeline, but nothing else moved there. For the moment, at least, this fellow was alone. But that meant nothing. He might have twenty comrades stowed back in the trees, waiting to see the company's headcount.

The man was tall, as tall as Gasca, though nothing like as broad. In fact he had a gaunt, hungry look. His chiton was worn and stained, ripped open at the neck in the grief-mark, and he had a blanket slung bagwise about his torso. There was a knife at his waist, hanging from a string. A scar marred the middle of his lower lip.

"I mean no harm. I hoped to share your fire," the man said.

The two merchants and the young husbands joined Gasca at the roadside, wielding clubs and knives. "Shall we kill him?" one of the husbands asked eagerly.

"He's not robbed us yet. Let him speak," Gasca said.

He was young, this fellow. Now that they all had a chance to see him up close they realised that he was not much more than an overgrown boy. Until one looked in his eyes. He stared at Gasca, and in his hooded gaze there was utter indifference.

I could kill him right here and now, Gasca thought, and he would not raise so much as a finger.

"What's your name?" he asked, more gently than he had meant to.

"Rictus."

"Of what city?"

The thin man hesitated. "I was of Isca," he said at last, "When Isca still stood." His eyes hardened. "I seek only to travel with you to Machran. I have no ill intent. And I am alone." He raised his hands, empty.

"Come on to the fire," Gasca said. "If we can raise a flame."

"Isca?" one of the merchants said. "What happened to Isca?"

The man named Rictus turned his head. He had eyes like grey shards of iron, cold as the sea. "Isca is no more."

"Really? Gods above. Come, boy—come sit and tell us more."

The strangeness had been broken. A threatening shape walking out of the woods had become a tired young man, who spoke civilly. They gathered around him, glad perhaps of some new story; news that was not shopworn, but fresh and raw. Gasca drew away, still watching this gaunt apparition. The man Rictus did not move. Something flickered in his eyes; pain. He was regretting this already, Gasca realised. He spoke again. "Let me go back for my spear."

They tensed. He looked at Gasca.

"Go get it," Gasca said, and shrugged.

Some humanity in the eyes at last. The man nodded, and went back the way he had come.

"You think he's not a ruse, a roadsman?" one of the young husbands asked.

Gasca was about to answer, but it was the fat merchant who spoke first.

"Look in his face—he tells the truth. I've seen eyes like that before." The merchant's face tightened. For a second it was possible to see the soldier he might have been in younger days.

"We've nothing to fear from this lad. He's already made his gift to the goddess."

They got the fire going again, digging out of its black carcass a single red mote of living heat. This they conjured into a blaze, and with the addition of copper cauldrons they had boiling water soon after, and set the barley to swell in it. The campsite regained some of its usual cheer, though the newcomer, Rictus, had an armspan of cold air between himself and the rest. This was remedied when one of the urchins edged close, and finally sat defiantly within the crook of his arm. Rictus appeared startled, then pleased, then grim as a blacksmith's washbowl. By his posture, one might think he had a spear-staff for a spine. And he was so cold that the warmth of the child next to him finally set him to shivering, with ground teeth.

The fatter of the merchants, the one Gasca now knew to be a true man, threw the wineskin to Rictus.

"Drink, for the gods, for all of us. Have a drink, lad. Pour a libation if you will. Ease that look in your eyes."

Rictus took the skin and drank. He drank as though it were the last thing he would ever do. And while his cheeks were still puffed full of wine, he poured a stream of it from the mouth of the skin so that it might puddle on the ground.

"That's good wine—" the thinner merchant cried.

"Shut your mouth," the fatter one told him, and Gasca nodded when he met his eyes. There were proprieties. There was decency. A man could not weigh the price of all things, and yet ignore their value.

Teeth bared for a moment against the vileness of the wine, Rictus looked at Gasca, and jerked his head towards the thickets on the western margins of the road. "Back in there, maybe two pasangs, or one and a half, there are eight men about a dead campfire arguing over the best time to ambush you."

Silence about their own fire. The procuress asked, "And they're friends of yours, are they?"

"If they were, would I be here?"

The fat merchant rubbed his fingertips through his beard. "Eight you say? Why did they not attack us before now? Dawn and dusk are the best time for these things."

"They were quarrelling over who would have the women—these two younger ones. They had a fight over it last night, then got drunk and slept the time away. Now they are arming, meaning to take you sometime today, before you get much closer to Machran."

The two husband-brothers stared at one another, white-faced, and then at their new wives. The look on the women's faces reminded Gasca of a rabbit he once caught alive in a snare.

"And how were you privy to their discussions?" the fat merchant asked.

"I have been travelling with them. I, too, was drinking last night at their fire."

"A roadsman," the thin merchant spat, and he whipped out his slim-bladed eating knife. "It's out of his own mouth."

"Stay," his colleague said. To Rictus he said, "What brings you here to warn us?"

"I have seen my fill of killing—that kind of killing. I will fight them with you, if you'll have me."

Gasca rose from the fire and went to the roadside again. The sun, mighty Araian, had climbed out of her bedclothes; she broke out now in a wrack of crimson and golden cloud, and the glare of the thin snow was broadening moment by moment. He looked about himself, at the wide spaces around them, then at the hills ahead which framed the road, the ruins of long-sacked Memnos rising white and dark with shadow and snow.

"We must pack up," he said. "If they catch us on the move we'll have no chance. We must make for the hills, put our backs to something. Those broken walls; we can climb them and fight from a height." He turned again. "What weaponry do they have?"

"Spears, swords, javelins. No bows, or shields either, not even a pelta."

"Are they up and about?"

Rictus considered. He was eerily calm. He does not care, Gasca thought. He thinks to do the right thing, but most of him could care less if he lived or died today.

"They're slow, hung-over. You have time. Not much, but enough perhaps."

"We'll do as the boy says," the fat merchant said abruptly, rising. "Time to be moving."

"We'll outrun them," one of the young husbands said desperately. "It's thirty pasangs to Machran; I can run that."

"And your wife?" the merchant asked. "These children? If we splinter up, they'll take us in mouthfuls. Fighting together, on good ground, we can hurt them, enough perhaps to make them think again."

"You care only for the wares on your donkey's back."

"Among other things. Run if you wish. They have legs too. You'll be dead before sundown, and your wife will be a raped slave."

They packed up their bedrolls, the younger women snivelling, the children subdued by their elders' fear. They left the fire burning and struck out for the south at a fast pace. The fat merchant was the slowest. Gasca took his donkey's halter and tugged the animal on while the big man clung to the animal's tail, sweating. They left the road, and the going became much harder as they forged up the hillside to the ruins above. When the youngest child began to fall behind, Rictus slung her up on his back, and she clung there with a wide smile on her face, hooting triumphantly to the other urchins. The thin merchant paused to catch his breath, and looked back into the lowland below. He cried out, and they all paused, turned their heads. A group of men had come out of the trees, moving fast, black as crows against the snow.

The company's fear lent them speed. They passed though the massive broken arch which had once been Memnos's main gate and raised a startled flock of sparrows out of the stones. The snow was deeper here, high as a man's calf. Gasca dropped the donkey's leading rein and ran ahead, his shield and helm bruising his back as they bounced there. The ruins were extensive, and had there been no snow it might even have been possible to hide the party amid them and avoid any fight at all; but now their tracks were clear as a line of flags. He cast about like a hound near a scent-line, and nodded as he found what he was looking for.

"The walls," he said, rejoining the others. "There's a stair leading up to a good section of them, and a tower that's still got a doorway. We go up there, the men defend the stairtop, and the others hide in the tower."

"What about our animals?" the thin merchant asked, gasping.

"They must stay below."

"I'll be ruined," the thin merchant groaned. But he did not argue.

From the wall-top they could see for pasangs. Their attackers were still toiling up the snowy slope below. The road was empty; no fellow travellers to provide allies or diversions. The world was a vast, bright stage ringed by mountains, snow blowing off their peaks in ribbons and banners, the sky above them flawless, pale blue, blue as a baby's eye. Only the pine forests provided a darker contrast, the shadow deep beneath their limbs.

"Look," Rictus said. He stood beside Gasca and pointed. There was a light in his eye.

Machran. To the south the mountains opened out in a vast bowl, perhaps fifty pasangs across, and within this ramp of highland the country was a patchwork of wood and field, the lower hollows of it untouched by snow, and green, green as a dream of spring. Machran itself was a sprawl, a smudge, an ochre stain upon the rolling mantle of this world, and from it the smoke of ten thousand hearths rose in a grey smear to sully the sky. From these heights it looked as though a man with a fair wind behind him might lope there in a matter of minutes. Gasca found himself smiling.

A shout from below. Their attackers had seen them standing up here. There were indeed eight of them. They had knotted their cloaks up over their elbows; sheepskins, fox-hide caps with the fur still on, and high boots. Their beards were black, long and tangled as the tail of a cow.

"Goatmen," Gasca said, using the contemptuous term reserved for those who had no city, who frequented the high places of the Harukush and were reputed to sleep in caves and hold their women in common. "You travelled with these?"

"I chanced across them," Rictus said.

"I'm surprised they didn't kill you out of hand."

"They tried," Rictus said, still in the same quiet tone. "Isca trained me. They came round to thinking that might be useful."

"Ah, Isca," Gasca said. He had heard the stories. It was hardly the time to hear them again. "You will need that training today."

They took their place at the stairtop. It was broad enough for two, but slippery with trodden snow. Gasca put on his father's bronze helm, and immediately all sounds became washed out by the sea-noise within. He had thought to leave it off, but knew how fearsome a crested helm would look to the men below. It would make of him a faceless thing, and hide whatever fear might fill his eyes.

He took the weight of his shield off his shoulder and balanced it on his arm. The bronze-faced oak covered him from shoulder to thigh. "They'll start with the javelins," he told Rictus. "Get behind my shield until they're done."

"I'd rather stand free."

"Suit yourself."

Behind Rictus and Gasca stood the fat merchant, face still shiny with sweat, and one of the husband-brothers. At the rear, the thin merchant and the other husband. Only Rictus and Gasca had spears. The rest were armed with knives and cudgels, the eternal stand-by of all travellers, but of little use today unless the enemy made it up onto the wall.

A harsh braying from below. The thin merchant cursed in the name of Apsos, god of beasts.

"They'll eat the damn donkeys. *Goatmen*—worse than animals themselves." Behind the six men, the sounds of wailing children came from the doorway of the ruined watchtower.

"I wish those brats were mutes," the thin merchant said.

"I wish you were a mute," his fat colleague murmured.

The goatmen sidled up to the wall-bottom, watching out for missiles. When it appeared the defenders had none they grew more brazen, edged closer. Two spoke together and pointed up at Gasca, in full panoply, as stark and fearsome as some statue of warfare incarnate.

"If I had some rag of red about my shoulders they'd walk away," he muttered to Rictus. There was no response from the Iscan. Despite the cold, Gasca was sweating, and the heavy shield dragged at his left bicep. Wolves he had killed, and other men he had broken down in brawls, but this was the first time he had ever hoped to plunge a spearhead into someone's heart.

He jumped, as beside him Rictus shouted with sudden venom. "Are you afraid? Why be afraid?" For a second, fury flooded his limbs as he thought the Iscan was talking to him; then he realised that Rictus was shouting at the goatmen below. He turned his head, and saw through the confined eye-spaces of his helm that Rictus was red-faced, angry. More than angry. He was feral, hate shining out of his eyes. Gasca shifted away from him out of sheer instinct, as a man will give space to a vicious dog.

"Is it too much, to fight men face to face, who have weapons in their hands? Can you not do that? Or will we send out children with sticks, and let them taste your valour? Come—you know me. You know where I hail from. Come up here and taste my spear again!" Now Gasca was thrust aside, and Rictus stood alone at the top of the steps. There was spittle on his lips. He opened out his arms as if to pray.

The javelin came searing up from the men below. Gasca, by some grace, saw it coming, even with his circumscribed vision, and managed to lift his shield crab-wise. It clicked off the rim of the bronze, pocking it.

"What in the gods are you doing?" he shouted at Rictus. He had half a mind to shove this madman down the steps.

"Now keep your shield up," Rictus said, and his face was rational again.

A flurry of javelins. They came arcing in: one, two, three. Two bounced off Gasca's shield. The third struck the ground between his feet, making him flinch. His panoply seemed impossibly heavy. He wanted to rip off the damned helm and see what was going on. His eye-slots seemed absurdly small.

But now Rictus was smiling. In his hand he held two javelins. The tips were bent a little; soft mountain-iron.

"Well thrown. Now have them back." His arm swooped in a blur. He had looped the middle-strings of the weapon about his first two fingers and as he loosed it the javelin spun, whining. It transfixed one of the goatmen below, entering under his beard and emerging from his nape for half a foot. The man crumpled, and his comrades scattered around him as though his bloody end were contagious.

The second sped into them three seconds later. This one missed a man's head by a handspan but struck the fellow next to him just above the knee. He yelped, dropped his spear, and grasped his spitted limb with both hands, mouth wide and wet.

"Even odds now," Rictus said, perfectly calm.

"Boy, the goddess has you under her wings," the fat merchant said behind them.

"Isca trained me well. They'll rush the stairs now. We stop the rush, and they'll break. Then we go after them. Agreed?" The men around him mumbled assent.

"They come," Gasca said, and raised his spear to his shoulder.

The rank smell rose before them as they scrabbled up the snow-covered stone of the stairway. Jabbing with their spears, snarling, they did not seem like men at all. Gasca crouched and took the impact of one blow on his shield. It jolted him, but the heavy wood and bronze shrugged off the spearpoint. His mouth was a slot of spittle as he breathed in and out, and all fear left him; there was no time for it. He felt his own spear quiver in his hand as he grasped it at the balance point and poked downwards. The goatmen were trying to come to grips with the defenders, get under the spearheads. One got a fist about Gasca's spearpoint but he ripped it back through the man's hand, the keen aichme shearing off fingers as it came free of his grasp. The man shrieked. Then

Rictus stabbed out with his own weapon, transfixing the fellow through the mouth, the shriek transforming horribly into a gargle. He toppled backwards. Behind him, two of his fellows roared and swore as his carcass rolled down the stairs and took their legs out from under them. A tumble of foul-smelling flesh encased in fur, flashing eyes, a snap as a spear-shaft broke under them. They rolled clear to the ground below, and bounced to their feet again as enraged as before.

Three remained on the stair. One had eyes that were different colours. Gasca was able to see this, notice it, store it away. He had never known that his own senses could be so keen. Two spearpoints jutted up. One came below the rim of the shield, scoring the metal. Gasca felt a sting in his thigh, no more. He thrust his own spear down at them and felt it go into something soft. Recovering the thrust, he felt warm liquid trickling down the side of his leg. Thrust, recover, catch another point on the shield. A goatman came up bellowing, dropped his spear and sought to grasp Gasca's shield in his fists and pull it away. Gasca felt his balance go, and fear so intense flooded him as he felt himself fall that he urinated hotly where he stood.

Then Rictus had embedded his eating knife in the goatman's neck, right up the hilt. The man wailed, his grasp loosened. He scrabbled at the knife handle and tumbled backwards. About to follow him, Gasca's chiton was seized from behind. There were arms about him, a stink of sweat and cheap scent.

"Easy there," the fat merchant said. "Find your feet, lad."

Recovering himself, Gasca blinked sweat out of his eyes. On the steps below him his blood had trickled in a thin stream, now diluted with his urine, steaming, all the stuff of his insides turned to liquid.

The goatmen backed down the stairs. Three of them now lay still and dark on the snow, and two more were grasping their wounds and struggling to keep the blood inside their flesh.

"I believe they've had enough," Rictus said.

"It was so fast," one of the young husbands said behind them. He had been four feet from the struggle, and it had not touched him, nor had he so much as raised his arm. Dimly, Gasca had some insight of what real phalanx fighting might be like. The proximity to violence of some, so close to the spearheads, and yet not part of the fight.

"Now, after me," Rictus said. There was a kind of joy in his face as he started down the stair.

"No, boy!" the fat merchant shouted, and he seized Rictus's chiton in much the way he had Gasca's. "Let them go. You go down those stairs and they'll fight you to the death. You may win, but there's no need for it, and you're likely to take a bad hurt before the last goes down."

Rictus suddenly looked very young, like a sullen boy denied the treat he had been promised. He hesitated, and the look vanished. That calm came across his face again, and a smile that was not entirely pleasant. He gently lifted the fat merchant's hand from his clothing, and then turned to address their enemies.

"Take your wounded and go," he called down to the goatmen.

"Come down and fight us here," one shouted back in the guttural accents of the high Harukush. "We will wait for you."

"You will die, all of you, if we do," Rictus said. And he was still smiling.

The goatmen stared at him. One spat blood onto the snow. Then they began to methodically strip their dead, whilst one remained at the foot of the stairs, spear at ready.

"You've done well, lads," the fat merchant said. "Now with a little more help from the goddess, we'll be in Machran by nightfall. We've nothing left to fear from these ugly wights."

They stood upon the wall, watching while the goatmen bundled up the belongings of their dead comrades. When they were done, the three bodies lay nude in the snow, their hairy nakedness taking on a bluish tinge already. Then, without ceremony, the five survivors took off, the leg-hurt one hobbling and hissing in the rear. They turned a corner of the ruins and disappeared.

"They may hide and ambush us," Rictus said. "I would."

"You and your friend have put fear in them," the fat merchant said. "I know these sorts. I come from Scanion, in the deep mountains. We used to hunt them like they were boar. Good sport, if you've a strong stomach. They're brave when they're in numbers, with an easy kill in sight, but you kill one or two and the rest lose heart right quick, like vorine. This pack is spent. Though what they're doing so close to Machran is anybody's guess. I've never met them so low." And then, "Boy, that leg of yours needs attended."

Gasca took off his helm and closed his eyes as the cold air cooled the sweat on his head. "You saved my life between you. I am in your debt now."

"You saved mine by standing there," the fat merchant grunted. "Do not speak of debt to me."

"Nor me," Rictus said. "You took that first javelin on your shield when it was aimed my way."

Gasca and Rictus looked at one another. Both their hands rose in the same moment, and in the next they grasped each other's wrists in the warrior salute, smiling, seeming not much more than boys.

"Of course, you did piss yourself," Rictus said.

FOUR
MACHRAN

There was a legend that the Macht had once been ruled by a single King, a mighty soldier, a just ruler, an architect of ambition and vision. He had gathered together all the scattered cities of his empire and connected them with a series of great roads, hewn with titanic labour out of the very faces of the mountains. Bas Mathon on the coast, he had linked to Gan Cras in the very heart of the Harukush range. Thousands of pasangs of high-way he had carved across the northern world, the better to speed the passage of his messengers, his governors, his armies. But they also sped the feet of his enemies. An unruly, restless and stiff-necked people, the Macht had overthrown him, broken down his palace at Machran, and splintered his empire into a hundred, two hundred different vying polities. The cities had elected their own rulers, one by one. They had forged alliances and broken them, and they had bludgeoned their own passage through history, heedless of any larger call on their allegiances. The empire of the Macht was no more; the idea of a single King ruling all the great cities of the Harukush came to seem fantastic, then risible; a tale to be scoffed at in taverns. But the roads still stood. Some fell into disrepair, but the most important ones survived, and men still walked them to trade their wares and make their wars and indulge the lust of their wanderings. The King who had made them became a figure of myth, and in time even his name was forgotten, and the stones he had set up to commemorate it were worn smooth by the wind and rain of centuries.

The greatest of these roads led to the city of Machran, which had once been the capital of this vanished empire. Even today, it was the most populous and formidable of all the Macht city-states, and almost alone out of all others it had never fallen to siege or assault. What central institutions the Macht as a people possessed were housed in Machran, and competing cities might send embassies there for mediation, or to hire mercenary spearmen to bolster their flagging battle lines. For Machran attracted the shiftless, the penniless, the adventurous, and the downright criminal in ways no other city could, and these men put up their services for sale at the great hiring fairs held thrice yearly. In Machran, it was said, everything was for sale, and a man might find himself bought and sold there before he knew it.

The road which Gasca and his companions had tramped for so many days came to an end at the grey walls of the city. Once faced with white marble, the battlements had been battered by the centuries and the greedy hands of men. Now most of the good marble had gone except for yellowing pockets here and there, lonely teeth in a blackened mouth. For all that, the walls were impressive, perhaps five times a tall man's height, the gatehouse in which the road ended twice that. Gasca could glimpse the wood and iron scaffolds of ancient war machines atop the wall-towers. Ballistas and mangonels and other engines which were but half-known names to him. The flitting sunlight snapped in spikes off the bronze of helms and spearheads as sentries paced the catwalks.

The road broadened into a muddy field before the towering gatehouse, the stone flags of it lost in ankle-deep mud and the droppings of every animal tamed by man. Carts, wagons, and pack mules stood surrounded by a jabbering crowd of men, women, and children who glared and talked and gesticulated and seemed on the point of some communal violence while the bored guards in the gateway waved them through, beating the slower beasts of burden with the flat of their spearheads. Gasca, Rictus, and their company were swallowed up in this crowd, repaying thumps and shoves with interest until they had passed through the dark echo of the gatehouse itself. On the other side the city reared up over them, as sudden and startling to witness as a precipice. They stumbled out of the way of the entering hordes and gathered themselves together, a final headcount. Gasca bent his head back and gaped without shame, a perfect picture of the country boy in town for the day—if one ignored the armour on his back and the weapons he bore.

Well, he thought, there is, at least, no shit rolling down the middle of the street.

The company was scattering. The procuress actually kissed Gasca on the mouth, then cackled and strode off, the urchin children now secured to her waist with thin lengths of cord. These were so cowed by the sight of the great city however that they clung to her side. She was taking them to the slave-market in the Goshen Quarter. One child turned and waved at Gasca as he went, huge frightened eyes in a filthy face.

The young husbands shook his hand one after the other in the finger-grip of the artisan. Their wives had donned veils, the informality of the road abandoned, and they were as demure as matrons now. No more squealing in the blankets by a campfire for them.

The thin merchant spoke briefly to his colleague and departed without a word for the men who had bled for him. He was perhaps still bemoaning his lost ass.

"Ungrateful sod," Rictus said mildly.

"You boys will stay with me until you can shift for yourselves," the fat merchant said. "I will hear of nothing else. On the Street of Lamps, in the Round Hill Quarter, you must go to the Beggar's Purse, nigh the amphion, the speaker's place, and tell them that you are guests of Zeno of Scanion. You tell them that, and you'll save yourself an obol or two. I will meet you there later and we shall wet our throats in memory of the Defence of Memnos." He grinned.

"Zeno of Scanion," Gasca said, smiling, "it shall be so."

"Ah! Till later then. Be careful, boys. No goatmen here, but plenty of jackals. One hand to your money and the other on a good knife."

Zeno—now they knew his name at least—left them with a wink and a wave. He was bowed under a heavy pack, for the goatmen, though they had slaughtered the donkeys, had not had the time to loot all the merchants' wares.

Staring, Rictus and Gasca moved aside to let the torrent of humanity move past and around them. On all sides, like white cliffs, buildings rose faced with marble. The streets were shadowed by them, made into narrow channels through which the people of the city flowed and whirled and turned. Rictus and Gasca were like twigs in a millrace, snagged for a moment by their own irresolution while the current broke around them.

"That's the Empirion," Gasca said, pointing. "I've heard of it. Gestrakos himself lectured there, back before my city had even been founded." This was a white dome, the sun blazing off it and the golden statue that surmounted it. The structure looked like some lost element of a dream brought to earth; it did not seem that its foundations could be planted on the same ground that bore their feet.

Handcarts rattled by them in convoy, bearing all manner of foodstuffs. Boys hauled them, while their fathers or elder brothers walked alongside, quirting the fingers of the avaricious with olive-wood wands. Machran had a vast hinterland about it, some of the richest soils in the Macht. It was famed for its olives, its figs, and its wine. The only place in the Harukush where the stuff did not have to be sweetened with pine resin, it was said.

"All these people. There's the whole Gosthere Assembly here in this one street. But I see no scarlet cloaks," Gasca said. "Where might all the mercenaries be found?"

"We should ask, I suppose," Rictus said. But he stood motionless, strangely intimidated by the great city, the teeming crowds who afforded him not so much as a greeting or a glance, but who all, it seemed, had somewhere important to be.

"What say you we wander and let our feet have their say?"

"A fine idea," Gasca said sourly, "for those not bowed under the weight of a panoply and carrying thread stitched in their leg."

"Give me your shield then. We'll hobble at any pace you care to set."

"A lame soldier," Gasca said, handing over his father's shield. "What a prize I'll be for some centurion to sign up."

"It's a good gash. It'll heal quick. Here; look at mine." Rictus lifted up the hem of his filthy chiton so that Gasca could see the purple scar on his ribs. It was oozing clear fluid and looked only half-healed.

"How long have you had that?" Gasca asked, shocked.

"Long enough to grow tired of it. Come; let's find someone who knows about the hiring of soldiers. This place is making me weary already."

They forged a pass through the press, twigs in the millrace. Rictus led the way, using the blunt bowl of the shield to shove the unwary out of his path. It helped that both of them were tall, raw-boned men of the inner mountains. Here, the Macht as a people were shorter and darker of hair and skin. The women were very pretty though, and they did not veil their faces in public as many of the mountain folk did, but strode about the streets as freely as any man, sometimes showing their arms and legs as well. In among the foot-walkers and cart-haulers there were also closed boxes with curtained windows, carried by men on poles. Rictus wondered what they contained, until he saw one curtain twitched aside and a fat white-faced woman shouted abuse at her bearers, her thick fingers alight with rings. He broke into a laugh, for he had never seen anyone borne about in a box before.

It was Gasca who had the best view about them, he being taller than almost every other head in the street. He tugged Rictus to a halt in the middle of a broad, column-lined thoroughfare. On either side of them there was a clangour of metal on metal, for amid the columns were scores of one-man shops, each with a blackened smith hammering out metal on small anvils before which they knelt cross-legged. These were not farriers, or armourers, but silversmiths, and their hammers tapped out intricate designs on argent sheets which were to become some fripperies to ornament a rich man's house.

"Look, Rictus—up front. Do you see him?"

Rictus leaned on his spear—the butt was becoming splintered—and peered through the coursing crowds. A black shape, like a shadow cast on a bright day.

"A cursebearer. What of him?"

"I've never seen one before."

"Really? A sheltered life you've led."

"If my eyes are right, he wears scarlet too—at least I think so. We should speak to him." He paused. "Can we speak to him? Can one do that?"

"He's not a god, just a man who inherited his father's harness. Come; if he's truly wearing scarlet then we must have a talk."

"Where did you see a cursebearer before?" Gasca demanded, a little put out at Rictus's non-excitement.

"We had maybe half a dozen of them in Isca, the *mora* commanders, mostly."

They pushed through the crowd none too gently, and received angry glances. "Strawheads!" someone called out, the ancient insult. Rictus smiled at the shouter and saw him blench, then kept going, but using the shield with a little more gentleness. Along his side of his chiton the blood was expanding in little circles, and he had sweat shining on his forehead.

"Sir—a word if we might!" he called out, for their quarry was getting too far ahead of them, people making way for the black armour.

The cursebearer halted in his tracks, turned round. He was a lowlander, shorter than them, middle-aged, with a peppery beard and deep-hollowed eyes. He had a scarlet cloak hung on one shoulder, the end of which was wrapped around his left forearm. No weapons of any kind. The man did not speak, but looked Rictus and Gasca up and down appraisingly, as a man would upon buying a horse. The two of them stood silent before him, breathing through their mouths, feeling the appraisal, lost for any more words.

The cursebearer saw two tall boys who were almost men. They might have been brothers. Both were light-skinned and fair of hair, the colouring of the inner mountains. One had grey eyes, the other blue. The blue-eyed fellow was broader, heavier, and had an open, friendly face. Grey-eyes looked underfed and ill-rested. In his glance there was some knowledge of the world, hard come by.

"What is this word you want?" the cursebearer asked. He had thick eyebrows, black as soot, and they moved more than his mouth, which was a thin-lipped gash in his beard with bad teeth behind it.

It was Rictus who must needs reply. Gasca was still staring at the black cuirass which the man wore. It seemed to soak up the very daylight, a midnight black so lightless it appeared a hole in the fabric of the afternoon. This was the Curse of God, one of the ancient armours which dated back to the origins of the Macht as a people. None knew how they had been created, but the legends said that Gaenion the Smith had made a wager with God Himself, betting that he could fashion a darkness which not even his wife's gaze could penetrate. His spouse was Araian, the lady of the sun, and she was both an inquisitive and indolent creature. When she rose from her bed her eyes saw all things, and when she left the skies of Kuf in the evenings she would tell God Himself of the day's doings.

Gaenion won his wager, but God took the black stuff he had forged and gave it to Antimone, Goddess of the Veil, for she was enamoured of darkness, and her two sons, Phobos and Haukos, loved to ride the horses of the air through the sky when Araian had left it for her bed.

Antimone wove Gaenion's hammered darkness into a chiton with which to clothe the first man of the Macht, whom God had set down upon the surface of Kuf naked and afraid. Antimone, in pity, gave this first man, whose name was Ask, the chiton to protect him, for Gaenion's fabric, though light and flexible, was more impenetrable than stone. When God realised what Antimone had done, He was angry, for He had intended that Ask and his kind should treat the other denizens of the world with respect, and show them courtesy through fear of their own vulnerability. But now Ask was unafraid, with Antimone's Gift to clothe him, and he set out to master the creatures of Kuf which God had created. And so, through Antimone's pity, Creation itself had been set awry. So God cursed the black armour of Antimone, and stirred up the hearts of all the other races of Kuf against Ask and his people. The Macht would be warriors without compare, He decreed, but they would never know peace, and they would have need of their black armour over the course of the world's turning, for they would pay in blood for their desire to master the earth.

Antimone was punished also. She had erred in pity, in softness of heart, and so God set her down on Kuf itself to watch over the Macht in all their travails down the millennia. She would foresee the fate of those she loved, but would not be able to change it, and so would weep bitter tears, for she would be witness to every crime that man would commit in his tenure of the earth.

Her sons, Phobos the elder and Haukos the younger, wished to follow their mother to Kuf, but God forbade it as part of Antimone's punishment. So they drew as near as they dared, riding their great black horses in shadow across the night sky, when Araian the sun was not there to tell God of their doings. Phobos hated the Macht for causing his mother's exile from heaven, and his white face leered down upon men from the depths of the night sky. But Haukos had inherited his mother's soft heart. To his pink countenance men prayed for intercession with Antimone, and hence, with God Himself.

Such was the legend.

Whatever their origin, there were some five thousand sets of Antimone's black armour abroad in the world, and those who bore them were known as cursebearers. The armour was passed down through families for centuries, though many had changed hands in battle. None were ever given up willingly, and a city might go to war for possession of a single black cuirass. Ageless and indestructible, some said that in them resided the very essence of the Macht as a people, and were they to disappear, then so would mankind.

"We saw your scarlet cloak, and the harness you bear, and wondered if you might be hiring," Rictus said to the man who stood before them now with one of these ancient artefacts on his back.

The man cocked his head to one side. "If I am, I do not hire in the middle of the street. Nor do I like to be shouted at there by boys who still have their mother's milk about their gums." One eyebrow rose at this, a mockery, though the rest of his face remained grave.

Gasca took a step forward, but Rictus tilted out his spear to bar his way.

"You're right, of course," he said to the cursebearer. "You have our apologies. Would it be acceptable for us to ask you—to ask you where it would be appropriate to look for employment?"

The man smiled at this. "You've not done much apologising in your time, boy. But you want employment you say. As mercenaries?

"Yes, sir."

"And is this all the panoply you possess?"

"What you see is all we have," Gasca said. "But it has done good service before now."

"No doubt. But it's not enough to get you both in the phalanx. One of you, perhaps, but the other will have to apply to the light arm, or else be a camp servant. Go to the northern gate, the Mithannon they call it. Outside the walls there's a marshalling square surrounded by tents and shacks. That's where they hire spears in this town."

"Thank you," both Rictus and Gasca said at once, eyes bright as those of children promised some treat.

The man chuckled. "You came to the head of the snake. I am Pasion of Decanth. Drop my name there and you may not get as hard a time. It's late in the day to be touting your wares. Leave it till the morning, and you're less likely to be manhandled."

"Thank you," Rictus said again.

"You're from Isca, boy, aren't you?"

"I... How do you know?"

"The way you met my eyes. Most men outside the scarlet drop their gaze for a second on meeting a cursebearer. You've had Iscan arrogance bred into you. Let slip that at the hiring—it will do no harm. Now I must go." He nodded at them both, then turned and resumed his way through the crowd, the people parting before him as though he were contagious.

"We have luck with us," Gasca said. "That's a meeting the goddess had a hand in if ever anyone did. And I have seen the Curse of God at last."

"I didn't come all this way to be a camp servant," Rictus said.

"Let us go to that merchant's inn. We'll set ourselves up there and see about joining a company tomorrow. We shall eat and drink and wash and find ourselves a bed."

Rictus smiled. He looked tired, older than his years, pinched with hunger and bad memories. "Lead on then. And take this shield for a while—fair's fair."

* * *

The Mithannon faced north towards the Mithos River, a grey flash of cold mountain-water that ran parallel to the walls of the city for five or six pasangs. The open plain there had long ago been flattened out and beaten into a dirt bowl around which there clustered irregular lines of wooden shacks and stalls, hide tents made semi-permanent with the addition of sod walls, and hundreds of low-roofed ramshackle shelters brought into being with the connivance of a bewildering variety of materials. The place seemed a mockery of the stone and marble majesty of Machran itself, but if one looked closer there was an order to the encampments. They ran in distinct lines, and some were cordoned off with rawhide and hemp ropes mounted on posts. Flags and banners snapped everywhere, a kind of ragged heraldry splashed across them, painted on signposts, daubed on the skewed planks of shacks and cabins. And everywhere in the midst of these crude streets there walked knots and files of men dressed in scarlet of some shade or other. These were the Hiring Grounds, and the Marshalling Yards, and the Spear-Market, and half a dozen other names besides. Here, men might join the free companies, those soldiers who sold their spears to the highest bidder and who owed allegiance to nothing except their comrades and themselves.

In the quarter of the city closest to the Mithannon there was the greatest concentration of wine-shops and brothels in all Machran. Here, the gracious architecture degenerated into a hiv-ing labyrinth of lesser buildings, built of fired brick and undressed stone, roofed with reed-thatch from the riverbanks rather than red tile, and lacking windows, often doors. Men had built upwards here, for lack of space in the teeming alleyways about them. It seemed, looking up from the splash and mire of the noisome streets, that the buildings leaned in on each other for support, and a mason with a plumb-line might look around himself in despair.

Up in the swallow's eyrie of one of these there was an upstairs room. A man might spit through the gapped planks of the floor there onto the heads of the drinkers below, but somehow the place stood, stubborn and askew and seething with all manner of babel that wine could conjure out of men's mouths. It was a place where conversations could be had in shouts, and still no one an armspan away would make sense of them.

"When is Phiron to return?" one of the men asked. This was Orsos of Gast, whose face had writ across it the dregs of every crime known to man. He was known as the Bull to friends and enemies alike. Now his deep-set eyes glinted with suspicion. "I have a firm offer from Akanos, me and my centon. Time is money, Pasion. Promises never fattened a purse."

The cursebearer named Pasion cast his gaze down the long, wine-stained table. Twenty centurions sat there in the faded red chitons of mercenaries. Any one of them alone would have made a formidable foe; gathered together they were a fearsome assemblage indeed. A jug of water sat untouched on the tabletop. Pasion knew better than to buy them wine before the talking was done.

"He is in Sinon," Pasion said casually, "Putting the final touches to our arrangements. With fair winds and good weather, he'll be here in a week at the outside. What's the matter, Orsos; do you have trouble holding your men to the colour?"

"Not since I stopped shitting yellow," the Bull said, and about the length of the table there were grunts of humour.

"Then have some patience. Pity of the goddess, this is the biggest fee you'll ever earn and you're havering over the matter of a few days here and there. If this thing comes off, we will all of us be rich as kings."

Greed warmed the air of the room a little. The men leaned forward or back as the mood took them, chairs creaking under a bulk of scarred muscle. From below, the raucous slatternly din of the wine-shop rose up through the floorboards.

"Quite a little army your Phiron is digging up, Pasion," another of the men said. This fellow was lean as whipcord, with one long brow of black across his forehead, and eyes under it that made a blackbird's seem dull. He had a trimmed goat's-beard, and a moist lip. No father would trust his daughter to that face.

"I hear that this is only the tip of the spear, this host of ours gathered here. There's more down in Idrios, and others in Hal Goshen. We've near two thousand men in the colour, here in Machran, and that's the biggest crowd of hired spears I've ever heard tell of. What employer is this that can hire such myriads and keep them kicking their heels for weeks as though money were barley-grain to him?"

"Our employer's name is not to be spoken," Pasion snapped. "Not yet. That is one of the terms of the contract. You took the retainer, Mynon, so you will abide by it."

"If you do not mean to take Machran itself I would do something to reassure the Kerusia of it," another man said, a dark-skinned, hazel-eyed fellow with the voice of a singer. "They're more jittery than a bride on her wedding night, and wonder if we have designs on their virtue. There's talk of a League being gathered of the hinterland cities: Pontis, Avennos and the like. They don't like to see so many of our kind gathered together for so long in one place."

"Agreed, Jason," Pasion said. "I will talk to them. Brothers, you must keep your men outside the walls, and in camp. We cannot afford friction with the Kerusia, or any others of the city councils."

A rumble went down the table. Discontent, impatience. The room crackled with pent-up irritability.

"I've had my centon here the better part of a month," an older man said, his beard white as pissed-upon snow and his eyes as cold as those of a dead fish. This was Castus of Goron, perhaps the wickedest of them all. "I've lost eleven men: two maimed in brawls, one who's gotten himself hung by the magistrates, and eight who took off out of boredom. Most of us here can say the same to some degree. It's not lambs we lead, Pasion. My spears are losing their temper. Where in Phobos's Face are you taking us anyway, if we're not to annoy Machran itself? The capital can muster some eight thousand aichme, given time. If we're to strike, it must be very soon, before these farmers get themselves together." There was a murmur of agreement.

Pasion smashed his fist down on the planks of the table.

"Machran is not our goal," he said with quiet vehemence. "Nor are any of the other hinterland cities. Hammer that into your heads and those of your men. You've taken money from my hand—that makes me your employer as much as anyone else. If you cannot hold to your half of the contract, then refund me your retainers and be off. Go pit your wits in some skirmish up north. I hear Isca has been sacked at last, so there's not a decent soldier up there to stand in line. Rape some goatherder women if you will, and boast of killing farmers' sons. Those who stay with me will find real flesh for their spears, a true fight such as we've not seen in the Harukush in man's memory. Brothers, stay to the colour here and I promise you, we shall all become forgers of history."

The centurions looked at the wine-ringed tabletop, frowning. At last Mynon said; "Fine words. Eloquent. I put them in my head and admire them. You always had a way with words, Pasion, even as far back as Ebsus. You could make men believe their own shit didn't stink, if you had a mind to, but we've all grey in our beards here, and rhetoric to us is like a middle-aged wife. You can admire it, flirt with it, but you're not going to let it fuck with you. Take my advice and speak plain now, or you're going to start bleeding spears."

Someone guffawed, and there was a chorus of assent. As Pasion looked down the table he realised that Mynon was right. Mercenaries would put up with many things and, contrary to popular myth, they would not desert the first time their pay was late. Stubborn bastards, proud as princes, and sentimental as women, they could be held to the colour by many things beyond money. Sometimes they would believe in promises, if those promises were grand enough, and if they flattered their own vanity. Mercenaries had their own kind of honour, and a fierce pride in their calling. It was only to be expected. Once a man donned scarlet, he became *ostrakr*, and abandoned whatever city had spawned him. It had to be so, or else allegiances to different warring cities would tear every centon apart. To replace that allegiance, the mercenary committed himself to his centon and his comrades. They became his city. The centurion was their leader, but could not commit his men to any contract until they had voted for it among themselves. It was the law of the Assembly writ small, and it gave each mercenary company the cohesion and brotherhood that all men craved in their hearts. To become a sellspear, a man might forsake his ancestors, his memories, the very place that gave him birth, but in return he was admitted to this brutal brotherhood and given a new thing to fight for. A city in miniature, clad in bronze, and dedicated to the art of warfare.

"Very well," Pasion said at last. "You scorn rhetoric, so I will give you fact. More words, but these are set in iron. I will tell you this now, and it will never leave these walls." He looked the table up and down, checking that he had each of their attentions. Had he been a less restless man, he would have loved the stage, the faces hanging on each word he chose to give and withhold.

"We are not gathered here for some city fight. We are making an army, a full-sized army, and all of it composed of mercenaries. Brothers, we have a journey before us, and its destination lies far, far outside the Harukush."

There was a pause as this sank in.

"Brothers, we are—"

"*Phobos*," Orsos swore loudly. "You mean to take us into the Empire."

FIVE
TAKING SCARLET

For Jason of Ferai, the morning clatter of the Marshalling Grounds was a piercing agony he could as well have done without. Rasping his tongue across the roof of his mouth he sent one hand out to find the water jug and the other down to his waist, where his money-pouch still hung, as flaccid as an old man's prick. He poured the contents of the jug over his head in the bed, getting some down his rancid throat and causing his bed-mate to squeal and dart upright in outrage.

"It's only water, my dear. You had worse over you last night."

The girl rubbed her eyes, a pretty little thing whose name he had not bothered to learn. "It's dark out yet. You've the bed for another turn of the jar if you want it."

Jason rose and kissed the nape of her neck. "Consider it a bonus. A turn alone."

She threw his scarlet rag of chiton at him, and stood up, stretching. "Have it your way."

Jason stood up also, the room doing its morning-after lurch in his eyes. The girl was striking flint on tinder and making a hash of it. He took the stones from her and blew on the spark he clicked out, first time, then lit the olive-lamp from it. The grey almost-light of the pre-dawn receded. It was night in the room again. He pinched the girl's round white buttock. "Any wine left?"

"There's the dregs of the skin, bought and paid for."

"Like you."

"Like me."

"Join me in a snort."

They sat back down on the bed, naked and companionable, and squirted the black wine into one another's mouths.

"So when is it to happen?" the girl asked. Her fingers eased the bronze slave-ring about her throat.

"What's to happen?"

"This war of yours."

"I wish I knew. What's the word in the stews?"

The girl yawned. She had good teeth, white as a pup's. "Oh, Machran is to be attacked by all your companies, and sacked for every obol."

"Ah, that war. It may wait a long time yet."

Suddenly earnest, the girl grasped Jason's nut-brown, corded forearm. "When it comes, I will hide and wait for you, if you like. I would have you as a master."

Jason smiled and stood up again. "You would, would you? Well, don't be hiding on my account." He dug into his pouch and levered out a bronze half-obol, flicked it at her. She caught it in one small, white fist.

"Don't you know what war is like, little girl?"

She lowered her head, a greasy, raven mane. "It cannot be worse than this."

Jason lifted her face up, one forefinger under her chin. All humour had fled his face.

"Do not wish to see war. It is the worst of all things, and once seen, it can never be forgotten."

Buridan was waiting for him, faithful as a hound, and they fell into step together as they made their way to the Mithannon amid gathering groups of red-clad mercenaries who were staggering in streams to the roster-calls. There was a floating mizzle in the air, but it was passing, and Phobos was galloping out of the sky on his black horse, his brother long gone before him.

"Gods, it's enough to make you wish you were on the march again," Jason groaned, splashing through unnameable filth in his thick iron-shod sandals and shoving the more incapable of the drunks out of his way. "After this morning, there will be no more city-liberty. I'll confine them to camp; Pasion's orders. The citizens are becoming upset."

"Can't have that," Buridan said, face impassive. He was a broad, russet-haired man with a thick beard, known as Bear to his friends. Jason had seen him break a man's forearm with his hands, as one might snap a stick for kindling. Under the beard, at his collarbone, there was the gall of a long-vanished slave-ring. Not even Jason had ever dared ask him how he had come by his freedom. He was decurion of the centon, Jason's second. The pair had fought shoulder to shoulder now for going on ten years, and had killed at each other's side times beyond count. One did not need to share blood to have a brother, Jason knew. Life's bitterness brought men together in ways not mapped out by the accidents of their birth. And even the blackest-hearted mercenary was nothing if he had no one to look to his back.

They passed through the echoing, dank tunnel of the Mithannon, the gate guards eyeing them with a mixture of hostility and respect, and as they came out from under that vault of stone the sun broke out in the sky above them, clearing the mountains in a white stab of light. At the same moment the roster-drums began to beat, sonorous boomings which seemed to pick up the glowing pulse of last night's wine in Jason's temples. One thing to be said for Pasion: once he stopped talking, he was free with his drink. Most of the twenty centurions would be too wretched to lead their centons out of the encampment today. Their hangovers would keep them under the walls. Perhaps that was Pasion's policy, the canny bastard.

Jason's troop lines were fifty spearlengths of hand-me-down lean-tos from which the fine fragrance of burning charcoal was already wandering. Before them was a beaten patch of earth, muddy in places, cordoned off from similar spaces by a line of olive-wood posts which had hemp ropes strung between them. Over all there flapped his centon's banner, a stylised dog's head embroidered on linen, with further layers of linen glued to the first to stiffen it out. Where the embroidery of the symbol had worn away, the pattern had been completed with the addition of paint. It was an old standard. Dunon of Arkadios had given it to Jason on retiring, and with it a few greybeards who had fought under it time out of mind. They were all gone now, but the Dogsheads were still here under that rag; different faces, same game.

Below the banner there now stood ten files of yawning, belching, scratching, glowering men, all clad in chitons that had once been bright scarlet, but which now had faded to every shade north of pink. They were a sodden, debauched, sunken-eyed crew, and Jason looked at them with distaste.

"How many?" he asked Buridan.

"Eighty-three by my count. One or two more may still wander in."

"That's four down on yesterday."

"Like I said, they may yet wander in."

"Another month of this, and we'll be hard put to it to get together a single file."

"There's fresh fish coming in all the time," Buridan rumbled, and he gestured to where a small knot of men stood unsure to one side, looking around them with eyes wide one second, narrowed the next. Though they bore weapons, none wore scarlet. The red-clad mercenaries filed past them without so much as a glance, though with the inevitable epithets flung out.

"Shitpickers."

"Goatfuckers."

"Strawheads."

"Too damn fresh. I like my fish stinking," Jason said.

"Like your women," Buridan said mildly.

"And your mother," Jason added. The two men grinned at one another.

"You call the roll," Jason said. "I believe I'll go check on the fish."

"We're short an armourer," Buridan reminded him.

"Fat chance we'll get one of those."

Would-be mercenaries. They came in two distinct categories. There were those with dreams and ideas of their own place in the world. These saw themselves as men amongst men. They craved adventure, the sight of far cities, the clash and clamour of war as the poets sang of it, and that bright panoply the playwrights made of phalanx warfare. Of these hopeful souls, perhaps one in four would last past his first battle. In the *othismos* there was no room for dreamers. Those who stayed to the colour soon put aside their illusions.

The second category was more useful; and more dangerous. These were those men who had nothing to lose. Men running from the things they had seen and done in their past, or running from those who wished to bring them to account for it. Such fellows made good soldiers, and were generally fatalistic enough to be brave. That, or they no longer valued their own lives. Either way, they were useful to any commander.

One of each, Jason thought, as he approached the two foremost of the fresh fish. Mountain lads, one with the bright, hopeful gaze of the ignorant, the other with old pain etched about his eyes. The bigger one, he of the broad, half-smiling face, had an old-fashioned panoply: cuirass, shield, close-faced helm at his hip, and spear. The other had a torn chiton and not much else.

"Names," Jason said, rubbing his forehead and cursing Pasion's cheap wine.

"Gasca of Gosthere."

"Rictus of—I was of Isca."

Damn. Iscan training too. What a waste. But without proper gear he was of no use to the centon—no fighting use.

"Famed Isca, breeder of warriors. I hear they've levelled the walls now, and all the women are being fucked six ways from yesterday. And what did you do when they were burning your city?" This Jason asked Rictus, sliming the question with a fine-tuned sneer. "Were you herding goats, or clinging to your mother's knees?"

The boy's eyes widened, grey as old iron. "I was in the second rank," he said, his voice quiet, at odds with the anger blazing on his face. "When we were hit in flank and rear I threw down my shield and ran."

There was a pause, and then Jason nodded. "You did the right thing." And he saw the surprise on the boy's face—and something else—gratitude?

Jason looked the two boys—for that is what they were—up and down. He wanted the Iscan. He liked the pride and pain in the boy's eyes. How to phrase it—they were friends, obviously. The big smiler could go cry to the goddess for all he cared. He might make a good soldier, but the odds were against it.

Ah, he thought, rubbing his aching temples again, let Phobos sort it out.

"All right; I'll take you both. You, Gasca, report to Buridan the decurion. He'll set you a file to join. Iscan, you cannot take a place in line of battle, not without a panoply. I'll rate you camp servant and skirmisher, but as soon as you get some bronze on your back you'll join your friend. His pay is twelve obols a month. Yours is half that. Do you find this acceptable?"

Rictus nodded without a word, as Jason had known he would.

"Buridan will give you your scarlet. Once you join the Dogsheads you may wear no other colour, and you will be *ostrakr*, cityless. We swear no oaths, and draw no blood, but if you lay down the colour without my permission, your lives are forfeit. We flog for stealing from comrades. For cowardice, we execute on the field. All other crimes are between you and the gods. Any questions?"

"Yes," Gasca said. "When do we eat?"

They drilled first, or at least Gasca did, whilst Rictus watched from the eaves of the encampment. All the centons had taken on fresh recruits that morning, and these unfortunates were marked out by the vivid colour of their new red chitons. They drilled in full armour, bearing spear and shield, and before an hour had gone by the new men had red dye running down in the sweat of their thighs. While they stamped and strode their comrades in the long files shouted abuse at them, called them women, and offered them rags to staunch their monthly flow.

Centon by centon, the gathered companies came together on the wide, blasted plain to the north of the Mithannon. There, between the Marshalling Yards and the Mithos River, the numbers of the assembled mercenaries finally became clear. Twenty companies, all under strength but still within nine-tenths of their full complement. Jason was out there with the Curse of God on his back, barking orders and clubbing with the bowl of his shield those slow to obey. Perhaps a third of the centurions wore the black armour, and as many as fifty of the rank and file. Possession of Antimone's Gift was not a prerequisite of command. It was worn by fools as well as heroes.

The companies and files came together one by one, evolving from discrete bodies into one long, unbroken snake of bronze and scarlet. All their shields, except for those of a few newcomers, were without device; when their employer made himself known they would paint his sigil on the shield's metal facings. The phalanx that evolved from their marching and counter-marching was eight men deep and two hundred and fifty paces long. In battle the line would shorten, as each man sought the protection of his neighbour's shield. As the formation was called to a halt the file leaders and closers, hardened veterans all, were haranguing some of the new recruits in low hisses. Nevertheless, as drill went, it was a good show, better than any city levy could provide. It was, Rictus had reluctantly to admit, almost as good as the Iscan phalanx had been. His heart burned and thumped in his chest. More than anything else in this life, he wanted to be out there in those profane, murderous ranks, to be part of that machine. His mind could imagine no other destiny, not here, not now.

"The Bull is drunk yet," one of the other skirmishers said beside him. There was a long cloud of them, hard faced youngsters with slings in their belts and the scars of old beatings on their bare arms. Many had peltas strapped to their backs, the leather and wood shields of the high mountains. These fellows were the light troops of the company, as well as servants to the spearmen.

"Drunk or sober, he'll keep them in the line, the cocksucker," said another, old, old eyes in a small face not too high off the ground.

"Who's the new fish?" a third asked, and the attention of a stunted crowd left the assembled spearmen to settle on Rictus. He was the tallest there, though by no means the oldest. Now that they had all turned to face him he saw that amid the boys there were small, hard-bitten men with grey in their beards, but they, too, had a wary, hungry look, like that of a mistreated dog. Too small for the phalanx, he supposed, but still dangerous. There were as many of these ragged soldier-servants milling about the encampment as there were men in armour on the drill field.

"He's too pretty to fight," one of them said with a leering grin.

"Let's us find out where his talents lie then."

They edged towards him, some half-dozen of them, old and young. The rest of the throng looked on without much interest. In addition to their own wargear, most were bearing wineskins for when the spearmen came off the drill field, leather covers for their masters' shields, linen towels for the sweat.

"Back in line!" a voice snapped. "Face your front and shut your mouths. He's wearing scarlet now, one of us. Save it for the stews."

The knot broke up magically and dissolved into the waiting line of skirmishers as though it had never been. Pasion stepped forward, black cuirass gleaming. He was unarmed, picking the seeds out of a pomegranate with reddened fingers. He raised one eyebrow, gaze fixed on the line of spearmen.

"Welcome to our merry band, Iscan."

Around noon the centurions gathered together as the weary centons trooped off the field. A clot of black and red, they collected about Pasion like a scab. Rictus had been looking for Gasca in the crowd, but lingered nearby, listening. It was cold, and from that great throng of sweating men the steam of their exertions rose thick as a morning fog. The rank cloud enveloped Rictus, and for a moment he was back on the drill fields of Isca with the rest of his *lochos*, his father's spear in his fist. The sensation, the memory staggered him, and for a moment he was blinded by it, and stood blinking, grimacing. Armed men walked past him, and he was jostled by armoured torsos, shoved out of the way and cursed for a half-witted strawhead, but he stood on oblivious. In the time it takes a famished man to eat an apple, his short life flickered past him. Boyhood in the hills about the farm. Beating the olives off the trees with long sticks. Gathering in the grape harvest, the round black fruit as big as walnuts, a broken ecstasy in the mouth on hot, dust-filled days. That scent of thyme on the slopes, and the wild garlic down by the river. And the river itself—plunging into its clean bite at the end of the grimy day with his father wiping wine from his mouth on the bank, talking of oil-pressing with old Vasio. The way Zori fed the fire in the evenings, twig by twig, the barley-cakes hardening on the griddle above it and the smell filling the house.

Rictus closed his eyes for a second and gave thanks to Antimone for the memories, the sight and smell of them. He put them away in a new corner of his mind that he had found, and when his eyes opened again they were dry and cold as those of a man just back from war.

They were fed late in the afternoon. Hidden away in the ramshackle lines of the camp were four great stone-built kitchens attended to by gangs of surly men and boys whose sole purpose in life was the tending of the black company cauldrons, the *centoi*. These were cast in solid iron, and of great antiquity. Each company might march under its banner on the battlefield, but off it, the men gathered about these immense pots at every meal. Traditionally it was around the centoi that the centurions addressed their men, and votes were taken on any new contracts. The pots had given their name to the companies that used them, for traditionally a centon numbered as many soldiers as could be fed from one centos.

All this Gasca and Rictus found out within minutes of joining the food-queue, for their fellow mercenaries became more congenial with the toothsome smell of the day's main meal eddying about them. They were handed square wooden plates and had a nameless stew ladled within, then grasped the butt of hard bread shoved into their free hand. Spearmen and skirmishers mingled indiscriminately as the meal was distributed, rank set aside. Last to be fed was the centurion himself. This was to make sure that there had been enough for every man. If the cooks ran short, it would be Jason standing there with an empty plate, and there was no excuse acceptable for that, short of an act of God.

But Jason was late. The evening of the short day had begun to swoop in before he appeared in their midst, and the wind had begun flapping at the dying flames under the centos. Men gathered around that ruddy wind-bitten light, and when Rictus felt a soft touch on his face he looked up to see that snow was falling, fat flakes spinning out of the dark in the grip of the wind.

Jason stood at the centos scooping cold stew out of his trencher. His second, Buridan, handed him a wineskin and he squirted the black army wine down his throat. He wiped his mouth, looking round at the assembled soldiers. There must have been seven score of them squatting about him, cloaks pulled up against the snow, buttocks stone-cold from the bare ground beneath them. They watched him without a word, spearman and skirmisher alike. The crackling firelight played on the faces of the nearest, but outside it dozens more were standing in darkness. Up and down the Marshalling Yards other centons were gathering in like fashion, like winter moths drawn to the flame-light of the cooking fires.

"Four sennights we've been here, or a little more," Jason said. He had raised his voice so that it carried to those peering in at the rear. "We have waited, and grown soft in the waiting. You're all poor now, money squandered in the stews of Machran. You've drunk each cup to its lees and grown to know the face and arse of every whore in the city. That time is at an end. My brothers, at dawn tomorrow we march out, every company of us. We make for Hal Goshen, on the coast, two hundred pasangs by road. We will cover that distance in six days. At the Goshen there will be ships waiting for us—"

A low murmur ran through the centon, and died away just as quickly when Jason held up his hand. "There will be ships waiting for us, and these ships will take us to our destination."

"And where might that be?" someone shouted out of the darkness of the rear ranks.

"I'll tell you when we get there," Jason said, his voice mild, but his eyes flashing.

"We should vote on this. I never volunteered for no sea voyage," someone else said.

"We voted to take up Pasion's contract. We took his money, and we will see it through. Unless, that is, you have the means to repay your retainer, and you wish to leave my centon." Jason left the last words hanging in the air. No one else spoke up.

"Very well. Assembly is a turn earlier in the morning. You will all be packed and ready to march out. Burn what you cannot take with you—only wargear will be carried on the wagons. And brothers, anyone too drunk or poxed to march in the morning will be dismissed from the company, on the spot." He paused. The snow whirled around his head, spotting his dark hair white. He looked up at the sky, blinking as snowflakes settled on his eyes.

"I don't care it if it's waist-deep. We march in the morning. File leaders, on me. All others dismissed."

The tight-packed crowd of men broke apart. There was little talk. They walked back to the company lines in the guttering glare of torchlight, spearmen and skirmishers mingled. Buridan called away some two dozen of the light troops to the rear of the lines, where the wagons stood like patient beasts. They hauled out harness from the wagon-beds and filed off after him to the city itself, where all the centon's draught animals had been quartered this last month.

Gasca was limping as he and Rictus regained the shelter of their shack. Inside, one of the other spearmen had lit an oil lamp and the wick smoked busily, catching at their throats. "How is the leg?" Rictus asked.

Gasca took off his cloak, laid it on the earth floor, and sat gingerly down upon it, breath hissing out through his teeth. "That drill today opened it up a little. I'll be fine. I'll strap it up."

"Let me have a look at it." Rictus lifted up Gasca's chiton. The red dye had leached out of it and streaked all his lower limbs. It was hard to tell what was blood and what was not. He touched the black-stitched wound in Gasca's thigh, feeling the heat of it. Some of Zeno's stitches had popped free and the whole purple line of it was swollen. Rictus leaned close, sniffing.

"It smells all right. Hold still. This'll hurt."

He made two fists and pressed the knuckles in on either side of the wound, squeezing it. Gasca uttered one strangled yelp, and then at the amused looks of the other spearmen in the shack he clenched shut his teeth until they creaked.

The wound popped, and out spat a yellow gush of pus. Rictus kept pressing until the pus ended and clean blood began.

"Where's your old chiton? Give it here." He ripped off a strip and bound it about Gasca's leg, knotting it loose enough that a man might slide two fingers underneath. His father had taught him that, the day the boar had ducked under the aichme. One had to let the blood keep flowing.

Rictus wiped his sticky hands on his chiton and sat back. "Now you can march with the best of them."

Gasca did not meet his eyes. His gaze flicked over the other men in the hut. More and more were coming in, and the shadowed space was becoming crowded and raucous. The other soldiers had leather bags into which they were stuffing their belongings with careless enthusiasm, high-spirited and talkative, throwing memories back and forth, insults, requests to borrow kit. No one spared a glance for the two youths in the corner.

Finally Gasca levered himself to his feet, spurning Rictus's hand but offering a smile. "This is life now, I suppose. Best to get used to it."

He looked around himself at the squalid hut, at the crowd of profane, battle-scarred, foul-smelling men that filled it.

"This is life," Rictus agreed, "and tomorrow we march out to see a little more of it."

SIX
KUFR

The port of Sinon was a relic. For those who had a smattering of education, an inkling of history, it was proof positive that in some legends there were kernels of truth. The city was as ancient as any Macht polity in the fastnesses of the Harukush, but it lay across the sea from the Macht lands. It had been founded on the coast of that vast, endless continent whereon lived the teeming masses and untold races of the Kufr. Men called those places The Far Side Of The Sea, but while to the south the Sinonian Sea opened out into the vast Tanean, here the straits that separated the Harukush landmass from that of the Great Continent were only thirty pasangs wide. Once, the Macht had crossed these straits eastwards, in fleets of oared galleys, and had taken warfare and conquest to the lands of the Kufr on the eastern shore. Gansakr and Askanon had fallen to them, broad, hilly lands with fertile pastures and rich orchards that made a mockery of their own stony soil. It was said the Macht hosts had pressed even as far as the Korash Mountains, more than seven hundred pasangs to the south and east. There, they had been confronted by armies so vast that there was no hope of victory against them. They had been beaten back, and had retreated to the coast of the Sinonian once more, like a tide tugged by the two moons of Kuf. The city of Sinon had been a fortress then, built to retain a fingerhold on the coast of the Great Continent. Exhausted by years of bloody slaughter, Macht and Kufr had signed a treaty. The Macht had sworn never again to cross the Straits in panoply of war, and the Kufr had conceded the port-fortress of Sinon to them, as a gateway through which embassies and merchants and commerce might come and go. The Kufr warleader who had signed that treaty had been named Asur. He had founded a line of kings, had built an empire. His descendants now ruled the world, and called themselves Great King, King of Kings. And the Asurian Empire had endured over the centuries, until it had become part of the fabric of Kuf itself, its greatness ordained by God, and destined to endure forever. So said the Kufr legends.

One hundred and seventeen ships, Phiron thought. And that's cutting it fine. Perhaps too fine. Perhaps I should have insisted on more. He has the whole of the Tanis treasury to draw on now, if Artaka has truly declared for him. He could fit half the Macht in his pocket if he chose.

Phiron turned away from his perusal of the harbour, in which were moored his one hundred and seventeen ships. Like a forest, their masts were so thick together that from the quays they withheld the sunrise. There was no room for them all along the wharves, so dozens had moored out in the shelter of the harbour moles, made fast to bladder-buoyed ropes at bow and stern. These were the lighter ones, the troop-carriers. Made fast to the stone of the docks were the heavy, wide-bellied transports, with hatches in their sides so that animals might be walked aboard, two by two.

These ships represented the seagoing craft of several nations. Such a fleet had never been gathered all in one port before. Even the entire war-navy of the Great King mustered at most some two hundred vessels, and they were scattered in deep-water bases up and down the Tanean, the greatest of these the naval yards at Ochos and Antikauros.

It must happen now, Phiron thought, pacing the marble chamber. Things have gone too far for him to turn back; it is open treason. Either he takes the throne, or dies trying.

And we alongside him.

The room was warm with the heat of lamps and a wide-mouthed brazier stacked with charcoal. Phiron had been pacing up and down within it for the turn of a water-clock, the hobnails on his sandals doing little good to the mosaic of the floor. Periodically he broke off his wandering to stare off the balcony again, resting his big-knuckled fists on the balustrade. They built with pale, honey-coloured stone here. It made Sinon look warm in the flitting scraps of winter sunshine that came and went. Sandstone, he supposed, the colour of the beach at Hal Goshen in summer. Phiron had not seen a Macht city built out of the dark Harukush granite for going on five years. His home had been Sinon and the Sea. He had learned the high Kefren speech which was spoken at the Great King's court, and in the stews of the docklands he cursed and bragged in common Asurian, the tongue that carried a man across the civilized world. His friends were sea-captains and merchants and brothel-keepers and lost soldiers like himself. He had been a man of note once, a centurion to whom his peers deferred. Once, he had led ten centons through the hinterland of Machran, and they had been employed by no one. He had meant to take a city for himself, no less, and become one of the great folk of his world. That had ended in defeat and exile.

And so here he was; a conduit between two worlds. For once in his life, he mused, he truly had been in the right place at the right time. And now the months of intrigue and furtive meetings and go-betweens were over.

The tall double doors of the room swung open on hinges of oiled brass. Two household slaves stood there in sable and yellow robes, heads bowed so that their top-knots fell forward. They were Juthan, as were so many of the personal slaves of the Kefren. Grey-skinned, with yellow eyes and blue-black hair, each was broader than the brawniest of Macht warriors, but shorter by the span of three hands. Phiron knew the stories of the Juthan rebellions. Meek though these pair might look, their people were among the most stubborn fighters of the Kufr, and had risen up against the Empire again and again. After their last, abortive uprising, half their population had been exiled to the far east of the world, to Yue and Irgun, where they toiled in the mines of the Adranos Mountains. That was a generation ago. He wondered if the Juthan had the heart to play at this latest adventure.

All this passed through his mind in a second. Phiron was a tall man, whose father had been from the Inner Mountains of the Harukush. He had taken his father's pale eyes, but his mother's dark colouring. He wore the scarlet mercenary cloak as a nobleman ought, draped over his left arm. Beneath it, the black shadow of Antimone's Gift armoured his torso, giving back none of the light from the wall-sconces and the brazier.

Two more figures glided into the room, and behind them the Juthan attendants closed the double doors with a soft boom. Phiron bowed deeply, speaking in Kefren as correct as he could contrive. "My lord," he said. "I am honoured. Lady, I hope I see you well." He straightened, heart beating faster despite himself. Face to face at last.

The foremost figure towered over Phiron, topping him by the length of a man's forearm. It had a large, equine face, with human features, but the shape and size and colouring of these were like nothing any human ever possessed. The eyes were leaf-shaped, with long, amber lashes. The iris was a pale violet with no discernable pupil.

The nose was long, narrow, aquiline, the mouth below it small, turning down at the corners. The whole face seemed elongated, with an immensely high forehead from which the rufous hair had been braided back in knots topped with gold beads. The figure's skin was a pale gold, enhanced by the light of the lamps. This darkened around the eye-sockets and about the nostrils, and in the hollow of the temples became a pale blue.

"Phiron," the thing said, and it had a voice of which any actor would be envious, deep as the peal of a bronze bell. "And so we meet."

This was Arkamenes, High Prince of the Asurian Empire, brother to the Great King himself. This was a Kefre, the high race of Kuf. This was one of the rulers of the world.

Behind Arkamenes was a smaller shape, with feminine curves emphasised by a close-fitting robe of lapis lazuli. Slender as a willow, this creature was veiled, only the eyes to be seen, and these were a warm brown, brown as mountain wine. The lashes about them were black, and had been drawn out with some cosmetic.

Arkamenes saw Phiron's quick, interrogative glance and smiled. "The lady Tiryn is as close as a wife to me. We may speak without fear."

Phiron bowed again. He was counted a handsome man, well-made and not without grace, but in the company of these two creatures he seemed a thing made out of ungainly leather and iron, stocky and solid, a rook in the company of swans. He was about to speak, but Arkamenes clapped his long, gold-skinned hands, the nails painted lilac. The doors opened again and the two Juthan bowed deep.

"Something to sustain our spirits. And quickly now."

With great speed but no haste small tables were set up, and upon them were set trays of sweetmeats and flasks of silver and glass. On a stand to one side a crystal basin of steaming water was placed with a click, and linen towels. The Juthan left again, the doors were shut, and the smell of the food brought water to Phiron's mouth. His breakfast had been army bread at the break of dawn, and a mug of black wine.

Arkamenes opened his arms in a gesture of inclusion. "You must forgive our squalor, but these apartments were the best the city had to offer. And we are being discreet, I believe. Even now, discretion is still called for. Tiryn, pour the general some wine. We will stand at the window, and look down on our ships."

A momentary shock, like some frisson of life, as the female's hand touched his, settled within his fingers a warm, smoking glass. He met her eyes for a second; she, too, was taller than he. The eyes were full of life, but closed off. Like a locked door with sounds of lovemaking behind it.

Phiron sipped his hot wine, savouring the warmth, rolling it around his tongue.

"So the fleet has assembled," Arkamenes said, his own cup untouched. "Are they enough? Can it be done in one voyage?"

"Yes, barely. Some of the baggage animals will have to be left behind, but we can make good those losses in Tanis."

"And what of numbers? Tell me, General, how does my army grow?"

"The contingents are assembling at Hal Goshen. The muster is to be complete six days from now. One hundred centons of fully armed Macht heavy infantry. At full strength, that would mean some ten thousand men, but most companies are somewhat below their complement. With them are some thousands of light troops, camp-followers, artisans and the like—"

"Slaves? We have plenty of those this side of the sea."

"No, lord. Free men, for the most part at least. Many are capable warriors, but lack equipment. Traditionally, they help protect the flanks of the phalanx, and are used for scouting and raiding parties in rough terrain."

Arkamenes stared down at his general. "All very well. But mind me, Phiron. I am not paying a great fleet to float whores across the Tanean. I trust there will be no gaggle of soldier-families trailing behind the host. These men must move fast and travel light."

"No women, lord; that was agreed, and Pasion will see that it is so."

"Good, good. Then it only remains for us to embark ourselves and set sail in the van of our little expedition. I have a fast galley at the wharves. We can be on the wing in an hour if needs be."

"I have heard rumours, my lord." Phiron sipped his hot wine. It was heavily spiced, too smooth for his liking.

"About Artaka I suppose? Yes, the province has declared for me. One of my captains holds it.

I have Tanis in the palm of my hand, general. When your men disembark, they need fear no hostile welcome. All is in hand."

"Yes, that I had heard. But I wondered—what of your brother?"

Arkamenes's narrow nostrils flared open wide, like those of a winded horse. "What of him?" he asked softly.

"Your flight is known to him—"

"Of course. He sent half a dozen assassins in our wake. Had it not been for my guards and old Amasis I would be dead three times over."

"But will he contemplate a general levy, or take the field with the Household troops alone? My lord, does he know what we do here?"

Arkamenes turned away. Now he did sip his wine, as delicately as a man taking the sacrament. "It makes little odds. Once your soldiers disembark at Tanis the news will run through the Empire faster than the flux. It is almost three months' march from Tanis to Ashur—ample time to gather whatever he thinks he needs. We will raise the provinces we march through against him. Already, I have had meetings with the elders of the Juthan. They are with us."

"And troops, lord? What may we expect?"

Arkamenes smiled, finding his humour again. "Myriads, General. I will raise thousands to march at your side; but it is your people who will provide the core, a heart of iron. Imagine! Ten thousand of the legendary Macht, come across the sea to war, after all this time. That news will be worth half a dozen armies."

Phiron bowed slightly, dissatisfied with his answer but knowing that none other would be forthcoming.

"So tell me, General, how far from this port of yours to Tanis? What length of voyage are we speaking of?"

Phiron blinked. He had been through these details a dozen times with intermediaries.

"Twelve hundred pasangs, my lord. The fleet captain, Myrtaios, assures me that with the wind as it stands, the passage will take some ten days."

"Ten days." Arkamenes strode away from the window, fairly crackling with energy. He tossed aside his exquisite goblet to clatter on a table. "Ten days! I shall be there before you, General. I shall be standing on the docks of Tanis, watching the northern horizon for the arrival of my fleet." His mouth widened in a huge grin, and it seemed that behind his lips there were far too many teeth.

"We will march across the Gadinai Desert in winter, so it will be no hardship, and when spring comes and the snows in the Magron Passes have melted, why then, there we will be, in the Land of the Rivers, the richest farmland in the world. My brother will meet us there, I know it. He will not march halfway across the Empire to bring us to battle, but will wait for us to come to him." His face blackened. "I will impale him for the killer of kin that he is." The thought cheered Arkamenes instantly.

"We will dine together tonight, you and I, Phiron. You like our food? Have you ever seen a Kefre dance? I shall have a robe made up for you, something more fitting than that scarlet rag you insist on donning. I should be thinking of liveries for your men. I see them in gold, I think. My crest in black upon breast and back. What think you?"

Phiron thrust out his jaw. "I think not, my lord."

Arkamenes went very still. Phiron caught the gleam of the female's eyes watching him with sudden attentiveness, the first genuine interest she had shown since entering the room.

"What?"

"My lord, scarlet is our badge. We wear it all our lives, so long as we hold spear in hand and set it out for hire. The colour is of our blood, our calling. No matter the employer, we wear it to our deaths, and are wrapped in it upon our pyre."

Arkamenes smiled again, a false note. "Fascinating. And though I pay your wages, though you will be afloat in my ships, eating my food and drinking my wine, still I have no say in this?"

"No, lord," Phiron said doggedly.

Arkamenes covered the room in four strides. He set one long hand on Phiron's shoulder, and fingered the red-dyed wool of the cloak upon it. He looked incredulous, amused.

"It will, no doubt," he said, "take some time for us to become accustomed to one another's ways."

Only when the doors were shut behind him did Phiron wipe the sweat from his brow. He could feel it pooling cold at the base of his spine, and the wine he had drunk sat with a disagreeable heft in his empty stomach. The two Juthan stood impassive on either side of the antechamber, yellow eyes unreadable. Phiron had killed a wolf with those eyes above its muzzle. He glared at the nearest Juthan as though the creature had insulted him.

"*Kufr*," he said with cold contempt. And he spat at the thing's feet. Then he strode away, intent on seeking the company of his own kind.

Behind him the Juthan bent, and with the hem of his robe, wiped the spittle from the patterned tiles of the chamber floor.

"Was it your intent to bait him?" Tiryn asked. Gently, she righted the cup Arkamenes had cast aside, and with one long finger traced a sigil in the spilled dregs of the wine.

"It was my intent to make him think me a fool," Arkamenes replied with a shrug of his narrow shoulders.

"There is then some advantage to be gained by making yourself out to be a vainglorious featherhead?" Tiryn asked.

Arkamenes laughed. The beat of sound was enough to make the nearest wall-sconce flicker. "I'm no fool; you know that better than anyone. But I want to see what this Macht mercenary will do, if I saddle him with burdens. He hates us—did you see that?"

"I saw it. Hatred—and yet a kind of lust, too."

"Your eyes, perhaps. Even the animals of the Macht can be bewitched by them." Arkamenes bowed. It was impossible to tell if he were mocking her or not.

Tiryn unhooked one side of her veil. Underneath was a pale-skinned face, something like Arkamenes, but in a lower key. It was softer, paler, and the mouth was both wide and full. One might have said it was more human, though the resemblance was one of form, as a portrait echoes the sitter.

"Not lust of the flesh. This man is hungry. He desires power as a drunkard craves wine. He is dangerous."

"I should hope he is," Arkamenes said tartly, "or else my money has been wasted. He is a hound, Tiryn, like those coursers they breed along the Oskus. Turn your back on them, and they'll hamstring you. Beat them well, and they will die in your service."

"And will his ten thousand be happy to die in ours?" Tiryn responded.

There was a stately series of raps on the door, as though someone were knocking a cane against the heavy wood.

"Yes, yes," Arkamenes said, rubbing his forehead. "Amasis, you heard everything, did you not?"

An immensely tall, gaunt, golden-skinned creature stood undulating slightly in the doorway. Its eyes were mere blue glints deep in a crevice of bone. The nose was a pair of black slits. It held an ivory-coloured staff in one naked arm and the other was tucked in the breast of a seven-times wound bolt of blindingly white linen. Scarlet slippers completed the picture. The creature smiled, showing white teeth inset with tiny jewels.

"Every word, my Prince. What a presumptuous beast it was." Amasis strode over to the brazier and warmed his free hand over the red coals. "Breath of God, but I will be glad to leave this end of the world. Some warmth in the air; a blast of true sunlight! How can they live without it?"

Tiryn poured the old Kefre some wine, and he raised the cup to her.

"To learn Kefren speaks well of this thing's intellect and ambition," Amasis said. "He could have settled with Asurian, but chose to learn the tongue of the highest caste. I like this in him. It shows that he concerns himself with details, and argues for a more subtle mind than we have perhaps given these creatures credit for. Perhaps there is more to them than the bloody savagery which paints our legends."

"We'll see," Arkamenes said. "I intend to run him with a long leash until we enter Jutha, to see his paces. These red-cloaked warriors of his shall be the spearhead of the army. I shall hone them as a man does a knife; at every opportunity it shall be they who bleed, not our own forces. At the end, if any are left, then they should be a more manageable number."

"A curiosity," Amasis said, amused. "When the battles are done, we should perhaps erect cages for the survivors in the grounds of the palace, and charge admission."

Arkamenes held up a hand. "Let us not tempt God's wrath. I do not intend to end this adventure with a Macht army intact in the heartlands of the Empire, but I shall not squander them either. These fearsome, bloody men of bronze, they are half my treasury on the march. I intend that they shall see good service. My investment will be repaid in their blood."

SEVEN
THE LAND BEYOND THE SEA

The storm had blown itself out at last, and now from horizon to horizon the sea was a tawny, white-toothed and ragged plain upon which the ships tossed and pitched under a hand-me-down of sail. For perhaps twenty pasangs, the scattered fleet plunged in tattered skeins and clots of heavy-laden wood and flapping cordage. In the holds of the overworked vessels thousands of men sat shoulder to shoulder whilst the fetid bilge splashed around them, and from the bellies of the big freighters the mules could be heard shrieking in angry panic and kicking at the confining timber of their stalls.

"We came through better than I thought we would," Myrtaios said with a degree of satisfaction that Pasion found quite inhuman. He bent over the ship's rail, only to find himself manhandled by the captain. "No—the *leeward* rail, for Phobos's sake. Why can you soldiers never learn to puke away from the wind?"

Pasion gave a watery belch, his face almost the same colour as the water below. "Because we're past caring. Had it been up to me, I think I'd have wished us all drowned two days ago."

"Aye, well, you damned near had your wish. As nasty a blow as I've seen, this side of Gygonis."

"What of the fleet? What do you see?" Pasion wiped his mouth and straightened. He had left off his cuirass, and his red chiton was smeared with all manner of filth. Below-decks the stink was well-nigh insupportable, but the men down there were also beyond caring.

"I've lookouts up counting, but that's no easy job in this swell. There won't be a full accounting made until you're numbering them off on the wharves of Tanis itself. Be prepared though, my friend; some ships will have been lost—you mark my words. You don't come through a four-days' blow such as we just had without some poor souls finding it their last." The captain shook his head mournfully and ran his fingers through the matted grey nest of his beard.

"I'll bear that in mind. So how long now until we're out of these damn contraptions and back with our feet on the earth again?"

The captain tramped to the windward side of the deck, beckoning Pasion after him. The cursebearer picked a path through a tangle of snapped rigging and made way for the working party that was intent on reinforcing the cracked timber of one of the great steering-oars. Seawater washed up and down the deck-planking to the depth of a man's hand. From the black noisome depths of the open mainhatch more of the crew were hauling up great skins of water by tackles to the mainyard, helped by those of the mercenaries who were not incapacitated by sea-sickness. The skins were tilted overboard, and when emptied were flung down the hatch again to be refilled. The process seemed unending.

"There," Myrtaios said, pointing with one thick forefinger. "You see that line on the horizon to the west?"

"That's land, is it?"

"That's Gygonis, the south-eastern shore of it, and if you were at the masthead you'd see the snow on the Andrumenos Mountains. I thank Antimone's pity the wind didn't back round sooner, or we'd all be floating on bits of firewood by now, pounded up and down that bastard black-rocked coast. No, rough though it was, it was as good as I could hope for at this time of year. You set sail in winter, you're thumbing your nose at Phobos, and he'll stir up the seas against you. Why, if it were not for the fee, I'd have laughed in your face when you hired me."

"So," Pasion said patiently, "assuming Phobos has turned his face away, how much farther is there to go?"

Myrtaios grinned, a stale exhalation of garlic. He picked at what teeth he had with one thumbnail. "Why, we're past Gygonis, so that's the worst of it over, and we've a good wind now, fair on the quarter. If it's more than four hundred pasangs to the coast of Artaka, well then I'll kiss my steersman's arse. And we can rattle that off in three days, barring storms, shipwreck, and this old bitch under us taking on any more water."

"Thank you, captain," Pasion said. "I am obliged to you, and your crew."

Myrtaios laughed. "You keep your thanks, sell-spear, and make sure my fee stays in the hold where it belongs. Now that's ballast I'd be happy to carry more often." He raised his hands as though he were cupping a woman's breasts. "All those lovely little round bags a' clinking together, like the gold was talking to you through the leather. You live long enough to need a return trip, and I'm your man!" He stumped off along the deck, laughing with his head back. Pasion belched, put his palm across his mouth, and lurched towards the windward rail.

During the day the wind dropped an octave, and what rags of cloud remained about the sky went with it, off into the west. The fleet bowled along in an almost stately fashion, and as the ships began to behave more like sensible means of transport and less like contrivances of torture, so the men below began to make their way up on deck. Rictus and Gasca climbed up the hatch-ladders and staggered forward to the bows. Here, the salt spray was refreshing as rain, and there was a warmth in the sun which seemed a new and strange thing. They almost fancied they could smell some new scent in the air, as though the senses changed along with the world's geography.

"We're running south," Rictus said. "See the sun setting on our right? The Harukush are behind our heads, and before us—"

"Aye—what's that out before us, I wonder?" Gasca said. He had a light in his eye which had not been there since they had left Machran, and Rictus was glad to see it.

"The Sea," Rictus told him. "This is the Tanean we're floating upon. In the legends, it is said that it was created by Antimone's salt tears, as she wept to be exiled from heaven. And then the smith-god Gaenion, in pity, reared up the land of Artaka on its far shores and filled it full of spices and fragrances and flowers to comfort her."

"That's where we're going, it seems," Gasca said. He grinned crookedly. "This land of spices and flowers you speak of—if it's so damn nice then why did God let the Kufr have it and stick us with the black mountains of the Kush?"

"I think God has other plans for the Macht," Rictus said.

"I think God has it in for us," Gasca told him. "He gave us the shithole of the world to fight over, by all accounts, and the best bits He saved up for the damned Kufr. Perhaps our legends have it all wrong and we're the pimple on this world's arse, stuck out in the snow-covered rocks, whilst the rest of the crowd have it easy with all the flowers and the spices and such. Ever think of that, philosopher?"

Rictus smiled, but said nothing. He leaned on the wooden bulwark at the bow and watched the bowsprit as it reared up and down, like a willing horse at the canter. He watched the waves come rolling in to be smashed aside by the ship's stem, and savoured the sight, the smell, the clean salt water on his skin. There was a presentiment upon him, a knowledge that he must remember this time on the wide waters of the world. A gift of the goddess perhaps. Always, her gifts were double-edged. This one gave him a keen delight in the living movement of the ship, and the massive turning of the waters below it. He knew now to make a memory of this, for when it was gone, he would not see it again.

At his throat, he fingered the coral pendant he had taken off Zori's corpse. It had come from here, from the depths of the sea. In Machran it would have bought him a week's worth of whores, or a good knife, but he had held onto it. It was the only thing he had left of that quiet glen where his father had brought him up to be a man.

The wind stayed fair for the south, and before it the fleet coursed along at the clip of a trotting horse. Aboard all the ships, the mariners repaired the storm-damage with the phlegm of those accustomed to the vagaries of the sea, and the mercenaries washed their filthy scarlet chitons in salt water so that they chafed at thigh and neck and bicep.

In the evening, for the first time, the captains allowed fires to be lit in the sand-filled hearths amidships. Over them the scattered companies of the Macht set the rust-streaked centoi of the communal messes, and they threw into these whatever they could hunt up from the holds of their ships. The centons gathered about each fire-frapped cauldron as darkness drew in on the face of the waters, and the sailors looked on from their stations in the bow and around the steering-oars. They had eaten their fill of biscuit and cold salt pork earlier in the day and now watched with some interest as their red-clad passengers went through the ritual of the evening meal as thought they were all safe and sound on land. Myrtaios had raised some concern at all the bodies on deck, protesting that it made the vessel top-heavy, but Pasion had overridden him. It was a comfort to those who found the face of the sea a dangerous, inimical place, and besides, the men were as gaunt as beggars after puking their guts up for the better part of a week.

There were two centons on Pasion's ship: Jason of Ferai's Dogsheads, and Mynon's Blackbirds. The raised platform at the rear of the vessel—they called it a steerdeck, the mariners, every object on board, it seemed, had a name in a language of their own—was a fine place to lean and look down on the two hundred or so men below who crammed the vessel amidships with the centos in their own midst, a bubbling, steaming darkness that had fire licking about it.

The cooks had finished ladling out the inevitable boiled stew, and the men had eaten at least half of it. Mynon and Jason joined Pasion on the steerdeck and surveyed the packed space below.

"Lean and hungry," Mynon said.

"Better that than fat and bored," Pasion retorted.

Jason smiled. It was an old exchange, a ritual almost. "Tell me," he said. "How many have we lost, Pasion?"

The cursebearer frowned. "Hard to tell in all truth, Jason. Even the sailors can't be sure."

"Pasion—"

"All right. As of now, it looks as though at least a dozen ships went down in the storm."

"*Goddess*," Mynon swore, genuinely shocked. "Men or mules?"

"The big freighters, for the most part—in a bad sea, Myrtaios tells me, the side-hatches can be smashed open. But we figure at least three of the troop-carriers."

"Six centons," Jason said tonelessly. "The bulk of six hundred men. *Fuck*."

"Why this voyage?" Mynon demanded. "We could have made the crossing at Sinon and barely had time to puke over the side. Instead we're here ploughing along the sea-lanes of the world, and we're hundreds of men the poorer for it."

"Tanis is the only port where we can get ashore in strength without fighting a war to do it. You've seen ship-borne assaults before, Mynon; men floundering ashore, drowning in their armour, picked off in the shallows. Believe me, Phiron knows what he is doing. Besides—" Here Pasion paused, as if he had been about to say too much. At last he went on. "If we make landfall in Artaka, then our journey will be shortened somewhat, and we'll avoid the Korash Mountains, a hard bitch to get through by all accounts."

"The Korash Mountains? Where in the hell of the world is Phiron taking us?" Mynon demanded, dark monobrow thunderous above his black-beaded eyes. "I thought he was on another ship. Is he with the fleet at all?"

"He went on ahead," Pasion said hoarsely. "There were problems in Sinon. He was worrying about our logistics, and so went on ahead in a fast galley. He'll be at Tanis waiting for us."

Jason shook his head. "Pasion, we're dancing in the dark here. Enough of the secrets. We're out at sea with nowhere to desert to, so be clear with us now. This is not a bundle of centons any more. When we get off these bastard ships, we'll be all in it together, with just the Kufr to rub up against. This is us, here. This is all we have."

Pasion bent his head. Below, in the waist of the ship, the men had begun to sing. Some old song of the mountains. His tongue probed the aching, rotten teeth that had kept him up at nights more times than he cared to remember. He thought of them as his conscience, or at least some joke of Antimone's, set in his skull to keep him from sleeping sound with so much on his mind.

"I had only the one despatch from Phiron," he said at last. What was the name of that song? Even he, a lowlander, knew the tune. "He had met with our principal at last. He thought the arrangements for our reception in Tanis were not all they might have been, hence his early departure from Sinon. That's all I know, brothers."

"No," Jason said. "There's more. We're to be fighting in the Empire, that much has been plain—but who is this principal of yours? What's the mission, Pasion? We've come far enough to know."

Pasion told them.

Land came into sight three days later. So said the sailors at the mastheads. For the men on deck there was the merest hint of a darker line on the hem of the sky, and with it, some intensification of the smells on the air. They had not known that land could be smelled as though it were a meal preparing, or a fart let go in a corner. They smelled land, and packed the decks of the fleet as though by their presence there they could make it approach the more quickly. When it did, they found it to be a mustard-pale shore clinging to the hem of the world, a line of sand, it appeared. For men bred to mountains, it seemed a strange and unseemly thing that a whole new world could be opening up on the horizon before them and yet seem as flat as a man's hand for as far as the eye could see. Flat and brown, with no hint of spice or flower to redeem it.

The Great Continent. So it had been known, time out of mind. The Macht had never forgotten their attempt to conquer it any less than the Kufr had. As the Macht fleet came in close to the land, sails reefed and sweeps striking out on the smaller ships, so they found that the very colour of the water under them had changed, becoming brown as an old man's piss. Birds began to circle the fleet and cluster about the tallest of the yards, shitting white drops on all those below. The Macht mercenaries hunted out their armour and weaponry, and burnished the salt-rust off it, determined to present a fearsome, gleaming front upon landing. And Myrtaios took on board a Kufr pilot to steer the ships of the fleet through the sandbanks and eddying channels of the mighty Artan River, upon whose delta Tanis stood, one of the great and ancient cities of the world. This Kufr stood on the quarterdeck between the twin steering-oars and barked orders in good Machtic to left and right, whilst behind him the better part of a hundred ships followed meekly in line, afraid of grounding their bottoms on the pale sand and yellow rocks of Artaka. Even Jason, standing at the break of the quarterdeck with his black cuirass on his back and iron helm hanging like a pot at his hip, felt the history behind the prosaic moment. He had seen Kufr before, a few, but then he was accounted an educated man. For most of the centons the shape standing immensely, unfeasibly tall at the stern was like some picture brought bright and colourful out of myth. They gaped at it; the golden skin, the weird eyes, the face with human features that were in no way human. And the thing did not even sweat under their regard.

"Perhaps they don't sweat," Mynon said, looking on with scarcely more discretion than the newest fish in his centon.

"Ah, don't tell me you've not seen one before."

"Upon my heart, Jason, I have not. We're not all well-travelled scroll-scratchers like you."

And so Tanis opened out before them. The pilot brought them through a broad estuary where the sea turned brown, and on either side the banks began to encroach on the water, narrowing pasang by pasang. Ahead, a tall gleam of white appeared on the brim of the world, and as the day wore on—the long, wearisome day for those who had donned full panoply—so this white grew and lengthened and in some places soared, until there was presented to the men of the ships a sight they had not quite bargained on. They had seen Machran, and thus flattered themselves that they knew what a great city looked like, but what bulked taller on their horizon moment by moment was something else. It was like comparing the mud-forts of children to the project of an engineer.

Tanis. They built with limestone here, a white stone which time pocked and darkened. But still, the passage of the years could not dim the illusion. This was a white city, a gleaming jewel. It reared out of the dun delta which surrounded it. In its midst two dozen towers, and fifty towers within towers, and interlaced battlements, all vast in conception, unreal to see, reared up and up into the clear blue sky, a dream of architects. A marvel. The farther the fleet slipped up the delta of the river, so the higher the buildings became. Men on the ships craned their necks, striving to see the summits of towers which were still pasangs away.

"Our Mother's God," Mynon said. His little rat-face was ill-suited to awe, but it was filled to the brim now. His face screwed up, and the awe moved on into baffled resentment. He stared up at the white towers of Tanis like a man whose wife has just betrayed him.

"Pasion—I, I—"

"I know," Pasion said.

"Quite a little mission," Jason said. And even he, the urbane man of letters, had trouble keeping his teeth together. "*Pasion—*"

"I *know*," Pasion said. His face was as set as some statue hewn from stone. "Ready your centons to disembark. Leave nothing behind. We will assemble on the quays in full wargear. If we must fight our way off the ships, then so be it. Brothers, see to your men."

Up the backstays of the leading ship went pennants of coloured linen. The following vessels of the fleet modified their courses, taking in sail and coming forward up the channel, line upon line of them. On every deck the Macht stood in assembled companies with their weapons to hand. And still the shore glided closer and the immense towering heights of Tanis loomed.

The messenger flung himself down at the lip of the dais. Prostrate, he babbled, "Great One, they have arrived. The ships are sailing into the harbours now, in lines as endless as the sea. Hundreds, Great One, and on the decks of every one the warriors of the Macht stand in armour in their thousands, their spearheads bright as stars. It is a sight glorious and fearsome, like some picture of legend—"

"Yes, yes," Arkamenes said. "Get out. I have eyes in my head."

He stood up, swaying slightly as he took the weight of the Royal Robes. Amasis drew near a step and raised the space where an eyebrow should have been. "Shall I—"

"God, no. Thank you, Amasis. A king must needs have strong thighs it seems."

"Those robes would pay for a second army by themselves," Amasis murmured. Turning to look down the length of the audience chamber, he said, "Do you think we put on a brave enough show?"

There were fully two thousand people in the hall, and the heat was stifling despite the best efforts of the fanbearers posted in lines along the galleries above.

"Where is Gushrun?"

"He stepped out. Even the Governor of Artaka has to piss now and then, it seems."

Arkamenes smiled. As he had risen from the throne, so the occupants of the hall had bowed themselves before him, and all talk had stilled. There was a clear way down the middle of that vast, echoing chamber, and posted along both sides of it, in a fence of flesh, were two hundred of the highest-caste Kefren of the Bodyguard, the *Honai*. Armoured in corselets of iron scales, they had been chosen for their height, their strength, their ferocity. The tall, plumed helms they wore made them stand out head and shoulders above anyone else in the crowd—in any crowd.

Arkamenes went to the window at the rear of his throne. It was two spear-lengths in height, and had been glazed with true glass, every finger's-length of it. Through the blurred brightness, he could look down on the wide triple harbours of Tanis below. He could see the fleet make landfall, and watch the beetling crowds on the wharves, kept back by more of his own spearmen so that the fearsome Macht might once more walk the earth of the Great Continent.

"Have his officers brought to me at once," he told Amasis. "Let them come here on foot, armed or unarmed as they choose. But make haste. This crowd will start fainting anytime soon. And Amasis?"

"Yes, lord?"

"Find out where Phiron is."

The heat of the land was something they had not expected, not in winter. As they followed the men in front in endless file down the gangways, Rictus and Gasca pursed their lips and looked at one another in silent surmise. This was winter? They felt as though they had come to some place beyond the natural run of the seasons. And as Gasca stood on the quay with his armour on his back, the helm close upon the bones of his face and his spear becoming slick in his grip, he wondered if Rictus might not have some truth in his tales. For this heat could not be right, not at this time of the year. Perhaps there were flowers here indeed, and spices too, whatever they might be.

The centurions went bare-headed, the better to shout and be recognised by those they were shouting at. As ship after ship came in, and more and more men filed off them to stand in rigid rows upon the quays, so the crowds who had gathered to watch grew noisier and more packed. Lines of Kufr spearmen kept them back from the ranks of the Macht, but under their tall helms their eyes were as wide as those of the straining hordes behind them.

Jason went up and down the front rank of his centon in full armour, his iron helm with its transverse crest bumping at his hip. "Stand still, you bastards," he said in a low snarl. "Show them who you are. Buridan, kick those fucking skirmishers into line."

They were led off the quays by Orsos's Dolphins, a disreputable crew even by the standards of mercenaries. In some moment of grim gaiety, these had slathered their armour in black paint found in the hold of their ship, and so it was as though a whole centon of cursebearers led the army from the waterside into the teeming vastness of the city that awaited them. Pasion was up in the van, conversing with great reserve with a pair of Kufr guides, each inclining gracefully to hear his words in the hubbub of the crowd. Even at a distance, it was possible to see that he was fighting not to recoil as the fragrant, golden faces leaned closer to his own, the violet eyes in them gleaming bright as some stone found in the desert.

Rictus stayed with the ships along with all the other skirmishers. The off-loading of the Macht gear and animals was going to last some time. There was some shouting and weapons were brandished as a huge crowd of Juthan dockworkers swarmed up to the gangplanks, pushing wheeled cranes in their midst as though they were siege engines brought to the walls of a hostile fortress. The skirmishers closed ranks and spat abuse at the line of grey-skinned Juthan, who stood impassive, yellow eyes blinking balefully. Only when a centurion came striding down the waterfront, swearing at them for fools, did the skirmishers relent and let the brawny Juthan clamber over their ships and begin the hot and heavy work of winching the army's stores ashore.

"They smell different," one of Rictus's comrades said, upper lip rising over his teeth. "Do you get it too? Like a beach in the summer when the tide has left weed on the strand."

"That's the port you smell," Rictus told him. But he was not sure that the fellow was wrong. Jostled beyond irritation on the crowded deck, he climbed up the mainmast shrouds until he was fifty feet above the wharf. From here the press and din and heat of the city seemed no less overpowering. The great harbours of Tanis were crammed with ships—not just the Macht fleet, but half a thousand other vessels, all edging to the docks for off-loading or loading. And the streets leading up from the waterfront were a jammed chaos of pedestrians, carts, handcarts, wagons, and pack-animals. Only the thoroughfare up which the Macht army now marched seemed free of congestion, the inhabitants of the city making way for the river of bronze and scarlet as it wound its way inland to where the white towers gleamed. Suddenly, the world had become a place immense beyond Rictus's imaginings, and the army that had appeared huge and fearsome in its multitudes back in the Harukush was now swallowed up by Tanis as a bullfrog will snap up a gnat.

Sweating like a horse, Pasion nonetheless felt the cool relief wash over him as he recognised Phiron standing at the summit of the street, waiting for the glittering river of men to trudge their way up to him. Phiron was grinning, that handsome face of his burnt dark, the grey eyes flashing bright in the shadow of it. He fell into step beside Pasion and the murmur went back down the gasping column. The men lifted their heads somewhat, eyes flickering in the T-shaped slots of their helmets, crests bobbing and feet tramping up and down. They began to keep time, and the cadence grew as the hob-nailed sandals on their feet punished the cobbles.

Pasion had always resented Phiron a little for his good looks, his aristocratic ways, his easy grasp of larger things; but he was glad to see him now. The two men gripped each other's forearms without breaking stride. "Where are they taking us?" Pasion asked, nodding to the pair of Kefren striding easily ahead.

"Out to the Desert Wall; the *Kerkh-Gadush* they call it. It's a fair tramp, and you and I cannot go all the way. We're wanted in the Aadan, the High City. Our principal awaits us there, no doubt growing mighty impatient. I want ten centurions too, to make a bit of a show. Make sure one of them is Jason of Ferai; I need an educated man there."

Pasion smiled without humour. "He's ten paces behind you, Dogshead banner and all. What about Orsos?"

"No, for God's sake. I want quick-witted fellows who know how to keep their tongue behind their teeth. Mynon—we'll take him. Pick out the rest, Pasion. There's not a moment to lose."

Phiron and Pasion stood aside and let the men march past them. They snagged Jason and Mynon, called them out of the endless files. Marios of Karinth, a hardened killer who nonetheless had the bland face of a baker. Durik of Neslar, black-bearded and broken-nosed, a veteran with a love of music. Pomero of Arienus, red-haired, his freckled face peeling in the beat of the foreign sun. Five others; the younger, the comelier, the more presentable of the army's centurions. Phiron called them all out of the marching files, bade them smarten themselves up with a curtness he had not possessed six months before, and then led them up the man-made tell of Tanis's upper city.

Every centurion he had chosen bore the Curse of God black and lightless on his back.

EIGHT
RULERS OF THE WORLD

Twelve men walked up the echoing length of that great space, that towering weight of marble and gold leaf and limestone arrayed in odd and improbable swirling balconies and galleries clear up to its roof, the vaulted pillars wrought in unsettling sinuous curves which did not ought to lie within the art of the mason. They did not look up, but in their close and fearsome helms kept their eyes facing front. They bore swords, but had left their real weapons behind. In the legendary black God-given armour of the Macht they strode onwards, scarlet cloaks wrapped around their left forearms, scarlet transverse crests nodding to their shoulders. They came to a halt in one bracing crash of iron on stone and stood like things immutable and unworldly in all that varicoloured, fragranced throng which packed the walls of the hall, silenced by curiosity and a little fear.

Tiryn watched from one side of the dais. Phiron she had seen up close—and now she watched him bow and doff his helm before Arkamenes and Gushrun and Amasis, all regal as statues in a little tableau they had practised beforehand, Arkamenes sitting upon the throne, Gushrun standing on his right hand with the staff of the governorship in one manicured hand, Amasis on the left, a vision of white linen. Down the hall the two lines of Kefren spearmen stood tall and fearsome in full, shining armour. It was as good a show as she'd seen—even in Ashur the Great King would not do much better, not for the everyday business of meeting his commanders. So what was different?

Tiryn tugged her veil down a little, that she might smell. The Macht stink she caught at once. There was an acrid fullness to it. These things sweated like animals and smelled like animals. Even the incense in the overhead burners could not wipe it out. In her childhood, Tiryn had sat in the stables while the slaves rubbed down horses fresh from the circuit. The smell was like that.

But there was something else. Impossible to define, it might have been something to do with the way these things simply stood, in attitudes of easy attention before the dais, oblivious to the crowds behind them, the great ones they faced, the opulent and crushing grandeur of their surroundings. They seemed more solid than anything else in the hall. Perhaps it was that fabled armour they wore, which reflected no light. Even the tallest of them barely came to the shoulder of the shortest Kefren guard, and yet...

There was something unsettling about these mercenaries, far beyond the myth and rumour which surrounded their race. Tiryn felt, standing there with one hand holding her veil from her face, that she was in the presence of something *wrong*, something that did not belong in the world she knew.

Another stir in the crowded hall as Phiron spoke up in good Kefren, the language of Kings. He had worked hard on his accent and sounded foreign but not boorish. It was remarkable to hear this thing speak up in the cultured tongue of the nobility, that which they spoke in the very throne-hall of Ashur itself.

"My lord, I bring to you the flower of our people, the finest warriors we possess. I bring before you one hundred centons of Macht spearmen to swell the ranks of your armies, to aid you in the time ahead. My lord, we are yours, here and now. We will not quit your service until you stand supreme in the Empire, and are crowned Great King in the holy halls of Ashur. This we have all sworn." Here, Phiron bowed deep, and after an awkward, ugly little pause, so did the other Macht standing behind them, faces unreadable behind their helmets.

Arkamenes stood up, smiling. "My dear friends," he began, stretching out his arms in the gesture which was his wont upon making a speech.

Tiryn edged away. Beside her, some of Arkamenes's higher-caste concubines stepped aside to let her pass, as one would make way for a malodorous beggar. She was the favourite, but when it came to it, he would breed with them. One could not have a true heir with low-caste blood in him. Tiryn lifted her head and thanked God for the kohl and stibium she had applied about her eyes that morning. They felt like armour to her now as she made her way through the crowd. The other concubines would have bowed to her, had Arkamenes's eyes been upon them. Now they barely gave her room to scrape past them. The closer he came to power, the less he would look for his little low-caste whore, the *hufsa* from the Magron Mountains. Would he miss her? Probably not. He talked to her in the night because it did not matter what one said to a *hufsa*. One might as well confide in a stone.

And yet, she thought, I walk here in silk and linen with gold upon my forehead and wrists and ankles, a bodyguard five steps behind, and a maid behind that. Mother, I did well.

She remembered the white mountains, and the blue sky beyond. From there, one looked down on the brown and green plains below with the glitter of the rivers and thought of them as another world, a place to provide a sorry backdrop to the real existence of snow and stone. And yet those endless, horizon-spanning river-plains with their black soils and thrice-yearly harvest were the powerhouse of the world, and demanded tribute from those who lived on their borders. And so Tiryn had been sent, in lieu of a son for the army. One serviced the Empire in whatever way one could.

And now it had been so long that the mountains were mere distant pictures in her head. I have become spoiled, she thought. Too long in palaces. I was born in a place where people worshipped God out of doors, stood before fallen rocks on the heads of mountains and looked up and spoke their mind to him. Now He is hedged about with ceremony and sanctuary, candlelight and gold. One whispers to Him in the shadows.

One begins to doubt if He is there to listen.

Momentarily, she hated herself. This soft, well-clad creature with painted eyes and pointed nails, who now doubted all the good things her parents had fought to make her learn. Why? Because she had seen something of the world and had begun to count herself wise.

Her mother had sliced off a fingertip the day the Tax collectors had taken Tiryn away. Wordless, white-faced, and without complaint, she had lopped it off with the best of her cooking knives, making of Tiryn's going a bereavement. Tiryn had understood and had not wept upon leaving, so shocked was she by the knowledge that this was for real and forever, not some temporary exile. But she had cried herself to sleep later that night, after the Tax collectors had taken it in turns to rape her.

Leaving the hall, staring down a pair of sentries in order to leave by one of the bewilderingly situated side doors, she found herself walking downhill because it was the easiest way to go. The heat of the day was beginning to fade a little, and it was becoming colder. Many of the local folk were clad in wrapped burnooses, which made Tiryn smile unwillingly, remembering childhoods deep with snow, and frozen lambs set in the ash of the fire to bring back some warmth of life. This winter, as they called it, was as warm as an upland spring. Artaka claimed to be the oldest place in the world, and Tanis its oldest city. Tiryn could believe that, but she still felt that slight scorn the mountain-dweller harbours towards the lowlander. Higher the land, lower the caste, the old saying went. That also was true. The tall, golden-skinned Kefren from the humid and fertile river-plains; these had been rulers of the world time out of mind. They utilised the other races and castes as a carpenter will reach into his box of tools. It had always been this way, and most thought it always would. But for Tiryn, looking on that small group of black-armoured soldiers in the great hall of Tanis today, there had been a jolt of some strange emotion she could not quite bring to register. These things; these men. They had never been anything to do with that box of tools. They did not show deference; they did not care about caste. They were ignorant, and Tiryn sensed that in their ignorance they would be full of hate. But all the same—all the same—how good it was to see the mighty Kefren stand unassured for once, and somehow in awe of the fierce creature they had invited over their doorstep.

Rictus had always liked climbing, whether it was trees or hills, and thus he was quite at home in the rigging of the ship. He sat in the Top of the mainmast, a narrow platform of heavy, salt-scarred wood some six feet across, and listened with a smile to one of the crew tell a story of a certain lady's house in Kupr, the forested island of many springs in the northern Tanean which Macht navies had plundered time out of mind for the excellence of its timber, their own home-grown stuff being too gnarled and hard to work for proper masts and spars. This certain lady had entertained two sea-captains in the one evening, and had kept them amused in turn, going from room to room in her spacious apartments until one had followed her and found her in the arms of his brother. Neither had been much fazed by this (both being very drunk), and the two of them had married her, all three living in serene contentment for the rest of their lives. When one brother was at sea the other would be on land, and so the lady was kept occupied and the brothers had a fine housekeeper to come home to. But that's folk on Kupr, the sailor finished with a wink and a grin.

The ship below them looked like a gralloched deer. Every hatch was gaping, and in some places the planking of the deck had been levered up so that the stores in the hold might be off-loaded more quickly. Rictus lay on the wood of the Top and looked down on the avid activity below. He was hungry and thirsty, as were almost all those detailed to remain with the ships, but the heat of the day was fading at last, and all along the dozen crescents of sea-leaning buildings and warehouses and other edifices which formed this part of the harbour the lamps were being lit, both onshore and in the ships which were moored nearby and along the wharves. Never in his life before had he seen anything resembling the marvel of such a sight, such a high and multi-layered snowstorm of lights. He lay there staring at it, thinking about this Great Continent, this vast beast upon whose hide he now looked in the darkening of a foreign evening.

"Who's that asleep in the Top?" a voice snapped out below.

"That'll be the Iscan, Rictus."

"Get him the fuck down. There's work here that needs another back."

As Phobos rose in the sky and Haukos trailed after him, so Rictus laboured on the wharves amid crowds of his own people and a dwindled gang of Juthan. Most of these had left with the coming on of dusk, and hence the Macht must sweat now to get their own stores ashore. The two races worked together without any communication other than grunts, nods, and arm-waving, but managed to get the job done with little more than the usual profanity.

They had stacked the crates too high. One was teetering over now, like to fall on the bent figure of a Juthan below it. Always fast on his feet, Rictus dashed to the creature's side with a shout and shoved it out of the way. He reached up at the falling crate and the wood of it struck him hard in the breastbone. He knew in that moment that it was too heavy for him.

The Juthan he had knocked aside rounded upon him, eyes glaring, fists clenched. Then it saw what he was doing. The Juthan ducked in under Rictus's arms and set its own strength to work. Between them, they edged the crate to one side. It missed them both, falling to the cobbles with a crash. It broke open to reveal bundled sheaves of aichmes, iron and bronze spearheads wrapped in straw.

Rictus straightened, staring at the Juthan and rubbing his bruised ribs. He smiled.

The yellow eyes regarded him carefully. The thing shrugged, then went back to work. But after that, when a heavy piece of cargo was lowered his way, Rictus often found this Juthan close by, and they would handle it together.

Several hours of staring seemed to sate the curiosity of the dockyard crowds. Before the middle of the night, while the work went on unabated at the quays, they dispersed, and the Kefren spearmen who had been set there to control them relaxed their guard, setting their shields on the ground and doffing their helms to reveal the strange, long-boned faces of their kind. Tiryn stepped through their scattered line with her attendants ten paces behind, her bodyguard bright-eyed and watchful, the maidservant veiled and impassive as only a Juthan could be. There were untold pasangs of docks and wharves down here at the waterfront, and almost every one it seemed had been given over to the Macht ships and the thousands of their occupants and crews who had not marched up the hill to the Aadan. *How many of them have sailed here, really?* Tiryn wondered.

She approached the nearest ship and the hill of casks, crates, and sacks that cluttered the dockside before it. The Juthan were here, of course, as they were anywhere in the Empire where heavy work needed to be done. They were humming their deep songs as gangs of them hauled on the tackles of the dockyard cranes. How odd, how disconcerting to see them working side by side with these strangers. The Macht labouring here wore no armour, of course. They were all sizes and all ages. Greybeards with nut-brown skin and corded forearms worked side by side with slim-shouldered youngsters. Was it true, as Amasis had told her, that the Macht had no castes?

There—look at that. One of the younger Macht, tall for their kind, and with pale-coloured hair, was drinking from a waterskin. When he had finished he offered it to the squat figure of a Juthan beside him. And the Juthan took it, squirting liquid into the red gape of its maw. Tiryn stepped forward, fascinated. Her bodyguard, a tall Kefren warrior long past his youth, appeared at her side. "Lady, is this fitting?" he murmured.

"Leave me be, Hurth." She walked forward, long skirts trailing and grimed from the passage of the streets. The Macht and the Juthan stopped to watch her.

"How can you share this thing's water?" she asked the Juthan in the common Asurian of the streets. "It is an animal. Can you not smell it?"

The Juthan bowed low, having noted the jewellery she bore, the bodyguard standing hand on sword behind her.

"Mistress, I was thirsty."

Tiryn found herself catching the eyes of the Macht who was watching this exchange with wariness and curiosity. In the light of the dock-side cressets it was possible to see how gaunt it was, dressed in not much more than rags, and scarred about the mouth. A slave, then. But the eyes were undaunted. There was humour in them. The thing said something, and then had the effrontery to hold its waterskin out to her.

Hurth stepped forward and slapped the skin out of the Macht's hand, snarling. All about them work on the dockyard stopped. Macht and Juthan all paused to view the little incident. Others of the Macht came crowding forward, and some bore knives. Others were untangling slings from their belts, eyes hot and bright. A splash of shouting in their language, and in the middle the Juthan standing like stone, as if waiting.

"That's enough, Hurth. Leave him. He—he meant no harm, I think."

Hurth drew his sword and backed away. "Insolence," he said. "But there are too many of them. We should leave, lady."

They retreated from the wharf, pursued by catcalls and whistles. A half-cobble soared through the air to land at their feet. Tiryn jumped, and the Macht about the ships laughed. All save the one with the waterskin. He bent to retrieve it, and watched their hasty departure with thoughtful eyes.

Twelve men stood on a bare hill, every one in black armour with a red chiton underneath. Above them, the sky was blinding blue, and around them a host of untold thousands went about its business, covering the land about like some windswept plague of legend. Off to the west, the glitter of a great river could be made out. There the land was green and there were trees worthy of the name, but here the dust tumbled in ochre clouds before the wind, and only thorn and greasewood and creosote shrubs fought their way out of the cracked dirt.

"From Tanis to Geminestra is four hundred pasangs, give or take," Phiron said. He knelt beside the map, scanning the calfskin as a man might search a foreign horizon. In his hand a length of withered stick served as a pointer. "It's desert, scrub land—rather like the plains about Gast back home."

"Only a little warmer," Jason said, and there was a rattle of laughter about the map-table. Phiron waved the flies from before his face. There was a drop of sweat hanging from his nose, more glistening along his cheekbones.

"Fuck this heat," someone murmured venomously.

"I second that. We will march at night. I have already discussed this with our principal. We will lie up in the heat of the day. By all accounts, the Gadinai Desert is not to be trifled with."

"Four hundred pasangs," Orsos the Bull said. "Ten days' march, if all goes well." He had shaved his head, and the scalp was burnt pink. His face shone as if oiled.

"Fifteen," Phiron corrected. When the centurions stared at him he raised both hands palm upwards, like a stallkeeper accepting a bad bargain. "The Kufr cannot march as fast as we can, it seems."

"You march slower, you eat and drink more," Jason said. "This is their country; what makes them so bad at walking across it?"

"They are not us," Phiron said simply.

He looked up from the map, eyes screwed narrow against the glare. One hand eased the rub of his cuirass against his collarbone. "We will start out tonight. Pasion, you have the manifest. We will be in the middle of the column—"

"Eating his Royal Highness's dust," Orsos growled.

"Indeed. But the main part of the Kufr forces will be in our rear. We keep our own baggage train with us, in our midst. Brothers, whether we are part of this Kufr host or not, I intend to proceed as if were on our own. Skirmishers out to the flanks, heavy infantry in hollow square. Baggage animals in the centre."

"We need to sweat," Mynon said, blackbird eyes darting over the map. "The men are out of shape after the voyage, and they need to get the last of our employer's wine out of their guts."

"Agreed," Phiron said "Pasion? You are close-mouthed this morning."

"You keep your mouth shut and less flies get in it," Pasion retorted. He was rubbing the side of his jaw, like a man with toothache. "I was just thinking. So, we've divided the army into ten battalions, morai, with ten generals to command them; but we've only enough spearmen for nine. We should perhaps think of making up those numbers out of the skirmishers."

"What, kit out the old men and boys with panoplies? I'd rather be under strength," Orsos snorted.

"There's likely enough lads among them," Pasion said, glaring at the Bull. "We have the gear; it's weighing down the wagons as we speak. Better it sits on a man's back than in a wagon-bed."

"I'll bear it in mind," Phiron said quickly, smothering the birth of the quarrel. "Brothers, to your morai. Brief your centurions, and have all ready. Pasion will inspect each centon's baggage this evening. Let your men sleep this afternoon. Any questions?"

There were many. Phiron could feel them hanging before him in the air, dancing in the heat-shimmer above the hill upon which they stood. Finally, inevitably, it was Orsos who spoke up. Despite his years, the mass of kneaded flesh which formed his face made him look like some huge, brutish child.

"You put this whole deal together, Phiron, and for that we all here give you credit"—a collective murmur of assent, but grudgingly given. Phiron raised an eyebrow, and moved his feet like a man about to receive a blow—"but you're not to forget that this here is now a Kerusia, an Army Council. The men elected ten of us out of a hundred centurions, but no one elected you—or Pasion there, if you come to it. We know you're the only one among us speaks Kufr, and so there's no thought of pushing you out of the way; but when it comes to decisions made for the army, we make them together now."

"You're not a king, brother." This was white-bearded Castus. Old as he was, he had the blackest heart of any of them. The scar that ran into his beard turned his smile into a leer. "You know these foreigners, it's true, but me, or Argus here, or Teremon, we all have more campaigns under our belt than you."

"And in battle, Castus, shall we take a vote on it every time I want a centon to hoist their shields?" Phiron asked lightly, but there was a wire in his voice.

"Don't be stiff-necked. We'll be working with these here Kufr when the time comes, so it makes sense you give the orders. Yonder would-be King will be sending you couriers by the dozen once the fur begins to fly. But for other things, for the ways we march and the places we stop, you come to us, this here Kerusia, and we puts a vote on it. Fair's fair."

"All right." Phiron bent his head a little. Castus, Orsos, Argus, and Teremon. The most experienced centurions in the army, a little quartet of killers. The younger generals—Pomero, Durik, Marios, and Jason—these formed another group. They even stood a little apart from the rest. And the crowd-pleasers, the talkers: Mynon and Gelipos. These would watch the way the wind blew, and make their votes the deciders.

"Anything else?" The ten generals looked at each other, nodded, shrugged. Pomero cracked his knuckles with a show of nonchalance. Argus spat into the dust and rubbed the liquid into a little turd with his foot.

"Very well then, brothers. Let us go about our business." And as the knot of men broke up, "Jason, stay a moment."

Three remained. Phiron, Pasion, Jason. The tell upon which they stood was no more than three spear-lengths high, and looked to have been made by man; there were ancient clay bricks peeping through the dirt at their feet. It made a fine vantage-point to survey the encampments of the army. They had not erected tents, but each centon had marked out its bivouac with cairns of heaped stones. The men had laid their bedrolls on the rolling dust of the plain in neat rows, two paces per man, and the company wagon in the middle. All told, the Macht camp was two pasangs long and somewhat wider. Not even Phiron had ever been part of so large an army before, or seen it spread out before him as it was here on the sere plain that bordered the Gadinai Desert.

But that was not the whole. The Macht lines were drawn some six pasangs from the eastern walls of Tanis, but between them and the walls was an even larger encampment. This was less ordered, a hiving, chaotic and many-tented city of some tens of thousands. A haze of dust hung over it, along with the smoke of a thousand cooking fires, and out upon its western borders great herds of animals darkened the earth. These were the beasts and soldiers of Arkamenes himself, his own household and the troops which Gushrun of Artaka had granted him. There were perhaps thirty thousand of them all told, and that did not take into account the camp-followers. Their camp was closer to the river, where there was still some grass. In the spring, all this would be a lush plain and there would be reed-beds down by the Artan, for the river flooded twice a year, swelled by some unknown source far back in the uncounted wildernesses of the interior. For now, the Macht were using a series of ancient wells out here on the plain and getting used to the sensation of sand in their teeth.

"If yonder host is ready to move at nightfall, then I'm a lady's maid," Pasion grunted, still kneading his jaw. "What is it, Phiron? There's a lot to do."

"Our elders in the Kerusia made a good point, Pasion, about talking to the Kufr. It had occurred to me also. To that end, I have something here." Phiron had bent and was rolling up his calfskin map. It was a gift from Arkamenes, and detailed the lands from Tanis to the Magron Mountains. Sometimes he wished he had never seen it. Four hundred pasangs on that calfskin was no more than a handspan. He thrust it into the oxhide bag he had been carrying on his back for twenty years, and dug out something else instead. "Jason, for you. Pasion, you may use it too if you've a mind to."

A close-written scroll. Jason opened it in his hands, dragging the spindles apart. "What's this? I see words here, Machtic script, and then some gibberish opposite."

"It's a word-hoard, a dictionary. Arkamenes's vizier, Amasis, had a scribe in Tanis write it out plain and fair for me. It tells you Machtic words in Asurian, the common tongue of the Empire, written as they sound in our own script." Phiron grinned, for Jason's face had lit up like a boy's. "We need someone who can understand what these bastards are saying besides myself. We can't always be relying on interpreters, or the charity of our allies."

"The charity of our allies..." Pasion mused on the phrase a moment before continuing. "We'll need that charity by the ton ere we're done, Phiron. What food will take us across this desert we can take on our backs, and you say there's waterholes out there too. But when we get to Geminestra, the bag is empty. I hope our princely employer has some skill with logistics, or we'll be eating mule before a month is out."

"It's been arranged, Pasion," Phiron said testily.

"I'm quartermaster. I like to arrange these things for myself."

Phiron tapped a finger on the scroll Jason held. "Then read this. Learn these things. If you cannot speak to the Kufr, how can you tell him what you want?"

Pasion set his jaw. He smiled a little. "As you say. Jason, I wish you joy of your studies. I go to count up sacks of grain, and hope they have multiplied in my absence." He turned and descended the hill, shielding his eyes against the glare of the sun.

"He's a professional, and thus dislikes being brigaded with amateurs," Phiron said, watching him go. "Can't say as I blame him. We march on the word of a Kufr, and from now on will eat and drink on his say so."

"If we run short, there are always other ways of making up the difference," Jason said. He rolled up the scroll and set the closer in place. "Thank you for this, Phiron. I'll put it to good use."

"What? No, no. I know what you're saying, Jason. But we cannot pillage lands we hope to win to our side. Arkamenes will look after us—it's in his own interest after all. I do not fear being betrayed or neglected, not by him. At least, not while he still lacks a crown."

The two men looked at one another, understanding. Jason sighed. "I was happier when I was ignorant—as ignorant as I shall keep my centurions. I never thought being a general would entail so much talk."

"It is always the way. He's offering us help with the baggage, you know."

"Help?"

"Eight hundred Juthan with broad backs. I've heard they're hardy as mules."

"I'd keep them out of our lines, for now, Phiron. Our men are not yet used to the Kufr cheek-by-jowl."

"As you say. We may be glad of them before long though. We march out tonight, Jason, whatever the Kufr do."

"And if they are late?"

"If they are late, then they can eat our dust."

From Tanis, the Gadinai Desert stretched out flat and brown, a parched plain that extended all the way to the Otosh River in the north, broken by wadis and gullies that the flash-floods of the rainy spring carved out deeper every year. To the south, the Gadean Hills stretched in line after line of broken, pale-coloured stone. White cliffs marked them out from afar, and dotted through them were the timeworn quarries from whence the very stuff of Tanis's mighty walls and towers had been hewn, in block after gargantuan block. Kefren shepherds roamed the hills, tending their goats as they had for time immemorial. Further south, tribes of hill-bandits made their lairs in the maze-like confusion of the bluffs and canyons.

These watched, amazed, from the highest of the crumbling escarpments, as now a great rash spread over the desert, a river of men, dark under the sun save where the light caught the points of their spears. They raised a dustcloud behind and around them, a tawny, leaning giant, a toiling yellow storm bent on blotting out the western sky. It seemed a nation on the march, a whole people set on migrating to a better place. The sparse inhabitants of the Gadinai drew together, old feuds forgotten, and watched in wonder as the great column poured steadily onward, as unstoppable as the course of the sun. It was as grand as some harbinger of the world's end, a spectacle even the gods must see from their places amid the stars. So this, then, was the passage of an army.

NINE
SERVANT OF KINGS

The news was brought to Vorus with a quiet tap on the door of his apartments. He grunted out some response, the dreams of the night still fogging his mind, and in came the morning-maid with her head bowed and a sealed scroll of parchment quivering like a bird upon the silver tray she held out.

He rose in the bed, the silk sheets whispering off his torso to reveal the broad form of an athlete—he had always been vain about his physique—and took the message from the tray. "I'll eat in the garden, Bisa."

"Yes, lord." The girl, a low-caste *hufsa*, bowed and left with the soft slap of bare feet on the mosaic floor. From outside, Vorus could hear the birds squabbling in the fountain, and the rill of the water got him thinking on other things. He reached the silver pot out from under the bed and stood pissing into it while breaking the seal of the letter. Astiarnes of Tanis—a good man. He remembered—

"*Phobos*!" He puddled the floor before collecting himself, and the parchment flapped in his fingers. "Kyrosh!"

A tall Kefren with skin the colour of birch-bark glided through the door. He bowed deep, azure eyes gleaming. In his hand he held a wand of ivory. "Lord."

"My best, and the Macht cuirass. A closed litter, and the swiftest bearers we know. No, wait; we must put on a show. I must go to the Palace, Kyrosh."

"It shall be arranged, my lord. I shall send in the dresser. Might I recommend the Arakosan silk?"

"No." Vorus was thinking clearly now. His face had become calm. "My chiton, the scarlet. And the Curse of God. My old gear, Kyrosh."

The Kefren blinked, and licked his thin lips. He moved forward a pace. "Lord, for the Palace?"

"Do as I say. And get that litter."

Kyrosh bowed deep and left, face impassive. Once outside the door, his voice could be heard like the crack of a whip. Other doors banged; the household came to life, a well-ordered panic. Vorus seldom rose this early.

Arkamenes is on the march from Tanis with twenty-five thousand foot and five thousand horse. Artaka has declared for him, and Gushrun is his creature. But that is not all. He has brought an army from over the sea—Ten Thousand Macht heavy spearmen, mercenaries under a general named Phiron. Arkamenes plans to raise up

Jutha against the Empire, and carry battle into the Land of the Rivers. He seeks nothing less than the throne itself.

The letter had been three weeks on the road. They must have killed a dozen horses to get it here so quickly. From old Astiarnes, one spy amid hundreds, thousands, which had been planted down the years in every alleyway and upon every highway of the Empire. But Astiarnes was not from the Royal Corps of Spies. He was retired. In his own youth, Vorus had used to boast sometimes that the Great King had a hand in every pocket. But they had missed this, somehow. A Macht *army*. Mercy of God.

The dresser came in, along with the muddled maid bearing bread and honey and a poached egg. Vorus smiled at her bewilderment. "Leave it here, Bisa. This morning, I eat on the wing."

This was the finest time of the year to be in Ashur. The Imperial capital lay on both banks of the Oskus River, and the water was full and high, a gleam of blue and silver instead of the midsummer brown. Ashur had been laid out in a grid, maybe four thousand years before. Vorus had studied on it, and believed the city to be twice as old; but always built on the same pattern. Imperial Ashur. Her walls were a hundred and fifty feet high, and sixty pasangs long. In their shadow lived some two million people. Kefren of all castes, Juthan by the scores of thousands, common Asurians, Arakosans, Yue, Irgun, Kerkhai. They were all here.

Dominating the skyline were what might first appear to be a pair of steep-sided hills in the midst of the city. These were Kefren-made tells, mounds of brick and stone reared up century upon century until they now loomed like mountains over the flat river-plain below. Upon these ziggurats were the Palace of the Kings and the high fane of Bel, as the Kufr chose to call their God. Each was a city within a city, and there were priests and slaves who had been born on both yet had never left either. The brick which supported these phenomena had been faced in dark blue enamel, laced with traceries of gold, and the walls of each were surmounted by battlements topped in silver plate. On the summit of the Temple ziggurat, the face of the Fane itself was covered in plates of solid gold, so that it caught the setting of Araian, the sun. Her beams were snared here at sunset by the grim teeth of the Magron Mountains to the west, but her last light was always caught by the temple walls, a beacon set ablaze by her farewell, a promise of her return. It was for this reason that the Fane ziggurat had been built, with tolerances of a few fingerspans.

The temple predated the palace, but those who dwelled in the latter had been making up for lost time over the last few millennia. The top of the palace ziggurat was perhaps fifteen taenons, and of those, ten were covered by the structures of the palace itself. The remainder was a green-walled park, a garden as big as five farms in which the great cypresses of Ochir had been planted, along with poplar from Khulm, plane-trees from the

Tanean coast, and date palms from the Videhan Gulf. Springs welled there, turning into clear streams that coursed around the roots of the ancient trees. These were not natural but torrents of pumped water, serviced by an army of Juthan slaves who inhabited the bowels of the mountain-ziggurat. Thousands of them laboured there in the dark so that the trees of the Great Kings might drink. Thousands never saw daylight, but were born, laboured there, bred their replacements, and died, and above them the serene parks and gardens swelled and bloomed under the sun.

In the lower city, the real city, as Vorus often called it in his mind, the teeming population went about its business with little or no thought of those in the ziggurats above. They revered the concordats of the priests, they were awed when the Great King chose to make a processional down the wide space of *Huruma,* the Sacred Way, but by and large they were intent on buying and selling, on eating and drinking and procreating, the same as any other creature with a brain in its head that walked the earth. And Vorus loved them for it. He loved the close-packed streets of the lower city, the shadowed canopies of the stallholders, the dark alcoves of the artisans where one might walk by and be showered in sparks, the spice-merchants, the carpet-bazaars, the metal-workers' plinths. He loved the slave-yards, where snivelling creatures of every race and type and colour were on display. He loved the packed busyness, the life, the arrogance, the insistence of this place. It was his city—he was more at home here than in any other place upon the teeming face of Kuf. No matter that he had been born in a snowbound mountain village of the Harukush; this was his home, had been for going on twenty-five years. He was no longer Macht. He was the servant of a Great King who ruled an Empire rooted in history—great, bloody, and enduring history. And he knew that he would fight to his death for it to remain that way.

When one alighted from the litter, there were the Steps to endure. These had been constructed so that horses could walk up them in swift, dignified strides, but for those with two feet they were a wearying experience, Added to this, on one's left as the ascent continued, there were carved upon the wall and inlaid in brilliant colour the spectacle of two hundred successive Kefren Kings of the line of Asur, subjugating their enemies in an unending series of sieges and battles. The Steps had been counted, and were something over two thousand. No one save the Great King might mount them on anything save their own two feet. Thus were the mighty made breathless who came to pay court on the Ruler of the Empire. But to Vorus now they were an irritating necessity that did nothing more than squeeze the sweat from his back. He passed more sedate supplicants on their way to the Audience Hall, striding upward and remembering mountains—real mountains—as he felt the strain in his thighs. There were quicker paths to the face of the Great King, of course, but he, as a hired foreigner, was no longer privy to them, never mind the fact that he had served the court for decades. And bled for it, and for the father of this Kufr he now had to meet.

"General Vorus of the Macht," he was announced. Always, of the Macht. It was that epithet that made heads swivel in the Court, that silenced the bullshit tapestries of conversation weaving their delicate ways about the King's ears. Vorus knew this Great King to speak to, but his father he had known better. Anurman had been a soldier, a hunter, a gardener. He had loved everything which nature had created, had planted bulbs with his bare hands, and with his bare hands had slain several assassins who had hoped to end his line. A plain Kufr, one of courage and honesty and humour, Vorus had learned generalship at his side. At first a novelty— the Macht renegade—he had progressed to errand-runner, and thence to warleader. But first, foremost, and forever, he had been a friend.

That was the pity of it—that Anurman's heirs were wood from some different tree. But Vorus served the son because of love for the dead father. It was why he was here now, sweating under the undulating air stirred by half a thousand fan-bearers. Because he owed it to the man he had known.

"You may advance," the outer chamberlain said with the great stately patronising chill of his caste. "Keep your eyes down, and always—"

"I know this dance," Vorus said and strode forward, scarlet cloak wrapped about his left arm, black cuirass sucking light from the hall.

The usual crowds, a long, useless length of them clad in the raiment that ten thousand villages toiled every year to produce. The Great King had entire towns devoted to the production of his slippers. One might laugh and disbelieve, until one saw it. Half a world given over to the luxuries of a few thousand; it was monstrous, until you realised that they were well paid and lived in peace. That was a good thing, was it not? To live in peace, even if that peace were servitude, and at the whim of the next high-caste Kefren higher in the preening order.

A phalanx of court officials stood on either side of the throne, and two Honai in full armour but for their shields. Vorus halted, and then went to his knees. He lowered himself further, until his forehead kissed the cool marble of the floor, then regained his feet with a swiftness that belied his years. The prostration was performed by those not kin to the King, or outside his favour. In the old days Vorus had performed a bow, no more, and then Anurman would stride forward and take him by the hand and look him in the eye.

"Great King, here stands General Vorus of the Macht, commander of the city garrison, who served under your blessed father and won high renown at the battles of Carchanis and Qafdir." The High Chamberlain rolled out the words with a fine, ringing relish, so that all in the hall could hear them. He met Vorus's eye as he spoke, and the two shared an imperceptible nod. Old Xarnes had been Anurman's High Chamberlain too, and had a fine sense of loyalty.

"He seeks an audience."

"I know who he is. He may speak, Xarnes."

Vorus raised his head. "My lord, I have received a message from the west. It might be better if its content were divulged in a more private setting."

"We are among our kin here, General, and our friends. You may speak freely." Ashurnan leaned one elbow on his throne and sat forward with a smile on his face. Taller and paler than his father had been, he had the gold skin of the highest castes, the violet eyes of the nobility. And his father's smile and easy manner. Vorus stepped forward a pace and lowered his voice.

"Your brother Arkamenes has raised the standard of rebellion against you. He has suborned Governor Gushrun of Artaka, raised an army of Macht, and is leading them east. He left Tanis the better part of a month ago; they will be in Jutha by now. If he is not hindered, he will be before the walls of this city in six weeks. He means to take the throne."

Ashurnan blinked, the smile freezing upon his face. "How do you know this before I?"

"Your father had me install trustworthy men in most of the major provinces. They reported to me alone, and some still do."

Ashurnan collected himself with admirable speed, but not before a flicker of the anger shone through. "What of our Royal spies in Artaka? There has been no word of this from them."

"My lord, they are either dead or have been bought by your brother. It is by the merest chance that we have this information in such a timely fashion. We must begin mustering the Royal Levy at once if we are to meet the traitor in battle."

The Great King sat back in his throne, his face blank. Only his fingers moved, gripping the arms of the massive, ornate chair until the blood showed blue about his knuckles. "You are quite sure about this, General? You are happy to stake your life on the word of this source of yours?"

Vorus's voice was harsh as that of an old crow. "Very happy, my lord." He lifted his head, defying protocol, and looked the king in the eye. "I served your father all my life. I serve his son now with the same measure of devotion. If I am wrong in this, then you may have that life, gladly given."

Ashurnan held his eyes as one man to another, rank, protocol set aside; he was setting Vorus on the scales of his reckonings, wondering if the son could truly inherit the loyalty that had been freely given to the father. Vorus knew this and stood very still, face set.

"Loyalty must be earned, if it is to be worth anything," the king said to Vorus. It was as though all others in the hall had disappeared and it was only the pair of them, equals, circling each other's intentions and memories and wondering how they would dictate the future entanglement of their lives.

"Trust is worth something also, my lord," Vorus said hoarsely. "Your father taught me that."

The moment broke. Ashurnan stood up. All down the gleaming length of the hall the talk stilled, and the brilliant creatures of the court bowed deep.

"Xarnes, summon my generals, and some scribes—good ones who write fast and clear. General Vorus, we will adjourn to the ante-room. Your second in the Garrison is Proxis, is it not?"

"Yes, lord." An old friend, and the only Juthan general in the Empire, Proxis would be drunk by now, it being mid-morning.

"Hand over your command to him. I have other uses for you now. Xarnes! I want runners, and the fastest despatch-riders in the city. Hunt them up. We must make use of our time."

Robes hissing on the floor, Ashurnan turned on his heel, beckoning them after him with just that abrupt, impatient jerk of his hand that his father had used. Vorus found himself smiling and wondering if there was not some of the old man's wood in the son after all.

Before noon, the riders began leaving the gates of the city with courier pennants flapping from their spines. These bobbing flags of silk opened up the roadways and sent all other traffic into the ditches as the couriers sped at full, frantic gallop down the good paved roads of Asuria, the heartland of the Empire. They went east, to Arakosia, south to Medis and Kandasar, north to the fastnesses of the Adranos Mountains, and westwards—by far the largest number went westwards. These riders galloped to Hamadan, the king's summer-capital in the heights of the Magron Mountains, and past that, the Asurian Gates, the narrow series of defiles that led out to the vastness of Pleninash beyond, and the Land of the Rivers with its many cities, lush farmland, and teeming millions of subjects and province governors, each of whom were mighty as kings in their own right. All the messages the couriers carried were the same. Raise your armies and stockpile supplies. The Great King calls you all to war.

PART TWO

PHOBOS'S DANCE

TEN
THE ABEKAI CROSSING

In the morning, the line of infantry stood in place as though they had been planted there. Three pasangs long, they had stood-to in the dark before dawn and now had their shields at their knees and were donning helms. Up and down the line water-carriers waddled, giving each warrior a glug from the bulging skins. Behind the line, cavalry moved casually in loose formation and in the centre-rear the baggage train sat like a lumpen mole on the plain, several hundred hand-carts and wagons full of gear and rations that were manned by a bewildering crowd of non-combatants.

To the front of the line the Abekai River foamed between its banks, raised by spring meltwater. This was a ford, or had been. After that there had been a bridge, but the Asurian engineers were now busy levering the last of its masonry into the river. So it was a ford again, and the only crossing-point for four hundred pasangs. The line of Kufr infantry were quite happy to stand before the ruined bridge and wait. They had reinforcements coming it was rumoured, the Great King himself perhaps. In the meantime, let the feared spearmen of the Macht grow fins, or chance the rocky riverbed in rushing water up to their chests. Either way, the Great King's levy would be pleased to receive them, should they be insane enough to try crossing.

The courier had arrived four days before with the fortuitous élan of some staged play. The governor of southern Jutha had a sizeable garrison of Kefren to play with, and as soon as he had dropped the Imperial scroll from his nerveless hands he had mustered these and set them on the road, no small achievement in the time allotted to him. These twenty thousand spearmen now stood in eight ranks along the ruins of the Abekai bridge, and had arrived there a scant two days before the appearance of Arkamenes's vanguard.

Out of the desert these invaders had come, their ranks shimmering in magnified blurs of scarlet and shine as they tramped amid the heat-haze of the Gadinai. It had been a spectacle to see, a life's event. Crowds had ridden out from Tal Byrna to watch, then had hurried away again. In the van of the enemy host had been the bronze and scarlet machine of the Macht, and when one saw them move unwearied into camp in perfect ranks, singing as they came, somehow the thousands of landlords' sons on the eastern bank seemed less reassuring.

That first night, the opposing banks had been dark and bristling, there being no firewood to burn on this edge of the Gadinai. The Kefren spearmen had stood by the riverbank and stared out into the darkness opposite and had tried, as all men have always tried, to look into the hearts of their enemy. A hundred paces away, the creatures on the western bank had done likewise, Macht and Kefren and Juthan alike, sidling down to the riverbank in the small hours to try and glean some wisdom out of the night and perhaps gain some courage. But on either side of the river, none truly believed that his adversary was doing the same. They walked back to their fireless camps with hearts as full of ignorance and hatred and fear as before.

"The skirmishers, in a mass, in the night," Phiron was saying. At his shoulders Pasion stood mute, and Jason listening. "We send them across in morai, and as they gain the eastern bank, so we feed in the spearmen. We must have space for the phalanx to shake out and reassemble, lord, else their impact is lost."

He had been giving this speech, or variations on it, for an hour now, a good two turns of the clock. And watching Arkamenes's golden face, he knew that it was all piss dropped down a drain.

"My lord, you perhaps overestimate the capabilities of our race."

"I do not," Arkamenes said with great good humour, speaking for the first time in too long. He was well wrapped in a scarlet cloak lined with the fur of hares, and the great tent within which they all spoke was warmed further by a series of braziers, all burning the black stones that passed for fuel hereabouts. They did not smell as fine as burning wood, but they did the job well enough, and were better than the camel-dung that had been their lot in the crossing of the Gadinai.

"In truth, General, all I want is to demonstrate the fighting superiority of this race of yours. Something, I might add, which I have been eager to witness at first hand. If your soldiers are all that hearsay makes them out to be, then you will do this thing for me—and you may even call it a demonstration of good faith. I have been paying your wages now for quite some time. I wish to see this machine of yours in full flow, as it were. I do not want to see a series of ragged boys wading through the river to sling stones at the enemy. Do you take my meaning? Or am I being unclear?"

Phiron bowed. What this Kufr said was almost just. The crossing of the desert had frayed all their nerves—especially since the Macht had been always in the van, by virtue of their faster marching. The Kufr host had been eating their dust for weeks, and this had not improved cooperation between the races.

We could have been here two sennights ago if it had not been for you and that ridiculous baggage train, Phiron thought, but his face remained blank. This, here, was where the contract cost the lives of his men. It had always been so—it was just a little more pronounced this time, and on a larger scale.

What fat-headed fuck sired him? he wondered as he bowed to Arkamenes and promised a heavy assault in the morning. And he promised himself that in event of disaster, he would find his way back to this warm tent, and see if he couldn't make Antimone weep a little.

They walked away from the king's tent in the chill desert night, and Jason explained with surprising accuracy what had just occurred—this to Pasion, who worked his mouth and said nothing until Jason was done. Phiron paused and looked up at the stars, closing his eyes for a moment to Phobos as one should, and nodding at Haukos for hope. As Pasion began to speak, he cut him off.

"We do it. He's paying us, and this is the way he wants it done."

"He's never led so much as a dance-line in his life," Pasion said. "Ignore him. Do it properly."

"No. This is a test he's setting. We do as he says, this time. We cross that river in full panoply, we beat those Kufr on the far bank. After that, we will do things our own way, I promise you."

"Who leads?" Jason asked. He, too, was staring up at the stars. He loves all this, Phiron realised. It's all just a vast education for him, a richening of experience. He felt a pang of envy, a memory of youthful energies.

"You do," he said.

So they attacked at first light, as so many of their fathers had. But the first thing they had to assault was the river itself.

Gasca was in the fifth rank, about as untried as one could be. He could not quite believe it when he saw them marching towards the river, but once he was in the midst of those foul-smelling, heavily armoured ranks of men, there were no ways in the world he was going to turn back.

"Keep that fucking sauroter out of my crotch, you hear me?" the man behind him said. "Keep your aichme up and out of the bloody way. You push when you're told, and you step up if you see a gap, all right, strawhead?"

Gasca said nothing. Green though he was, he already knew those who felt they had to talk going into the thing. It was a phenomenon, like having to piss, or wipe one's mouth every minute. Rictus had told him that. Where in the hells was Rictus anyhow? He'd find some way to get into the thick of it, Gasca was sure. That skinny bastard would never rest until he was in the front rank.

The water—they were wading into the river now. *Phobos and all his tits, it's cold. Antimone, look down on me now and—arrows—they're shooting at us!*

God in hell, the water is cold—ah, Phobos—it's on my balls. He raised his shield, casual and frantic at the same time. A lead-weighted dart banged off the rim. He actually found himself overcome by curiosity rather than fear. *What the hell was that? Do they make those in—*

The man next to him went down without a sound. They were waist deep now, and Gasca could only see a faint darkness of blood in the dark water. Where do you have to get hit, he wondered, to fall down all at once like that?

As the river deepened, so the current grew stronger. The column of men began to veer downstream as the vast volume of water pushed on the bowls of their shields. The man on Gasca's left was lurching into him, as he was into the man who had filled the gap on his right. Something entangled Gasca's legs, and he almost went down. It was a body, anchored to the floor of the river by the weight of its armour. The water was up to his breastbone now, and under his feet Gasca could feel the rolling stones and pebbles of the riverbed, more bodies, which he stepped over as though climbing stairs. Once his sandal slid on the smooth convexity of a shield. He gasped for breath; his helm seemed to be suffocating him. Anyone who even tripped up in this press, this rush of water, would drown in moments, dragged down by their armour, trampled by their comrades. It was insane—it was not war; how did courage avail anyone here? Gasca wanted to cry out, but none of the other men were making a sound apart from hoarse, ragged panting and curses hissed venomously into their beards.

Then a voice began up front. It was Jason, Gasca realised. The centurion had begun to sing, at first in fragments as broken as his breathing, then stronger, as if the very act of singing somehow helped the labour of his lungs. It was the Paean, the battle hymn.

More men took it up, spitting out the ancient words like curses, teeth bared against the assault of the river and the shower of missiles that was now raining down on them. The song travelled down the column until all at once there were thousands of them singing it. The slow, sonorous beat of the hymn grew in their blood, bringing them almost into step with one another. They lifted their heads and looked up at the far riverbank ahead and the waiting line of Kufr. Some men began to grin insanely. The Paean boomed out, implacable, a fearsome battery of sound. The men found their feet and settled their shoulders into the bowls of their shields, shoved forwards as if assaulting an enemy line. They attacked the river.

Amid a fearsome clattering of missile-points on metal, the water-level began to sink. There was squared-off masonry below their feet now, the remnants of the bridge. More men went under, stumbling to their deaths in tombs of bronze. The arrows and darts came falling in a black hail, finding the eye-slots of helms, the nape of necks, the fleshy muscle at the space between shield and cuirass. But the column was still intact. The water was thigh-deep, knee-deep—and suddenly the terrible press of the river was gone and there was the weight of the armour and shield dragging downwards again, the men exhausted and dripping and sweating and bloodied before they had even come to grips with the enemy. Now men were taking arrows in their knees or shins—no one had donned their greaves for the water-crossing—and there were gaps everywhere. Jason, up front in his transverse helm, began barking out orders. The head of the column halted, and centons began to deploy to the left and right of the Dogsheads, broadening the line. The Dolphins were on the left—Gasca recognised their banner—Mynon's Blackbirds on the right. Phiron had put his best at the van of the attack.

Men fell, shot through, and others stepped up from behind them. The gaps were filled, the line remained unbroken. Ahead, the enemy spearmen had donned their shields and were standing with spears levelled.

"Advance!" Jason shouted, and up and down the line the Centurions took up the call. In front and rear of the line the experienced file leaders and closers led the way or shoved on the backs of those before them. The line shunted into motion. The Paean, which had died away, now began again. One of Gasca's sandals was sucked off by the churned mud of the riverbank but he never paused, grinding forwards with the shield of the man behind him occasionally dunting him in the back, stepping on the heels of the man in front, fighting to keep his spear upright in the press and the wicked sauroter-spike from slashing his lower legs. So busy was he with these tasks, and so utterly exhausted by the struggle in the river, that he had not a moment to feel fear. Merely advancing took up all his energies, mental and physical. Around him, that sea of men and metal marched with the remorseless efficiency of some great machine, but on the level of the individual spearmen there was only the treacherous sucking of the mud underfoot, the shoving of neighbours, and the blinding sweat trickling down in the confines of the bronze helm. When the Macht battle line finally struck the Kufr defenders there was nothing that registered with Gasca, save the fact that they had halted at last. The man behind him leant into his back with his shield and said, "*Push.*" So he did so. Up ahead, in the leading ranks, he could see the levelled spears going in and out, stabbing at the Kefren ranks. The Macht were shorter than their enemies, but more heavily built. They shoved the enemy line asunder through sheer brute strength, and as the line splintered and gaps appeared, so the wicked aichmes licked out. There was no extravagance to the fighting; no glory, Gasca realised. These men were doing their job. They were at work. They did not raise battle-cries, or scream curses. They pushed with their comrades, they looked for openings, and they stabbed out with a swift, economic energy, like herons seeking minnows. The Kefren were shouting and snarling and trying to beat down the Macht shields, but their impetuosity fragmented their own line. One of their champions would physically batter down a Macht warrior's shield, but as the Kufr then raised his spear to strike, three Macht aichme would riddle him.

The Kefren could not match this remorseless efficiency. At first in pockets, then in struggling masses, they began to turn away from the Macht line and drop their shields in a frenzied panic. The Macht spearheads killed most of those in the first two ranks who did this, but those farther back were getting away. And now a great animal growl seemed to go up in the phalanx, as the tide of battle turned. The line surged forward, but still men kept within the shadow of their neighbour's shield, and the centurions could be heard shouting, "*Hold your line!*" Someone struck up the Paean again, and the hymn steadied them. They began to advance, dressing their gaps and putting their feet in step with scarcely a conscious effort. They stepped over corpses uncounted. Up in the front ranks the best killers in the army were still at their work, cutting down the hindmost of the fleeing foe.

It is over, Gasca realised. This thing is won. I have been in my first battle and I am alive, and I am not disgraced. A wave of cool relief washed over him. He felt lighter, and yet weak as a half-drowned pup. His spear was unbloodied, but that did not matter. He had gone into the *othismos*, the heart of battle, with the rest of the veterans and had come out alongside them with his shield still on his arm.

The Kefren army abandoned its baggage and became a hunted mob of individuals, all order lost as the line shattered and the Kufr looked to their own lives, tossing away anything that might slow down their flight. The Macht heavy infantry stood down and opened ranks. Through the gaps came the skirmishers, the light troops who were fleet as deer and who would complete the destruction of the enemy army. Gasca saw Rictus at the forefront of these wild, hallooing fiends, but to his friend he was just one more anonymous, helmed spearman, and his triumphant greeting was drowned out by the general cacophony. The skirmishers coursed after the retreating Kefren like a pack of hounds and began stabbing these tired warriors in the back as they caught up with them. They generally worked in groups of four: *fists*, they were called, and while the fleetest member of the fist would trip up their quarry, the rest would pounce on him and cut him into quivering meat. Then they would move on. Mercenaries did not loot the dead while the enemy was still on the field, and in general did not pursue their foe to the death; it was foolish, dangerous, and uneconomical. But they were not fighting in some inter-city battle of the Harukush now, and Phiron wanted to set an example. So he had loosed his Hounds with orders to slaughter every Kufr on the eastern bank who fell into their hands. And the bloody business was thus scattered over the plain to the east of the Abekai River, and carried on to the very surrounds of Tal Byrna itself. The gates of the city were shut in panic, cutting off a mass of the Kefren soldiery who had marched out the day before. The last remnants of this army had their throats cut within sight of the city walls.

That night the Macht camped before the towering battlements of Tal Byrna, the fortress-city of southern Jutha, made rich by the caravan trail that passed through it on the way to the Land of the Rivers. This had been a Juthan fortress once, in the far-off misty days when the Juthan had been a free people living under their own kings; then it had become a Kefren stronghold, garrisoned to hold southern Jutha for the Empire. Now, militarily speaking, it was a husk, a beautiful towered shell with half a million Kufr quivering inside it and barely a soldier left to man its walls. There were countless mud-brick villages in the region around it, and the richest farmland outside Pleninash, farmland watered by the tributaries of the Abekai and the irrigation systems of the Imperial Engineers. While the Macht gathered their dead and stockpiled the masses of enemy wargear left on the field, the Kufr elements of the host crossed the river and sent out a dozen foraging parties to gather food for the army. These covered southern Jutha like hungry locusts, sucking up the resources of the entire region to feed the hungry masses of Arkamenes's hosts.

"To the victor, the spoils," Phiron said. "What's the butcher's bill, Pasion?"

"Larger than it ought to have been," Pasion said sharply. "Almost two hundred dead or too crippled ever to lift spear again. And twice that wounded, though most of those will come back to the colour, given time."

The campfire crackled between them in the dark, and behind them Kufr servants, a whole company of them, were rearing up Arkamenes's tent, a laborious job which would take them half the night. In the morning, Arkamenes would receive the surrender of the city within it, and he wanted everything just so.

"It had to be done," Phiron said with unwonted gentleness. "Arkamenes was right. And now we have put the fear of God into these fellows. This one battle may have saved us a dozen more."

"I see it; I'm not some strawhead fresh off the mountain. It's good to take the measure of our enemy, too."

"Don't put too much store by their performance today. These were a levy, no more. The Imperial troops will be another thing entirely. And this lot had no cavalry. In the plains ahead we will be up against horsemen by the thousand, and our skirmishers will not be able to run riot."

"Beef up the centons then. There's good gear piling up head-high outside the camp. The cuirasses are too big, but the shields and spears and helms are a fair enough fit. Draft in a thousand of the Hounds to bolster the battle line."

"I will," Phiron said. Then he set a hand on Pasion's shoulder. "This was a good beginning, brother."

"It is only a beginning," Pasion said with a tight smile.

The Dogsheads were fewer in number that night, the crowd about the steaming centos somewhat thinner as the cooks ladled out the stew. Two dozen of them had fallen to the river or the Kufr in the morning and many of the remainder were carrying wounds, mostly punctures to the upper body, or lost eyes. Jason had gone the rounds of the hospital tents and now he and Buridan stood back as his centon wolfed down the good, hot food, the best that could be gleaned from the farms and storehouses of southern Jutha. The desert was behind them, they had a victory under their belt, and the army's quartermasters were busy accounting for every captured spearhead. Plus, there had been an issue of palm wine, the sweet, thick, intoxicating brew of the Middle Empire. As the men settled about their plates and jugs, so a raucous recalling of the fight began, all fear forgotten, blows dealt and received now part of a story that all had a hand in telling. This, while the stink of the Kefren army's corpses was beginning to rise from the water channels and dyked fields that surrounded them. They had trampled half a harvest beneath their feet and pitched their tents on the other half, but the granaries of the countryside round about seemed inexhaustible. Round, bee-hive mounds of fired brick built on columns of stone to keep them from the vermin, they held enough millet and barley to feed a score of armies. Herds of pigs and cattle and goats had been rounded up by the bloody-handed skirmishers. Many of these were now spitted and turning above broad fires, which in turn were fuelled by the felling of the innumerable palm trees which lined the irrigation channels. We may be freeing this country, Jason thought with a pang, but we're laying waste to it too. The Juthan have exchanged one master for another. That is the way of things. There is no such thing as real freedom, not here, on this continent.

The young Iscan, Rictus, was standing slopping stew into his mouth and listening to the boasting of his strawhead friend. He had filled out a little, and was dressed in a red Kufr tunic that had been cut down to size. He looked up as Jason approached and nodded, that Iscan arrogance dripping off him. Even by firelight, Jason could see the dried blood that still caked his hands.

"A good hunting?" he asked casually.

"A good hunting," Rictus said. Something twisted his mouth. He looked down into his stew. "Not much of a fight though, once they broke."

"Fight enough for me, getting cross that bloody river undrowned," his friend said, rising; Gasca, that was the name. This fellow was beefy, his face shining with fat. He was drunk, too, but then most of them were. Drunk with having survived. It came upon even veterans after a battle, and Jason thought none the worse of him for it. But Rictus interested him.

"You think we should have let them go?" he asked.

"I think the slaughter was excessive. If we're here to win an Empire for our employer, I don't see how we'll do it by killing every mother's son who stands up against us."

"Mother's son—listen to him," one of the veterans scoffed. "They're Kufr, lad. Not even human. What do we care how many of them bleed under our spears? The more the merrier I say." And there was a chorus of full-mouthed approval around the great black, steaming centos.

"You got to break eggshells to eat eggs," someone else said, spitting gristle into the fire.

Rictus shrugged. He was a self-contained young fellow, Jason thought. "I've not met many Iscan mercenaries," he said.

Rictus spooned his stew around his plate. "Isca is gone. It's barely a memory now. Here, we're all the same." He raised his head and looked about him at the catcalling, carousing company which filled the night, and there was a kind of hunger in his eyes. *He still wants to belong*, Jason thought. *Well, that's a good thing. I can use that, perhaps.*

Rictus spoke again. He was awkward now, some of the maturity dropping off him. "I found a good shield with a bronze facing. It's smaller than ours are, but sound enough. And I have a spear and a helm now. I could take my place in the battle line. I've drilled; I know the way of it." He met Jason's eyes, then looked away again.

"I'll think on it," Jason said, though he would not. He thought there were other things to be had from this young fellow, things that hunger in his eyes might make him good at.

ELEVEN
THE PASSAGE OF THE STORM

Tal Byrna, a great city, now scooped up as a man will stoop to lift a chestnut off the ground and put it in his pocket.

There it clicked with the others: Tanis, Geminestra. The south-eastern portion of the Empire had been secured by Arkamenes now, that change in ownership ratified in the blood of the Abekai Crossing.

The army marches, there is a slaughter, and a form of words is made to make the world change. But the world does not change; the water still flows, the seeds still sprout, and those who work the soil continue to work it, a little poorer, a little thinner and sadder than before. The storm moves on, and in its wake the world goes once more about its business. This is war, this passing storm on the land. This stink on the air, this dust-cloud which hems the sky. These creatures marching in their thousands, changing everything and changing nothing with their passage. This is war.

So thought the lady Tiryn as she pulled back the curtains of her bobbing litter to watch the green hills of Jutha roll past, their bases bedded in the glittering tracery of water-channels which enriched this earth and held it back from the embrace of the desert to the west. Nothing in her life had so sickened her as the sight of the broken Kefren army lying scattered for pasangs between the Abekai River and the walls of Tal Byrna. The corpses had been stripped naked, high-born Kefren some of them, all of them high caste, the masters of this world. As naked frameworks of meat they had been piled into mounds by the Juthan peasants and set afire, great stinking pyres topped with pillars of oily smoke that could be seen for pasangs. Thus did the mighty of the world pass away: as ashes, to be scattered into the dirt and nourish the seeds of next year's harvest.

She looked down at the heavy scroll in her lap. On one side, words in her own tongue—Asurian, the language of the masses. On the other, in the same script, odd-sounding gibberish, nonsense-words that were nonetheless somehow familiar to her. She had been bred in the Magron Mountains, and the tribes there had dialects of their own, words lowlanders did not know or could only half guess at. Some of these meaningless words sounded like the tongue of her childhood, the rough speech her father's goatherds had used.

It was the speech of the Macht, transcribed phonetically in good Asurian script. Amasis had given her this scroll, to keep her occupied perhaps. The sister-copy had been given to the Macht general some time before. Tiryn had been learning Machtic now for many weeks, since landfall in Tanis, and the more she learned of it, the more she became convinced that it was—or had once been—the same language the mountain-people of the Empire spoke in their snowy fastnesses. Whatever the Macht were now, at some time in the distant past they, too, had lived in the highlands of the Empire, and had spoken something akin to Asurian. This knowledge Tiryn had kept to herself—for who was there to tell? Arkamenes had barely spoken to her in weeks. Tiryn was a tool, once of great use in palaces, but now mere baggage in the midst of a marching army.

A line of men went running past the litter—Macht without armour. They were dressed in the interminable red tunics and carried leather-faced shields of wicker, javelins, and short stabbing spears. Arkamenes and his Household were at the forefront of the column for once, they being sick and tired of eating Macht dust, so these men were running up to the very forefront of the army. Tiryn eyed their passing ranks with some curiosity as they sped across her vision, sandals slapping in the muddy verges of the road. There were scores of them and they ran easily, like loping wolves.

A different sound in the air; the muffled thunder of hooves. Horses approaching—a troop of them cantering in the wake of the Macht—and there was Arkamenes himself at their head, jewelled breastplate flashing in the sun. He wore a *komis*, the cowled linen head-dress of the Kefren nobility, and there was a holster of javelins at his thigh. Then he was gone, and the plodding column carried on its way, the litter swaying on the shoulders of its Juthan bearers. Tiryn's maids squatted with downcast eyes opposite her in the perfumed compartment. Once again, the endless tramp of feet upon the earth, the army's heartbeat. Tiryn sank back upon her cushions, the scroll sliding from her lap, forgotten. He did not so much as look my way, she thought. I am no longer useful to him now, not even as a brood mare. And from the hot glare of her eyes the tears spilled, and trickled into her veil.

Arkamenes reined in, the high-bred Niseian prancing under him, nostrils flared. The tallest of the Macht would not reach its shoulder, and he felt that he towered over all of them. This put him in an even better humour. He set one hand on his hip and slouched in the saddle as one born to it.

"Well, Phiron, what plan is this you've hatched for me now?"

Phiron stepped out of the brisk-marching column. He wore his cuirass and carried a spear. Like all the Macht, he stored his shield and helm in the wagons while on the march. He was growing a beard; Arkamenes thought it did not suit him, but then no Kefren noble grew hair on his face. What an ugly race, he thought. So stubborn and steadfast, so small in mind, unprepossessing. They might be brothers to the Juthan, were it not for their colouring. And yet, these hairy, ugly little creatures were the stuff of Asurian legend. Deep down, Arkamenes knew full well that no Kefren army, not even the Great King's Honai, could have come out of that river and broken the enemy line as these things had. There was an implacability about them that had to be seen to be believed. His money had been spent well.

"I am sending forward a flying column to scout out the region to our front," Phiron said. His eyes ranged up and down the passing files of marching men, noting everything. The Macht winked or nodded at him as they passed by, no jot of deference about them. Arkamenes, they ignored entirely, and he swallowed the anger that welled up in him.

"I wish to send these scouts far ahead of us. They'll be on foot, as we are not a horse-people, but they can move swiftly if they're unarmoured. And my lord, I would like one of your staff to accompany them, someone who can speak Machtic and interpret for their officers."

"What is there to scout for? We have destroyed the only Imperial force in Jutha," Arkamenes said. The sun caught the polish on his nails as he held one reasonable hand palm upwards.

"Fast moving cavalry could cover a lot of ground. Levied in Pleninash, it could be on the Jurid River a week from now. I mean to seize the next bridge intact, my lord. I do not want my men to fight their way across another river."

Arkamenes was stung by the implication. Again, he found himself controlling the anger these creatures seemed to stoke in him. He affected disinterest. "Very well. But you are not in luck today, General. None among my staff speak your barbarous tongue. That is the reason Amasis had ours written down for you in Tanis—the costly labour of a dozen scholars, I might add. Your men will have to shift for themselves."

Phiron looked up at Arkamenes's golden face. He seemed thoughtful and almost puzzled at the same time. Even silent, he rebukes me, Arkamenes thought. He kicked his horse's ribs and the animal half-reared.

"You are in my Empire now, General. Your men will have to learn my language." The horse took off under him. He galloped away, raising a hand in mocking farewell, whilst a brightly dressed kite-tail of attendants and staff trailed after him, whipping their mounts to keep up.

The combined army trekked onwards across the fertile plains of southern Jutha, a moving city of some forty thousand souls. The Juthan peasants who worked the land straightened from their labour to watch as the phenomenon came and went. In the morning it would be a rumble on the air, a dust cloud at the horizon. As noon came, it would fill their world, an awe-inspiring host of hosts tramping the winter-sown barley under their feet and gathering up every hoard of grain, every herd of livestock in its path. The Macht army in the van held to its ranks and marched in disciplined companies. Behind them the Kufr troops spread out in skeins and crowds about the countryside, looting as they came, not just for food, but for anything they might carry on their backs. They rifled through the reed-thatch of the Juthan villages, poked holes in the mud-brick walls, kicked in the doors of smoke-houses, and made off with the hanging hams.

When evening came, the storm had passed. The army was no more than a blur on the dimming horizon again, marching into the eastern darkness. In the sky above Phobos and Haukos looked down in its wake, and the Juthan set about repairing their homes and salvaging what they could out of their gutted farms, rebuilding the broken dykes of the irrigation channels and comforting their weeping wives and daughters. And when they had finished, the Juthan menfolk gathered in quiet crowds about the squares in their villages with their billhooks and axes to hand, and talked amongst one another long into the night.

"He is crossing into Istar now, following the Great Road eastwards. It is the best route, quickest and in the richest country. He will not deviate from it. With that knowledge, we can plot his march with some accuracy."

Vorus stood looking up at the brilliantly lit western wall of the chamber. There, in mosaic pieces smaller than a moth's wing, was set a map of the world—or at least, that portion of it which mattered. The map was as accurate as the Imperial surveyors could make it, and the craftsmen had laboured over it for fifteen years, or so court legend said. The room was circular, with windows set high above his head. The map curved about half the room's circumference, and marked out in stone and tile upon it were not only the mountains and rivers and cities of the Empire, but the roads, the posting stations, the Imperial granaries, and the fortresses which nailed this immense expanse of territory together. Vorus had last stood before this map with Anurman and Proxis, planning the Carchanis campaign twenty years before. Now he turned to Ashurnan the Great King, the only person seated amid the crowd of others who stood silent in the room, and he clicked his ivory pointer from spot to spot on the map.

"We thought to hold him at the Jurid River by taking the bridges with cavalry before his main force had come up, but he sent ahead a body of light infantry and forestalled us. Esis has capitulated to him, the last major fortress before the Bekai River. All the Juthan cities have now declared for the traitor: Anaphesh, Halys, Dadikai—"

"I know the cities of Jutha, General," Ashurnan said quietly. "What of Honuran, Governor of Istar—any word?"

There was a silence. Somewhere, a woman's voice sang with exquisite sweetness. This chamber was near the harem—Hadarman the Great had built it here so he could be briefed on the Empire's doings without straying too far from his wives. It had the added advantage of being far from the audience chambers of the Court, and easy to secure against prying ears and eyes. The

Honai outside the door were high kin of the King himself. One turned to blood for trust, even when it was the blood one was wariest of. Honuran, Governor of Istar, was Ashurnan's cousin. They had played together in this palace as boys.

"There is no word from him, my lord," old Xarnes said. He cleared his throat slightly, leaning on his staff of office as though it were a thing of practical use now, not merely ceremonial. "Our messengers sent to Istar have not yet returned."

"He's equivocating, waiting. That means Istar is already lost," Vorus said bluntly. In the knot of people about the seated king, the wide, grey face of Proxis stared back at him, yellow eyes shot with blood. Proxis shook his head slightly, one old comrade to another.

"At least, lord, I believe it likely that—"

"My cousin has betrayed me for my brother. I know, General. You need not be too careful of your words." Ashurnan stood up, and approaching the wall he ran his hand along the mosaic of the map as though he thought he could gain information from its touch. "Not today, anyway. Today I must have truth in all its bitterness." He turned away from the wall abruptly. "Berosh, how is it in the Magron Passes?"

A high-caste Kefren with the violet eyes of the Royal house bowed deeply before responding. "My lord, the snow is still deeper than a wagon's wheel. The Asurian Gates are closed to all but the hardiest of our couriers. There is no passage yet for the army. Spring has not yet come to the passes."

"So we're caught here, whilst beyond the protection of the mountains he rapes half the Empire," Ashurnan snarled. "General, what of our muster?"

Proxis stumped forward, bowed as deeply as Berosh had done, though without grace, and handed Vorus a scroll. The Macht general opened it and scanned the tabulated lists that lined the parchment in the exquisite hand of the palace scribes. Even writing bald lists of numbers, their craftsmanship was a thing of beauty.

"My lord, the levies from Arakosia and Medis are in. With the Asurian troops and your Household, that totals some hundred thousand foot and twelve thousand horse. The marshals have done well."

"And now we must feed them all through what remains of this winter," Ashurnan said, rubbing his eyes.

"My lord, this works to our advantage. He must make the passage of the Asurian Gates soon after the spring melt. His men will be marching down from a mountain-crossing, tired, their supply lines strung out. We meet him here, on the plains before Ashur itself, where our cavalry will carve him up and our numbers can be brought to bear. Our men will be rested and well-fed, and we will outnumber the foe three or four to one. My lord, the traitor will die before the walls of the Imperial City, I promise you."

Ashurnan smiled. He stepped across the room in three strides and set one hand on Vorus's shoulder. The Kefren among those present stirred in shock. The Great King bent, and kissed Vorus on the cheek, the greeting of a close friend, or a kinsman. Vorus felt his face flush with blood. There were murmurings among those present.

"You will lead this army," Ashurnan said. He turned and looked over the high officers and courtiers of the Empire, who stood stiffly before him now, eyes downcast, heads bent.

"Who else could I choose that would better know how to kill an army of Macht?"

It was a bad place for a girl to be, this far into the bivouac-lines of the army. In the firelight she wore a komis pulled across her face, but there was no mistaking the curves that filled her silk robe, or the peep of her pale hand as it tugged the veil closer about her nose. She was as tall as the average strawhead from the mountains, and she was Kufr, wandering through a Macht camp at night. One of the other army's whores, Jason supposed, though she was well dressed, and more demure than most. The Macht did not copulate with Kufr—never had, never would. That was the chosen line they all took. But at night, when the camps of the Macht and the Kufr drew close for protection, there was a certain traffic of figures flitting back and forth that had nothing to do with the daytime commerce. It was hard to know. Even Jason could not say for sure, and he had a quicker wit than most. And even he, the scroll-scratcher, was beginning to feel the lack of female company. It had been a long time since they had taken ship, and now the Kufr did not look so outlandish as once they had.

Orsos, of all people, turned up in her path. He was middling drunk, as affable as a pig like him was likely to get. He grinned at her, shaven bristles standing up on his head, and took her by one slim arm as she tried to pass.

"Ha! Dearie, you picked the wrong spot to splay your legs. We're men here, not those ball-less calves you're used to servicing." He drew her close to his large, lumpen face, and leered happily.

"Let's have a look then, and see what the Kufr call a good fuck. Set aside that rag on your head." With a twitch of his wrist, Orsos ripped the komis from the Kufr's face. The girl cried out something in her own tongue, and twisted in his grasp. Tall though she was, her wrist was engulfed by his meaty fist. "You've come here, so you're looking to get a taste of—"

"What's this you've found, brother?" Jason asked lightly, stepping up. Around him, other Macht spearmen were rising from their camp-fires with anticipation shining in their eyes. If Orsos was starting something, there would be sport to watch ere it ended. Jason snapped out at them; "Back on your arses, and keep your eyes to yourselves!" And he could not quite account for the anger which bit through his voice.

"Centurion's meat," someone said with a shrug. There were a few catcalls around the farther fires, from those too far away to be identified, but in the main the centons settled down again. Orsos was about to rape something—it was not exactly news.

The Kufr girl had darker eyes and skin than the high-caste Kefren Jason had seen, in Tanis and about Arkamenes's tents. She was shorter too, though still a head higher than either of them.

"She could almost be one of us," he said to Orsos, surprised despite himself.

Orsos was turning her face this way and that, as though studying a melon at market. The girl was silent in his grasp now, clearly terrified.

"What do you think, Jason, is the rest of her as good-looking as her face?"

Part of Jason wanted badly to find out, but then the girl met his eyes. There was more than fear in them; a kind of pitiful resignation. And then, in clear and perfect Machtic, she said, "*Please.*"

Orsos dropped his hands from her face as though they had been burned. "Phobos! Did you hear that, Jason? It speaks our tongue. Kufr—say something else!" He was grinning, and he poked the girl with his finger.

Her face was still now, though tears had marked tracks down it, streaking the kohl about her eyes. "Please," she said again, "I am Arkamenes's... woman."

Jason and Orsos looked at one another. "She's well enough dressed," Jason said. He bent and retrieved the girl's komis. "Could be she's a household slave."

"Could be she's a liar," Orsos said, but the humour had gone out of him now. "Get her the hell out of here, Jason. Best to be safe. That Kufr bastard doesn't like to have anyone so much as look at his women." Orsos stumped away. "I'm going to find a goat to fuck." And he cackled, weaving his way off through the campfires and shouting insults at the men upon their bedrolls.

Jason studied the girl as she wrapped her komis back about that beautiful face. She looked so human. Then, in Asurian gleaned from his studies, he said, "I'm sorry."

The girl looked at him like a startled deer, and there came a flurry of Asurian too fast for Jason's limited scholarship. He held up his hands, smiling. "Slow, slow."

"You speak our tongue?"

"You speak ours?"

She hesitated. "I am been learning. I have a scroll."

"I have one also. I am Jason."

"I am Tiryn."

Jason gestured to the lines of men reclining about the campfires, their eyes catching the flames as they watched the little exchange. There was a pool of silence about them as the Macht watched, and listened.

"Why are you here?" he asked her. She shook her head, and seemed near to tears again.

"I don't know."

His head hurt from recalling the close-written phrases on his precious scroll. Eyes shut, haltingly, he said, "I take you home."

"Home," she said in wonder.

"Arkamenes."

"Ah. Yes. Take me to him."

"You are his woman?"

"His woman, yes."

Jason held out his arm, but she recoiled as though he had raised a fist at her. Cursing his ignorance, he led the way and heard the soft hiss of the silk about her thighs as she followed. Through the Macht camp, hundreds of eyes following their every move as they wove in unhurried fashion about the campfires. Everywhere they went the talk was stilled, and the Macht watched them in wonder and surmise: the handsome Macht general, and behind him the tall, veiled Kufr woman with the dark eyes.

TWELVE
THE MELTED SNOWS

They crossed the Bekai River in the early spring, and accepted the capitulation of Istar in the city of Kaik, another of those tall fortress-cities the Empire had reared up at every ford of the world's great rivers. The Bekai was fast-flowing with the meltwater of the mountain snows, for the year had turned at last, and in the east the green line of the lowland world was inching up the slopes of the mighty Magron Mountains, though their peaks were still wrapped in everlasting snow. Beyond those mountains lay Asuria, the heart of the Empire, and the Imperial capital itself: holy Ashur of the endless walls. The army had marched almost two and a half thousand pasangs since disembarking at Tanis, and they had been seventy-eight days on the road. The Kufr troops now marched almost as fast as the Macht themselves, and their numbers had been augmented by contingents from those provinces which had surrendered along the way. Honuran, Governor of Istar, now accompanied the army as one of Arkamenes's lieutenants. His family had been left behind under guard back in Istar, for their safe-keeping, and to assuage any regrets he might feel at his betrayal of his cousin.

Rictus led his fist up the smooth-sloped hill and stood at the top, breathing and sweating hard. The air seemed heavy, laden with the moisture of the great river at their backs. He turned and stared back into the west. The Bekai was a long, meandering curve of brilliant light upon the carpet of the world, spearpoint-bright where the sun took it, mud-brown and ochre where the passing clouds kept the sunlight from its banks. The city-fortress of Kaik rose high upon its tell west of the river, a pasang to the north, and from the many thousands of its hearths a thin haze of smoke rose to cloud the still air. Even at this distance the hum of its busy streets could be heard, filling the countryside all around. Kaik was a brown city, as so many were in the Land of the Rivers. Constructed largely of kiln-fired brick, it held within its walls a hundred thousand square houses which all looked the same, but on the flat roof of each was a garden, and each of these gardens was like a tiny, distinct little emerald jewel. The mighty Bekai had been bled by man-made channels lined with more brick, and an army of slaves toiled ceaselessly on the waterwheels to keep siphoning off the life-giving water for the greenery of the city. Earth and water, the very stuff of life itself. In this part of the world they were held in reverence, and the Kufr had river-deities and crop-deities by the score. Earth and water: the building blocks of the Empire. The only commodity that could match them in abundance was the labour of slaves.

Down at the river the army continued to cross by the Bekai bridges, as it had been crossing since the morning of the day before. All but the last of the Kufr baggage and the rearguard were now on the eastern bank and the Macht were already on the march for higher ground, seeking open country beyond the stinking, confined ditches of the lowland farms. Flies and all manner of flying filth haunted these moist fields, for the peasants hereabouts fertilised the land with their own excrement. Thus far in their journey the Macht had lost few men to disease, thanks both to the season and rigid latrine regulations. Phiron did not intend to relax these rules now. The sternest part of the march was before them, looming up at the edge of the world with every sunrise, a saw-toothed barrier now only some two hundred pasangs away. The Magron Mountains.

More lightly armed Macht troopers joined Rictus on the crest of the height. This was not a hill, but one of the ubiquitous tells which marked the sites of old cities all across the Middle Empire. By some unimaginable labour in the distant, legendary past, the inhabitants of these parts had reared up dozens of the things, each large enough to hold a fair-sized Macht city with room to spare. On these stood the most ancient Kufr fortresses and cities. But many were bare and forgotten now. Looking at the shape of the land below, Rictus realised that once the Bekai River had wound close to the foot of this tell, and thus the city built thereon had controlled the crossing. But rivers were fickle things, changing course even in the space of a man's lifetime. As the Bekai had moved away, so the people had followed it, to keep to the crossings, and they had built another tell for their new city where Kaik now stood, snug up against the steep riverbanks.

Rictus thought of a different river, a mere stream flashing through a quiet glen somewhere in the far west and north. The snowdrops would be gone by now, and there would be primroses and crocuses about the oaks in the valley-bottom. He fingered the coral pendant about his neck, slick with his sweat, and for a moment he felt as lost and bewildered as if he had only this moment left his father's farm and found himself here, in this immensity of strangeness that was the world.

"Where're we headed, cap'n?" one of the other men asked. Rictus collected himself. He pointed towards the distant mountains. "Out that way. There's an Imperial post house twenty pasangs along the road which is still manned. We're to take it, and everyone in it."

"Alive or dead?"

Rictus shrugged, and the men about him nodded and rubbed their chins or tested the edge of their javelin-points. These were Phiron's Hounds, the swiftest, ablest and most vicious of the skirmishers. For some reason, Jason had taken

Rictus and made him a Second, commander of a half-centon of them. Rictus now led ten fists into battle. Except that they never saw battle—not as Rictus understood it. They saw massacre and rapine and murder. They cut down the enemy when he was in flight, they seized bridges and gatehouses and defiles ahead of the main army, and they harassed any enemy they found who was too strong for them to destroy. They did not stand in rank, or bear armour, or meet their foes as equals. They fought their little war in as dirty a manner as they could. And Rictus was good at it.

They knew him now, these men—or boys, most of them were—and they trusted his judgement. He had a feel for the land and the manner in which it must be used—the way terrain could even stiffening odds, the value of surprise, of ferocity unleashed at the right moment and from an unsuspected direction. He was brave in battle, a rare hand with both javelin and long spear, and a captain who was not afraid to get up and close with his foe, sometimes charging into a wavering enemy without bothering to find out if the rest of his command had followed. Because of who he was, his men had taken to calling themselves *the Iscans*, and Rictus had neither approved nor objected. They had even painted the *iktos* sigil on the leather facings of their shields, though Rictus had left his own blank. After each of their missions, they would rejoin the main body—they were part of Jason of Ferai's mora—and Rictus would leave for the command tent to report and receive more orders. Buridan the Bear would see to it that they were fed and had dry ground to sleep upon, for if Rictus had one drawback as a leader, it was that he seemed singularly indifferent to such things. He would not let his men starve, but he would not go to special lengths to make them comfortable, either. If anything, this made the men he led respect him all the more, for all that he was a gangling strawhead with the slow twang of the mountains in his speech.

They took off down the slope at an easy run. This pace, they knew they could keep up for many pasangs. Phiron called them his foot-cavalry, and they revelled in the title. The heavy troops might garner the glory of pitched battle, but for those who liked to be ahead of the column, unfettered by too many officers, the light arm was the unit of choice.

Twenty pasangs, half at a run, the other half at a brisk walk. The day wheeled its way through morning and afternoon and into dusk. They arrived before full-dark, as Rictus had intended. In the last light of the sunset they saw the post-house ahead of them, the land around as flat as the bread the Kufr ate, then rising up as steeply as rocks out of a calm sea towards the white-topped mountains in the east, now blushed pink with Araian's last light. The Imperial Road arrowed up into the Magron foothills, too straight to be quite real, and off it smaller roads of red dirt were carved out which led to villages and towns of mud-brick, none important enough to warrant a tell to perch on. In these, lamps had already begun to be lit. Not many—poor folk went to bed with the sun—but enough to mark them out upon the darkening face of the land.

Rictus raised his hand, and all about him his men came to a halt, blowing and panting, spears upright in their right fists, their left arms hung with the leather and wicker peltas, and in the left hand of each a bundle of slim javelins. Rictus nodded at an older man, a bald-headed, gap-toothed veteran of the skirmishers. "Whistler, take four fists and hang back left. You're the reserve. Keep a taenon or two between us. We meet something big, and we'll pull back through you." The man nodded, grinning. His name was Hanno, but he was known as Whistler because when he breathed though his mouth, as he did now, the air shrilled through the gap in his front teeth.

A younger man, a mere boy with eyes dark as blackberries and the beauty of a girl, spoke up. "What of me, Rictus?"

"Go out on the right with two fists and keep a lookout on that flank, Morian. Get up on the higher ground there. When the thing is done, we reassemble here." They nodded at him, impatient to be off. "Very well. Now we go. Arrowhead, all of us."

Half the men spread out in formation, Rictus at the point. They loped forward, eyes darting left and right, staring ahead. There was no Paean sung, no feet marched in time. This was warfare on the fly, as much a hunt as anything else.

The post-house was in fact a complex of several buildings with a corral beside them that had half a dozen swift horses nosing at the earth within.

Rictus's men sped through the buildings and out the other side. A single Juthan slave who walked out of a doorway was spitted through the neck and dropped without a sound. On the eastern edge of the post-house Rictus raised his hand again. "Move in." He waved at Morian; the boy nodded and spread his own tiny command in a line off to the right. As he took to the rising ground there, they became silhouetted against the stars.

Rictus stood fast as his men went through the buildings. There were shouts now, a scream cut off. He stood watching in the dark, noting in his head the position of every fragment of his little command. Moments like this, he loved—when one directed the men like the elements of some dance and saw the efficiency of it at one remove. Phobos's Dance, mercenaries called it, making light of war as they did of most things.

This kind of killing, though, Rictus had seen enough of. He did not count it valour to slaughter men struggling out of their beds.

Morian came pelting back down to him. The boy's eyes were so wide they almost had a shine about them in the gathering starlight.

"Off to the south and east, maybe three pasangs, there's a camp, a big one. Scattered fires spread out wider than the walls of Machran. Rictus, it is *huge*."

Rictus paused a second. Morian was young, but as clear-headed as they came.

"All right. Bring in your men. Finish the work here and then join up with Whistler. Quickly now." Unable to help himself, he grabbed the boy's arm. "Morian, are you sure?"

"Antimone's tits, it's bigger than our own, Rictus."

"You're sure it's not a town?"

"It's campfires, not lamps, enough of them for a city. Rictus—"

"Enough. Off you go." Rictus released him. His heart had begun to hammer. When he opened his mouth he could hear the rush of it beating in his throat. He looked around him, gauging the situation. No more cries from the houses; the work there was done. Now the men were ransacking the place for food and drink and trinkets. If he was quick... He hesitated a split second more, then took off at a run.

The ground rose under his feet. Not a steep slope, but enough to hide what lay beyond the rise. He sprinted, slinging the pelta on his back by its leather strap. In one hand he held his spear at the trail; his javelins he clenched together in the other. His feet barely felt the earth beneath him. He topped the rise and found fragments of brick under the soles of his sandals. Another tell, vast as a long hill out of nature, but so ancient that it had worn down to a low slope in the ground, no more. And on the other side—

On the other side the world had changed. The quiet starlit night was fractured apart.

"*Phobos!*" Rictus swore. The boy was right. Two pasangs away, not three, more campfires were extending the perimeter minute upon minute. How many taenons? A hundred, two hundred? It was a sea of campfires back to the foothills.

It was an army.

The Great King had come west over the mountains.

Twenty pasangs back at a hard run, the men blowing and winded now, heads down. When Whistler and a few of the older ones began to lag behind, Rictus split his command, going forward with the youngest and fleetest. They stumbled in the dark and went headlong, got up and started running again. The two moons rose, and in the blushed silver light they made better time. It seemed in the moonlight that they were making no distance at all, but were mere staggering men running on the spot, while all around the dark world sat still under their feet. But at last the other campfires hove into view: the lights of their own camp. Running down into it, swallowing vomit, Rictus knew by the comparison that the army camped back in the shadow of the Magron was many times larger than their own. Gasping, he told his men to make for their own lines. He tossed Morian his weapons and kept running, making for the taller cressets that blazed above the rest of the Macht camp, marking the large tent of Phiron where the Kerusia met. When he reached it he bent over and spewed out what remained of his last meal, whilst in front of the tent two of Arkamenes's Honai stood watching in disgust, flanking the open tent-flap. From within there came the sound of music, a woman singing, and voices engaged in stately conversation.

Rictus staggered askew, spitting out the foul taste of his vomit, mind wheeling. The sight of the Honai had completely thrown him. Was he not in the right place? He wiped his mouth on his arm and went up to the tall Kefren. "Phiron," he said. "Get Phiron."

The guards stared at him, alien eyes set within the bronze masks of their helms. "Phiron," Rictus repeated faintly, and sank to one knee.

A voice spoke up, louder than the blood thundering in his ears. He was taken by the arm and shaken roughly. Not Phiron but Jason, the ivy-leaves of a party in his hair, wine on his breath. He wore his finest chiton, still scarlet, but embroidered with gold sigils on the shoulders. In his pale eyes there was instant recognition.

"What's happened? Speak, Rictus."

Rictus regained his feet, swaying. Jason's hands grasped his shoulders, transfixing him to the spot.

"What are the Kufr doing here?"

"Arkamenes is within—Phiron is hosting him. You picked a rare night to puke on his doorstep. Now speak it out."

"Twenty-two or three pasangs to the east, there is an army encamped. It is huge—many times bigger than ours."

Those eyes, strange in so dark a face. Pale as flint. Jason studied him for a long moment, breathing wine into his face. Gods, he could do with some wine. But he was collecting himself now, his heart hammering out a less insane beat.

"You're sure, Rictus?"

Rictus smiled. "I know an army when I see one."

"How close did you get? How many campfires? Were you seen?" The questions were shot out like barbed darts. Rictus answered them as well he could. When Jason was satisfied he released him. Even in the torchlight it was possible to see how his face had lost colour.

"They stole a march on us it seems—a campaigning season of marches. I thought Ashurnan did not have it in him."

"The snows in the Magron," Rictus said. "They must have melted early."

"Yes. You've done well, lad. Antimone had her eye on you tonight, on us all. Now it's Phobos we have to worry about. Follow me."

"Where? In there?" Rictus asked, dismayed.

"In there. You're going to stand up straight in front of Phiron and our generals and the Kufr and tell all this over again, and you'll not miss a beat."

Rictus rubbed at the vomit on his front. His chiton stank with sweat and his legs were spattered dark with the muck he had run through. "I could use some wine," he said in a low tone. Jason grinned.

"You and me both. Come now."

He might have been an after-dinner freak-show. Phiron's tent had been hung with tapestries and hangings looted from half a dozen cities; it was lit with many-armed lamps of gold and silver. The couches of the great and the good were circled round an empty space below them, through which musicians and slaves came and went. Now Rictus stood in this space, stinking, filth-stained, rank, and told them all that the enemy had come over the mountains and was half a day's march to the east. An enemy in his many tens, perhaps hundreds of thousands. He was brought wine and sipped it standing as one after another of the generals questioned him, many sharp with disbelief, and even angry, as though Rictus were playing some joke on them. Orsos and Castus denounced him as a spy, planted by their foes; they were rather drunk. Phiron and Pasion, side by side, questioned him as parents would a prodigal son. And Arkamenes sat rigid, watching, listening to Phiron interpret, his eyes glowing with a light that was utterly inhuman. Behind him, on a lower couch, a Kufr woman reclined. As he spoke, Rictus was sure she understood some of his words, for she reacted before Phiron translated. Her eyes were stark with fear.

Jason took his arm. He had tossed away his ivy crown. "Sit down before you fall down." Rictus was led out of that focused space in their midst, to the periphery of shadows. A cane stool was found for him, and more wine. A Juthan girl poured it, her blue-black hair in a pigtail that touched his wrist as she bent. He smiled at her, but there was no answer out of the yellow eyes. Jason stood at his side and watched the wrangling, the debating, and the barely restrained animosity go their inevitable way about the banqueting couches. Phiron stood at Arkamenes's side now, speaking swiftly to the Kefren prince and hammering his fist into his palm.

"What a marvellous thing a Council-of-War is," Jason said, shaking his head.

"Jason. I saw what I saw. I am not a fool."

"I know that, Rictus. But all they see is a young buck out on his feet and covered in shit."

"We need to get more of the Hounds out there, quartering the ground, or some of the Kufr cavalry."

"Oh, I agree. But the Kerusia must stop talking first."

Rictus sank back against the heavy leather wall of the tent. The wine had lit up his insides and fogged his mind. He was nodding where he sat. He fell asleep with the clay winecup still clenched in his fist, the endless sound of the voices beating about under the flickering glare of the golden lamps, and the strange perfumes of the Kufr filling his head with dreams.

THIRTEEN
THE OTHER SIDE OF THE MOUNTAIN

"He has made good time," Vorus said, reading the end of the despatch. "I had thought we might catch him still on the western bank of the Bekai, but he is across with all his baggage."

"Arkamenes's troops have learned how to march," Proxis agreed grudgingly. "But it is no matter. We have the numbers, and the ground is adequate."

"The ground," Vorus mused, "is bad for cavalry; too many ditches. And it's wet. The Macht will like this ground, Proxis. It will give them something to stick their heels in." He slapped shut the despatch scroll.

"There are ten thousand Macht, I hear. Even ten thousand cannot prevail against the force we have brought into the west."

As one, the pair of them turned and looked eastwards, back at the looming wall of the Magron Mountains. Memories. Fighting to force double-axled wagons through the drifts, whole companies roped together, heaving them onwards by main force. Kefren huddled in windbreaks of flesh as the snow whirled around them. The bodies of those left behind, stark against the snow in their wake, waymarkers of carrion.

"I never thought he had it in him," Vorus admitted.

"Yes. He is his father's son after all. We can be thankful for that, at least."

They turned back to the warmth, the sunlit world of the lowlands and the rivers to the west. Wide and green, it now had carved across it brown scars of churned-up mud where the columns of the army had marched past. Too large to keep in one formation, the levy of the Great King had been split up into four separate entities, each pasangs long, each with its own flanking forces, vanguards and rearguards. The baggage train was back in a fortified camp five pasangs in the rear, a stockade larger than most cities which housed several thousand wagons, and another small army to guard them. This was campaigning on a scale no one had seen before. It was nothing less than a catastrophe for the inhabitants of the entire region, for foraging parties were systematically stripping it bare. They could reap three harvests a year here. In Pleninash, such was the bounty of the soil and the clement generosity of the climate; but to sow one had to plant, and to plant one must have seed. When the war was done and the battle won, there would be famine this winter, here in the breadbasket of the Middle Empire. That was the price paid to stymie one man's ambition.

They fell into step together, the worn, athletic Macht general and the squat Juthan with the bloodshot eyes. Waiting for them at the base of the slope were a knot of Kefren horsemen, Honai cavalry of the Royal Guard. Beyond them a Juthan Legion stood patiently in the mud, five thousand of the grey-skinned creatures with the round shields and heavy halberds of their race. Many had been squatting upon their hams, talking quietly. They rose now as Vorus and Proxis came closer, a quiet mass of flesh and bronze, their banners limp above their heads. About their faces the river-flies buzzed in clouds, new-hatched by the spring warmth.

Juthan grooms stood in the middle of the magnificent Honai cavalry grasping the halters of two less grand mounts. Vorus could ride a horse, but for him the animal was a means of locomotion, no more. He had Niseians on his estates back in Ashur, but would sooner ride something a little nearer the ground. Proxis habitually rode a mule, its grey pelt the same colour as his own. The magnificent Honai looked faintly offended at their proximity to such poor equine flesh, but then they looked faintly offended by most things, Vorus thought.

Screens of light cavalry were operating on every front of the army, gathering what information they could and sending it back to the high command in an unending stream of mud-slathered couriers. Looking south, Vorus could see some now, a pennanted column of them, as gaily dressed as if going to a fair. All the Kefren loved finery, and war called out the dandy in them in a way that even court ceremonial could not quite match. Even the Juthan legions were in gaudy liveries of the various Kefren lords, and the mighty Qaf had painted their faces with all the barbaric enthusiasm of children. Added to this, the various provincial factions called up to the standards wore versions of their national costumes. The Medisai trimmed their harness with feathers from the parrots of the Panjir River valley, the Arakosans preferred the white fur of mountain-leopards. The Asurians of the heartland made no bones about it, and had all their wargear inlaid with gold and lapis lazuli dredged from the bed of the Oskus. If one of their nobles went down in the mud a prince's ransom in bullion and gems would fall with him. Vorus did not approve. In Anurman's day such extravagance was saved for the court. On the hunt, and in war, his soldiers had left their armour unadorned.

It was our deeds marked us out in those days, Vorus thought, not some brooch or robe or crown. But even Anurman might have donned his finest, were he to go out and meet a Macht army in battle. Such events seemed a part of myth rather than historical reality.

Another courier came galloping up, the muck flying from his horse's feet like a flock of startled birds and the ranks of the Juthan making an avenue for him. He threw up an arm in salute, a *hufsan* from the mountains with the dark eyes of his caste. He was grinning, face alight with the joy of his position, the armies massing on the plain, the good horse under him. Simple folk, the *hufsan* Kefren, and the most vicious warriors in the army, bar the Honai.

"General! I find you! I bring a message from the Archon Midarnes." The *hufsan* proffered a leather despatch-case, spattered with mud from his passage. Vorus took it with a nod, breaking the seal. Midarnes was up front some five pasangs, feeling out the terrain with his soldiers' feet, and claiming space should the army need to shake out into battle line. *Dominating the ground*, the manuals of Vorus's youth had called it. For the earth upon which they fought would have its say in their lives and deaths as surely as any tactic of the enemy.

Vorus paused for a second as he realised his hands were trembling. He clenched his jaw, the muscles jumping under his face, and read the scroll.

To Vorus of the Macht, officer commanding the armies of his excellent majesty Ashurnan, King of Kings, Great Kings, Lord of—

He skipped the pleasantries. Midarnes was commander of the Household Guard, and sometimes he let protocol get in the way of haste, for all that he was a capable fellow.

The vanguard of the traitor's army has been sighted ten pasangs east of the Bekai River. I hold high ground two pasangs to their front, and have put all my forces into line of battle. There is good space here for the rest of the army to deploy to my right and left. The Macht are out on the enemy right, the traitor and his Bodyguard in the centre. They, too, are deploying into line. I shall hold this position until further orders.

Vorus swore under his breath, though he kept his face blank, aware of the Honai guards watching, Proxis's eyes upon him. He passed the scroll to the Juthan. "Things move fast, my friend." He looked up at the sky, squinting into the sun and gauging how long it had to meet the flat river-plain of the western horizon.

Proxis, too, uttered some profanities in his own, dark tongue. "This is the King's work. If we don't move fast he'll be up there alone. He has his father's courage, but as for judgement—"

"Mount up. We must get to Midarnes."

"It's too late in the day for battle, surely."

"Phiron of Idrios commands the Macht, a canny bastard if ever there was one. We must gather up the army at once, and concentrate on Midarnes. Courier—courier, there! Proxis, have you ink and quill?"

Ashurnan had left all his finery behind on the back of another tall Kefre who might have been his twin. This officer, lucky or luckless according to opinion, now stood in the royal chariot, his head shaded by the royal parasol-bearers and the Great King's standard waving slightly with its long plumes above his head. Ashurnan himself had taken two close companions for a horseback tour of his mustering army. They were coming up into line by their thousands, and he galloped along their front on his grey gelding in the brilliant robes of a staff officer, no more, whilst a gleaming white komis kept most of his face covered, and soon became black with the tiny flies hatching out of the river-mud. He had mud on his arms and legs also, thrown up by the exuberant passage of his horse. Beneath the komis he was grinning like a child, so happy to be young, and a king, and well-mounted to the front of a mighty army that would halt or move or march into battle at his will. He raised his eyes to the sky as his horse sped over the tightly-packed earth of the Middle Empire—his empire—and he gave thanks to the Creator Himself for all this, for the breath of Kuf that had given life to them all, for the ability to be glad at this time, to find worth in the great issues and bloody struggles of the world. For if a man could not savour such a dish, then he was no man at all.

The Household troops, the Honai, were ten thousand strong in themselves, and in eight ranks they had a frontage of some thirteen hundred paces. Unlike the other Kefren contingents, they did not rely on the horse or the bow, but on the spear. Like the Macht, they were close-quarter killers, trained to prevail in the most demanding mode of warfare known.

They were magnificent. Ashurnan had never seen them gathered all together before, and now it seemed that there could not be a force in the world to contend with them. All through the passage of the mountains, they had hid their wargear under leather campaign casings, but these were discarded now, and the effect made Ashurnan rein in his horse and stare, Great King though he was. Their arms and armour were gilded and inlaid with every precious metal and gem known to exist; the sun caught these now and made their line a scintillating blur of varicoloured light. They did not seem things made of flesh at all.

And more troops were coming up minute by minute, thousands of them. Kefren from Asuria, *hufsan* from the mountains, Qaf from the north, Juthan Legions marching in dour ranks, and files of brightly clad cavalry from the Oskus valley. A world in arms, it seemed; an army which could no more be fought than could the passage of the moons.

Ashurnan wheeled his horse and stared back down the long slope towards the river valley of the Bekai. Far in the distance, the tall hill of Kaik could be made out, a shadowed hummock on the edge of the plain, and beyond it the westering sun had begun to lengthen the shadows. Closer to hand there was the enemy, a line of armoured troops with the sun behind them, who had come here to kill him and take his throne.

Arkamenes is there, he thought. My brother sits his horse somewhere in that line, and watches, and wonders where I am.

In the harem there had been many wives, and many children, all sired by great Anurman. The boys had been taken away soon after birth, so that the court might not poison their upbringing. They had been reared as sons of simple fathers, and hence had been taught those things the Kefren still held essential to hold true the course of life: to wield the bow, to ride a horse, to speak the truth. Such things were their heritage, and no matter how depraved and indolent the ruler of the Empire might become, he had the knowledge of those values buried in his soul, to reproach him when he fell short. Such simple things.

To tell the truth.

At age thirteen, Ashurnan had been brought back to Ashur, and told of his true parentage by matter-of-fact tutors his mighty father had hired to complete his education. Illiterate as the *hufsan* couple who had fostered him, he had been thrown into a world of palace protocol, vicious conspiracy, simmering feuds, and poison—the weapon of choice for wives, concubines, eunuchs, and courtiers. No bows or horses here, and precious little of the truth, either. That was the palace.

The Great King stood above it all, or at least Anurman had, and at his shoulders he had two creatures he trusted. The Macht, Vorus, and the Juthan, Proxis. These two were faithful as dogs, and were treated like dogs by the Kefren nobility, outraged beyond fury by the Great King's reliance on them. All this, Ashurnan had known, had seen at first hand and heard at second whilst growing into his manhood within the confines of the ziggurat. His father had been a distant, stern figurehead, hardly connected to him at all, but Vorus had looked in on him from time to time, to make reports he supposed. He had hated Vorus, knowing that Anurman, his own father, loved this alien Macht as though he were his son. He would see the two of them together at state occasions, Vorus elevated to commander of Ashur's very garrison, made greater than the highest-caste Kefre of the Great King's own blood. He had hated Vorus for his patience, for his honesty, for his loyalty. The very qualities any King needs in a friend.

Arkamenes, my brother. Ashurnan reined in and sat his horse a hundred paces forward of his Household's line, the foremost man in the army. His companions he waved back as they approached, to remonstrate with him about security, no doubt. He sat there and watched the ranks of the enemy thicken, a hedge of spears and shields, a mass of pushing and jostling and stumbling people all intent on finding some patch of earth upon which they could stand and muster their courage. These were Kefren opposite. He saw the banners of Tanis, of Artaka there, and with a tightening of his mouth he beheld the sigils of Istar, and his cousin Honuran.

What price bought you? he wondered, for he had loved Honuran, had counted him a true friend. They had stayed together as best they could through the palace upheavals, Ashurnan the serious, Arkamenes the proud, Honuran the trickster. A little triumvirate of resistance, dedicated to foxing their tutors and making some space outside the palace for themselves. They had all lost their virginity on the same whore, had planned it that way so as to avoid the slick and murderous concubines of the palace. They had drunk in wine-shops of the lower-city together, their bodyguards fretting and nervous at every door. They had hunted together, boated down the Oskus, broken horses as a team, been beaten by their tutors with all their rumps bare in the air at the same time. Boyhood, and friendship. One thought it was supposed to mean something. Perhaps it did. Perhaps I was too serious—the Heir of the Great King. Did I wrong you, Arkamenes? It was not through spite, only ham-fistedness.

Friendship. I do not have it. My father was a lucky man. I take his leavings, worthy as they are, and out of them I spin what I can. But I was never one to make great friends, it seems.

The glory had left him now. Ashurnan sat his horse and looked out at the enemy battle line with eyes as cold as glass, noting the depth of rank, the armour, the level of drill. My brother, he thought. I made you ruler of one third of this empire, in fact if not in name—and it was not enough. I did it for love, for boyhood friendship. I was mistaken. I shall kill you now, and weep not one tear when I stare upon your corpse.

He kicked his mount's ribs savagely, and as the animal reared in fear and startlement he calmed it with kind words, ashamed of himself.

The bow, the horse, the truth. Very well. Even if it is only to please the memory of a dead father, it is good enough.

He stared back down the sloping ground to where his brother might be, then scanned the enemy line, hunting out the legend, the much-vaunted mythical Macht. The familiar half-made ranks of Kefren troops opposite had been a kind of comfort; one saw this calibre of soldiery all over the Empire, and they were faintly risible compared to the stern ranks of the Honai. He had a half-smile on his face as he peered up the enemy line, the anger and betrayal in his heart fuelling a kind of arrogance, the shield which few saw through, and which meant he would never make the friends his father had.

The Macht.

Harder to make out because they were not moving. They stood in patient files on the enemy right, eight ranks of heavy infantry resting their shields on the ground so that they leaned against the right knee. Their bronze was different. Ashurnan could not quite puzzle it out, until he realised that it was old metal, tarnished and dimmed. These men had carried their harness a long time. It was not a matter of burnishing; it was a matter of years. And there was no decoration to it. They did not take joy in their turn-out. They wore their panoplies with all the pride and élan of labourers set to a day's heavy shifting. Ashurnan's mouth began to sneer under the komis as he regarded them, and then his lips straightened. Their formation was perfect, as though someone had gone running along their front with a plumb line. They stood at ease, almost unmoving. They were watching the armies moving into place to their front, but none of the Kefren's flinching restlessness went through their ranks. They seemed almost bored.

Ashurnan turned his horse around and cantered back to his own lines, his mind brewing all manner of phantasms. To kill his brother—that was the self-evident mission of this campaign. But now there was another filtering into place within his thoughts. These Macht; they could not remain within the bounds of the Empire. They, too, must be utterly destroyed. This legend must be brought to heel here in the mud of the Middle Empire.

The Great King's levies, drawn by a skein of frantic couriers, drew together on the sloping ground east of the city of Kaik. Here, the land rose out of the floodplain of the Bekai River and crested into a series of low heights that might once have been the foundations of ancient cities, but which now had disappeared utterly and were mere shapeless mounds. The heights had a name though; locally they were known as the Kunaksa, the Goat's Hills, and goats had indeed grazed there in happier times. Now they provided dry footing for the Great King's battle line, and a vantage point from where the whole expanse of the plain could be made out right back to the river itself. Below, in the sodden ground of the farmlands, the traitor's army had finished deploying and now occupied a solid front of some six pasangs. The Macht out on the right made a line of shields just over a pasang and a half long, and curled round their open flank was an amorphous crowd of light infantry, skirmishers with spears and javelins and no armour to speak of. The traitor Arkamenes had set a renegade Juthan legion on the Macht left. There were his personal troops, his Honai, and behind that a mounted Bodyguard of perhaps a thousand heavy cavalry. Further left, there were the levies from Artaka, the Tanis garrison, and more Juthan troops. Between forty and fifty thousand all told. On this wide plain their formations were as perfect as could be imagined. He was short on cavalry and archers, but had a solid wall of heavy infantry to fight with. If their morale held, that line would take a lot to stop.

So thought Vorus, looking down on them. Again and again, his eyes were drawn back to the unyielding, insouciant line of blank bronze that was the Macht. Something ached near his heart, a kind of pride. The Macht heavy spearmen had retained their cloaks. They knew that battle might not be joined today and that they would most likely have to sleep in line, so they had brought the scarlet badge of their calling on their backs. They would die tomorrow with their red cloaks on their shoulders. For a single, insane moment, Vorus wished with all his heart that he was down there with them, part of that sombre spectacle.

Only for a moment.

FOURTEEN
KUNAKSA

Off to the north, the Arakosan cavalry had begun to move, six thousand horsemen with the mist of the morning grey about the bellies of their mounts. The ground was packed red and hard under them, the chill of the night holding it firm. The rumble of the horses could be heard and felt over the earth for pasangs on every side. A harbinger of what was to come perhaps, a dark music borne upon the waking world.

The noise woke Gasca from an uneasy sleep, and many others around him. They rose from their cramped ranks, cursed the snag and jab of bronze on their shins, and tugged their cloaks tighter about their torsos, the mist all around them, deep and unknowable as the currents of the sea.

Old Demotes raised his hawk nose to sniff the pre-dawn air and cocked his grey head to one side. "That's cavalry," he said. He spat on the ground and bared what remained of his teeth as he stretched his worn and warped limbs into function.

Around him more men rose ahead of reveille, that dark murmur in the earth bringing them out of what scant sleep they had endured. Close on ten thousand spearmen had lain down the bright evening before with their heads pillowed on their shields and their cuirasses biting their hips. Now it was almost a relief to stand up, to make the blood work about the bones and face the thing which had brought them all here.

Gasca checked all his gear automatically, touched the upright planted length of his spear for luck and tried to shiver some warmth into his limbs. The cloak had helped, but his father's layered cuirass had been stiffened by the cold. His flesh would have to warm it into some kind of compliance before it stopped biting him.

Buridan was walking down the line; he had taken over the Dogsheads after Jason's promotion and now had the transverse crest of a centurion on his helm. "Up, up, get in rank you motherless fucks. We've a big day ahead of us."

"I hope you slept well, centurion."

"I dreamed of your mother last night, Bear."

"Aye, she fucked half the centon in her dreams!"

They rose, pissing where they stood and garnering curses and shoves and the ribaldry which was the meat of an army's morning. The file-leaders geared up and strode forward a pace or two, bitching and murmuring to each other about where precisely the line should run, and behind them the hastily armouring men fell into their files one after another, pushed, cajoled, and threatened by the file-closers, who counted in each man. When he had six ahead of him, he clapped the shoulder of the man in front, who did the same to the man before him, until the file leader felt the thump on his own shoulder and knew that behind him the file was complete. Buridan then strode down the front of the centon and as he passed each file the leader raised his spear. All down the mist-choked length of the Macht ranks, centurions were doing the same. In the half-light of dawn, the Macht had reformed their battle line in a matter of minutes, whilst to their left the Kefren troops were still milling in bad-tempered disorder, and their officers were cantering up and down among them on horse-back, waving swords to get them into place.

The sun rose through the mist; mighty Araian who loved her bed in the north, but in this country seemed eager to rise and reluctant to quit the day. The mist thinned. There was not the breath of a breeze. Even before the sun was well clear of the Magron, the heat had begun to simmer out of the ground itself, and with it the tiny black flies that plagued the low river-country. The ground softened as it warmed, and the Macht spearmen sank an inch into it with all the weight of arms and armour pressing upon their flesh. Gasca heard the file-closer, big Gratus, talking to the light-armed skirmishers who had remained to the rear. "You keep that water coming today. I don't give a fuck if you have to fetch it all the way from the river, but you keep the skins full, lads."

"Any word from up front?" someone beside Gasca asked. He was yawning himself, the bronze of the helm constricting his skull. There was a worn spot in the padding within; he should have replaced it before now.

"They're on the hill, same place as they was last night, except there's more of them now."

"Where's Phiron, I wonder?"

"Licking Kufr arse." And a mutter of hard laughter went down the ranks.

Arkamenes met with the ten generals of the Macht to the front of their battle line. Phiron and Pasion were there also, every one of them in the transverse crested helm of officers, and every one wearing the Curse of God. They carried their shields on their shoulders and bore spears the same as the lowest infantryman on the field. Arkamenes looked down on them from his horse and when the eyes in the T-slits of the close helms stared back at him he felt a kind of shiver trail down his backbone. He was glad, so very glad, that he was not up on the hill above, waiting to fight these things.

"We will attack," he said crisply. "My brother has the high ground; he will not leave it, so we must go to him. Phiron, as you have suggested, your people will lead an echeloned advance into his right, and smash that wing. The Juthan have been told to hang back, and only follow on once you have engaged. Then the rest of the line will move up in turn from the right. That way we are less likely to be outflanked. My bodyguard and I will be in the centre. As soon as I mark out

Ashurnan, we shall attack him. If the King dies, it is all over. Any questions?"

"When?" Phiron asked.

"I leave that to your discretion. But it should be soon. The heat will be punishing today."

"Thank you, my lord."

Arkamenes bent over in the saddle and pulled his komis aside a little. He smiled, his golden face disconcerting so close to theirs. "Good luck, General. If all goes well, when evening comes we shall be rulers of the world." Then he straightened and kicked his horse, wheeling away to where his bodyguard awaited him in bright and gaudy ranks back at the centre of the army.

Phiron looked round at his fellow officers. "He's leaving it to us to make the first dent in their line. We must hit them hard as we are able, then wheel left, towards their centre. There the battle will be decided. Arkamenes was right; if we kill their king, they'll fold."

"There was cavalry on the move before dawn, Phiron," Pasion said. "Could be a flank move."

Phiron nodded. "I'm sure it was. That's why your Hounds are out on the far right. They'll have to cover our arse. I need every spear up front if we're to break these bastards before noon. Jason, your mora is right-handest. The Hounds will be under your orders. If they need help during the morning it is you who will be detailed to assist them. You lead off when you're ready and we'll follow on."

Jason nodded, eyes bright within his helm. He had donned his party-chiton under his armour, and the gold embroidery of it gleamed out incongruously in that sombre gathering.

The twelve of them stood silent a moment, eyes flickering back and forth among themselves. Some of them were smiling.

"Brothers," Phiron said simply, "let us start the Dance."

Starting on the right, the Macht line began to move. The men kept the bowls of their shields on their left shoulders, to save their strength, and carried their spears down the length of their right arms, snug against the body. The mud sucked at their feet and broke up their step until they had marched clear of the last night's ground and were on packed earth and pasture once more. File-leaders and file-closers barked out the time. The men began to march in step, and with that the ground began to echo under their feet, ominous thunder. Jason's mora, close to a thousand men in eight ranks, led off. After it came Mynon's, then Orsos's, then Castus's, then the morai of Pomero, Argus, Teremon, Durik, Gelipos, and Marios.

To their left the Juthan Legion stood watching as the Macht line moved up the slope towards the King's army, close on two pasangs of tight-packed men marching in almost perfect time, and now in almost complete silence. Above their heads the centon banners hung heavy in the morning air. Hardly a breeze stirred about the plain, but the heat of the sun had already burned away the last of the mist. The men in the ranks had the sunlight in their eyes for the first few hundred paces, until the shadow of the heights above them cut it off.

The light troops kept pace with the phalanx, and in their midst Rictus strode easily along, his heart thumping so hard it seemed the beat of it would leap up his throat.

"We'll fight like spearmen today, if we have to," Agrimos, overall commander of the skirmishers had said. "There's cavalry out on the right, and we're to hold our ground against it. No retreating today, boys; no falling back. We fight where we stand."

At long last, Rictus was to be part of a real battle, not some honourless skirmish fought with knives and javelins. Today would be a spear-fight, and he was wholly glad of it.

Look down on me today, father. Grant me your courage. Help me live or die well before the sun goes down.

Jason, in the midst of his thousand, struck up the Paean. It was taken up by the whole mora almost at once, and travelled down the line until the entire Ten Thousand were singing it, the slow mournful beat of the ancient song clenching their feet in time with one another. As always, Jason felt that cold thrill in his flesh at the sound. The Death hymn of the Macht. It had been millennia since a Great King had heard it, and now here in the heart of the Empire, ten thousand voices were rolling it out with a fine relish, their feet providing the beat. Ten thousand voices, the sound of them echoing off the heights of the hills to their front, the ground rising under them as they marched, and the ranks of the Great King's army awaiting them at the crest.

This, Jason thought, is what the poets sing of; it is what it means to be truly alive. And as he marched, singing, the tears trickled down his cheeks within the tall-crested helm.

Seated on his quiet mare, Vorus watched the line of spearmen march up the hill with a wall of sound that was the Paean preceding them. He thought he had never seen a sight so fearsome in his life: that moving battlement of scarlet and bronze, that wave of death approaching. All along the Kefren ranks, there was a kind of shudder as the troops moved in restive increments, as a man will flinch before a blow.

"Lord," he said, "let me go out to the left."

Ashurnan shook his head. For now, he was standing in the Royal Chariot again, shaded by a parasol and surrounded by bodyguards, couriers and staff officers.

"Stay here, Vorus. They may be coming our way soon enough."

The Kefren troops on the left had begun to shout and jeer and batter their spears against their shields in an emboldening din of defiance. To their rear the archers had nocked arrows to their bows. A flag went up to show that all was ready. Ashurnan waved a hand, as gracious as a greeting to a friend, and the archers loosed.

All at once the air filled with another noise; the swoop of clothyards blotting out the sun. They rose in a cloud, and then arced down towards the Macht line.

The sound of their strike came even to the Great King's position, a hammering, clattering madness of metal on metal. Gaps appeared in the ranks of the Macht. Men folded in on themselves, dropped as if pole axed, staggered as though struck by a gale of wind. For a few seconds the line wavered, and the Kefren cheered and shouted in derision and triumph. Then the gaps were closed, the phalanx drew itself together, and the Macht came on.

An order was shouted, carried down their line, and the first three ranks of the Macht levelled their spears. Another series of orders, and they picked up the pace to a lumbering trot. Ten paces from the Kefren line they uttered a hoarse roar, and then plunged forward.

The crash of the battle lines meeting, a sound to make the hearer flinch. It carried clear down the valley, and close on that unholy clash there came the following roar of close-quarter battle. The ten thousand Macht slammed into forty thousand Kefren like some force out of nature. In the rear of the Kefren left the archers loosed another volley, twenty thousand arrows overshooting to pepper the ground behind the Macht army. Before them, the ranks of their spearmen were shoved bodily backwards, pressing in on each other. Vorus could see the glittering aichmes of the Macht darting forward and back at their bloody work all along the line, like teeth in some great machine, whilst the men in the rear ranks set their shields in the back of the man in front, dug their heels into the soft ground, and pushed. The Kefren phalanx staggered under that pressure, as a man's stomach will fold in on the strike of a fist. The battle line was simultaneously chopped to pieces and pushed in on itself. Vorus found the breath clicking in his throat. It had been a long time. He had forgotten what his people looked like in battle, and what savage efficiency they brought to war.

Now the Juthan legion on the Macht left was marching up the hill, and to the left rear of it the traitor's entire battle line was on the move, pinioning the King's troops with the threat of their approach. An advance in echelon; brilliant. This Phiron knew his tactics. All along the plain below, for fully six pasangs, great formations of troops were on the move. For the moment, the traitor's armies had the initiative, but that was part of the plan.

Gasca had moved up from the fifth rank to the third, and now was stabbing overhand with his spear whilst the crushing weight of the men behind him forced him forward. In the frenzied press of the phalanx he periodically felt his feet lifted off the ground and was borne along bodily by the close-packed crowd. He ducked his helm behind the rim of his shield as an enemy spearhead came lancing out at his eyes, was jolted by the impact of the point on his helmet, and stabbed out blindly, furiously. Under his feet, bodies squirmed in the gathering muck and the men behind him with their spears still upright were jabbing downwards with their sauroters, finishing off the wounded, grinding their heels into Kufr faces. The heat was indescribable, the sound deafening, even over the sea-noise of the bronze helm. This was the *othismos*, the very bowels of warfare. It was where men found themselves or lost themselves, where all their virtues were stripped away, leaving only courage; for one could not endure the *othismos* without it.

The line lurched forward as the Kufr ranks shrank from the Macht juggernaut. The file leaders shouted hoarse, half-heard commands and from the rear the unrelenting pressure of the file-closers ground the phalanx onwards. Dead men were carried upright in the files, held there by the press of flesh and bronze. The aichmes of the first three ranks stabbed out endlessly. *Shearing the sheep* this was called, the decimation of the front ranks of the enemy with skilful spear-work, a hedge of wicked metal plunging into the enemy's faces, shoulders, chests, bellies, anywhere there was an opening. The Kufr infantry were not so heavily armoured as the Macht, and the spear-points were drilling clear through their wooden shields, the leather caps and corselets of their panoplies. Gasca found himself stepping over a layered mound of corpses and half-dead, squirming things that the rear ranks spiked through and through with their sauroters.

A spear-blow to his shield-rim stretched the metal. The men in the front ranks had their heads down as though sheltering from a storm. Many had gashed and bleeding spear-arms from the thrusts of their own comrades behind them. Gasca rested his spear on the shoulder of the file-leader, three ranks ahead; it seemed insufferably heavy. The file-leader's spear broke off in the body of a Kufr maniac who threw himself at the line of shields, and he flipped the shaft round, tearing up the thigh of the second-rank man as he did so. With the sauroter now facing forward, he began stabbing out with as much energy as before. In this mass of sharp bronze and iron the flesh of men was a fragile thing, to be scored and sliced without comment or complaint. They were expendable parts in the machine, and they would endure their role without complaint until the thing was done. That was part of the philosophy of the *othismos*.

Ten thousand Macht, pressing forward with all the professionalism of their calling. The Kefren spearmen could not hold back that mass of murder. The deep formations of troops here on the left, stacked up to absorb the Macht assault, became a weakness rather than a strength. Reserve regiments, moving forward to the aid of their comrades, became close-packed by the ordeal of the men at the front, packing lines of bodies against the enemy spearheads.

The Kufr army was pulling back; no, it was in flight—but the flight was so constricted as to be a mere shuddering of movement, no more.

But the Macht felt it. A lessening of pressure, like pushing on a stiff-hinged door past the point of equilibrium. A knowledge that the back of this thing is broken.

Those in the Kefren front rank were showing their backs now, pushing and clawing at the men behind them to get away from the spears. These whose courage had failed were stabbed to bloody quivering meat and their toppling bodies entangled the legs of the next rank; the struggling mob that resulted was cut down without mercy. Gasca found himself hiccoughing with a manic kind of laughter as he stabbed out over the shoulders of the men in front of him. The pressure from the rear had eased somewhat, and the Macht ranks were opening up as the enemy to their front disintegrated. Now Gasca felt the rasp of his tongue about his teeth, the taste of salt about his lips: sweat and splashed blood. His legs were scarlet to the knee, and the ground under all their feet stood pocked with puddles of blood where it was not carpeted with the enemy dead. The Great King's left wing had been smashed asunder.

A gap opened up between the fleeing Kufr and the remorseless, ordered ranks of the Macht. The order to halt was ferried down the line by men whose throats could barely sustain speech. And the phalanx halted, the men breathing hard, many bending to vomit. Up through the opening files came light-armed skirmishers with skins of water hanging from their shoulders. These were passed up and down the line. Gasca managed a few swallows before passing it on, and closed his eyes as the stale, warm liquid set his tongue to moving in his mouth again.

Now the centurions left the ranks and came to the fore. Jason was up front with them, gesticulating, his black armour all ashine with blood, half his helm-crest hacked away. The Kufr left wing was a mob of retreating figures running downhill in their thousands, cavalry mixed in with infantry, officers beating their men with the flat of their swords. The ground they left behind them was littered with cast away shields and weaponry, and straggling wounded by the hundred were dragging themselves at their rear, limping on spear-shafts or crawling on hands and knees, crying out to their fellows not to leave them behind. A few centons of Macht skirmishers went chasing after them, hurling javelins into their spines or finishing off the wounded where they crawled and screamed on the ground. A centurion called them back, cursing them for ill-disciplined fools, and they came trotting up the slope again shame-faced and with arms bloody to the elbows. A few had severed heads hanging from their belts. Gasca wondered where Rictus was, and if he had been anywhere near the meat of the fighting. He would have a story to tell him tonight, by Antimone's Veil.

A trembling took him, and he had to clench his teeth tight against the sob which ballooned in his chest. A whimper made it out his mouth, and another. He disguised it with a fit of coughing, but then felt a thump on the back of his cuirass. Old Demotes, his white beard dyed rust-red as it trailed out the bottom of his helm. "It's all right, lad. It's the Goddess. She must have her say. Let her out, and you'll be better off."

"Back in line—back in line you fuckers!" someone was shouting. It was Orsos, running up and down the relaxed ranks with his helm off and his spear resting on his shoulder. His shaven head gleamed white with sweat in the sunlight and there was spittle flying from his mouth. "Jason! Jason—we've cavalry coming up on our right and rear, maybe ten morai of them. Wheel your men about to the right. We're taking the rest into the Kufr centre. Do you hear me, Jason?"

* * *

The cavalry came on in a wave, tall horses bearing shrieking Kufr with luminous eyes and billowing, multi-coloured robes. They had scimitars, javelins, and a few stabbing spears. Their line extended two pasangs to left and right. Had the ground been firmer, they would have made it into a gallop, so frenziedly were the riders beating their wild-eyed and snorting mounts. But here the earth had been churned into a mire by the infantry battle, and the hillside was strewn with dead and dying of both sides and bristling with spent arrows, like the hair on a man's forearm when the cold hits it. So they advanced at a fast trot, some horses tripping up and toppling even at that. There were thousands—Rictus had not believed there could be so many of the beasts in the world. The ground shook under their hooves, and the blood rippled in its muddy craters.

They rode down their own wounded. At a hundred paces the skirmishers threw their first volley of javelins. There were perhaps three morai of light troops out here on the Macht right, and for the moment they were entirely unsupported. The heavy troops were at the top of the hill with their backs to the cavalry.

A second volley. Fifty paces. There would not be time for a third. "Spears!" Rictus shouted. "Close up, close up!"

They had not been drilled for this, unlike their heavier brethren. They did not come together in a solid line, but in clumps and knots of men and boys, pelta shields on their left arms, single-headed spears thrusting out on the right. Rictus felt a moment of pure, almost incapacitating terror. He had never been charged by cavalry before; none of them had.

The big horses struck home. Some, confined by their fellows on right and left, charged straight into the spears. Most streamed to left or right of the broken, scattered line, their riders hacking at the heads of the skirmishers as they passed by. Rictus and his comrades were islands in a raging sea of horseflesh and hacking steel. They stabbed out at the bellies of the animals and in moments had a bank of the injured beasts thrashing around them, riders pinned beneath their carcasses or finished off before they could rise out of the mud. But more and more cavalry kept streaming past, turning and coming back again, hooves hammering the ground into a bloody morass, bogging themselves down. There was no fluidity to the fight; the cavalry did not charge and counter-charge. They slogged through the light troops of the Macht in bursts of pure mass and muscle, and bore down the defenders by numbers and bulk.

Rictus's half-centon was now facing out on all directions, surrounded. In their midst a dozen dead and dying horses made a sort of bulwark. Thrusting his spear at a passing rider, Rictus leaned his foot on the equine carcass before him and felt the warmth and heartbeat of the animal as it lay dying in the bloody mud, not comprehending why it should have to endure the agony of such an end. He killed it with a spear-thrust to the brain, unable to listen to its screaming gurgles. When the Kufr went down they screamed no less piteously, but that afforded his conscience no trouble at all.

The sun climbed higher on that endless morning. It topped the hills upon which the Great King's armies now struggled and came bursting over the battle, setting alight a million tiny shards of reflected light, caught on helmets, spearpoints, and sword-blades, on the sweat of men's flesh and in the madness of their eyes. The Kufr cavalry fought in a cloud of their mounts' steam and the sun caught it and made wands and bars of restless light that speared through the carnage in a bitter kind of beauty. The Arakosan horsemen had been brought to a bloody halt by the amorphous ranks of the Macht skirmishers, and now some eight or nine thousand soldiers were embroiled in a charnel-house of blood and muck and animals screaming out on the Kefren left wing. For perhaps two square pasangs the tortured, sucking ooze that was the earth could not be seen below the maddened press of men and animals contending there. All thoughts of higher tactics were lost as the base struggle went on. But though the skirmishers were being steadily destroyed, they had protected the flank of the heavy infantry. The Macht spearmen were wheeling left on the crest of the hill, by morai, and were now advancing once more, their ranks thinner now, but as ordered as they had been at the beginning of the day. Before them, the Kefren centre was pulling back, threatened now by the Ten Thousand to the south and the advancing Juthan Legion to the west. The Kefren right wing was being hurled forward, courier after courier urging the Great King's generals there to advance at the double, to support the King's position on the right. A line of troops four pasangs long thus began to wheel inwards to try and catch the echeloned regiments of Arkamenes's army before they could close the pincers of their formations. More cavalry led the way, this time the heavy lancers of the Asurian heartland with their blue and gold enamelled armour. These burst forward out of the Kefren line with all the dash and brilliance of a king-fisher's strike, and began thundering down the slope towards the contingents from Tanis and Istar below, five thousand strong, fresh and unblooded.

"We should move back," Vorus said to Ashur-nan. He had taken off his helm the better to dictate to the battle-scribes and now his gaze swivelled back and forth between the advancing Macht on their left and the Juthan legion to their front. The Kefren left wing had been beaten up so badly it was beyond rallying; the plain behind the hill was black with fugitives for two pasangs, thousands of troops throwing down their weapons and their honour in a bid to escape the Macht killing-machine. What had once been their centre was now a flank. Forty thousand men, blown away like dead leaves in autumn. He would not have believed it had he not witnessed it with his own eyes.

"We should perhaps have hired some of these fellows ourselves," Ashurnan said. There was a smile on his face, and though fear had paled the gold of his shining skin, the humour in his tone was genuine. "No matter. We shall just have to do the thing with what remains."

"My lord, you must pull further back from the front line," Vorus grated.

"Look down there, General, to the right of their Juthan troops. You see the horsetail standard? That is my brother. I have a hankering to meet with him. It has been a long time since we looked into one another's eyes."

The Macht had started up the Paean again, and their line was lengthening as mora after mora came up to right and left. Their discipline was incredible. Just over a pasang separated the spearheads of their front rank from the Great King's chariot.

"Bring me my horse," Ashurnan said. He was not watching the Macht, but the horsetail standard that bobbed above the press of advancing men on the slopes below. "Vorus, I want you to hold on here. Retreat if you must, but slow your countrymen down. Buy me time."

For what? Vorus wondered, thoroughly alarmed now. The Great King had climbed out of his chariot and was mounting a tall Niseian. An aide brought him his cedar-wood lance. Prancing with impatience around them were the great horses of his bodyguard cavalry, and in their midst the standard-bearer with the winged symbol of the Asurian kings upon a twelve-foot staff.

"I go to greet my brother," Ashurnan said; he smiled again as he said it. His father's smile. The protests died in Vorus's throat.

He bowed. "I will hold them, my lord, or I will die trying."

Ashurnan leaned in the saddle and grasped Vorus's shoulder. "Do not die. I have too few friends already." Then he straightened, raised his hand, and around him the great mass of cavalry, a thousand at least, began to move, the Kefren nobility following their king down the hillside and into the maw of war.

The battle lines had veered round. Both the rebel right and the Great King's right were advancing, as though following agreed-upon steps in some cataclysmic dance. Arkamenes's centre was now almost upon the Royal line at the crest of the hill. The Great King led his thousand-strong bodyguard of heavy cavalry straight into this, the roar of that meeting coming even to the Macht spearmen two pasangs to the south. The rebel advance halted, recoiling from the impact of these, the finest cavalry of the Empire, whilst another three pasangs to the north the Asurian cavalry had also made contact with the rebel left. The entire field was now a milling scrum of troops, and where the fighting was heaviest the earth beneath their feet was tormented into a calf-deep morass of sucking mud in which the wounded were trampled and suffocated beneath the feet of those still fighting.

Young Morian had fallen; his neck hacked half-through by a shrieking Kufr horseman. Beside his corpse, Rictus had taken the second blow on his pelta, and the keen blade had sheared off half of it even as he raised his own spear and took his attacker in the armpit, above the leather corselet. The Kufr tilted and slid down the side of his horse, the animal maddened with rage and fear. It reared up and Rictus stabbed it in the belly, a twisted rope of intestine springing out of the hole the aichme made. Then the poor beast lurched away, hooves caught up in its own entrails as it strove to run from the agony, trailing its dying master by one hopelessly entangled stirrup. It careered into two other riders, their mounts already hock deep in the bloody mud. Rictus discarded his shattered shield, staggered forward, and jabbed his spear at these two in turn. He caught one in the thigh, the other about the groin. They shrieked with a sound not remotely human, their eyes bright as some gems dug out of the mountains. Rictus let the flesh-stuck spear go as their horses staggered and tilted and fought the mud. On his hands and knees he crawled over carcasses and through the bloody mire to regain what was left of his centon. Whistler left the ragged ranks to pull him back in, over a rampart of horseflesh. There were spears and shields aplenty about it in the hands of the dead and so Rictus re-armed himself for the third time that morning, his palms sticking to the spear-shaft, some other man's blood the glue. He looked at Whistler; the older man's bald head was a cap of blood, his scalp hanging down one ear. But he managed a gap-toothed grin all the same. There was no need to speak.

At the start of the morning this had been a bare and smooth slope of scrub-peppered earth, wide and open enough to have run footraces upon.

Now the work of war had transformed it into a swamp within which the corpses piled up in banks and outcrops of carrion like soft, rotting boulder-fields. It was no longer ground for cavalry, but the Arakosans were slogging it out to the end, their horses almost immobilised under them. *What bastard brings a horse to war?* Rictus wondered, outraged to the brim of his exhausted mind, shattered by the slaughterous waste, the stunning profligacy of the enemy.

Nevertheless, the Macht had been beaten here. Of the three thousand skirmishers who had held this slope at the start of the morning, there might be a thousand left who were still standing weapon in hand. And these would soon follow their fallen friends into the mud. They knew this, but they fought on because they also knew that behind them, up on the hill, the line of their heavy kindred had its back to them. Should the enemy break through their ranks there would be a slaughter on the hillcrest which would make this one seem trivial by comparison.

So the skirmishers, who had not been trained or created for this task, stood their ground. Because they were Macht, and it was what they had been ordered to do.

For Arkamenes the morning had been a marvel of sensation, the ultimate spectacle. Not even the most jaded libertine could fail to have his senses aroused by this, the grandest kind of theatre. *I say go*, he thought, *and they go. They die in thousands, the lines move, the thing is done. I have said it shall be so, and so it becomes.*

He had never been so happy in his life.

He had seen the Macht march up the hill and had watched them annihilate the Great King's left wing, an army in itself. The cavalry which had ambushed the Macht had been fought to a standstill by their camp-servants. He could see that struggle still going on, a dark stain on the land some three pasangs to the south. He could also see the Macht battle line reforming on the hilltop. Soon they would advance and take on the Great King's centre. When that happened he would lead his personal bodyguard up the hill to complete the victory, to be in at the kill.

It was hot, now that the sun had climbed. He could feel the heat of it even through the fine linen of his komis, and the jewelled breastplates of his bodyguard were too bright to look upon. He held out his hand, and a Kefren attendant placed within it a cool goblet of spring-water.

The water was never drunk. Halfway to his lips, the goblet stopped, and hung there in the air, his fingers suddenly cold about it. There it was, the Great King's standard, the holy symbol of Asuria. And it was coming down the hill towards him in the midst of a great cloud of fast-moving cavalry.

The goblet spun through the air and the tall Niseian half-reared under Arkamenes, catching its master's shock. He wrestled and beat the animal to quiet, staring. It could not be.

The enemy cavalry took a loop out to the north a few hundred paces, to avoid striking the ranks of the Juthan Legion now making its dogged way up the hillside. They wheeled back in like fish in shoal, not in ordered ranks, but a crowd of superb horsemen following their leader—and that leader was out in front now with a bright scimitar raised up to catch the flash of the sunlight.

Arkamenes drew his own sword and waved it forwards. "Go, go go!" he cried to the Kefren horsemen about him, his mind reaching for words but not finding them in its tumult.

The enemy cavalry struck his own at a gallop, a thunderous crash of flesh and metal; suddenly the war came near and to be smelled and felt and feared. Back, the stationary ranks of the rebel horse were crushed by the impact, some bowled over in the first onset, others smashed onto their haunches, riders pinned in the melee, legs broken between the ribs of the maddened animals. From these platforms of plunging flesh their masters hacked at each other with bright swords or stabbed overhand with their lances, the points and blades clashing amid flurries of sparks. Asurian steel struck Asurian steel, Kefren killing Kefren, and the momentum of the enemy charge was still felt through the horseflesh and the confusion, the King's standard rearing up like a raptor above the killing.

Ashurnan's bodyguard were the finest warriors of their race, mounted on the mightiest warhorses the Empire could breed. And they had momentum on their side. The Great King fought his way forward, and those who died under his blade saw that there was a kind of gladness on his face, a recklessness. He did not expect to live long, and so meant to live well for what remained of this life to be measured in moments, the mere drips of an almost empty waterclock. His followers had caught his mind and were with him in the moment, wholly reconciled. Even Arkamenes, watching, thought there was a kind of beauty about it. And for one broken second, he found himself loving the brother he had known as a boy, who had been his conscience and his ally. That familiar face, transfigured so as to be a boy's again.

The second passed, and there was only the murderous insane violence of the present and the task in hand, something to grasp through the fog of fear and confusion. Arkamenes's bodyguard had been pressed back in a mass by the concussion of the King's charge, and now there was nowhere to go. Even if a man were able to dismount in that milling crush he would be trampled underfoot within seconds.

The currents that moved the melee were created by killing, by the sheer brutal struggle of one against another. The Great King moved forward, horses going down as he and his guards stabbed at the big veins in the neck, or transfixed them through the eyes. Arkamenes's bodyguards fought back with the savagery of the trapped, but though they were Honai, they were not the Honai of Ashur, and they gave ground, dying and falling and turning their faces from their own deaths instead of trying to deflect the killing blades as they realised they had become carrion.

And so Ashurnan and Arkamenes met in the middle of that vast bloodletting, in the end both willing that it should be so, in the end neither afraid, in the end brothers again.

Their eyes met but they did not speak, though both of them had words they would have said. Their blades clicked off one another. Under them the tall Niseians charged at each other's shoulders and tried to bite and rear, but were reined in by both their masters as the swords flickered out and clashed and sought the life of the other in a kind of dance, in its way a splendid thing. But Ashurnan had always applied himself better to the learning of such skills, and it was his blade which sliced home first. Though he had put his strength into the blow, he tried to take it back as he saw it would go home, not even conscious of the reason. But the keen blade did not need much muscle at its back to do the work, and the edge took Arkamenes under the chin, severing the big arteries there and the windpipe, before sliding free.

The rebel prince dropped his sword and clasped both hands to his gaping throat. His mouth worked, frog-like, and in his eyes there was terror, and a kind of regret. Then he toppled from his horse. Around him, his bodyguards saw the death of all their hopes, and sent up a kind of wail. Some threw down their swords and raised their eyes to the sky as if in prayer, others turned their horses around and tried to fight their way to the rear. The horsetail standard that signified the presence of the pretender was cast aside, disappearing in that great mass of bloody, struggling flesh. And as the standard fell, a kind of shudder, more felt than seen, went through the ranks of Arkamenes's army.

FIFTEEN
A FAREWELL TO THE KING

Phiron walked out to the front of the phalanx and held up his spear. Up and down the endless lines of the heavy infantry the order was passed along: "*Halt.*"

Pasion joined him, and as the minutes passed so did a few other centurions, standing like curious spectators at a street fight. "Is that the—?" Durik began to ask.

"The Great King has proved himself a man, it seems," Phiron said. He levered off his stinking helm, his black hair plastered down flat as a seal's back beneath it. "They're at it hand to hand, bodyguards and all."

"And what about these bastards?" Pasion asked, gesturing to the enemy ranks not half a pasang from them along the hilltop. Kufr spearmen now as irresolute and fascinated as their officers by the close-packed cavalry battle in the valley below and the two standards waving in the midst of it, mere yards apart.

"If they fight it out, that's the whole battle down there, won or lost in a moment," Orsos said. He joined them, breathing heavily. "Jason covers our rear, Phiron. He's seen off the Arakosan cavalry. It's a fucking slaughterhouse down there." Even he seemed shocked by the carnage of the day.

All along the ridge-top, thousands of men were standing still, watching while the contest went on, the sound of it a dull roar that echoed off the face of the hills. The Juthan Legion had come to a halt halfway up the slope and now stood in a rankless mob of several thousands, all looking back the way they had come rather than up to where the enemy centre stood above.

"We stand here like virgins in a fucking marriage chamber!" This was young Pomero, come striding up to them with a face full of baffled anger. "What's halted the lines? We should be pitching into them right now, and the Juthan should be hitting them from the flank. We have the battle won, here and now!"

Phiron did not turn round. He closed his eyes for a second. "The battle is lost. Can you not hear it?"

They watched, silent now. The crush of cavalry which composed the battle below was opening out. To the Macht, all Kefren looked the same, but it was possible to see that their employer's horsetail standard no longer waved above the ranks. The Great King's winged banner was advancing, whilst before it clouds of cavalry were streaming away. All along the field, there came from Arkamenes's Kufr troops an eerie collective sound, half groan and half wail. It trailed for pasangs along the flatlands of the valley floor.

"The son of a bitch has gone and gotten hisself killed," Orsos snarled.

Remarkable, how that information seemed to disseminate about the battlefield faster than a man could run. The Juthan Legion disintegrated first, just as the first knots of fleeing bodyguard cavalry came galloping past them, the riders beating their horses beyond reason, throwing away priceless breastplates to ease their load. Back down the slopes towards the Bekai River in the distance, what had been an army was now in the process of breaking up. Here and there, ordered formations survived and held together—they could see the troops from Artaka under Gushrun, who had marched all the way from the shores of the Tanean with them. But for the most part Arkamenes's forces became a formless mob now running for their lives, and hoping to make the Bekai crossings before the Great King's cavalry cut them off. Already, the superb ranks of the Asurians had given chase, thousands of richly clad horsemen yelling like maniacs and starting the grim sport of the pursuit. The Macht centurions on the hill watched in horror and something approaching awe. It was Phiron who collected himself first.

"We may well be fucked, brothers, but that does not mean we leave this world like lambs. Orsus—about-face your mora and link up with

Jason. Tell him to pull up the hillside, and bring the skirmishers with him, what's left of them. Brothers, we go into all-round defence and see what transpires. We do not run, nor do we retreat. The Bekai bridges are about to become a chokepoint, and the Great King will destroy the rest of the army before them. We must do otherwise." He donned his helm once more. They stood looking at one another, all thinking the same thing. The battle had been won; another half hour of fighting and an Empire would have been gained. One Kufr's stupidity had lost it, and with it, their lives.

"We are Macht," Orsos said, spitting out the word like a curse. "We do not show our backs to Kufr. The morning is done, brothers; now night approaches. We will go into the dark together."

In the Kefren centre, Vorus watched the death of Arkamenes's army with a kind of wonder. Beside him, old Proxis set his fist on his heart and prayed a moment to the Juthan smith-god, in whose forge the world had been hammered out.

"I knew he was his father's son, but even Anurman would not have staked all on one throw, Proxis. He is either a genius, or a fool."

"He did right; the snake's head is severed. He has saved his Empire."

Vorus called over a battle-scribe and a courier. He scribbled quickly on the portable desk the *hufsan* scribe wore about his neck. "We are not quite done," he said to Proxis, still writing. "There are men on this hill who will not be running."

"The Macht? They are finished. They fought well, but their legs are cut out from under them now."

"We must contain them at once." And to the courier, "Take this to all the legion commanders in turn. Tell them they must not hesitate or break ranks; give them those words as well as the despatch."

The courier nodded and ran off.

"We will surround them, and then destroy them," Vorus said, and despite the resolve in his words, he looked sick to his stomach.

Out on the southern edge of the battlefield Jason's mora stood easy now, shields at their knees, helms off. Around them what remained of the skirmishers went over the mounded corpses looking for wounded, for loot, for Kufr whose throats could still be slit. The runner found Jason sharing a skin of water with Rictus and Gasca, the three of them not speaking, just drinking in turns from the skin, their eyes glazed with that blasted look of men who have seen enough. The runner told them of events on the rest of the field, a strawhead youth who had cast aside all his wargear to run this errand. His account was tortured by the effort to breathe. Jason listened to him without comment.

"Rictus, what do you have left here, you suppose?"

Rictus's face was an unknowable mask of dried blood, black gobbets streaking it, the only clean spaces about his lips and where he had wiped his eyelids. He looked around them at the shattered hillside and its ghastly carpet of bodies. "I'm thinking maybe eight hundred fit to fight, another two or three hundred lightly wounded, and as many again who will not see tomorrow unless they're seen to right now."

Jason rubbed his forehead. "We must get back up the hill and rejoin the other morai at once. We don't have time..." He turned and looked northwards up the valley. Six pasangs away, the bulk of Arkamenes's army covered the ground like a creeping rash from which glints of white light sprang out, reflected metal. Behind them the hillcrest was bare, the bulk of the Macht centons having moved beyond it. Standing here, it hardly seemed possible that the battle was not over.

Jason beat the black flies from his face, grimacing. His grey eyes were cold as a spearhead, but he closed them as he spoke, like a man tired to the marrow. "Kill the severely wounded. Bring along the rest. We'll cover your retreat. Bring along what spares you can scavenge off the dead; arm heavy, if you can. It's spearmen we need now, not stick-throwers."

Rictus shared a glance with Gasca. "Kill them?"

Jason's eyes broke open, shot with blood. "You heard me. We can't take them all with us, and the Kufr will torture them. It's a kindness. Besides, we'll likely be joining them soon enough."

Rictus blinked rapidly. "Who am I to be giving such orders?"

"You're in fucking command is what you are. Agrimos and everyone else above you are dead or maimed. You take these men now, Rictus, and you get a grip of them. Do you hear me? Now start them at it." Jason strode away. There had been a quake in his voice. Rictus watched him go, aghast.

"Promotion. Ain't it grand?" Gasca snorted, and drank from the skin again. He wiped his mouth, and with a half-smile said, "Tonight you'll be a centurion in hell."

The Great King sat his horse and looked down on the thing that had been his brother. Arkamenes had been a handsome creature in life; his face now seemed nothing more than a mound of meat, for the horses had trampled it. Below what had been the chin a blackberry-dark gash gaped wide, a black mouth smiling at the sky, running with flies.

"Cover him up," Ashurnan said unsteadily. "Bear him from the field. His bones will be buried in Ashur, where they belong."

The Honai bent and laid a cloak over the battered remnants of Ashurnan's brother. The Great King wheeled his horse away and pulled his komis up over his face.

"Midarnes!"

"Yes lord?" The commander of the Household troops drew level, bowing in the saddle.

"Leave the pursuit to the cavalry. Tell Berosh to take our Juthan to the river also, and make sure he takes and holds the bridges. The Household and the Honai are to remain opposite the Macht lines, but are not to engage. Is that understood, Midarnes?"

"Yes, lord."

Ashurnan looked up at the sky. It was past noon. The morning had ended at last and the day was on the slide, but there was enough daylight left for the things which had to be done.

"I need scribes and couriers, the best we have. We will send word to Istar, to Jutha, to Artaka. The pretender is dead. These provinces must come back to me without delay. If they do, there will be no repercussions. If they do not, I will bring fire and the spear among them."

"Honuran died on the field," Midarnes said, "But Gushrun of Tanis has not yet been caught."

"Find him. Bring him to me. He will be made an example of. I will impale his body upon the very gates of Tanis."

Midarnes bowed again.

"Amasis also, the chamberlain—he will be back with the baggage. We must take their baggage train, Midarnes, without it these Macht will be without food, without water, without so much as a spare spearhead."

"It shall be done, my lord. I shall send word to the cavalry. It is rumoured that Arkamenes travelled with a fortune in bullion also, half the treasury of Tanis to pay these mercenaries with."

"Secure it. The day is far from over."

The Great King rode sedately up the hillside that he had so recently charged down, surrounded by hundreds of heavy cavalry, Kefren who had pledged their loyalty to him in blood. He warmed to them now as he had not before, for they had followed him down into the great gamble, not knowing it would pay off. He felt slightly dazed, dazed by the victory, by the aftermath of the violence still singing in his ears and shaking in his muscles. Today, he thought, I proved myself my father's son. I have earned my throne at last. And he gave thanks to God, there in the midst of that vast slaughterhouse, for the way the morning had passed.

"It's twelve pasangs to the river, and five back to the baggage train," Phiron said.

"The baggage is gone," Pasion growled. "We need not trouble ourselves over it. All we have left in this world are the spears in our hands and the bronze on our backs."

"Then we are still rich men," old Castus said. "I'd as soon die with wargear on my back as staring up the arse of an ox. What's the plan, Phiron? Do we stand here and let them come to us, or do we charge down into them and try and make a story out of it?"

Thirteen men, all in the Curse of God except for the youngest among them. Rictus had unstrapped a battered bronze cuirass from a corpse and now wore full panoply for the first time since the day he had fought in the ranks of the Iscan phalanx. Jason had insisted he be admitted to the Kerusia, as his skirmishers had rearmed themselves similarly, and now constituted a Macht mora. Rictus had not become a centurion; he had become a notional general of several hundred men. For all that, he was entirely ignored by the true veterans of the Ten Thousand who despised him for a strawhead upstart, Iscan or no. He held his tongue as the older men debated.

The Macht had come together again on the ridge-crest of Kunaksa and now their centons were facing out in all directions. In the hollow heart of the formation several hundred lightly wounded were strapping themselves up as best they could, helped by those of the skirmishers who were too young or too old to bear the weight of a full panoply. A few hundred paces away, the Kufr lines were extending to east and west, a shallow crescent of troops thickening moment by moment. On the plain below the great hunt went on, Kefren horsemen riding down and slaughtering the last of Arkamenes's army before they could come to the Bekai bridges. There were so many figures on the move that the plain seemed to be crawling with life for pasangs to the west, as though someone had tipped up a termite mound and let the occupants spill out in their busy, frantic tens of thousands.

Phiron wiped the sweat from his face. What remained of the water had been given to the wounded, and his tongue was rasping against his teeth like something foreign in his mouth. "We go to them," he said tersely. "Otherwise they wait for thirst to do half their work for them."

"What way?" Pomero asked.

"Not to the river; they'll be expecting that. We hit them here, as hard as we can, and beat them back off the heights. Their cavalry is still busy down on the plain, so we stick to the hills. We head north, parallel to the river. There are big cities up there, on the river. One called Carchanis maybe eight, ten days' march from here. We get there, take that city and hold it, regroup and resupply. Then—"

"Then?" Orsos demanded.

"Then we decide what to do next."

"If we get to decide how to die in the next two hours we'll be lucky," Mynon snapped, black eyes flashing. "Ten days' march? And we eat and drink what on the way? And won't the Great King have something to say about us tramping off through his Empire?"

"Mynon's right," Pasion said quietly, kneading his jaw. "We fight and die here and now, or we sue for terms. Ashurnan knows we'll take ten times our number with us when we go down; he may be amenable to some kind of compromise. Otherwise his army could well be wrecked by our last stand."

"You think he cares?" Teremon spoke up. An older man, a close friend of both Castus and Orsos, he had taken an arrow in the face during the morning's fighting and now a bloody rag was stuffed in the socket where his left eye had been. "He can call up a million spears against us if he wants; the whole Empire sits around us. What does he care if he loses another ten thousand, another fifty thousand, so long as he sees the end of us?"

"Calling up more levies takes time," Pasion said patiently. "For now, the only army in the Empire that the Great King can rely on stands opposite us, on these hills. Don't forget that Jutha, and Istar and Artaka are still in rebellion. He'll have to send troops to recall them to the fold. No, Teremon, he cannot afford to see this army of his wrecked upon these hills. I say we send him an embassy under a green branch, and see if we can come to some arrangement. Who knows, he may need Macht spears as his brother did. We fight for pay, not for any cause. He must learn of this, and quickly. If the fighting starts again, then the moment is lost. We will leave our bones here, and the Kufr will pick Antimone's Gift off our bodies."

There was an angry murmur at this. The thought of the black armours falling into Kufr hands was unthinkable, impious; there were scores of them in the ranks of the army.

"All right then," Phiron said. He seemed shrunken, as if the turn of events had done something to his insides. "We'll send out an ambassador. Someone who can speak their damned language." There was a pause. "That's—"

"Me, you fucks," Jason said. "Yes, I know. I'll do it. And I'll take the strawhead here with me."

The heat of the afternoon was an enervating oven which must be struggled against physically. The corpses had already begun to add something to the brew, and their luckier comrades had to piss and shit somewhere. So for pasangs all around, the stink on the unmoving air was a thing that hung heavy in the stomach. It was as if the bloodletting had fouled some essential balance in the earth itself, and now the face of Kuf was revolted by it. The Macht had a name for this miasma, as they had for most things connected with warfare: *the soup*, they called it. By naming it, joking about it, they made it more bearable. For the carrion birds circling and the black flies laying their eggs in the eyes of the dead it was a field of bounty, and their claims upon it would soon make of this place a plague-pit.

Jason and Rictus strode forth unarmed under the withered stick that was the nearest they could come to a green-leafed bough upon the field. They walked out across the sucking, steaming morass of mud and carrion which occupied the space between the armies and planted themselves there whilst the sweat stung hot in their eyes and the stink of the place seemed fair to choke them.

"Why me?" Rictus asked as they watched the Kufr lines and saw figures run back and forth behind them.

"I might ask the same myself," Jason said equably. "Phiron speaks Asurian better than I, and Kefren too. My guess is, he's so indispensable to the army's survival he's counted himself out of gambles such as this. As for you, I picked you as a companion for several reasons. You're not stupid, you know how to listen, and you're a big bastard who might be able to look one of these gangling fucks in the eye. Now shut up and prove me right on all counts."

Their presence in the field between the armies had set individual horsemen to the gallop behind the Kufr phalanx. There were more horsemen there now; fine looking fellows in all the finery the Empire could provide. Jason stared at them and said; "I believe the King is there. No standard or chariot, but that's his bodyguard, or I'm a blind man."

"What happens if all this is moonlight?" Rictus asked. "What if they're just set on finishing it today?"

Jason looked at him, cocking his head to one side. "We die fighting."

Strangely, Rictus smiled.

The Kufr ranks broke open, and someone came walking out across the mud to meet them. He wore black armour, and as he drew close, they could see that he was Macht, clad in the Curse of God. Jason's mouth opened in astonishment.

"What are your names?" the strange Macht asked. He was middle-aged, spare and lean and bearded. He bore no weapon, and stared upon them with a barely restrained hunger of curiosity. Jason and Rictus stared back at him with something of the same expression on their faces.

"Jason of Ferai; Rictus of Isca," Jason said, collecting himself.

The man smiled. "My name is Vorus. I am general of the army behind me."

This fell into silence, Jason and Rictus too thunderstruck to reply. Vorus looked them up and down, not without kindness. "You wish to negotiate on behalf of Phiron, I take it. Well, I am authorised likewise on behalf of the Great King. You may speak to me freely."

"*Phobos*," Jason said under his breath. "We wish to discuss terms under which we may leave the Empire in peace." Still staring he added, "Our employer is dead, and now we just want to get home. Vorus you say—Vorus of where?"

"Son, I left the Harukush long before you hefted your first spear," Vorus said. And more formally, "My King has divined your intention beforehand. We have no wish to see further bloodshed—the issues which set us at each other's spearpoints have already been decided. Now it only remains to see how this army of yours can be repatriated as quickly and easily as possible. To that end, we wish to invite the entire Kerusia of your generals to a meeting tonight, down on the plain, where terms for your departure from the Empire shall be discussed. Would that be acceptable to your commander, you think?"

"I believe it would," Jason said, and he could not help the smile that broke about his face. "I take it all parties shall be unarmed, and that the space where the meeting takes place be equidistant from both army's lines?"

"Of course. We will prepare a suitable venue at once. The Great King will attend, with myself and two or three others. There will be slaves also, of course. You may bring your senior officers only; there is no need for a large crowd at an event such as this. Things become too easily misunderstood. What say you?"

"I think I may say on behalf of Phiron that we can attend as you suggest. Might I request in the interim, as a gesture of good faith, that water could be brought to us here by your—your people? We have wounded in our ranks who would bless your Great King's name for a single sip."

Vorus's face clouded. "I am afraid that's out of the question. We remain enemies in name at least, until your generals agree to some arrangement tonight." His jaw worked, and he looked away for a second. "I am sorry."

Jason stiffened but his tone remained perfectly civil. "I quite understand. We will rejoin our comrades now."

He turned away, exasperation and relief warring on his face. Rictus paused a moment. He stared Vorus in the eye, that Iscan arrogance coming out once more. Vorus met him look for look a long moment, and then moved with an odd jerkiness, walking back to his own lines. He moved with the stiff onerous gait of a man ashamed of what he has just done.

SIXTEEN
THE MEN ON THE HILL

Many of the wounded died during the day, and the healthy were reduced to dipping their helmets in some of the less noisome puddles which dotted the hillside, drinking down mud and blood as much as any water. They threw it up again directly, until Phiron forbade the practice.

The Great King's army continued to follow its own evolutions, with regiments marching here and there in the shimmering heat, and pack-trains of laden mules bringing up supplies from the baggage-camp to the east. From the ridge-crest it was possible to see through the heat-haze to the bright glimmer of the Bekai River twelve pasangs away, but beyond a certain shadow upon the earth about the mound of Kaik, it was impossible to tell what had transpired there. Arkamenes's army seemed to have vanished from the face of the world, leaving behind only corpses, a windfall of carrion scattered across the earth for as far as a keen eye could see. Juthan soldiers were methodically clearing the plain, stripping and looting the dead, piling up the bodies into pyres. The work went on all day, until the light began to fail and the shattering heat at last eased a little. On the ridge-line of Kunaksa, the Macht stood in stubborn ranks, shields at their knees, helms at their belts, and their throats as parched as burnt bread. They had piled up all of their own dead that they could come at, though there was nothing to burn them with. Every spearhead and belt-buckle that could be gleaned from the battlefield had been gathered. The corpses now lay stacked, almost three thousand of them in several long mounds. Ravens and vultures were already clustered on these knolls of rotting flesh, heedless of any outraged shout or thrown stone. And the *soup* thickened about the hills as evening drew on and the blood congealed in gobbets about the very stones half-buried in the ground.

The Great King's standard was set up on the plain some pasang and a half from the Macht lines, and about it hundreds of Kufr had erected a tented compound, labouring through the heat of the day until it seemed that a veritable village had sprung up in the space of a few hours. As the light failed, a trio of Kefren horsemen rode up to the Macht lines under a green branch and gestured with it to the tents below. Phiron shouted assent at them in their own language and they galloped off again, komis held close to their noses.

"Well, there's the invite," he said. "Shall we take him up on it?"

"It's that, or charge his lines," Castus retorted. His seamed old face appeared to have withered in the space of a day, like an apple in an oven, but his eyes were as fierce and clear as always. "Can we trust these bastards?"

"We trust them or fight them," Phiron said simply.

"Let's move, before it gets too dark to see where the fuck we're going," Orsos rasped.

Thirteen of them walked out from the Macht phalanx. They had left off their armour and weaponry and walked in the cool lightness of their sweat-sodden chitons, with short swords in their belts. Many of them bore crudely bound wounds. All were plastered with dried blood and shreds of flesh and bone, and their legs were caked black with filth to the knees. They looked more like defeated slaves than the generals of an army. There was an uneasy murmur in the ranks as they picked their way down the broken hillside to the tents below. The Kufr army had drawn back somewhat for the night and had lit campfires, breaking their lines and laying out pickets every hundred paces. As the light faded and the stars began springing out above the black heights of the Magron, these campfires described an arc some eight pasangs long. In the centre of the arc the Macht army stood by its arms in fireless darkness, the wounded shivering as the heat of the day evaporated and a coolness poured down out of the mountains in the east.

There were horses hobbled by the meeting-tent, but apart from that the plain seemed wholly deserted now, the Juthan having given up their corpse-gathering for the night. The thirteen Macht officers paused at the lightless bulk of the tents until a flap was lifted to let light spill out from within. They entered in single file, Rictus at the rear, his hand on the hilt of his cheap sword.

"Up on the hill, the wounded are dying for want of a cup of water, and this twisted bastard has set us out a *feast*?" Teremon whispered, venom in the underscored rasp of his voice.

"Behave yourself tonight and the wounded may drink before morning," Phiron told him. "This is the Great King we deal with now, not some usurper with ideas above his station. Brothers, we must be humble—do you hear me now? We stand in a foreign land, not as some conquering army, but as interlopers."

"Interlopers, my arse," Orsos said.

The tent within which they stood was as tall as a great tree, and had been floored with planks of cedar. It was hung with lamps up and down, all burning sweet oil. On a low table to one side a vast array of breads, meats, fruit, preserves, and wines had been set out, as well as a great earthenware bowl full of clear water, as big as a centos. The generals eyed it with some anger, licking their cracked lips, but not one made a move towards it. They stood in two rows behind Phiron.

Opposite them were some of the low-caste *hufsan*, Royal attendants in the livery of the King, and in the darker corners of the tent a trio of towering Honai, unarmed save for stabbing short-swords—this being the only form of weapon permitted at a parley, and more a ceremonial badge than a useful adjunct to a fight.

"So where is the renegade?" old Argus asked.

"And the King," Mynon added.

Jason stood, head cocked to one side in that way of his, listening. He was about to speak when a flap in the far side of the tent was lifted and Vorus entered. He was wearing his black armour and his helm sat in the crook of one arm.

"There's more behind him," Jason hissed, and started to draw his sword.

"Peace, brothers," Vorus said, holding up one hand. But the Macht generals were all drawing their weapons now, except for Phiron, who stepped forward with both hands up and empty, palm out.

"Listen to him," he said loudly. "Sheathe your swords, damn it all. Think of the men on the hill, for Phobos's sake. Stand down."

The men behind him paused, and one after another the twelve blades were slid back in their scabbards. Vorus nodded. He stepped forward. "Phiron of Idrios," he said. "You have led your men well, and they have acquitted themselves honourably. I salute you, one man to another, one general to another." He held out his free hand, and after a moment's hesitation, Phiron took it in the warrior grip. The tension in the tent sank swiftly. Pasion, just behind Phiron, shook his head and began to smile.

Vorus brought up his helm, that bowl of iron, and smashed it into Phiron's face, breaking bone.

Phiron staggered, and Vorus struck again, still gripping the other man's hand in a white-knuckled fist. As Phiron crumpled, Vorus shouted out in the Kufr language. All around the walls of the tent, hitherto unseen flaps were lifted, and pouring into the space around the Macht there filed fully-armed Honai of the Great King's bodyguard.

Vorus released Phiron's hand, and the Macht general crumpled to the planked floor, his face a broken mire of blood. Vorus stepped back, donning the gore-flecked helm, and shouted in Kufr once again. The Honai moved in.

Pasion had leapt forward, sword in hand. He bounded across Phiron's body with a full-throated roar and stabbed out at Vorus. The blade struck the renegade's black cuirass and scored harmlessly off to the side. Vorus's own blade came up from his waist and transfixed Pasion through the ribs, hilt-deep.

Rictus did not see much more. He and Jason were at the rear of the Macht. As Rictus started instinctively to advance, Jason thumped him backwards to the wall of the tent. "Cut it open!" And then he turned to clash aside the thrust spear of a Honai guardsman.

Rictus scored his blade down the tent-leather, admitting a bloom of cold air from the night outside. He turned once, to look back at the one-sided melee that was now raging in the tent. The Macht had come together in a tight knot of blades and were beating down the spears of the Honai. Vorus had disappeared. Phiron and Pasion lay dead, and as Rictus watched, Teremon followed them, his one eye not quick enough to catch the spearhead that took him on his blind side. Orsus's bull-roar filled the air as the shaven-headed general lunged forward, stabbing the Honai below the corselet and opening his bowels. This Kufr's fall entangled the legs of two more, and the Macht blades licked out at once, opening their throats and groins. The air was full of blood; the tall Honai with their raging eyes seemed like some smith-made automatons set whirring into clockwork life, jabbing down with their spears and butting into the Macht with the bowls of their shields.

Then Rictus was through the opening he had made. The night was dazzlingly dark about him, full of feet running, plashing through the mud, Kufr voices calling to one another, screams echoing out of the tent. He stood one moment, and then turned back and was about to push his way back inside when Jason burst through the rent, dragging Mynon with him. "Get his other arm. Up the hill, now. *Move*!"

Mynon had taken a blow to the head. He was supporting his weight with all the craft of someone very drunk. They dragged and carried him away from the tents, the breath sawing in their lungs, their brains white with the enormity of it all. Rictus felt as though his mind had been locked down in some box, and his body carried on its necessary work without it.

"Down," Jason said. And all three of them lay flat in the mud. Kufr with torches ran back and forth across the plain and clustered around the tents like fireflies. The three Macht lay not thirty paces from the nearest, but so slathered were they with mud that only their eyes gleamed clean of it. These they shut when the Kufr torchbearers looked their way.

"Is this all?" Jason asked hoarsely. "That cunting renegade. I will have his life, before this is over." He rested his forehead in the clammy ground and his body shook in silent spasm for a few seconds. When he raised his head again his features were a mask of mud and hatred.

Mynon's eyelids fluttered. He groaned loudly, and Rictus placed a hand over his mouth. The dark-browed man glared at him, then collected himself. He levered Rictus's palm gently from his face. "Who is this? Rictus?—and Jason."

"Quiet," Jason whispered.

A chariot trundled forward and about it gathered a body of Kufr cavalry, well-armoured Kefren of the bodyguard. In the chariot were a *hufsan* driver and a tall Kufr with a snow-white komis about his face. Juthan warriors lined up and held their torches above their heads, making an avenue of torchlight leading up to the chariot. Up this avenue came a file of Honai, some bloodied and limping. Each of them bore something dangling from one hand. Vorus was at their rear, his black armour gleaming.

The Honai lifted up their burdens. First the Juthan and then the mounted bodyguards gave a great shout and clashed their spears against shields and breastplates. Ten severed heads, held up dripping in the torchlight to stripe the arms of their bearers. The leaders of the Ten Thousand, their features frozen in death, eyes blank and glazed.

"I've seen enough," Jason said. "We go now, while they're having their party. Up the hill."

The three of them began crawling up the muddy slope in the darkness, whilst behind them the Kufr shouted and cheered their King and the heads of the ten generals were set upon poles as trophies.

"Is that all?" Ashurnan asked. "Did we get them all, Vorus?"

The Macht general had a face like some grey mask carved out of stone. "I believe one or two escaped. But we got Phiron, and Pasion, all the senior officers of experience. The Macht are leaderless now. We must attack them at dawn, a full assault."

The Great King stared at the pole-mounted heads that snarled at him in the torchlight. Bred to war though they were, his chariot horses stamped and snorted uneasily under the regard of those dead eyes. "You know what to do with these," he said briskly. "I will return to the camp. Take them at dawn, Vorus, and wipe them out. If any are alive by the moons of tomorrow, I want them in capture yokes."

"Yes, lord."

Ashurnan regarded his general more closely, dropping his komis from his mouth. "Would you rather some other officer undertook this mission? I would understand. They are your people, after all."

Vorus drew himself up, anger sparking out of his eyes. "I serve the Great King. I do his bidding, whatsoever it might be. I have served the Great King for twenty years, and never yet have I begged off a mission or disobeyed a command. I will continue to serve the Great King until the day of my death."

Ashurnan smiled. "I do not doubt it, my friend. Send word of events to me. Midarnes, you will place the Household troops under Vorus's command, and obey his orders as though they were my own. I go now, General, to see what remains of my brother's baggage train and the riches he brought from Tanis. Should you need me, seek me there." He raised a hand and the charioteer slapped the reins on the horses' rumps. The vehicle moved away, and with it a great cloud of Honai cavalry, their hooves thumping out a triumphant tattoo on the ground. Vorus stood and watched them go for a long while, the Juthan and Kefren guards standing around him in the torchlight, the dead eyes of the Macht watching all.

"Proxis," he said.

"Aye." The old Juthan stepped forward. He was somewhat drunk, but steady as an oak, and his yellow eyes were as shrewd as one sober.

"You know what to do with these?"

"I know," Proxis said, heavily.

"Then see to it. I am going up the hill to meet with our officers." Vorus strode away from the circle of torchlight, out into the stinking darkness of the Kunaksa heights, where the Kufr army waited around its campfires for the bloody work yet to come.

The heads were to be transported to Kaik, just across the plain, where they would be embalmed, and then a powerful escort would take them through the rebel provinces of Istar, Jutha, and

Artaka under a green branch, to declare that Arkamenes was dead and the invincible Macht had been destroyed. A special wagon was already being constructed to display them to best advantage on their travels. It was a calculated barbarism. Vorus saw the purpose behind it, and approved of it. But for all that, it turned something in his stomach.

The army was restless about its fires, the Honai sitting on the bowls of their shields, their eyes catching the firelight like the polished bulbs of brass lamps. In the *hufsan* lines, the mountain folk were singing their dark croon of lament for the dead, celebrating and remembering those of their kin who had fallen during the day. The Juthan sat in quiet circles, their halberds on their knees, talking in their sonorous tongue. Farther back, on the less broken ground to the south, the cavalry were quartered. These had seen the brunt of the day's fighting, and up and down the horse-lines the Arakosans and the Asurians were tending their animals. They took their mounts down to the river to drink in shifts of a thousand, and many of the Arakosans did not come back from these trips. Vorus suspected that they were deserting in large numbers, for their assault on the Macht flank had broken them, and hundreds had no horse to ride at all. They had been in the centre of the day's carnage, and seemed haunted by it. None of the rest of the troops who remained on the hills had yet fought the Macht, and the Arakosans were telling gloomy tales of slaughter to visitors from other quarters of the camp who came to find out how exactly these creatures made war. All of the army had seen the left wing disintegrate under the Macht assault, and had heard the Paean sung in great and bloody splendour. That part of the battle was already becoming a kind of legend.

In the morning, Vorus promised himself, we will make another.

"They'll attack at dawn," Jason said, the cracked mud falling from his face as it dried. He buckled on the Curse of God without looking at his fingers, staring out at the Kufr campfires burning in their sleepless arc across the hills.

"Mynon, we need new mora commanders. Get the senior centurion in each and bring him here. Buridan will do for mine. I know Mochran and Phinero will do too. Get them here fast; we don't have time to fuck about."

Mynon seemed about to say something; his keen eyes were almost buried by the frowning bridge of his brows. Then he nodded and trotted off.

"You, Rictus, take one of these," Jason said, gesturing to the neat lines of black armour upon the ground.

Rictus stood looking down on them, priceless relics with no one to claim them.

"They should have been worn," he said.

"Then they'd be in Kufr hands by now. It was a sound decision. Take one for Antimone's sake. For the sake of those that wore them. They do not bite."

All around the pair the Macht had gathered a little closer to watch and listen. Bad news was the easiest thing in the world to disseminate about an army. It flew on the swiftest of wings. Antimone saw to that; it was part of her curse. This news had travelled through the centons like a wildfire. Their leaders were dead, some of the ablest and most popular men in the army. There had not been a panic, but the ranks had broken all the same. The army had begun to revert to is constituent parts, the centons clustering together, the line abandoned, the men talking in quiet groups among themselves. They did not even have the communal centoi to gather around any more, nor any wood to burn. They stood in the darkness, separate entities whose loyalties now took little reckoning of any overall command. They were on the edge of disintegration, and Jason knew it.

"Take one, Rictus," he repeated, more gently now. The big, blood-masked strawhead stood looking down on the dead generals' cuirasses as though they were the naked wife of a friend.

"I have no right to it," Rictus said. Tears had cut white streaks down his face and in the light of the two moons he looked like some warpainted savage from the Inner Mountains.

"You have every right. I intend to mark out the new morai commanders with these. It will give them authority in the eyes of the men. Now take one and fucking *put it on*." Jason's voice cracked on the last words. Around them, the men of his old centon stood murmuring. Finally Gasca spoke up. "Take it Rictus. You're as good as any of those as wore it before." And there was a rumbling of assent from the Dogsheads around him. Whistler raised a spear. "Take it lad. You earned it fair, coming back alive from those murderous bastards."

So Rictus bent and grasped the shoulder-flaps of the nearest cuirass. He did not know whose it was; Antimone's Gift was the same for every owner, and could not be modified or customised in any way. Whatever material it was made of shrugged off violence and age and the tools of men. It remained inviolate and anonymous.

And it was light—so light that Rictus was startled. He straightened more quickly than he had intended as it came up in his hands, hardly heavier than a winter cloak. The two moulded plates of it cinched together under the left arm with strange little black clasps, and then the shoulder flaps, the *wings* they were called, were tugged down into place and clicked into others of these fastenings on the breast. Rictus tugged at the neck of the armour where it cut into the flesh of his neck, and Jason pulled his hand away.

"Wait a moment."

As the cuirass took warmth from his body, so it seemed to ease upon his bones. Rictus looked up, astonished, and Jason smiled. "They mould to the form they find within them. Something inside them shifts and melts and then hardens again. Give it a while, and you'll barely know you wear it."

I am a Cursebearer, Rictus thought. It may be that I will be one for only a few hours, but I will die with Antimone's Gift upon my back, fighting fearful odds, in the company of my peers. Father, you could have wished nothing better for me.

"Don't forget the helm," Jason added, gesturing to the line of transverse-crested helmets the generals had left behind. "We must all of us look the part if we're to play this thing out to the end."

The centurions Jason and Mynon had picked to be the new generals of the army trickled in, grim, blasted looks upon their faces. As they did, Jason handed each one of them a black cuirass, and they hesitated as Rictus had before donning them.

"Reform the line," Jason told them. "We attack them now, under cover of darkness. We break this army of theirs and make through it for the river."

"It's twelve pasangs, Jason," Mynon said quietly.

"We take the Bekai crossings and hold them, and base ourselves in Kaik. There, we resupply. One more thing: we take back our baggage on the way. I want our bloody pots back."

"They'll cut us to pieces on the plain with their cavalry," Buridan said, a rumble in his beard.

"Their cavalry did a lot of fighting today, even the Great King's bodyguard itself. And no one takes cavalry into battle in the dark. We have three or four hours until dawn; we must use that time."

"The wounded?" one of the new generals asked. This was Phinero, whose brother Pomero had died in the Great King's tent not two hours before.

"Five morai up front, one on each flank, four in the rear. The wounded in the middle. Those who cannot walk must find someone to carry them or take their own lives."

A pause. No one dissented. They were all half-crazed with thirst and exhaustion, and did not expect to live for much longer themselves.

"This is how we move out," Jason began.

SEVENTEEN
THE SECOND DAY

In the dead hours of the night the weary Kefren pickets posted along the hills of Kunaksa looked up to the star-spattered sky. Clouds had come shifting in from the mountains in the east and were now building up overhead to blot out the welkin. One by one the moons disappeared: first pink Haukos with his blessings of hope and compassion, and then leering white-cold Phobos, moon of fear. The night closed in and the rain began, a steady drizzle that did not put out the campfires of the army, but which made all those tens of thousands who lay beside them in the mud edge a little closer to the flames. The spring rains were early. It was a gift from Bel, the Renewer. Mot, god of death and dry-baked summer soil had left the world to his rival for a night, and the cold rain pattered bitterly down to deepen the mud of the war-scarred plain.

The rain brought Tiryn round, pattering into her open mouth and prickling a chill tattoo on her skin. Forgetting where she was, she sought for a moment to wipe it out of her eyes, but then remembered and blinked herself fully awake.

Blurred torchlight, shadows moving before it, back and forth, as they had moved in her nightmares. She shivered convulsively for a few moments under the cold, intimate kisses of the rain, and blinked her vision clear. The hub of the wagon-wheel had gouged a bruise deep into the small of her back, and her bound hands were blue and numb, roped to the rim. She was naked. She no longer knew or cared how many times she had been raped.

The camp was all astir, not the night-time routine of sentries but full, chaotic, crowded, and shouted movement. Some new thing had happened, some new chapter in the savagery of the earth. Tiryn closed her eyes again, meat tied to a wagon-wheel, the mind within drawing back from the world, gnawing on itself, unable to give up the obscenities it had seen.

They were five pasangs from the battle lines here, the humid heat-shimmer of the day before not even allowing them the chance to spectate. Tiryn had walked out of the flimsy stockade with only her maid beside her and had watched the great creeping darknesses of the armies move across the surface of the earth. Faint on the still air had come the awful roar of their meeting. The Macht were winning, she had heard, and she watched Arkamenes's army advance up the hillside. And she had thought it over, the thing done, the day behind them. My Prince, she thought, is now a King.

Incredibly swift, the disintegration of those complacencies. First there were the stragglers, the cowardly, the broken, the walking wounded. And then had come the great mass of infantry, the Juthan Legion, the Kefren of the main line. These had poured past the camp with barely a glance to spare for those inside, too terrified even to try their hand at the paychests. Because behind them the enemy were snapping like vorine on the heels of sheep.

The Asurian cavalry had been first into the camp, tall high-caste Kefren on magnificent horses, statues of gold and iron and lapis lazuli with bright eyes and bloody swords. The Juthan baggage-bearers had fought them off with whips and sticks and ladles and any object that came to hand. When none did, they leapt on the horsemen and used their teeth. They had fought to the end and Tiryn, even in the grip of her terror, had wondered at their ferocious courage.

Her bodyguard, Hurth, had never thought much of her; she had known that. High caste as he was, he thought it demeaning to watch over a little *hufsa* whore. But he had tried to get her out of the camp, and when they had been caught, it was with his own life that he had bought her the time to run away. This had shocked her, that he had done such a thing. She and her remaining maid had gone to ground after it, too cowed to try again. They had been like rabbits, cowering in knowledge of their own end and unable to do anything about it.

The end had come, the Asurians had prevailed, and the sack of the baggage camp had begun.

Arkamenes was dead, that much was made clear by the triumphant enemy troops who now began to loot the tents and wagons of the army, searching always and foremost for the paychests containing the gold of Tanis. These found, they had time to attend to lighter matters, and one of these was discovered in Arkamenes's tent, a curved mountain-knife in her fist. A single wound Tiryn had inflicted, and that only enough to earn her a beating. At first she had been set to one side as the looting went on, and the higher-caste concubines of the harem were ferreted out. But once all these had been claimed they came back for her, killed the Juthan maid who threw herself at them, and began the sport of the evening.

Perhaps her own caste would have been gentler; perhaps not. In any case, Tiryn had ended the long, long day tied to this wagon-wheel, and used by any passing soldier who did not mind the blood, the muck, the bruises, and the shining slime of other Kufr's leavings which now painted her skin.

Arkamenes is dead, she thought. Why can it not be over? And she prayed to Mot, the dark god, for the blessing of her own release.

One hundred paces away, in the tent that had been his brother's, the Great King was roused out of sleep by old Xarnes. No ceremony; Honai were lighting the lamps without being given leave to do so, and Xarnes had actually touched the royal shoulder to bring Ashurnan into the present. He sat up at once, still fully dressed, though wearing his brother's silk slippers.

"What's happened?" Fear of the event had taken away their fear of him; it must be bad.

"The Macht have attacked, my lord—all along the hills."

Ashurnan blinked. A Honai held out a goblet of wine and he waved it away, frowning. "How long did I sleep?"

"Three hours, my lord, by the turn of the clock."

"Any word from Vorus?"

"Nothing as yet."

"Then how do we know?"

Xarnes hesitated. He looked very old in the gathering lamplight, an elderly man kept from his bed. "Some of the troops up on the Kunaksa have already fled this far."

There it was, cold water down the spine. Ashurnan rolled out of bed and straightened with the quicksilver poise of a dancer. "Stand-to the bodyguard," he said. "Couriers to Vorus. Where is Proxis?"

"In the camp, my lord, but we have not yet located him. He was supervising the transport of the paychests across the river until the middle night."

"Find him, Xarnes."

"Yes, lord." The ancient chamberlain bowed and withdrew.

The Honai were watching him. We had victory, Ashurnan thought—we had the glory of it, the thing sitting in our very hands. What in the depths of hell have these animals done to me now? Can they not lie down and die?

* * *

They were dying indeed. They were dying by the hundred, but they were on their feet and advancing over their own dead. In the rain-drenched dark of the starless night they were singing the Paean of their race, and never had it seemed so apposite as now that the battle-hymn of the Macht should also be the song sung in the hour of death.

They advanced on a frontage of some seven hundred paces, a compact mass of interlocked centons and morai. The line was ragged as men tripped in the dark or wove around obstacles half-seen until a boulder barked their shins, but it came together again always, the clash of bronze in the blackness guiding those who lost their way, the mud sucking the sandals off their feet, the rain—the blessed rain—trickling down their bodies so that whole morai raised their heads as one and opened their mouths to let the life of the water spot their tongues. Antimone had fluttered her Veil, men said. She wept above them, and so they had her tears to moisten their mouths here, in the shadow of strange mountains. The rain gave them new strength, new heart. It did not convince them that they would live, but it persuaded them that they could make a good end.

The Kufr pickets had been swept away in the first moments, and now the Macht had pushed deep into the scattered ranks of the King's army, catching hundreds, thousands of his troops before they had gathered into formation. The Macht heavy spearmen stabbed out in the dark at half-guessed masses of milling bodies and kept advancing. It was not the casualties that mattered but the fact of their advance, that remorseless tide of flesh and bronze welling up out of the night, the Paean rising with it, the feet of the infantry keeping time. This was an army the Kufr had already made a story of. As the morai advanced, so the Great King's forces streamed away from the forefront of that line. For pasangs up and down the hills a panic took root. This—an assault on this scale—could not be happening in the dark of a moonless night. It was impossible. And so the Kufr troops assigned mythical properties to the half-seen battle line of the Macht spearmen, and the song which accompanied their relentless advance.

Only the Honai of the Great King's bodyguard stood firm. Ten thousand heavy infantry, superbly armoured, they moved into rank with a discipline that baffled their fellow soldiers and took up position like a rock around which the waters of their lesser brethren whirled and rippled. Midarnes, their general, stood at their rear, and here Vorus found him standing as stolid as some ancient reared-up stone.

"Hold them," Vorus said. "We must stop them here. Dawn is not far off. When the sun rises, things shall take a different turn."

Midarnes was a nobleman of the old school, as high a caste as one could come at in this Empire without becoming a king. In the dark his eyes shone pale, looming over Vorus. He looked down on the Macht renegade without rancour, with even a shade of respect. "Your people," he said, "are worthy of the stories." Then he straightened. "You had best see to the flanks. Here in the centre, I shall hold them."

In songs and stories, the lines met with a great clash and roar. Sometimes this was true. But in the dark of that rain-swept night on the hills of Kunaksa, the Macht and the Great King's Honai melted together in a wicked hedge of spearpoints lit up by the kicked sparks of dying campfires, a cataclysm introduced at walking pace—blind, savage, and bloodier than any legend.

Rictus was in the front rank. The initial contact was a glimpse of pale gold, and then a massive impact of some great creature's shield upon his own. He felt the breath of the thing on his eyes as they were pinned there, breast to breast, by the weight of the ranks behind them both. He stabbed out with his spear, as did his opponent, but they could not stab at each other. They were held there in a vice of flesh and blood, this thing a foot taller than him, its thighs moving against his own in a strangely intimate struggle through the muck underfoot. He butted the thing in the windpipe with his crested helm, and its weight gave a little. Immediately, the press of the men behind sent him forward. His opponent slid downwards. There was the smell of blood, the scrape of bronze, and the thing was at his waist, his knees, and then under his feet. He stamped down on it with his bare heel, one strike encountering the hard jar of bronze, the second snapping something of flesh. Then he was propelled along again, and he knew that the sauroters of those behind him would take care of it. Another face, another form, impossibly tall, with the same eyes. The panic to be fought, until he locked down the fact that the aichmes of those behind him were at work. One of the great eyes went dark, and again, the thing slid down, clunked earthwards to be kicked and stabbed in the ankle-deep muck, the flesh robbed of the spirit, the advance continuing. Those in the rear ranks were still singing the Paean, a hoarse, dry-throated rasp of defiance. Rictus smashed his shield forward into the line, aware now of the light indomitability of the cuirass he wore, the different balance of the transverse-crested helm. *I lead these men,* he thought calmly. *They look to me—to this black armour, this crest.*

I must be better than this, he thought.

And so he used his gangling strength to butt forward into the enemy line, his feet sinking deep into the mud, the foreign silt splaying his toes as they took the weight. He pushed his way into the Honai ranks with no skill or courage, merely a black determination to see the thing done. And before him, the Honai were shoved backwards, lowering their shields as their balance went—and into that gap the aichmes of the Macht stabbed pale and dark, silver and bloody, and a gap was opened out, and the shield-wall of the Honai was ruptured.

Vorus felt the balance of the thing shift, even in the dark, even in the epicentre of that great, flailing cauldron of violence. The lines of Kefren spearmen before him seemed to shudder, like a horse twitching off a fly. And then there was a sullen, agonising falling back. It scarcely seemed possible that the tall Kefren of the Honai could be physically pushed back by the Macht, but this was happening. They were not retreating; they were being killed up at the front of the line faster than they could be replaced, and they were being physically shoved backwards.

They will break, Vorus realised. He was not entirely, intellectually surprised, but he was still shocked. After all these years in the east, he had thought the Honai of the Great King unbeatable. He had forgotten too much about his own heritage.

The line broke. Not the wholesale rout of the day before, but a bitter, sullen retreat. It was like watching a flock of starlings, at one moment so black and dense as to fill the sky, the next, a scattered shifting cloud opening up into something else. The Honai did not turn their backs on the enemy, but fell back step by step, and as they retreated so their formation was scrambled. No longer a battle line, it was fast becoming a mere dense crowd of individuals.

Vorus reached up and took Midarnes by the upper arm. "Withdraw. Pull back your companies and reform."

Midarnes looked down at him, and actually smiled. "Never." Then he raised his voice and shouted in the Kefren of the Court. "To me! Rally to me!" He raised his spear and smote it upon the brazen face of his shield. Around him, the Honai began to coalesce in a formless crowd. Further away, the Macht were still pushing them back, wedges of their troops battering through the ranks and stepping over the dead. And all this in a darkness lit only by the hellish glow of a few neglected campfires, and the rain silvering down to hiss in meeting with the sparks flying up, as though fire and water were at war also.

Jason stepped out of the front rank. There was a gap opening up before his men, a space. He held his spear up horizontal above his head and shouted until he thought the veins in his throat would burst. "Hold! Hold here!" He jogged up the line. The Kefren were streaming backwards, beaten for the moment, and the front ranks of the Macht stood on hummocked mounds of their dead.

A transverse crest. He grabbed the man's shoulder. Who was it? It did not matter. "Wheel left—pass it on. All morai to wheel left starting with Mynon on the extreme right. Pass it down the line!"

The minutes passed. He looked up at the sky, but saw only blank darkness, felt the rain on his eyes and licked it off his lips, his mouth and throat heaving-dry. He had gone past exhaustion. He must stay upright now, keep moving. If he stopped or so much as laid down his shield, he would never be able to lift it again.

At last the movement, and the Paean out on the right, a thousand tortured voices. Thank the goddess the line was short, five morai long, six hundred paces. And behind it, what was left of the wounded, and the rear companies. The Macht were in an immense square, ragged, incomplete, but compact. Cohesion, Jason thought, that's the thing. Mynon will keep the right-hand lines together. Phobos, we're too slow!

The Macht line wheeled westwards, pivoting on Buridan's mora. The movement was ragged, hesitant, performed by exhausted men in the dark, but they kept shoulder to shoulder with one another, the formations drawing together and gaining cohesion from the human contact of those to each side, those in front, those behind. The men in the front rank had the hardest task. Jason was able to watch them by the stuttered illumination of a few still-burning fires. They looked like ghosts walking past the flames, men already dead and in the hell of all lost souls. The Macht did not have a god of war; they had Antimone to watch over them instead. For though they gloried in combat, they knew the price it exacted. A true man did not need help from the gods to kill—that was in him from birth—in all of them. He needed their help to face what came afterwards. He needed the pity and compassion of the Veiled Goddess. And she was here tonight, Jason was sure. If he shut his eyes he thought he might even be able to hear the beat of her black wings.

Further to the right, the Macht morai struck those Honai who were struggling to reform about Midarnes. There was a bitter fight and the front ranks of Mochran's mora were actually driven in, but then the centons to right and left piled into the Honai flanks, leaving the line to lunge forward. The Honai broke, a small knot of them fighting to the end about their standard, the rest driven beyond their capacity to endure and in danger of being cut off. They threw away their shields and ran down the hillside. Midarnes disappeared under a pile of bodies, and on the Kunaksa ridge, the Macht dressed their lines yet again and continued the advance. None of them were singing now. Their tongues had swollen in their mouths. They were things of unsparing sinew and bone, barely able to conjecture an end to the night or the possibility of rest.

There was one new thing about their travail though: for the first time since the battle had begun, they were marching downhill, towards the river. This realisation gave them some heart. They stepped out, centurions forward of the main line. The ridge-crest was theirs, and they looked down on the fire-dotted plain that led to the Bekai River, now some ten pasangs away. They fixed their minds on that thought, the possibility of water, of something like sanctuary, and they marched on.

Many thousands of Kefren and Juthan troops were now in flight across the Bekai plain, but most had fled eastwards, towards the Magron Mountains and their own baggage camps pasangs behind the Kunaksa Hills. It was in this direction that Vorus had gone, striving in vain to rally the second-line Kefren units. In the dark, it was impossible. They would run now until they thought pursuit had stopped, until their own tents brought them to a halt. The Macht army had completely routed the main body of the Great King's forces, and had all but annihilated his Household troops, the best there was. There was nothing left for it but to wait for the panic to subside and then begin picking up the pieces. As Vorus kicked his tired horse into a lumbering canter, he pulled a fold of his cloak about his head and wore it like a scarlet komis. In the midst of that great, maddened, frantic crowd of armed Kufr, it was not good to have a Macht face.

But where was Ashurnan? That question brought cold sweat to his spine. The Great King had decided to rest for a few hours in the enemy's captured baggage camp. It lay now square in the path of the Macht advance. Vorus reined in. It was no good; there was no one to send who would get through alive.

He spun the horse on its haunches and took off back the way he had come. Someone has to get through, he thought. And who better to try than one of the Macht?

Behind him, the paling sky in the east broke open pink and bloody with the day's dawn, the Magron Mountains standing like black titans on the edge of the world. A wind from the west picked up and began to shunt aside the heavy cloud of the night. In the gathering light the Macht army marched stumbling down off the bloody, muck-churned heights of the Kunaksa and began to plash wearily through the wet lowland below. Before them the stragglers of the Kefren army scattered like quail before a fox, no longer a coherent whole, but a beaten remnant. Some ran for the Bekai bridges, some scattered to north and south, parallel to the river-line. From the tented square of the Macht camp, they flooded out like cockroaches from under an upturned stone, abandoning their loot, their women, their arms. From a distance the Macht formation looked as disciplined and indomitable as it had the day before, going up the hill. It came down from the heights in silence, no voice left able to raise the Paean. At a distance it was impossible to see the staggering weariness of the spearmen, the broken shafts of their weapons held up for want of anything better, the crowds of wounded being dragged along in the middle of the morai, rags stuffed in their mouths to stop their screams. They had taken thirteen and a half thousand men up the hill the morning before, and now some ten thousand were marching back down. Many of those would not see another morning.

Ashurnan watched them come, sat on his tired horse to the south of the camp. About him a motley crowd of aides, bodyguards, and sundry officers had gathered, all mounted, all shattered by the sight of the advancing phalanx, the disappearance of their own mighty army. It did not seem real. The half-light of the gathering dawn made it into some nightmare from which they must try and waken.

Ashurnan leaned in the saddle and grasped old Xarnes's arm. The elderly Chamberlain had begun to slide from the back of his horse.

"My lord, you should not—"

"And let you fall? I think not, Xarnes." Ashurnan smiled, but his face was empty as that of a glass-bound fish. He looked at his feet, at his brother's mud-spattered slippers, then up again at the advancing army.

"All the gods in their heavens, what incredible creatures these are," he said, shaking his head in genuine wonder.

"My King," one of the bodyguards said. "We should—"

"I know, Merach. I see them too. Watch them march! Our legends did not lie, did they?" His face tightened. "Someone else to join us, I see, some other lost soul."

It was Vorus, on a blown, shattered horse. He dropped his cloak from his face and held up a hand. "My lord—"

"Is Midarnes dead?"

Vorus could only nod.

"I knew he would not run, not Midarnes. He was my father's friend also." Suddenly the Great King looked away, pulled his komis up over his eyes and choked down a sob. They sat there on their horses, appalled and afraid and understanding as he bit down on his grief, knuckles white on his reins, and before them the Macht marched on, scarcely half a pasang away now.

He collected himself, the tears shining on his face, his violet eyes still glittering. "General Vorus, I rejoice to see you alive. What do you suggest?"

Vorus's tired horse was moving restlessly below him now, for it had picked up the vibration beneath its feet, the tramp of the approaching army.

"We flee, my lord," Vorus said. "We flee, and we pick another time, another place, to finish what was begun here."

"Your brother is dead, my King," old Xarnes added. "This Empire stands. The Macht are a problem for another day, as the general says. But you, you must not come to harm. Your place is no longer here."

Ashurnan's mouth twisted. He looked at the oncoming Macht spearmen. Now he was close enough to see the stumbling weariness of their stride, the blood that soaked them, the broken spears and dinted shields. These were not a legend; they were men at the end of their strength. They were not invincible.

"Let us go," he said. "Merach, lead on. Take us back to camp. We leave this field to the Macht."

The girl was bound naked to a wagon-wheel. At first he thought her dead, but when he took her by the hair and raised up her head, he saw the eyelids flutter. She was Kufr, one of the shorter ones. What were they called?

Gasca reached for his knife. Once, his father's best hound had been gored by a stag, its entrails spread far and wide. He had done then what he would do now, not out of anger or vindictiveness, but out of pity. He set the knife at the Kufr girl's throat, thinking how much a pity it was, for she did not look so inhuman at all. He sighed heavily. The knife was blunt.

"Stop there!" This was Jason of Ferai, doffing his helm and striding forward. He set down his shield. "Lower the blade, son. Lift up her face again."

Dumbly, Gasca did as he was told, cursing the fact that he had stopped at all. The mora had retaken the camp and lost all order in its search of the remaining tents and wagons. Water, they were after, more than anything, but there was none to be found. The centurions had set them to loading up the wagons with the centoi instead, and as there were no draught animals left alive in the camp it would seem they were to draw these across the river with the yokes on their own necks. Had it not been for the semi-sacred regard the mercenaries held the great cooking cauldrons in, there might have been trouble, a last straw to break the back of their discipline; but for the most part, it had held. The camp was a gutted wreck and there was nothing else in it to ease their passage, but even the most bloody-minded of the Macht would be glad to have those damn pots back.

And this girl... Gasca looked at Jason curiously.

"I believe I know this one," Jason said. He knelt before the girl and moved her face this way and that, as though studying a sculpture. "*Phobos*, what have they done?" he whispered, taking in her abused form. Anger lit his eyes. He unstrapped his cloak from the back-belt and threw it down. "Who is it—Gasca? Cut her free, wrap her in that, and bring her with us. Keep her alive, Gasca."

Gasca set his jaw. "General—"

"Don't fucking argue with me, strawhead. And don't try fucking her, either." At the expression on Gasca's face he laughed, and thumped the wing of the younger man's cuirass. "All right then. Just humour me—bring her along. She may be useful. Where's your friend Rictus?"

Gasca was sawing methodically at the ropes binding the Kufr to the wheel-rim. "Haven't seen him since he stuck on that black armour. He could be dead, for all I know."

"That one? Never. He'll see old bones. You know why? Because he doesn't care if he will or not. Look after her, Gasca!" Jason rose, collected his shield with an audible groan, and then was off shouting at a group of spearmen who had dropped their weapons to rifle through some sacks.

Rictus stood at the Bekai Bridge with his shield leaning against his knees and his forehead leaning against his spear-shaft. He thought that if the spear slipped, there would be nothing in the world that would keep him on his feet. He would topple down the steep bank, through the mizzling clouds of mosquitoes, and into the brown water. He would drink that water, no matter if every Kufr ever born had pissed in it, and he would die bloated and happy.

His head jerked up, and a spike of pain transfixed his skull as the helm came with it. Another man's helm, not set to the bones of his own face. The pain woke him from the half-doze. He stamped his bare feet and looked down on the endless column of men crossing the bridge before him and half a pasang away, the same on the other bridge. They were crossing the river again, back the way they had come only some—what—three days ago? It seemed like a month.

Jason found him there, nodding in and out of a kind of sleep.

"Bastards took my scroll, all my gear," he said. "You're still this side of the Veil I see."

"Still this side," Rictus said thickly, his tongue rasping against his teeth like meat rolled in sand.

"We take the men into Kaik, and we get whatever we can out of the city. But we can't stay there long. The Empire did not disappear in the night. Rictus, I will need you for light work again."

Rictus stared at him, bloodshot eyes crusted within the T-slot of the helm. "Why?"

"We will need light troops, more than ever now, and you're half-good at leading them."

Rictus said nothing. Talking was too painful. All he could think of was water.

"Join your mora—get into the city. I'll stand over the rearguard."

But Rictus did not move. "What do we do now, Jason?" he asked. "Do we look for another employer, set up shop in some city?"

"We'll talk later," Jason said. His hazel-green eyes caught the light as he looked back eastwards to the dark heights of the Kunaksa. How many bodies left there? In a few days the place would be fetid. Then he looked west, to the unending plains and farmlands of Pleninash. They seemed to go on for ever, flat and lush, with man-made tells pimpling up out of the heat-haze, each one a city. This teeming world, this alien place, and here he and these half-dead men were lost in it.

"We beat those bastards. We beat them fair and square," Rictus said, and it was as if the younger man had caught the current of his thought.

"If we beat them once, we can do it again."

EIGHTEEN
THE LAND OF THE RIVERS

Tiryn opened her eyes on a brown, heavily-beamed ceiling. A gecko was sidling across it, head turning this way and that every time it paused. A faint roaring came on the air, the sound of many voices, but at a distance. It was quiet. She lay in a decent bed, with sheets and a coverlet of linen, and there was light flooding in a west-facing balcony, drapes drawn back and shutters wide open. Dust danced in the sunlight, motes of it hanging in the air. The heat of the lowlands filled the room and she was thirsty, above all else, thirsty.

She made as if to rise, but the racking pains in her shoulders and arms caused her to lie back again. At once, there was movement on the far side of the room. A Juthan girl came forward, yellow eyes gleaming as she passed from shadow into light. She dipped a gourd into a clay pot hanging in one corner, and cradling Tiryn's head said, "Drink. Slowly now." She spoke Asurian with the guttural accent of the Juthan, but her hands were gentle. Tiryn sipped the water slowly, relishing every drop, her mouth suddenly a thing of movement again.

"Where am I?"

"You are in Kaik, the city," a strange voice said with an even stranger accent, the words clumsy and ill-used. A man approached the bed, a Macht. He was dark of skin, hazel-eyed, and he wore the felt tunic of a *hufsan* peasant.

"Do not be afraid. I saw you once, before."

Before. Before what? She dimly remembered being carried or dragged in a huge moving crowd. Before that, the wagon-wheel; before that, the knowledge of defeat.

"You are safe here," he said. A flicker of something passed on his face. "You are *safe*," he repeated.

"Arkamenes is dead," she said. She switched into the Macht tongue she had learned for months on the long road east. "What has happened? What is to happen?"

At that, the Macht smiled. He had a good face, though it was worn to the bone by privation and worry. "I don't know," he said in his own tongue.

"Why am I here?"

"Would you rather we had left you where we found you?"

She felt heat in her skin, a blush mounting up her face. She was naked under the bedclothes, her body clean but bruised and aching. Dressings had been tied in neat, tiny knots about her wrists where the ropes had galled her. All of that came back to her now, that long night, that black obscenity. She shut her eyes and tears welled under them. "Better you had left me," she said.

He came closer. She felt his hand in her hair, a light touch, with nothing but pity behind it. She turned her head away.

"This Juthan will look after you," he said, his voice gruff now, the anger back in it. But it was not directed at her. "You need rest. Do not worry about things. Do not think or remember. Drink the water, eat, and enjoy the sunlight."

She looked at him again, baffled by the compassion in his voice. He smiled at her, eyes dancing. In better times he would have humour about him, a lightness. Now there was a shadow.

"Who are you?" she asked, genuinely puzzled.

"Jason of Ferai, once centurion of the Dogsheads centon, now a general of the Macht that remain. You are..."

"Tiryn."

"That was it. You told me once."

"A long time ago."

"Not so long. It seems long, sometimes. Last week seems a long time ago to me." He smiled again. There were indents of purple flesh below his eyes. He looked like a man who had forgotten how to sleep.

"Why did you help me? I am Kufr; you are Macht."

Again the anger. The tiredness sparked it out of him, she felt that quickness, that flare. She liked it.

"I would not have left a dog like that." Her heart fell. He rubbed one big-knuckled hand over his face, and chuckled, rueful. "Or a beautiful

Kufr." Then he sat on the side of her bed. The sudden closeness of him startled her, that smell they had, the Macht. It was not like that of a Kufr; it was earthier, both repulsive and oddly interesting. Not quite that of an animal, for all she had thought in the past.

"I need you to teach me your language," Jason said simply. "We are lost in your world now and must learn your tongue in order to make our way through it."

Some strange little hope within her withered. But she nodded slightly. She wanted him to move away; he was too close. The memories were fighting round the corner. Soon they would be back in full flood.

He sensed it somehow and rose at once, backing away a step. "You're alive," he said quietly. "Many thousands died on those hills, but you are still here. Thank Antimone for that, at least."

"Who?" she asked thickly, throat closing, eyes burning.

"Our goddess, the guardian of the Macht. She is the goddess of pity. Her tears salt every battlefield. She watches over every crime."

"A goddess? I was told you worshipped a monster with black wings."

Jason nodded. "She is that too. Sleep now, Tiryn. There are ten thousand of us guarding your bed." He turned away, his bare feet padding lightly on the warm stone of the floor as he left.

Strange to say, it was an actual comfort to Tiryn, that thought. She could sleep now. These ten thousand who had been to her little more than animals, let them be her guardians. Her own race had forfeited all loyalty.

The Kerusia met in the Governor's house near the summit of Kaik's hill. It was a tall-ceilinged structure of fired brick, massive black beams of river palm and cedar supporting the roof, and high windows letting in a little of the humid air to move lazily above their heads. They gathered round the long table where the Kufr Governor had been wont to entertain, and by each man there was an earthenware jug of lukewarm water from which he sipped almost continuously, without thinking, the parched flesh of his body soaking it up without pause or distraction.

Jason was too tired to stand, too tired almost to register the names of those present. He knew their faces, and those faces were marked in his mind with ink-stabs of impression.

Rictus, perhaps the best of them all, though Jason would never have told that Iscan straw-head such to his face. Jason had seen greatness before now, on a small scale perhaps, but he could smell it out. This overgrown boy had it. Except he was nothing like a boy any more. Kunaksa had burnt out what remained of his innocence.

Old Buridan, grey in the russet glory of his beard, a friend from what seemed a past life. Mynon, extremely capable, the best intriguer of the lot, perhaps the brightest of them all, and utterly untrustworthy anywhere but on a battle-field, for all his smiles.

A clutch of half-known faces. Phinero, very like his dead brother, a hound with good teeth and little brain. Mochran, a dogged old campaigner, one of the few remaining old crew who had been centon-leaders time out of mind. His shaggy head was devoid of imagination, but he would hold to the letter of an order until he bled white.

Aristos, a younger pup well pleased with his elevation. His uncle, Argus, had indulged him too much, put him forward for Second despite arrogance and ineptitude. He had been told to hold the bridges, but had left his men behind to do it while he sat here, ready to kick off this new Kerusia. A rod for my back, Jason thought with an inward sigh.

Four others: Dinon, Hephr, Grast and Gominos. Just names and worn young faces. Jason knew nothing of them. At the moment his body craved sleep, and his thoughts were still dwelling on the face of the Kufr woman he had lately visited.

They were talking, half of them at once, mostly the younger ones. Buridan and Mynon and Mochran watched them with a kind of detached wariness. Rictus looked out of a window at the pitiless blue of the sky. It was hot, so hot it got a man to shouting in an instant, weather for argument and lovemaking.

Again, the Kufr girl's pale face, those dark eyes.

Jason thumped the long table, not hard, but enough to rattle the jugs, to shut them up. He pinched his eyes as though squeezing water out of them; they stung like lemon-juice under his fingers.

"Mynon," he said into the sudden quiet. "Talk to me. And I swear by Antimone's cunt, that if any one of you interrupts him, I shall kick you up and down this room."

Mynon smiled a little. His one brow rose up his forehead, the red skin peeling above it, his black eyes sunken in lines of weariness. Still, he held onto that sneering jauntiness which was his trademark. He produced a slate and a knob of chalk and looked the table up and down.

"We have the paychests; the Kufr ran before us too quickly to take them along. But a man cannot eat gold. And for that reason, we cannot stay here."

A splutter of argument. Mynon and Jason looked at one another.

"We will bleed this city dry in a matter of days, the countryside round about in less than a month. We stay here, we starve, and we starve the Kufr all about us. Is that clear enough for you, brothers?"

"I'd like you to be Quartermaster, Mynon. You have a knack for it, a head for figures and the like. Do you accept?"

Mynon considered, head to one side in that bird-like way of his. He shrugged fractionally. "All right."

"You will retain command of your mora. We need your experience in the battle line too."

"Who are you, Jason, to be elevating and appointing without so much as a say so from the rest of us?" Aristos spoke up, his freckled face burnt dark by the sun, bright hair shining. Another strawhead. Some of the younger ones rapped the table with one knuckle in agreement.

Who am I indeed? Jason wondered. For a cold moment, he saw himself packing a horse and taking off across the Empire alone, making hell's leather for the west and the shores of the sea. But that would leave his Dogsheads here, and Buridan. That would leave behind the best part of what he had earned for himself in this life. A name, and respect for that name. If he left that behind, he would be worthless. Go back to soldiering in the Harukush? Why? He had the adventure of his lifetime here and now.

"Aristos makes a fair point," he said lightly. "Shall we vote on it, then? I put myself forward to take Phiron's place. Who will have me?"

His own hand went up first, those of Buridan and Rictus in the same second; then old Mochran, and Mynon. And then a pause. Finally Phinero joined them. "I don't see no one else here I'd take orders from," he said with a shrug.

Aristos made no sign of acceptance or anger. He flapped his hand on the table. "You have a majority, Jason. You are our warleader." He had a smile even less pleasant than Mynon's. "Some proprieties must be preserved, or else what are we?"

"We're in shit up to our necks, so we'd best start shovelling," Buridan growled. "What's the plan, Jason?"

He got up from the table and paced over to one of the great openings in the wall. From here one could look down on the garden-rooves of Kaik, green squares retreating down the hill's steep slope amid a sea of brown brick, all shimmering in the heat. A steady train of refugees was leaving the city, heading along the roads to the west. Running before the storm. His men had wrecked this city simply by entering it and taking what they needed—not loot, or women so much—but water, food, a place to lay their heads. This army would wreck many more before they made it home, he thought. And home is where we must be going. There is nothing for us here, in the Empire.

For the first time, perhaps, he understood the real abilities of Phiron and Pasion. They had collected these centons, had fed and watered and supplied them, had held them together to the end. Until one Kufr's death had turned their certainties upside-down.

"We go home," Jason said simply. "That is all we can do. "The Great King has shown he cannot be trusted or negotiated with, so we will not try." He turned back to face the others, the sunlight behind him making of his form a black shadow, faceless.

"We must march to the sea."

There was a square below the Governor's Palace, built up on one side like a massive terrace to make level the slope of the hill. All around it, the fired-brick buildings of the city reared up three and four stories tall, and on their rooves could be seen date palms, juniper bushes, vines, a cool green horticulture three and four spear-lengths above the cobbles of the square itself, ivy and ferns trailing their tendrils down the faces of the houses. In the centre of the square was an oasis of cedar and poplar trees, a sizeable copse surrounded by the beating heat of the open stone around. This was where the city's markets had been held, and there was still the wreckage of a hundred, two hundred stalls scattered far and wide across it, melons rolling underfoot, pomegranates broken open like bloody relics of battle, pistachios scattered like pebbles on a sea's shore. Here, a great many of the exhausted Macht had set up a camp of sorts, burning the market-stalls in their campfires and roasting anything four-footed they could find over them. There were public wells at the four corners of the square, and running up to each of these were ceaseless queues of thirsty men bearing buckets, pots, and skins to fill for their centons. It was orderly, in a way, though to the terrified inhabitants of the surrounding district it must have seemed as though some great shambling beast of the apocalypse had wandered into their world and collapsed with a tired groan. Perhaps six thousand men were bedded down on the cobbles, their heads pillowed on the ragged red rolls of their cloaks. They had all claimed their own centoi again, and congregated round the black cauldrons like acolytes stunned by their oracle. The pots were not being cooked in, but were full of drinking water. The alleyways and streets leading up to the square were already stinking with the army's effluent, and centurions were clustering here and there, haranguing each other about where each centon should piss. Tired men were almost as ready now to fight each other as they had been to fight the Kufr, the uncertainty of their plight finally looming through the receding haze of thirst and exhaustion.

Gasca had been to the Carnifex to have a wound stitched, but the charnel-house stench of the buildings set aside for the wounded drove him away. Groups of gagging Kufr had been pressed into disposal of the bodies, and were hauling them out of the city on flat-bed wagons, to be burned down by the river. The walking wounded rejoined their centons as soon as they could; in this heat, an injury gained in the filth of the Kunaksa went bad very fast, and the flies choking the air about the infirmaries were too fat and blue and insistent to keep from every wound. Men were lying with maggots crawling upon their flesh, their eyes sunk in blackened sockets of pain. Their comrades stayed with them as long as they could bear it, but their fate was written in their eyes; already they could see the land beyond the Veil.

The youngest, the fittest, the most venturesome of the Macht were scattered throughout the city, ostensibly to gather what supplies they could find. In reality there was a lot of discreet looting going on. But from what Gasca had seen, it was not gold or jewels the men were after, but footwear, clothing, weapons. Anything which might speed their pilgrim way across the Empire. A mora was guarding the city gates, but some of the Macht were making off across the walls, leaving Kaik, their centons, their comrades, and striking out alone across the vastness of the Empire, believing in the madness of their hearts that they could somehow trek all the weary pasangs back to the Harukush. No one stopped these fools, and nearly all who remained recognised them for that. But all the same, the army was creaking and fraying and breaking down. There were a few would-be orators in the main square, arguing that their contract was null and void now, and they were no longer beholden to anyone but themselves. They would hold to their centons for now, but some of them had begun to think in terms of their cities. Lines were developing, even among the Cursebearers.

Gasca found the Dogsheads close to the shade of the trees in the centre of the square, and was handed a waterskin without a word. Bivouacked around them were the Dolphins and the Blackbirds; these three centons had worked as one since the Abekai crossing, and stuck together.

Astianos lifted up a hand to shade his eyes. "You get it seen to?

"There were too many. It's not much more than a scratch anyways."

"I'll stitch it for you later, if you like."

"You can kiss my arse."

Astianos grinned. He was Gasca's opposite, as dark as the strawhead was light, and he had few teeth left to fill out his smile. "Bend over, sweetie, and I'll see what I can do."

"Even a Kufr arse would be something to look upon right now," big Gratus said with feeling. He was Gasca's file leader, and lay now with his hands clasped on his stomach.

"Go take your pick; they're all around," said another.

"But let us watch, Gratus," old Demotes cackled. "I want to see what a Kufr makes of that skinny little dog's dick of yours."

Desultory, reflexive, the profanities were thrown out upon the air. These men had lately fought two great battles, and had found themselves cut off two and a half thousand pasangs from home, but give them a drink of water, and a few hours sleep, and they would be trading insults again, just for the fun of it. Their shoulders had been right next to Gasca's through the Abekai, through Kunaksa. Their aichmes had kept him alive, and he had taken blows meant for them on his own shield. They had shared water with him when their own mouths were cracked and dry for the lack of it. Sitting down upon his cloak, Gasca reflected that the men on either side of him were more his brothers than those he had grown up with. Whatever happened, he was glad he had come here, and had known this. He thanked Antimone silently, whilst laughing at the obscenities thrown among them like balls for boys to catch and fling back. It may be I'm meant to be here after all, he thought.

Rictus found him as the afternoon had begun to shade into the swift-dwindling twilight of the lowlands. He stepped over sleeping bodies and picked his way across a carpet of battered humanity until he stood over Gasca and held up a small skin. "Palm wine," he said. "Are you ready for it, or is this crowd still drinking water?"

"Make a space there," Astianos said, shoving the man sleeping next to him. "I've drunk enough water to float my back teeth. I'll have a slug of that, centurion, if you're willing." Rictus tossed him the skin and squatted cross-legged before Gasca. He wore the Curse of God over a Kufr chiton, and was barefoot.

"Jason told me you had come through it," he said.

"Strawhead luck," Gasca replied. They watched one another, not quite sure what to say. At last Rictus spoke. "This is a long way from the Machran Road."

"I never thought I'd miss snow," Gasca admitted.

"Did you piss yourself this time?"

Gasca grinned. "Me and every other one of these bastards here." They smiled at each other, but the smiles did not take.

"I just wanted to be a spearman, like you," Rictus said at last. "That's all."

Gasca gestured to the black cuirass that fitted Rictus's torso like a second skin. "You were born for that, and for what you're doing now. It's plain to me. I don't mind it at all."

Rictus stared at him. He seemed in need of something, some word, a kind of forgiveness perhaps. "They're going to make me a skirmisher again, my own mora of lights. I don't suppose you'd want to come and—"

Gasca shook his head. "My place is here, with this crowd. I belong here, Rictus, holding a spear and following the man in front. It's all I want."

Rictus nodded. He looked very young in the failing light, though as the dusk grew about them all and the campfires took life from the dark, it was possible to see the lines and bones graven in his face.

"Have a drink, centurion. Antimone's tits, what is this we have here? A love affair? Take it somewheres else." Astianos grinned, and thumped the wineskin against Rictus's shoulder.

"What's going to happen?" Gasca asked him. "What did the Kerusia decide?"

Rictus wiped his mouth. Around him, even in the gathering dark, he was suddenly aware of men pausing in their conversations, cocking an ear to listen.

"We have to stay together," he said. He raised his voice as he said it, and like a stone dropped in a pond, he felt the ripples of his words grip men further and further away across the square as they listened in. I should stand up and shout, he thought. But then it would be a speech, and they'd not listen anymore.

"If we break up, they'll cut us to pieces. Together we are an army, a Macht army. On the Kunaksa we beat their best, all by ourselves. If we stay together, hold to the colour, then we can do it again. And we'll have to, if we're to make it all the way back. We're marching home by the shortest route, across Pleninash and Kerkh and Hafdaran, through the Korash Mountains, across Askanon and Gansakr, until we find ourselves back on the shores of the sea, at Sinon. That's what we're doing. And we'll march as an army, the whole fucking way. All of us."

PART THREE

THE MARCH TO THE SEA

NINETEEN
THE GENERAL'S KUFR

Three pasangs long, the column stretched straight as the Imperial Road would allow across the soggy lowlands of the plain. Up front, a mora of light-armed troops spread out on a kind of shapeless crescent before the head of the main body, a thousand men with javelins and light spears and a weird confection of shields. None wore scarlet; none in the entire column wore scarlet any more, for those chitons had been too soaked in the mud and gore of past battles to be of further use. They wore instead the felt tunics of Asurian peasants, or cut-down linen robes looted from some Kufr's household. But upon these rags rested the bronze of their fathers, and on the shoulders of that armour they leaned the long spears their race had carried from time immemorial.

The column was composed almost entirely of marching men, until one came to the latter third.

Here, light wagons and single-axle carts trooped, drawn by mules and horses and asses and oxen and any beast which could shoulder a yoke. There were some two hundred of these vehicles, and perhaps a thousand men walked among them, leaning their shoulders against the wheels when the animals up front faltered in their relentless haulage. Behind this cumbersome train there marched a further two thousand spearmen. These two morai, like the two in the van, did not keep their heavy shields in the wagon-beds, but wore them on their shoulders. And periodically they would halt, about-turn, and present a bristling, impenetrable front to whatever or whoever might be approaching the army from the rear. Thus the Macht marched, away from the Bekai River, and into the heart of the Pleninash lowlands.

"I see them as a dark line on the horizon, no more," the Juthan, Proxis, said, frowning. "They collected themselves as if they have a purpose."

"Of course they do," Vorus told him. "They are marching home."

"We slaughtered their high command, and yet..."

"The Macht vote on things," said Vorus. He smiled a little. "They vote, and create new things out of that collective will. It is not a good way to run an army, and yet here we are and there go they, marching as though nothing had happened. They have another leader, Proxis, someone they all respected before we slaughtered their generals. He must be a good man to have wrought such wonders out of them at Kunaksa. I wonder if I know him."

The two generals were ahead of the main body some pasang or so, seated on their long-suffering mounts. Behind them, Kaik rose above the Bekai River on its ancient mound, the gates of the city wide open, lines of Kefren troops streaming past it, crossing the river by the two undefended bridges.

"They stripped Kaik bare," Proxis said, a hard gleam in his eye. "Food, water, wine, horses, oxen, and hundreds of my people to be taken along as slaves, beasts of burden. But then that is what we have always been."

Vorus looked at his companion and nodded. "Yes, you have. But I hear tell that in Jutha now the people are arming, and it's not to fight the Macht."

Proxis allowed himself a small, humourless smile. "I have heard that also."

"These fine fellows we're after, if we let them they'll tear up half the Empire in their wake."

"Perhaps the Empire's day has come and gone," Proxis said and looked away, not able to meet Vorus's eyes.

"If it has, then so has ours," Vorus said angrily, and he kicked his horse forward.

The Great King took up residence in the Governor's Palace of Kaik. His immense baggage train was moved forward from the east bank of the river, and for the space of a day the unfortunate inhabitants of the city watched as the endless line of wagons and carts and pack mules entered their gates. They were to have the honour and blessing of the King's presence among them for some time to come, as he had designated Kaik his forward headquarters. What crumbs the Macht had left them were now ferreted out by the stewards of the Royal Household. Skeining out across the bountiful lowlands of Pleninash, the foraging parties went in their columned thousands, more troops set to gathering supplies than marched behind Vorus in pursuit of the enemy. These were the realities of warfare. Even the diminished host the Great King still held to his standards represented another three or four cities of hungry mouths set down in the middle of the region. And more troops were arriving by the week: levies come late to the campaign, summoned from every crevice of the Empire which would produce and arm warriors.

"I want reports from Vorus every day," Ashurnan said. The fanbearers wafted perfume into his face. Lately, the very hall in which he sat had been used as a meeting-place by the generals of the Macht. It had been scrubbed clean by Juthan slaves and sluiced down with well-water, but still the Great King could not get out of his mind the picture of those creatures sitting up and down the long table before him. He ordered the table taken out and burnt.

"They have made of Kaik a sewer," he said to himself. And when old Xarnes leaned closer to catch his words he waved a hand. "No matter. General Berosh, we are certain that the messengers went off before the Macht took possession of the city?"

Berosh, the new commander of his majesty's bodyguard, bowed by way of affirmation. "They and their escorts were on the road before the battle on the hills had ended, my lord. They are well on their way."

"So much the better." Ten heads, ten dead men's faces pickled in jars, to be shown around the Empire like so many signposts of warning. That, at least, had gone to plan.

"A pity we could not have been so quick with the gold," he said, and Berosh bowed again.

"When the Asurian Horse has refitted and rested they are to join Vorus. We need cavalry to keep pace with these animals. We must get ahead of them, pen them in." Ashurnan thumped his fist down on the elbow of his throne. "They must be rounded up and destroyed to the last man."

"All possible steps are being taken, my lord," Berosh said, inclining his head.

"Taken—yes—taken *now*. Now that the foe is on the wing." He stood up, and the whole chamber full of courtiers, slaves, soldiers, and attendants bowed deep. All his life, this had been the protocol, the way things were done, but right now he felt it suffocating him.

His brother's face, as the blade took him under the chin.

"Clear the room," he said. "All but Xarnes and Berosh. *Now*."

They went out in a hushed queue, even the fanbearers. Ashurnan stripped the heavy robe from his shoulders. In the long linen singlet he wore beneath, he went to one of the great wall-openings, a tall window without glass. There was a breeze up here, and it played cool on the soaked fabric of his undergarment. He pulled off the royal komis and felt the air on his face, breathed deep. Even here, he could smell the foul stench of the lower city.

"Great King," Xarnes began uncertainly.

"I was too hot, Xarnes, nothing more. Leave me be. There is nothing to fear. Nothing at all." To Berosh, he spoke over his shoulder. "Have couriers sent to the north-west provinces, all governors. If I find one city which opens its gates to the Macht, I shall raze it. Do you hear me, Berosh?"

"Yes, my lord."

"I shall have no more Kefren cities defiled as they have defiled this one, filling the streets with blood and excrement. I want the streets washed. Turn out the whole population if you have to, but make this place clean again."

He turned to face them, and closed his eyes, the breeze cooling his back, unwrinkling the sodden linen.

"We must wash them from our world, Berosh. They do not belong here. I do not think they ever have."

When they camped for the night, the Macht dug a shallow ditch all around their camp. It was not so much a defence as a demarcation. The ten morai laid out their bedrolls in a great hollow square, and in the centre of this were the baggage vehicles and the draught animals, the paychests full of the gold of Tanis, and the Juthan slaves that had been led out of Kaik in chains with sacks and barrels and jars balanced on their heads, the way in which the Kufr had carried their burdens since the world had been created.

The men slept on the ground, wrapped in whatever blankets and hangings they had been able to loot from Kaik. Most had managed to keep hold of their scarlet cloaks also, and so in the evenings there was almost a uniformity about their appearance. The foraging parties usually made it back into camp around dusk, each two or three centons strong, each—if they had been lucky—resembling a rural circus, for the procession of braying, bleating, clucking animals they drew along in their ranks. By the time they returned, the wood-gathering parties would have come in, and the water-haulers. The fires would be lit under the big centoi with the water bubbling within. In all, perhaps a third of the army was scattered across the surrounding countryside by late afternoon of every day, stripping it clean of anything the Macht could possibly make use of. By the time the army were a week out of Kaik this had become routine, and despite the Kufr scouts watching them from the tallest of the surrounding tells, there was as yet no other sign of the Great King's pursuit.

Tiryn sat near one of the central fires in the midst of the baggage, her Juthan slave heating something in a copper pot over the flames. Jason looked out for them, making sure they had food at the end of each day, and the common soldiery knew better now than to try and molest the general's Kufr. When he could, he would join them at the fire in the later part of the night, and he and Tiryn would trade words in each other's tongues, she teaching Asurian and learning Machtic as he did the opposite. It was a little piece of routine which anchored Tiryn to some kind of reality in a bewildering world, and she had come to look forward to those quiet nights by the campfire, even the animals asleep in their rope corrals, Jason and she exchanging quiet words, using their minds for something other than the day to day business of survival.

He was frowning as he arrived this night. He wrapped his cloak about his knees as he took his usual place by the fire, as if to keep out the memories of the day as much as the cool night air. He looked around at the wagons and carts parked in lines, the hobbled horses and mules, the nodding oxen, and the lines of chained Juthan sitting silent and exhausted by their day's labour.

"They're damn near as good as mules, these people," he said to Tiryn, nodding at her personal slave. The Juthan girl sat eyes downcast on the other side of the fire, a hemp slave collar about her broad throat. In her hands the copper pot sat forgotten.

"Her name is Ushdun," Tiryn said. "She was born in Junnan, in northern Jutha, and was given to an Imperial Tax Collector as part payment for her father's debt."

Jason considered this, disgust on his face. "These people give up their children to pay a tax?"

Tiryn's eyes burned. "It is the way the Empire works. Arkamenes told me it was good for the... the circulation of the population, and it avoided beggaring the smallholders. Most have too many mouths to feed as it is." Like my father, she thought but could not say—would never say.

"Then they deserve their Empire," Jason said with contempt.

"Do you not have slaves in your homeland?"

"Yes, but they're taken in war, not freely given up by their parents." He thought again, shrugged a little. "Well, maybe the goatherder tribes—but they're little better than animals."

"And are we, then, little better than animals?"

Jason looked at her, head cocked to one side. "Your Machtic is very good now. What say you, we try and get my Asurian up to the same mark?"

"The word for slave is *durun*. The word for animal is *qaf*. Have you heard of the Qaf?"

Jason smiled. "I see I am to be educated in several ways tonight. I have heard of them, yes."

"They are taller than the tallest Kefre, and broader than Juthan. They live far north of here, in the snows of the Korash Mountains. They do not like the heat of the lowlands, but I saw some in Ashur."

"They sound like fearsome creatures indeed."

"The word for angry is *irghe*. You are angry tonight."

"Did Gasca bring you that jar of wine? I'd have some, if there's any left."

She ordered the Juthan to get it out of the wagon. Jason clicked off the clay lid and drank straight from the lip of the jar. He wiped his mouth, nodding. "That's the right stuff. I was sick of palm wine. It's a relief to know someone here makes a drink out of the grape." He caught Tiryn's eyes still upon him. "Yes, I am angry."

"Why?"

"I do not come here to discuss my day."

"I know. You come here to receive language instruction from animals. Why are you angry?"

He laughed at that. "Was this why Arkamenes kept you by his side? To needle him out of a dark mood?"

"Perhaps. You like to talk to me, Jason. You lead this army. I do not think you can talk to others."

"You've met Rictus. No? I talk to him. I talk to my friend Buridan. And I talk to you. I do not know why. I do not know why I trust you, but it happens that I do."

He was in all seriousness, the laughter gone. He stared into the fire and nudged an errant faggot closer to the flames with his foot.

"We are not one army, but two," he said at last. "For now, we are together, because if we split up, we will no doubt die here. But if the Great King forsakes our pursuit, there will be factions in our ranks. They will tear us apart."

"Kill the leaders of the other factions," she said. She took the forgotten pot out of the Juthan girl's hands and began ladling the lentil stew within onto three earthenware plates.

"The Macht do not conduct their affairs in that way," Jason said. He seemed displeased.

"Are you hungry?"

"I'll eat."

He ate with his fingers, as did the Juthan. Tiryn scooped up her own food with a horn spoon. The taste took her back to the hearth of her father's house, in the mountains. The fire in the centre of the round room, the woodsmoke tainting every mouthful. She stared at her plate and across her mind a flickering pageant of childhood images played themselves out, stealing away her appetite.

Jason set down his empty plate. He lay back in his cloak and stared up at the stars. "I see Gaenion's Pointer," he said. "It shows the way north. Many's the night march I've made with it to guide me. It seems strange, somehow, that our stars are here, in this land."

"Your stars?" Tiryn asked.

"Gaenion the Smith made the stars out of Antimone's tears. When she wept he loved the way his wife's light caught in them—his wife is the sun, Araian. So he caught some of Antimone's tears, and set them in the heavens in patterns and chains ordained by God Himself. And there they stick."

"The stars are the gems of Bel, thrown into the sky as the god celebrated the killing of the great Bull, Mot's beast of the dark," Tiryn said. "The eyes of the Bull he set in the sky also, though one was full of blood from the beast's death-throes. They are our moons, Firghe and Anande, Wrath and Patience."

Jason grinned. "Each to his own gods, I suppose. I don't know about your Bel, or bull, but I have heard the beat of Antimone's Wings upon the battlefield, like some black flutter in the core of my heart. And then of course there is this." He cast aside his cloak, and sitting up, he thumped the black chest of his cuirass, the Curse of God.

"I do not know how these things were made if they are not the work of some god, because assuredly, there is no smith on earth who can fathom their creation."

Tiryn raised an eyebrow. "Perhaps there was once."

"What is the word for stubborn?"

"*Kura*. A mule is a *Kuru*. I am thinking it a good word for *Macht*, also."

Jason got to his feet, and bowed. "Thank you for the wine, the food, and the instruction in humility, my lady."

She lowered the komis from her face, looking up at him as he stood there. She did not want him to go. "I will see you on the march perhaps, tomorrow?"

"Perhaps." He reached out his hand, and for an unthinking second she did the same, her fingers longer than his, pale in the firelight. They did not touch. She drew back, startled by the temerity of her own impulse.

"Tomorrow," he said. "I wish to learn the words for hearth, home, and happiness, in case I should ever need them." Then he turned to go.

"I hope you may need them, one day," Tiryn said, watching his cloak-wrapped shape disappear into the firelight and shadows of the sleeping camp. She did not think he had heard her.

The next day, a large tell loomed out of the morning mists before Rictus's trudging skirmishers. All about, the flatlands of the Middle Empire croaked and clicked and buzzed as the sun began to warm the air. A solitary Kufr farmer, leading his ox out for a morning's work, saw the Macht appear out of the mists and fled, leaving his puzzled animal behind. Rictus slapped the beast's rump as they passed it, and Whistler grinned. "Rictus, shall I?"

"Leave it. The foragers will pick it up. Cormos—take your centon out on the right, but stay linked."

"Look," Whistler said, swinging his pelta from his back to his left arm.

A city reared up before them, afloat on a white sea of mist. Steep-sided as a spearhead, it was a vast black shadow on the edge of their world, coming to life as they watched with the flicker of a hundred, two hundred, a thousand lamps. The inhabitants were rising with the sun.

"Ab-Mirza," Rictus said. "So Jason says. All centons at the double—pass it down the line. They'll open the gates at sunrise—we must secure them."

They ran at a fast jog through the mist, javelins in their shield-fist, short spears in the other. They were nearly all barefoot, for sandals could not compete with the sucking ooze of the farmlands they had passed through. Nine hundred-odd men, their eyes as bright and eager as those of a hunting wolf, no formation to their number, a mere fast-moving, shapeless darkness in the mist.

Another astonished farmer. Someone speared him and he splashed to the ground with a sharp cry. Rictus bared his teeth. No point shouting back at the pack behind him. Leading these men, one took the rough along with the smooth.

They passed clusters of farm buildings, mud walled and thatched with reeds. A line of stout palms planted along an irrigation ditch. Mud walls, knee-high, chest-high. They poured over them with scarcely a pause, the clay brick crumbling under their feet and elbows and scrabbling fingers.

And at last, the great smell of the city itself, to be sensed with the nose, and felt as a shadow upon the mist around them. They were at the walls, fired brick, slimy, veined with ivy. "Follow them round—this way. On me, brothers," Rictus panted. He heard the slap of their feet behind them, the sound women made when washing clothes on the stones of a river.

And here was the gate—a tall barricade of wood, reinforced with green bronze. It was closing in their faces. Rictus screamed something—he knew not what—and sprinted forward. His men roared out a wordless howl of anger and sped up with him. They crashed into the gate at full tilt, heads knocking against the wood with a ripple of cracks.

"Push, you bastards!" Rictus yelled, and they set their shoulders to it.

He backed out of the ranks of his struggling men, made for the dark, thinning gap, and squeezed through there. On the other side were a crowd of Kufr, tall, angular shapes, grunting and shouting. He stabbed the short spear into their bodies, hardly aiming the head of it. Behind him, more of his men were squeezing through the gap. Whistler was beside him, using a javelin as a spear. A sharp point keened off Rictus's armour, the blow hardly felt. Then another. Someone was loosing arrows into the press, careless of who they hit.

The gates were opening now, and on the far side of them the Macht were a great mass of shouting men, shields held up over their heads, spearheads lancing out below, going for the bellies and groins of the Kufr. They poured into the city, the momentum on their side now, the gates all the way open, that torrent of muscle scraping them across the flags of the gatehouse floor. The Kufr fell back. There was torchlight here, mixed up and competing with the mist-bound glow of the rising sun. The morning was fighting its way into life. Rictus's men were through the gatehouse and in the streets. Buildings reared up all around like red cliffs, Kufr running everywhere, showers of arrows hissing through the air, men going down with the feathered shafts skewering them. The Kufr were up on the rooftops, archers bobbing up to loose their shafts, others beside them hurling down bricks and stones and all manner of other debris. A dozen Macht were down now, and the cobbled brick of the roadway was puddled with their blood. The rest of the mora, still pushing and pulsing through the gates, set up a great shout as they saw their fallen comrades and lunged forward. The knot around the gatehouse broke up. The Macht leapt over their own dead and wounded and streamed up every street, cutting down all who stood in their way, kicking in doors and hauling out Kufr women, cutting their throats or stabbing them through the heart, the eyes. They pounded up the internal stairways to come out on the rooftops, and on the flat hard-packed earth above they slew their attackers without mercy, throwing them down to the street. Rictus saw two of his men catch a tall Kefren woman, pinion her arms and violate her with a javelin, laughing with a fierce, insane hatred as they did so.

He shouted orders, but they went unheard. The men were slipping out of his command, scattering into the maze of streets, pursuing any Kufr who dared show their face. And still, on the farther rooftops, the inhabitants of the city were popping up to shoot arrows and fling spears and stones, and carts were being wheeled across the roadways to bar the passage of the invaders. There seemed to be no soldiery resisting the Macht; it was the population itself. Rictus's mora was being soaked into the city. It was disappearing in chaos and murder before his eyes.

He grabbed a young Macht by the scruff and clouted aside the knife which was raised in his face. "Get out of here, back to the army. Find Jason and tell him to bring up some of the other morai. Tell him we're fighting in the streets, and like to be swamped if he does not hurry. Do you understand? Repeat it to me." The boy did so, sour and resentful.

"What's your name?"

"Lomnos."

"Lomnos, if Jason does not get this message, I will come looking for you—you understand?"

The boy nodded, snarling, and then ran back the way he had come.

"Whistler, is that you? Not the head again." Whistler's bald pate had yet another slice out of it. He raised his hand and touched the blood. "Never felt it—I don't feel nothing there no more—lucky for me, eh? Rictus, we've got to rein in these stupid fuckers before they burn the place down around us."

"I know. Discipline is all to hell. Do what you can. I'll try to get to the head of them." Rictus took off up the steep city street at a run, grabbing men here and there, any face he recognised, any name he could shout out. Called like this, the men remembered their duty and followed him up the hill, but hundreds of Rictus's mora were scattering through the city, killing and looting as they went, beyond the reach of their centurions. The bodies began to pile up in the streets.

The boy Lomnos panted out his message with the spittle spraying from his lips. Jason set a hand on his shoulder. He looked around, saw Aristos in the midst of the marching column, and called him over.

"Take your mora into the city, at the double. Rictus may need help." Aristos grinned, face flushing with pleasure. He turned to go.

"And Aristos—keep them in hand!"

The lead mora broke into a run, clapping on their helms and sliding their shields from back to shoulder with the neck-strap. Jason looked round again, saw Buridan two hundred paces away. He pointed to the city and pumped his fist up and down. Buridan nodded, and shouted at his men. Immediately, this second mora began to pick up their pace as well. Two thousand men, sweating and gasping in their armour, now streaming towards the open gates of Ab-Mirza at a run.

"Shields!" Jason cried. The centurions around him took it up, and the five middle morai of the column immediately broke ranks and made for the baggage train, where their shields were stored on the wagons. Morai took it in turns to provide the shield-bearing rear and van guards, because to march all day with the shield was punishing. It would thus be some time before Jason could send more fully-armed morai into the city. For the moment, whatever was happening in there was the concern of Rictus and Aristos and Buridan alone.

Perhaps two hundred men held around Rictus in a body; all that he could gather out of his mora. These were mainly veterans who had been close to him at the Kunaksa, older men with more level heads, but even they were eager to be off and join their comrades. He could feel it. Some fool had knocked a cresset into a stable, and half a street was burning. Rictus found himself frozen, staring at the flames, remembering Isca, the sound of the city's torture roaring up into the pine-shrouded hills.

Up the steep city streets more troops were advancing, hundreds of heavy spearmen, a curse-bearer at the head. He doffed his helm and became Aristos, lithe, olive-skinned, his face alight with happiness. "Well, lads," he shouted, "Let's finish what Rictus has begun. Remember my uncle Argus—remember Phiron! Teach these Kufr their names!"

Vorus was woken by an orderly, a young *hufsan* with a set face. "General, I was told to wake you. Outside, there is something you must see."

Mystified, Vorus threw a blanket about his shoulders and padded barefoot out of the tent. Dawn was almost upon them, and the great camp around him was stirring, the smell of woodsmoke and horseshit mingling on the air.

"General Proxis is on the mound, sir," the *hufsan* said.

Vorus laboured up the slope of the small tell, all that was left of some indescribably ancient city. There was a lookout post at the top, this being the highest point for miles around. Proxis stood there now, along with three other Juthan of the Legion.

"Proxis."

"Look west, General. What do you see?

A glow on the brim of the sky, red in the white mist-sea which blanketed the plain. Vorus's face hardened.

"They're burning a city," he said. "Where would that be?"

"Ab-Mirza. It's sixty pasangs from here; two days' march."

"I know it. The King's messenger got through, then; they must have made a fight of it."

"That, or the Macht are simply setting an example."

"I don't think they would," Vorus said quietly. "What purpose could it serve? No; there's been a fight in that city, Proxis."

"And the city has lost. The Governor of Ab-Mirza has brought ruin down on himself. And his people."

"Would you suggest we order all governors to throw open the gates of their cities to these brigands?" Vorus asked, angry now. "The King was right. We must make them fight every step of the way."

"Then they'll be treading on Kufr bodies every step of the way," Proxis retorted. Vorus turned from the silent spectacle on the horizon. Up here, on the tell, they were above the mist, and below they could hear but not see the army about them. As though it were a mere phantom.

"Proxis," he said quietly. "My friend, what is the trouble?" He knew it went beyond this morning's revelation. The three Juthan behind Proxis stared rigidly out to the west, but there was something there between the four of them, something Vorus felt had excluded him.

"Proxis?"

"Nothing. I do not like to see a city burn, that's all." Proxis was stone cold sober, with not a breath of wine about him, which meant he had not drunk the night before either. Vorus had known this Juthan for two decades, and he could not remember the last time Proxis had gone to bed without at least a cupful of something, if the cupful could be found.

"Join me in my tent. We'll have some wine, warm our livers."

"I have things to do," Proxis said with a shake of his head.

"It's not like you to turn down a drink, Proxis."

The Juthan stared at him. He came up to Vorus's chin, but was half as broad again about the shoulders. His yellow eyes had veins of blood shot through them, and in the dawn light his skin looked dark as charcoal. "Perhaps I will swear off wine. As a slave I drank every gut-rotting brew I could pour in my mouth," he said. "Enough for two lifetimes."

"You are not a slave now," Vorus said hotly.

"We are all slaves, Vorus. Even you."

He turned and left the summit of the tell and the three other Juthan followed him, silent and sombre as all their race. But now there was something missing—a certain regard for the general they passed by on their way down the hill. A deference which Vorus had scarcely remarked before, and only knew of now it was gone.

"Damn him," Vorus whispered. "Twenty years too late, he becomes proud. Damn him."

He looked back at Ab-Mirza's ghost, burning in the mist of the far away horizon. We'll be treading on bodies now, all right, he thought. Every step of the way.

TWENTY
INTO THE DARK TOGETHER

A campfire, and about it, eleven men who wore Antimone's Gift.

"Why should we not?" Aristos demanded, eyes blazing. "We have the spears to take what we want, when we want it. This Great King of theirs is hiding off behind the eastern horizon somewhere. Why should we not rape his Empire as we march through it? Let us send him a message on the wind and make him smell the stink of his burning cities. Why should we not?"

Several of the other generals thumped their fists on their thighs in agreement. Jason noted their faces. Gominos the stout, Grast the ugly, Hephr the snide and Dinon the ass-licker. Thus had he labelled them in his mind. Then Mynon spoke up, bird-eyed Mynon, always drifting with the wind.

"Aristos may have a point to make, Jason. What does it gain us to negotiate with the Kufr, when we find their gates closed to us anyway?"

Jason was about to reply when Rictus spoke up. The boy's eyes were like two windows of white glass in his darkly tanned face. The fury could be smelled off him. But he kept his voice even.

"Every time we sack a city, a little of the men's discipline goes. Every time we let ourselves loose on the innocent and the unarmed, we poison a little of the soldier in us. We make ourselves into brigands and rapists and murderers. If we are to make it to the sea, then we must be soldiers before all else. We must have discipline, and the men must obey their officers. If that goes, that obedience, then we are finished. And we deserve to be finished, for we will be nothing more than criminals."

Aristos snorted with laughter. "Well, listen to this, a strawhead with a sense of honour! Where did you pick that up, Rictus? Did your father tell you tales of bravery whilst fucking his sheep?"

They saw a blur, a shadow leap across the campfire. Then Aristos was on his back with Rictus atop him, a knife at the prone man's throat, drawing blood. The other men about the fire froze for a second. Then Gominos drew his sword.

"Hold!" Jason bellowed. He strode forward and grasped Rictus's shoulder. "Off him, boy—that's an order. Rictus!"

Rictus rose and thrust his knife back in his belt. He looked down on Aristos and said quietly,

"You ever mention my father again to me, and I will kill you."

The knot of men opened up. Aristos rose, hand clenched on his own sword-hilt. The younger generals drew closer to him. "You had best leash this dog of yours, Jason," Aristos spat, a mite unsteadily. "He is like to get a whipping if he keeps snapping at his betters."

"Shut your mouth, you damn fool," Buridan growled, more bear-like than ever in the firelight.

"Enough," Jason snapped. "Aristos, do you contest my authority?"

"I say we vote for warleader again."

"On what grounds?"

"On the grounds that some members of this Kerusia are not fit to command a mora."

"I agree. But we are not going to start swapping generals right now, with the Great King on our tails and the supply-carts half-empty."

"I say we put it to the vote, here and now!"

"And I say you shut your mouth, or I will demote you."

"You can't do that!" Aristos said, wide-eyed.

"I can. The generals were not voted in by the men. I simply gathered up the Second in every mora when we were down on our tits at Kunaksa. At the proper time, the men should have a say in their generals, but now is not that time. Do you agree?"

After a long moment, Aristos nodded.

"Then my orders are still to be obeyed. There will be no more sacking of Kufr cities. That is to be made clear all the way down the line. We're in a hole as it is, without digging it any deeper.

Make it clear. I will begin instituting field punishments for any man who thinks otherwise." He paused, looking them up and down, remembering Phiron and Pasion, Orsos and Castus, and the other dead men who had once stood where these striplings stood now. He felt old, he felt as though they were all diminished in some way. That sense of brotherhood that had taken them so far was gone now. He wondered if even Phiron could have brought it back after this.

"Brothers," he said, "we are Macht. Remember that."

Some of them returned his gaze. Old Mochran nodded, the memories in his eyes also. Young Phinero, who had loved his dead brother. Even Mynon had the grace to look somewhat ashamed. Rictus was lost in simmering rage, unreachable. Aristos and his supporters—the words meant almost nothing to them.

"Dismissed," Jason said heavily. "Mynon and Rictus, stay behind if you please."

He looked up at the stars—his stars. He smiled, remembering. They were half a pasang out of camp, the better to have their debate without the whole army hearing it. To the west, the Macht bivouacs were a square of campfires, a pasang to a side. And to the east, Ab-Mirza still burned on the horizon, behind them now. He had marched the army hard today, made them sweat out the wine they had looted from the city. Jason closed his eyes, remembering that awful moment when he had felt the army slip out of his control and become a mob. Aristos and his mora had poured through the gates without discipline or order or thought for anything except satisfying their basest desires. Buridan's men, the best in the army, had come upon what they thought was a battle, and had joined in the slaughter.

And he, Jason, had sent them in there.

It was no battle. Aristos's and Rictus's troops had been killing Kufr women and children and old men at that point, spilling blood for the sake of it. By the time order had been restored the city was aflame, a burning charnel-house. Nothing for it then but to leave it burning, to walk away.

Jason did not know why it bothered him so. Rictus had seen Isca go up; no doubt his family had been slaughtered—his father, if tonight were anything to go by—so he had an excuse. But Jason had been at the death of a city before this—a Macht city, too. He could not fathom why this one bothered him so.

"*Phobos*," he whispered, baffled and angry. Now at least the Kufr knew what it was like to have a Macht rape them. Another phenomenon for this changing world.

"It was my fault," Rictus said. He was rubbing his eyes as though their brightness pained him. "They got away from me and wouldn't come back, except for a few. It was my mora started it. Aristos is right. I am not fit to command."

"You lead too near the front," Jason told him brusquely. "You must stand back a little and grip the centons behind the assault. They are the key. You are a general, Rictus, and you were the first man through the gate. This is not a story out of legend we are making here. A general must hang back and consider the larger play of things. Do you understand?"

"I wish to be demoted."

"Shut up. Go back to your mora and make them obey you. Get out of my sight."

Rictus left them, trudging into the dark with the slow gait of a tired old man.

"That boy has strange ideas," Mynon said. "Perhaps it is the Iscan in him."

"He wants to think well of men, to believe they are better than they are," Jason said. "His men love him for it; Buridan told me. When they let him down, he takes it bad. He's young. He's learning."

"Nothing like learning the hard way," Mynon said, yawning. "You're wondering what's left in the larder, I suppose."

"Most of what was in Ab-Mirza got burned, which fucked the supply situation all to hell. What do we have, Mynon? Be nice."

"Three days' full rations. We go on half, stint the slaves, and we can make it a week. The place is picked clean for pasangs around, and from what I hear—"

"Our Macht friend has an army galloping up our arse. I know. He's two days behind us now, and there's cavalry with him. It's eight hundred pasangs to the mountains. If we push it, we can do it in twenty to twenty-five days. In the mountains, we will turn and fight. Until then, we march as hard as we can."

"Our bellies flapping."

"It's tongues I'm worried about now, as much as bellies. Rictus was right; we make a habit of cutting loose like we did yesterday, and we'll be nothing more than rabble inside of a month. Those young pups would be happy that way, but it would mean the death of the army, pure and simple."

"Some would say the best part of the army is dead already," Mynon said, sombre for once.

"Antimone is still with us, Mynon, believe me. We are still—"

"Macht. I know. I was here earlier. What was it Orsos used to say? It was a quote, from Sarenias I think. '*Brothers, let us go into the dark together, in the shadow of Antimone's wings*'."

They stood, remembering, the fire cracking at their feet, beginning to sink now. Around them the teeming insect life of the lowlands chittered and clicked, filling the night with meaningless sound.

"We do not belong here," Jason said softly.

"I know. I see the same stars overhead and wonder why they are not different. Even the water tastes strange to me here. I think sometimes, Jason, that the Kufr have more right to this world than we."

Jason tried to laugh, but the humour died in his throat. "The water? Yesterday the gutters of Ab-Mirza were full of blood. It poured over the walls. How many thousands, Mynon? More than died at Kunaksa, I think. Whatever wrongs have been inflicted on us, we have repaid them many times over."

* * *

Before dawn, the army was on the march again, the men sullen and subdued, like a drunk remembering the antics of the night before. Jason had the centurions go through the camp and have all the loot from Ab-Mirza flung in the embers of the campfires. Those Kufr women which had been brought along in capture yokes were freed and left by the wayside like naked, whey-faced ghosts. The men marched with empty bellies and sore heads; up and down the column the centurions bellowed at them to pick up the pace. When pack-animals failed, whole centons were detailed to bear their loads. Dozens of men were assigned to the heavier of the wagons and levered them through the muck of the Pleninash lowlands by main force, thrashing the exhausted mules and oxen that strained alongside them. Half the army, it seemed, laboured under a sense of disgrace. The other half simmered with resentment, like a man wrongfully accused. Up and down the trudging ranks men argued amongst themselves. Periodically some would fall out of the column to brawl in the mud of the wayside, until the centurions broke it up.

"I wish it all to the back of the fucking Veil, this fucking country," Gratus said, slapping his neck. He peeled something black from his skin, regarded it with distaste, and wiped his bloody fingers in his hair. "I mean, we're not into high summer yet, and this heat would make a fish sweat. How do they bear it?"

"It's their country," old Demotes said, a wizened vision of white beard and blackened face, blue eyes bright and out of place in the middle of it. "They're bred to it, like we're bred to the mountains. Besides, it's not so bad. At home, in the winter, my knees lock up after a march and I'm rubbing on them like a boy who's just found out how to work his piss-tube until I can stand up again."

"I saw you grab that Kufr girl, Gasca, how'd that work out?" Astianos said. "Me, by the time I got to anything with a slot between its legs, it was dead. And I draw the line at carrion."

Gasca marched on, saying nothing.

"He's shy," Astianos said, slapping him on the back. "It was his first time, and so fucking a Kufr doesn't count. He's a virgin yet."

Gasca's broad face remained impassive. The sun had burnt his blond hair white and his skin was dark as boot-leather, the freckles about his nose and cheeks a black tattoo. He had indeed grabbed that girl, to keep her from the others. She had seemed pretty to him, the first Kufr he had ever regarded in that way. In the chaos of the sacked city he had hauled her into a quiet alley-way and stripped her. The excitement of the city's fall had invaded his brain, and he had drunk some grain-spirit that Astianos had ferreted out of a tall-sided house. He had run his filthy hands up and down her skin, had poked and prodded her. But her eyes had halted him. They were dark and hopeless. She was weeping silently, just like a real woman. So he let her go. Oddly enough, he felt no less of a man for not raping her. He felt only relief, that he had come out of Ab-Mirza the same man who had gone in. His friends would not understand that, but Rictus would. He knew

Rictus would. So he bore the good-natured chaffing of his fellows with a slight smile, no more. Had he but known it, the last of the boy had left him. He marched along now with a veteran's face, his smile that of a full-grown man who knows his own mind.

They were all of them thinner than they had been, all scarred in some place or other, all sun-blackened and with bird's-feet fans of white skin at the outer corners of their eyes. Their nails were broken and ingrained with dirt, their feet bare, the soles as tough as any leather. Their bodies were as worn and lean as a man's can be, and the muscles of their very faces could be seen cording and bunching at jaw and temple every time they opened their mouths. They were soldiers, creatures of appetite and routine with a core of indefinable restlessness at their heart. They were callous, brutal, sentimental, sardonic. They were selfish and selfless. They would knife a man over a copper obol, and would share with him the last of their water. They would trample a masterpiece of art in the dirt and be brought to tears by a veteran's voice raised in song. They were the dregs of the earth. They were Macht.

Four days, the army marched at the punishing pace Jason set for it. Broken wagons and played-out beasts littered the Imperial Road behind them, and foraging parties gathered fodder for the animals, wood, and water—nothing more. As the days went on, so the scarlet memory of Ab-Mirza receded, and the brawling in the ranks sank to a more normal level. The last powdery, rat-gnawed remnants at the bottom of the wagons were scooped out and set to boil in the centoi, and what meat remained was chopped up, green and slimy, to bubble with them. For the first time, men began to drop out of the column to void their bowels outside the time allotted at rest stops. A week passed, and even though the pace of the march slackened somewhat, the wagons began to fill with those whose bowels had flushed away their strength. And those who marched on, supporting their sick comrades, grew ever leaner.

"Enough," Buridan told Jason. "They know. They're not sure they know why, but they know."

"What do they know?" Jason asked him.

"That you are in command."

"Send out full foraging columns, Jason," Mynon said. "Phobos's sake, the men have to eat."

"There's a city called Hadith, another three days' march to the north-west. We get there, and we can restock our supplies." To answer the other men's looks, Jason said, "We will encamp outside the city, and send a delegation to speak with its governor. He will have heard of Ab-Mirza. We will make its fate work for us."

It was two more days before Jason could bring himself to visit Tiryn again. He found her in her wagon, a lamp lit and drawing smokily, almost out of oil. Her Juthan slave was asleep in her blankets under the vehicle's axle. Tiryn sat in the guttering lamplight, staring at the flame as though it were saying something of import to her. She looked up once as the wagon creaked under Jason's weight, then back at the lamp-flame, tugging her komis closer about her face.

"The conqueror comes," she said in a low voice. "Have I taught you the word for murder, Jason? It is *jurud*. It is a word you should know."

Jason stared at her, the muscles in his jaw clenching and unclenching. "I'm sorry," he said at last. "It was not meant to have happened in that way."

"It is war. I should have expected nothing more. In war, what's a city, here or there?"

"Tiryn—"

"Did you sate some appetite at Ab-Mirza? Your men did. Now they know that Kufr women are very like the Macht in some respects. We have holes in all the right places."

"I shall need your help in the days to come, Tiryn."

"My help? What amusement can I afford you that the Kufr of Ab-Mirza could not?"

"Enough! I need you to speak for us, for the Macht. I need you to talk to your people. I do not want any more cities to burn."

She looked at him, eyes blazing. "I should help you now?"

"You will be helping your own folk too."

"Betraying them, you mean."

"When I found you, your own people had made quite a mess of you themselves," Jason said, angry now. "Since you've been with us, there's not a hand been laid near you. I would kill the man who tried."

That cooled the air between them. She tugged her komis away from her mouth. He saw the dark lips move. "Why?" they said, though they made no sound.

"I ask myself that too," Jason said, more softly now. "I have seen cities burn before. I know what it means. I think I am like Rictus now; I have seen enough of it. I am sick of it, Tiryn. I believe I am sick of soldiering." He leaned back against the side of the wagon and exhaled, a long sigh. He stared up at the stars overhead. "Hearth, and home," he said.

"*Orthos*," Tiryn said. "*Amathon*. Now you know the words for them."

Jason smiled. "I give you my own word," he said. "Help us make our way home, and I shall try to get us there without the burning of cities, the deaths of the innocent."

The lamp winked out with a tiny hiss, leaving them in the dark under the stars. Jason leaned forward and touched his mouth against hers, just for a moment, a dizzying second. She sat like some fine-boned statue of marble, fists suddenly clenched in the blanket that covered her lap. Slowly, she replaced the folds of the linen komis about her face, and then sat as unmoving as before. Jason opened his hand, as though he were about to make her a gift. Then he turned and clambered down from the wagon without another word.

The gates of Hadith were shut, and the walls were lined with defiant citizenry. Jason strode up to the kiln-fired brick of the battlements with only a single companion, whilst half a pasang behind him the Macht stood in line of battle. He waved a green branch as he approached, remembering the last time he had tried to negotiate with Kufr. The sweat dripped down his face.

"Drop your veil," he said to his companion. "Let them see what you are."

Tiryn did as she was told. Her skin, normally the colour of a hazelnut shell, was pale now. She was trembling with fear, eyes wide and fixed on the spears and javelins and bows in the hands of the defenders. Jason took her hand. It was cool in his, fine-boned and slender. She tugged it away, some colour coming back to her face. "Keep your word," she said quietly. "That is all I ask."

"If they do not open their gates, we will march away. I swear it."

She turned and looked down on him, managed to smile. "Very well then."

The Macht general and the Kufr woman stood under the loom of the city walls, and Tiryn called out in her clear, carrying voice. She asked for food, for wagons, for draught animals. And in return she promised the defenders that the Macht would leave their city be, and would march off with the following dawn. If the requested supplies were not forthcoming by dusk, she said, the city would be assaulted, and would suffer the fate of Ab-Mirza.

An hour later, the gates were opened, and the folk of Hadith began hauling out the contents of their granaries and their stables and their byres. The Macht stood like an army cast in bronze, motionless. As night fell, they moved in to collect their spoils, and by dawn they were gone, a mere shadow on the western road, the dust rising in a cloud to mark their passage. The gates of Hadith were opened again, and the more valiant of its citizens went out to inspect the beaten earth of the Macht camp. As they stood there, marvelling, they saw in the east another dust-cloud, hanging high in the still air and moving westwards in the wake of the Macht. A great army was on the road.

TWENTY-ONE
BROTHERS IN ARMS

"The land is rising," Rictus said. He leaned on his spear and stared westwards, into the endless shimmering haze, the blue of distance. He stamped one heel into the ground. "It's drier here, better going for man and beast. Could be the lowlands are coming to an end at last."

"Those hills on your left are Jutha," Jason told him, consulting the calfskin of Phiron's map. "The province capital, Junnan, is three hundred pasangs to our south-west." He raised his head, staring westwards with Rictus, a look not unlike hunger on his face. "From here, it's two hundred pasangs to the mountains. Five or six days' march, if the weather holds. Think of that, Rictus, mountains again."

"How high are these mountains?" Rictus asked, ever practical. He was looking at Tiryn, kneeling on the short-cropped turf of the hillside and running her hand across it as a farmer will feel the ears of his crop.

"Not so high as the Magron," she said. She stood up, taller than either of them. "The Korash are much colder though, and there is only the one pass through them which is fit for the passage of armies: the Irun Gates. It is defended by two fortress-cities. On the eastern side, Irunshahr, on the western, Kumir. And it is said the Qaf live in the mountains between the two."

"Beyond the mountains is the land of Askanon," Jason told them, still staring westwards. "Beyond it, Gansakr, and then the sea."

Rictus had turned and was now looking back the way they had come. Below them the camp of the army sprawled in its rough square, the grey ribbons of a thousand campfires rising up from it in the still air. They led the oxen out to graze, and he could hear the armourers at work in the smithies, hammering upon their field-anvils. At this distance, the measured strokes could almost be the tolling of bells.

He looked farther along the horizon and there it was still, the yellow cloud on the air that was the army of the Great King in pursuit, as dogged as a sniffing hound.

"When we fight them again," he said, "we shall hold the high ground."

Jason rolled up his map. "Indeed. And we must fight them this side of the mountains. We must break that army before we enter the Irun Gates."

"Another battle?" Tiryn asked.

"Another battle," Jason told her. "The last, perhaps, if we do it right."

"I'll take the men ahead a ways, and see what these hill-villages have in their larders," Rictus said. He bent and picked up his pelta, slinging the light shield across his back. He nodded at Jason once and then set off at a swift jog. Further along the slope his mora awaited him, some eight hundred men scattered across the grass enjoying the cooler air, most lying on their backs asleep. As he approached they began to rise, the movement rippling out across the hillside. All of them had the *iktos* sigil painted across their shields, the badge of Isca.

"He's so young, to lead so many men," Tiryn said.

"He's not so young as he once was." Jason set a hand in the small of her back, and set it travelling upwards, feeling the flesh of her through the silk. It came to rest on her nape, slid under the fabric, and brushed the tiny hairs there, as silken as the robe she wore. Her skin goosepimpled under his fingers.

"If you want me, why not have me?" Tiryn asked him, standing very still.

"I will not take what is not freely given."

"It's been taken before, many times."

"That makes no difference." Jason slid his hand away, brought it up and grasped her chin through the thin material of the komis. "I want what is in here," he said, shaking her head gently. "Here." He set his hand gently on the warmth of one breast, and felt the thudding of her heart within, the heat of her. She moved infinitesimally closer, pushing her breast into his palm so that he could feel the nipple through the fine stuff of her robe.

"You are Macht," she said. "I am Kufr."

"I don't care, Tiryn."

She bent her head, and after a moment's hesitation she kissed him through the veil. "Others will."

"I don't care," he repeated.

"Let it be so then," she said. "For a while. Until we come to the shores of the sea." Her hand came up and caressed his face, touching lightly on old scars.

"Until then," he agreed, and kissed her again.

Within the yellow cloud to the east, Vorus rode his old mare deep in thought, his eyes narrowed against the dust. Inside the smoking fume of their passage he felt detached from the army he led, and let the mare pick her way in the wake of the vanguard with little more than a nudge of his heels every now and again to keep her on her way. The scouts told him he was three days' march behind his quarry, and no matter how hard he pushed the troops, it seemed that gap never narrowed. He was leading a dust-caked, phantom army of trudging ghosts, chasing something even more phantasmal than themselves. Chasing an idea perhaps, a marching symbol which with every step it took, broke open new thoughts among the people it passed, among the people who had merely heard of it, and sowed garbled stories of its journey. He was chasing down a myth.

So it seemed, every evening, when he read the letters sent at horse-killing pace by Ashurnan to plague the few moments of rest he allowed himself after the army had bedded down for the night. The Great King had kept fifty thousand soldiers as his bodyguard, hoarding the new levies which were still arriving in Pleninash and encamping them around Kaik as if the Macht could somehow still surprise him there. He had lost something: a kind of courage perhaps. Even through the long-winded flowery language of the scribes, Vorus could read it. Ashurnan wanted this thing done and over with and forgotten. He wanted to forget, perhaps, the carnage of Kunaksa. His brother's death. Why else send the corpse of Arkamenes back to Ashur for a Royal funeral? Vorus would have fed it to the jackals.

But there were still enough here to do the job. The column in which Vorus rode was twelve pasangs long. The van of it went into camp two hours before the rearguard every night. And he still had the Asurian cavalry, six thousand of them. Every day they rode out on the flanks and to the front, not so eager as they had been once, nor so brilliantly turned out, either. Many were now mounted on local scrub ponies, for the tall Niseians had died by the hundred at Kunaksa. But they were still the best he had.

As for the rest, there was a remnant of the Honai, which Vorus kept as his reserve and commanded himself; the *hufsan* levies, still intact, though they hated the humid flatness of the lands they were trekking across; and the three Juthan Legions, twelve thousand of the squat, dour-handed warriors under Proxis. Close to fifty thousand warriors, all told. And Vorus had Kefren officers out among the plains cities day and night, conscripting more. He would need them. He would need them all.

He left the column and kicked his unwilling horse into a canter, eating up the ground alongside the marching files. Near the head of the army he found the Juthan contingent, their grey skin tawny with dust, halberds resting on their shoulders, shields slung on their backs. He trotted along their ranks, staring into the lines of squat, dust-caked warriors, as intent as if his eyes could somehow fathom what was travelling through their heads. He almost ran into Proxis, who sat by the side of the road on his slate-coloured mule, watching the legions pass by.

"We're low on water," Proxis told him.

"Anaris is ten pasangs away, and there are wells there. We halt before the city for the night."

"The plains cities have been supplying the Macht with fodder and water, all of them along the road, all of them since the sack of Ab-Mirza."

"I know." The knowledge had angered most of the army, and had made relations with the city-governors tetchy. Feeding one army was bad enough, but when a second, five times larger, turned up in the wake of the first, there was not much left to go around.

"Will you punish them?" Proxis asked. "The Great King would wish it so."

"I will not sack our own cities, not until Ashurnan expressly orders me to do so. They are our people, Proxis."

"Are they now?" the Juthan said, and a grimace flitted across his broad face. "You've heard the rumours from Junnan?"

"I have heard them." Vorus sat very still in his saddle. He did not look at his old friend, but studied the marching files of Juthan as they marched past. Slave-soldiers, hoping to earn their freedom through service in war; as Proxis had done twenty years before, saving a general's life on the battlefield. The general had been Vorus.

"It may be that once the Macht are destroyed you will have to move on to the Juthan," Proxis said.

"Many things may happen," Vorus said stiffly. "We cannot foresee all of them. We can only keep putting one foot in front of the other." If the rumours were true, then the Juthan had risen in open rebellion, and the entire ancient province of Jutha was lost to the Empire. The slave-race had rediscovered their pride at last, and from the Gadinai Desert to the Jurid River they had expelled all Imperial garrisons, even those rebel ones Arkamenes had installed in his passage though the province. Rumours of battles, of bloodshed on a massive scale. The Empire was creaking on its foundations.

"You have always been my friend," Proxis said. "You made me free."

"You earned your freedom. You saved my life at Carchanis."

Proxis rubbed his mule's ears. He seemed about to say something, then stopped. That Juthan reserve came down again. "As you say, we can only keep putting one foot in front of the other." He swung his mule around and joined the column of Juthan troops, becoming part of that dun-coloured crowd of trudging warriors. Vorus watched him go, knowing now that some decision had just been made, and there was nothing he could do about it.

Out of the western horizon, the white-tipped peaks of the Korash Mountains rose now to stand stark against every sunset. This was the province of Hafdaran. At long last, the endless lowlands of the Middle Empire had been left behind. The land grew more broken and rugged, with knots and fists of stone thrusting up through the soil on all sides. Here, the irrigation systems of the plains came to a halt, for the earth was poorer, and the local Kufr grazed herds upon it rather than planting crops. These were *hufsan* folk in the main, the hill-peoples of the Empire, and they lived in unwalled towns and sprawling villages rather than fortified cities. They herded goats, sheep, upland cattle, and scrub ponies. As the land rose, so the air grew cooler, and the Macht found themselves able to breathe a little easier. The wind came off the mountains in dry waves, flattening the upland grass and reminding them of their homeland. To the thousands of marching men, it seemed that they must be drawing closer to journey's end, though those who had some notion of geography knew this to be wishful thinking. As the crows flew, it was still twelve hundred pasangs to Sinon.

The fortress-city of Irunshahr rose up on a spur of outlying rock from one of the lower Korash peaks. It overlooked the Irun Gates, the only way through the mountains to the wide lands of the Outer Empire beyond. Within sight of the city the Macht halted, set up camp, and sent out foraging parties to scour the land around for anything four-footed which might be put in the pot. To their rear, Jason posted the morai of Aristos and Mynon to keep an eye on the pursuing Kufr army. They had marched over a thousand pasangs in the last five weeks, following the Imperial Road as if it had been constructed to speed their passage out of the Empire. In the lowlands it was summer now, while up here in the hills the gorse was in full blossom, and there were bees by the million crawling around the heather-strewn slopes and amid the rocks. Overhead, the great raptors of the Korash foothills circled endlessly, wide-winged sentinels of the mountains.

"This is good ground," Jason said. All the generals of the army were clustered about him on the hillside, leaning on their spears.

"This is where we fight. We have two days before the enemy comes up. I want a position prepared here, where the hills break up into stone. We will place our line along these heights and let him come to us. If we break up his army here, he will take a long time to reorganise, and we will use that time to get through the mountains." Jason paused and looked his companions up and down.

"Any thoughts, brothers?"

Mynon spoke up. "The city has closed its gates behind us. We'll need to watch our rear. Irunshahr has a garrison; they may well sortie out in the middle of the battle, just to annoy us."

"Agreed. Aristos, your mora is to remain to the rear of the main battle line, both as a reserve, and to guard against any mischief. Rictus, your lights will be back there with him, and behind you will be the baggage train. The enemy still has a large force of cavalry. I don't want your men engaging them, or they'll get cut up like at Kunaksa. Leave the horse to the spears. Clear?" Rictus nodded. He and Aristos looked at one another for a second. Jason saw the hatred between them, and wondered if he were being a naïve fool, making them work together. Even men who loathed each other sometimes found the unlikeliest of likings developing on the battlefield. He hoped it might be so.

"The main body will deploy on this hill south of the road," Jason went on. "My mora will be on the extreme left, next to the road. Mochran, you will be the right-most mora. Watch your flank; there's nothing beyond your right but grass and stones. Every mora is to keep one full centon to the rear of its line, as a reserve. No one breaks rank without orders, not even if their entire army turns and runs. Don't forget their cavalry. We lose formation, and they'll hunt us down one by one. Tonight we sleep in camp, everyone eats a good meal, and we sleep like babies. In the morning we take up our positions, wait for the Kufr to come to us, and with luck they'll soon be crying like babies." There was a rustle of laughter, an echo of fellowship.

"If the line breaks," Jason went on, "then we reform it. We plug the holes, and we stand on these stones and fight until the day is won, or we are all dead. There is nowhere to run to. Any questions?"

"Who looks after the baggage?" Rictus asked.

"I've culled two centons from the front-line morai, lightly wounded, footsore, and chronic shitters. They'll stay with the wagons."

"And the gold," big Gominos said, grinning.

They stood looking at one another, until Aristos said, roughly; "Let's get the damn thing done then," and the group of men broke up. Jason remained on the hilltop as they walked down the slope to their waiting morai. Even now, they separated into two distinct groups which seemed to take form around Aristos and Rictus. Once the spearheads were levelled, he prayed they would come together.

TWENTY-TWO
THE LAST OF THE WINE

Mid-morning brought the army in sight of the hills before Irunshahr. On the ridge-line before the city Vorus finally found his quarry standing at bay, a line of heavy infantry over a pasang long, their ranks undulating about every outcrop of weather-beaten stone to the south of the Imperial Road. Here, then, was where it would end.

He reined in, the placid mare chewing at the bit under him, throwing up her head as if she, too, could smell what was on the wind. He turned to Proxis. "We have them."

"So we have," Proxis said. He had been drinking, but his eyes were clear. "My legions are in the van—we'll take up the left, and then the rest can file in to our right."

"Very well. I'll send the cavalry out that way, and see if we can feel round their flank. The gods go with you, Proxis." Vorus extended his hand.

The Juthan leaned over in the saddle and took it in the warrior-grip, fingers curled round Vorus's wrist. "May they watch over us both," he said.

Noon came and went. Up on the hillside the lines of Macht infantry relaxed, eating their midday meal in shifts, barley bannock and cheese and the last of the wine. Below them the Kufr marched and counter-marched, their officers chivvying the tired troops along, the regiments fed into the line as they came up the Imperial Road. When at last they were in place it was mid-afternoon, and for a while the two armies stared at one another as in between them the bees clustered about the heather and the scrub juniper, and skylarks sang above their heads, heedless of anything but the warmth of the sun and the clear infinity of blue sky about them.

It reminded Vorus of his youth, late spring in the hills about Machran when at long last the snows eased their grip on the northern world. It had been a long time since he had breathed upland air and smelled gorse-blossom on the breeze. As he sat his horse to the rear of the Kufr centre, he felt a moment of pure clarity, a sense of exactly how the world was turning under him. At that moment he wanted to dismiss these soldiers of his to their homes and send word to the Macht that they might march away in peace. What was it, this notion of duty, of loyalty, of Empire, that kept them standing here in their tens of thousands, that would see this lovely summer's day soon broken up into a wilderness of bloody slaughter? What would it gain the world, the mountains, the very stones under their feet, to have these thousands shed their blood upon them?

In the next moment he had the answer. Twenty years of duty, of loyalty, of service. Those were worth something. If a man could not keep hold of those qualities, keep them in sight through all the murderous absurdities of his condition, then he was not much of a man at all.

Vorus turned to the banner-bearer beside him, a tall Kefre with skin of gold. "Signal the advance," he said.

In the Macht baggage camp the wagons were loaded and waiting, and the patient oxen stood flicking their ears at the flies. The Juthan slaves were strapping up the last packs of the mule-train watched by a small skeleton guard of Macht, older men, wounded men, and those for whom the flux had become a debilitating condition which had sucked the flesh off their bones. Tiryn sat atop her wagon and peered east, to where the land rose and the momentary glitter of the Macht spearheads could be seen at the top of the ridge-line. Kunaksa in reverse, she thought. Today, we have the high ground.

And she caught herself, shocked, as she realised who *we* had become in her mind.

Jason had given her a knife, a long, wicked iron blade with a leather-wrapped handle. It felt huge and unwieldy in her fingers, and she disliked it for the smell of someone else's sweat in the leather, the nicks on the blade in which old blood had collected, so wedded to the metal that the iron would have to melt before it was wholly gone. When would this thing start? When would it—

Now—there it was. The roar of many voices from the far side of the hills. Something, at least, had begun. She fingered the edge of the knife. Whatever else happened today, she promised herself, she would be ready for it. She would bury this iron in her own heart before she was tied to another wagon-wheel.

Restless, like a horse that smells fire, Rictus strode up and down the loose-ordered ranks of his mora. The men were shuffling from foot to foot, blowing their noses, twisting the shafts of their javelins in their palms. To stand wholly still was impossible it seemed, at least, if one were not wearing the panoply of a spearman. The men tossed skins of water to and fro, more for something to do than because they were thirsty. There was little talk. When Rictus paused in his pacing, he could hear the men breathing, those hundreds of lungs speeding up their work as the cold white loom of the battle rose through the men's blood. At times like this a man's heart would beat and beat until it seemed almost to be a shadow thudding in the corner of his eyes.

To the left of Rictus's men, a mora of heavy spearmen stood like graven images, helms on, shields resting on the ground before them, propped against their knees. To their front, Aristos was striding up and down in much the same way as Rictus. He had taken off his helm, the better to listen to that mighty surf of sound on the other side of the hill. Even through it, the bees were loud in their endless work among the stones, a peaceful industry which knew nothing of the murderous chaos to come. It was a day to take apples and cheese and wine and a sweetheart, and find a sun-warmed hollow in the shelter of the stones, there to eat and drink and make love and stare up at the hovering skylarks above, and count the passing clouds.

Phobos, Rictus thought, I hate this.

Up near the western crest of the hill, Gasca stood third in the file amid thousands of others. He tilted his head to left and to right, like someone striving to see a cockfight over the shoulders of a crowd. There was stone under his feet, something good and solid to bear him at last. He barely felt the weight of his panoply. This beats slogging up a muddy hill, he thought. This time, let them come up here and try and push us off these stones.

"They're on their way, brothers," the file-leader, big Gratus said. "Kufr to our front, spindly bastards a girl could kick over. Juthan on the right, a big damn crowd of them, and out on the left I see that bastard cavalry of theirs."

"Fuck, I hate cavalry," someone said.

"They won't come up here—too many stones for them to stub their toes on. I hope Aristos and his lot are ready to take on horses, because you mark my words, they're heading out round the flank for the baggage."

"How many of this crowd are there, Gratus?" someone back in the file asked.

"Maybe five times what we have here. Enough to go around, at all events. All right, brothers, here comes Jason. Shields up as he passes."

Jason strode past the front of the phalanx, helm off, nodding to those file-leaders he knew best. As he passed, so the Macht reached down for their shields and slid their arms through the bronze bands in the centre, gripping the strap at the rim.

"Hold fast," Gratus said. "Spears stand until we get the word."

The Paean began, out on the right, and it swelled as the eight thousand men on the hill took it up centon by centon. The Kufr army began to march up the rocky slope towards them, the neat lines of spearmen splintering and reforming, rippling around the larger boulders. To their rear, the archers opened their ranks and began sticking arrows in the ground at their feet, the swifter to pluck them for their bows.

Down the Macht line the centurions bellowed out the order: "Level spears!" The first three ranks of the phalanx brought down their spear-heads and gripped the weapons at shoulder-height. This time, Gasca was one of those who would be shearing the sheep from the start. His aichme thrust out just to the right of Gratus's helm. Behind him, he could sense the men of the rear ranks bracing themselves, jamming their bare feet amid the rocks, seeking purchase for the pushing match to come. He closed his eyes for a second, and saw the terrorised eyes of the Kufr girl at Ab-Mirza. All around him, the noise of the approaching Kufr army rose up, the tramp of their feet, the catcalls and cheers and inchoate screams of them. And then the hissing sound in the air above as the first wave of arrows swooped down and began the day's killing.

The Kufr line was the better part of four pasangs long. Vorus sat his horse in the centre rear, his head turning left and right as he tried to keep track of the various elements in the army. The archers were firing volley after volley now, and the main body of the heavy infantry was well up the hills, about to engage. The Asurian cavalry was out of sight, hidden by the rising ground to the north, but he could still hear the low rumble of the moving horses, even over the clamour near at hand. He meant to outflank the Macht on the right with the cavalry, and on the left with the Juthan Legions. In the centre he simply meant to hold them. He knew now that there were no troops in the Empire who could hope to prevail against the Macht in a stand-up fight, not even the Honai of the Great King. In the centre, he would feed in his troops line by line, and keep the enemy spearmen pinned in place, buying time with their lives. On the flanks, the decision of the day would turn. He had agreed the plan with Proxis the night before.

The Kufr centre made contact with the Macht. They were eye to eye up there, for the Macht were on the upslope. The spearheads of the Macht phalanx jabbed in and out, a long glitter caught in the sun. Before them, the Kufr formation rippled in and out as the front ranks fell, or recoiled, and then lunged forward again. Now the armies were joined together, two fighting dogs with their teeth locked in one another's throats. This was the time.

Vorus turned to one of his couriers. They sat their horses around him like eager children, the tall Niseians stamping under them.

"Go to Proxis. Tell him to move in."

"Yes, general," and the Kefre took off, his mount scattering clods of turf as it went.

Another one came in to replace him, his horse foaming and blown. "General, Archon Tessarnes is south of the Imperial Road with his command. He is in the enemy rear, and means to attack at once."

"Very well. Have yourself some water." Vorus felt a wave of relief flood him. The cavalry were in place. The building of the thing was done. He had set it up and loosed it according to plan. Now it was up to those at the spearheads.

The Asurian cavalry broke into view over the embanked line of the Imperial Road, a shining mass of horsemen two pasangs wide and many ranks deep. They were behind the Macht phalanx, ready to gut it from the rear. They were singing as they came, and the heavy Niseians were surrounded by a fog of their own sweat as the ranks separated out. They came on at the gallop, losing riders here and there whose mounts had tripped on the rough ground, but holding together, a brute mass of muscle and flesh and bone, a gold-flecked tide.

Rictus saw them burst into view and was staggered by their numbers, the momentum they carried with them, the true weapon of all cavalry.

"No," he said aloud. "Oh, no."

They curved in, wheeling like fish in shoal. Before them now was the rear of the Macht phalanx on the rocky hillside ahead. Bad ground for cavalry. But the Asurians seemed not to care. They gave a great triumphant cheer and kept the pace, spreading out and drawing their bright swords. The horses grunted as they hit the slope and powered on.

At last, Aristos's mora was on the move; to his right came Rictus, his men spreading out and already beginning to throw their javelins into the press of horsemen. Rictus sprinted over to Aristos, who was labouring along at a run in front of his men, his helm bobbing on his head.

"Thin out your line! Go in four deep or you'll just get bogged down!" He was ignored.

The heavy mora crashed into the right flank of the horsemen. The Asurians had wheeled several squadrons round to meet their advance, but the movement robbed them of all momentum. They were virtually at a standstill as the spearmen struck. The horses recoiled, staggering backwards, rearing, screaming as the lines of spearheads did their work. Aristos and his mora cut into the Asurians like an arrowhead seeking flesh. But like the arrowhead, their own momentum was burying them. They had engaged perhaps a third of the horsemen. The rest had kept going. Up on the hilltop, the bulk of that cavalry was about to hit home.

Rictus raised his fist. "Hold!" Behind him, his men came to a ragged halt. Javelins were still being thrown over his shoulder. He stopped, eyes wide, and looked around his portion of the battlefield.

Too late. The cavalry had made it to the top of the hill, and had crashed into the rear of the Macht spearmen. Thousands of horsemen. The left-hand portion of the Macht line seemed to simply disappear, engulfed.

Whistler came up beside him, panting. "Oh, *Phobos*," he groaned.

Lower down the hillside, Aristos's mora were embroiled in a bloody, futile contest with perhaps two thousand Asurians. The cavalry had surrounded them. The riders hacked with great courage at the heavily armoured spearmen, whilst underneath them their mounts were slaughtered by the keen aichmes. But Aristos had missed the main body. He was entangled now; he would be fighting there for precious time to come.

"Throw away your javelins," Rictus said. "We use the spear today."

"Last time we took on cavalry we got our arses fucked," one of the men said.

"This time it's we who take them up the arse. Brothers, they're killing us up on that hill. That's Jason's mora there on the left, and they're destroying it. I'll walk up there alone if I have to."

"My arse, alone," Whistler said, and tossed his bundled javelins aside. There was a clatter all around as scores, hundreds of men did the same.

"Lead us, Rictus," someone called out.

They started up the slope at a swift run, short spears in their right hands, peltas on their left arms, fear and hatred blazing out of their eyes.

* * *

Gratus had gone down, and so Gasca was now in the second rank, with Astianos in front of him. His spear had snapped in half, the fore part of it lost in some screaming Kufr's head, so he had reversed it and was now stabbing out with the sauroter, the splintered end of the shaft slicing out slivers of his palm as he thrust it into the faces of the Kufr in the enemy line before him. Under his feet, Gratus had crawled back from the forefront of the fighting, one eye stabbed out from his head so that it flopped on his cheek. He had made it back a little, the spearmen straddling him, protecting him, but then had died. Less spectacularly he had been pierced through the thigh as well, and had bled to death with his comrades fighting around him. Now they were standing on his corpse, their feet shunting it back and forth as they struggled to keep the line intact. His was not the only corpse the Macht spearmen were standing upon, but he had been well-liked, and his death had infuriated his comrades. Before them, the Kufr marched up the hill only to be cut down. Now they were climbing over mounds of their own dead, their heels set in the flesh of their comrades.

There was a shudder from behind, and Gasca was jolted off balance. He fought to stay upright, and before him Astianos was shoved forward. He beat back a Kufr with the bowl of his shield, head-butted another, and stabbed out blindly with his spear. "Easy—easy!" he yelled as he and Astianos fell back into the line.

A horse screamed, right in Gasca's ear it seemed. He half-turned, and as he did the files of men around him broke up, shouting. The whole mass of the formation, which had seemed so locked together a few moments before, was smashed open. The light of the westering sun was cut off by a mass of horsemen careering into the back of the spearmen, knocking them down, hacking at their backs, stabbing them through their napes.

"Rear ranks, face about!" a voice was thundering. It was Buridan, his russet beard trailing below his helm. "Stand fast brothers!"

He had dropped his shield and now hauled a Kufr horseman off his mount. The animal collapsed on him as one of his comrades speared it through the skull. Buridan went down, smashed between the horse and the unforgiving stones. The Macht around him set up a great shout. The Asurians' horses careered and stamped and reared, butting the line into pieces, bowling men off their feet. In the press it was hard to turn round and face this new assault, harder still to bring the long spears into play. The Macht line was splintered into chaos, and dozens of the heavy spearmen were hacked down before they could even bring their weapons to bear.

"Gasca!" Astianos was down. He had turned to see what was afoot behind him and a Kufr spear had taken him in the armpit. He toppled. At once Gasca moved forward, set his shield over the fallen man and jabbed out with the sauroter spike, his head snapping back and forth, trying to see what was going on beyond the confines of the helm-slot. The line was broken, in front as well as rear. He could not see what was happening.

"Astianos!" but Astianos had already been stabbed through and through, and as Gasca crouched there a trio of snarling Kufr thrust their spears at him. He beat off the first, killed the second with a thrust to the throat, but the third caught him in the instant before he could recover, spearing him right through his father's cuirass, the point breaking off in his flesh. He fell sideways, baffled at the turn of things, his feet scrabbling in the stones. Two more spears came down, transfixing him, fastening him to the earth. He squirmed there, his helm coming off, the upland air cooling his face. Confused, he thought for a moment that he was back with his brothers again, up in the high pastures, and they had bested him at some game. Then the last spearhead came down and, feeling the blow, he remembered where he was.

We have them, Vorus thought. It's working.

He had seen the left wing of the Macht army shudder as the Asurians charged them from the rear. They were engulfed now, that fearsome beast of bronze and iron. He watched, more intent than he had ever been in his life before, as the Macht line was chopped to pieces. The cavalry burst through it, hacking bloody gaps in the ranks of the spearmen. In the front the Kufr infantry, emboldened by the sudden apparition of the Asurians, pressed forwards.

Vorus turned to his nearest courier. This one was a *hufsan*, and he was looking up at the ruin of the Macht army like one who has been granted a glimpse of a miracle.

"Go to Archon Distartes. Tell him to send in the reserves—to send in everything."

"Yes, lord." The *hufsan's* teeth were a white flash in his face as he took off, the dun pony's hooves twinkling under him.

The Macht on the right were no longer a line, but bristling knots of infantry, fighting back to back. They could not run, for there was nowhere to run to. They died where they stood, fighting as long as their feet could bear them.

I have beaten them, Vorus thought. He watched the Macht dying up on the hill and knew it to be true. Many of them were now fighting with their swords, their spears shattered or lost. He saw a Cursebearer go down, the black armour standing out in that mass of bronze. And for a second he had to bow his head and choke back a kind of grief.

On the left, the Macht morai were creating a terrible slaughter among the Kufr pushing up the hill. Most likely, they were not even aware of the disaster unfolding on their flank. It was time Proxis moved in to finish it. His legions were standing out on the Macht right flank, facing empty air. Once they wheeled in as the Asurians had done, the Ten Thousand would be no more. That story would be ended at last.

Except that the Juthan were not moving. They stood in rank, all twelve thousand of them, and watched the battle lines struggling on the rocky hillside to their right, as stolid and unmoving as mourners at a funeral.

A chill went down Vorus's spine. Proxis, no, do not do this to me now.

He leaned in the saddle and physically grabbed the courier nearest to him, not taking his eyes off the ranks of the Juthan some pasang and a half away. "You must go to—" He released him again.

"They're moving, General," someone said beside him. "The Juthan are moving off."

"Slow, as always," another of his aides said with the hauteur of the high-caste Kefren.

And yes, they were moving at last. Twelve thousand of them, and with them his friend of twenty years.

"Where are they going?" the aide asked, puzzled, not yet realising.

Twenty years, Vorus thought. What was it to you, Proxis—something to be endured? Maybe that was why you drank, to keep the knowledge that you would one day do this toward the back of your mind.

For the Juthan were marching away, legion by legion. They were leaving the battlefield to turn south, marching in perfect ranks. Vorus saw a figure lead them away, seated on a mule.

"Where are they going?" his aide repeated, wild-eyed.

"They're going home," Vorus said. "Where else?" And you timed it well, Proxis, he thought. You left it until the perfect moment.

He bowed his head, leaning on his horse's neck, smelling the salt sweat of the patient beast under him. I have lived too long, he thought.

"General."

He straightened, looked up the hill at the battle once more, that all-encompassing roar of madness and slaughter which meant nothing to him now. More Macht troops had come up to hammer the Asurians from the rear, light-armed by the look of them. That corner of the battlefield was as confused and murderous as anything at Kunaksa. There, the Arakosan cavalry had been fought to a standstill by skirmishers too. He wondered if it was the same commander. Someone capable, at any rate.

The Kufr centre was collapsing. As the Juthan legions peeled away, abandoning them, so the Macht on that flank began to advance, finally aware of their brethren's plight out on their left. They came down the hillside in a ferocious, perfect line, tramping across the bodies of the dead and the living alike. The Kufr troops could not withstand that torrent of professional fury. They retreated, withdrawing in some order at first, and then casting aside their shields and running without shame. Behind their running backs, the Macht wheeled right, by morai, and moved in on the catastrophe that had overtaken the other half of their army.

Vorus's young Kefren aide was weeping in grief and fury. "General—my lord. We should move. This field is lost."

"Juthan bastards!"

Vorus sat upon his horse and stared up the hill at his own people, whom he had tried to destroy. Around him, the Honai stood uneasily, looking behind them at the pale length of the Imperial Road. On the slope ahead the lightly armed companies of archers were already running, their quivers only half-empty.

There is such a thing, Vorus thought, as a tradition of victory. Perhaps that is what does it.

Proxis, may I be forgiven, I wish you well. Take your people to freedom.

Aloud, he said, "Signal general retreat. We will pull back along the Imperial Road." He grasped the shoulder of his weeping aide. He was not much more than a boy. "Phelos, try and get through to Tessarnes. Tell him to break off, to get away as many of his men as he can."

The Kefre wiped his nose on the back of his gold-skinned hand. "Yes, sir. Where will I find you when I return?"

"Tell Tessarnes to take command, Phelos. I am stepping down. I have failed."

"My lord! General!"

"Go now. And try to stay alive." He clapped the boy on the shoulder. Was I ever that young? he wondered. As Phelos sped off the standard-bearer at Vorus's side was waving his banner to the rear. A formality. The army was already in full retreat.

It is stubbornness, Vorus realised. That is what sets us apart. We Macht will fight on when there is no hope of victory. We are stubborn bastards, worse than mules. It is not even a matter of courage.

He looked up at the chaos on the hill. The Macht morai that had wheeled north were the only intact troops on the field. Everything else was just a mass of struggling men and Kufr and horses, all lines lost, all order destroyed. In some places they were packed together like a crowd in a theatre; in others the masses were opening out in flight, in death, a collapse of the bonds that held armies together. As the Kufr companies streamed down off the hill they left behind a heaped and tangled line of bodies, like seaweed thrown up on a beach by a spring tide. On the left, the Macht had died where they stood, falling in line.

Stubbornness.

Vorus raised a hand and saluted them, his countrymen. Then he turned his horse's head and set off down the Imperial Road to the east, one more fleeing figure in a sea of them.

TWENTY-THREE
COUNTING STONES

The snow had started up again, flying in flurries about the camp and greying out the world. The only colour was in the heart of the campfires, a thousand of them dotted for taenons about the floor of the valley, motes of yellow light with the darkening mountains looming on all sides around them, like titans peering down upon the concerns of ants. No ditch had been dug, and there was no order to the scattered bivouacs. The encampment of the Macht no longer seemed that of an army, but was a disorderly conglomeration of individuals. Most centons stayed together and a few of the morai, but by and large it seemed the higher organisation of the army had been abandoned.

"How is he?" Rictus asked, ducking his head under the flap of the wagon-canopy. The wind was getting up, and though there was not much of a chill in it for those bred to the mountains, it made the leather snap and shudder like a snared bird.

"He's asleep," Tiryn told him. "I got some soup down him this morning, but nothing since. I need more water."

"I'll get it for you." Rictus made to leave, but Tiryn's cold fingers fastened on his wrist. "What is happening out there, Rictus?"

The Iscan's face did not change. "They're talking, still talking."

"Then you should be out there talking with them."

"I have nothing to say."

"Men look to you; many of them. You can't let Aristos have his way."

Rictus stared at her, his eyes the colour of the snow-darkened sky behind him. "I'll get you the water," he repeated, and was gone.

Tiryn tied down the canopy once more, and inside the wagon there was only the flickering glow of a single clay lamp. Beside it, wrapped in his red cloak and every other blanket that Tiryn possessed, lay Jason.

She smoothed the dark hair away from his forehead. The sound of his breathing filled the wagon, a harsh, stertorous battle of sound. A spearhead had gone in over the lip of his cuirass, just at the collarbone, and had angled down into the lung.

The breathing paused a second. Jason opened his eyes. His voice was a zephyr. She had to lean close to hear. "Rictus was here," he croaked.

"He's fetching water."

Jason licked his cracked lips. "Cold," he said.

"We're in the mountains now, the Irun Gates."

"Cold," he said again, closing his eyes.

She lay full length beside him, tugging him close, sharing what warmth she had. On the other side of his body his cuirass was propped upright, black and ominous. He could not settle without it near him. She hated the very look of it; that untouchable blackness, giving nothing, marked by nothing. It was as though his grave-marker already stood beside him in the back of the wagon, watching him fight for his life with cold indifference.

How many days since the battle? Four, five? Latterly they had all seemed the same. She had watched the Asurian cavalry strike home with unadulterated horror; it had seemed that the battle was lost, and the army destroyed. They had fought through the baggage carts, the Asurians and Aristos's men, whilst Rictus and the light troops had run up the hill to aid the main battle line. She was still not sure how the thing had turned around, but the men were talking of the Juthan deserting the field. They had been saved by the intervention of Antimone herself, many said. As it was, the victory was bitter enough. Over two thousand dead, and hundreds wounded. Tiryn had picked her way up the hill before Irunshahr, stepping in scarlet puddles, on the entrails of men and horses. She had climbed to the hill-crest to find Jason, for he had been on the left, where disaster had fallen. She had never walked upon a battlefield before, had never seen the ground hidden by stark and crawling bodies, Macht and Kefren moaning next to each other, horses screaming and trying to stand on the splintered bones of their legs. She had not known it would be like this, such a concentrated entanglement of lacerated flesh. In the end it was Rictus who found him, who had him borne down to the wagons on a litter made from spears. The only thing that warmed her was their automatic assumption that Jason should be with her. "*Look after him*," Rictus had said, his eyes as cold as the mountains.

With the rout of the Kufr army, the governor of Irunshahr had come to their camp under a green branch, to ask for clemency. He did not know just how badly the army had been hurt, but he could see the last of his hopes disappearing along the Imperial Road to the east in a broken panic. He went on his knees before those blood-slathered, bronze-clad men, and begged for the life of his city. Had he but known, he could have kept his gates closed with impunity. The Macht were in no condition to assault the walls, and did not have the stomach for it either. Rictus and Aristos made a good two-man act, the big Iscan as taciturn as a marble pillar, Aristos as arrogant as a Kefren prince. Thus the army had been supplied, after a fashion.

"Buridan," Jason said. "Where is Buridan?"

"He is dead," Tiryn told him. "Remember?"

Jason's eyes opened. For a moment they were clear, though whatever he was seeing it was not in the gloom of the wagon-bed. He smiled a little, a bitter smile, not looking at her. "Phiron would have done it better. He tells me so." His eyes rolled in his head, "I hear the wings. She is close now." He drifted off again.

The lamp went out, and there was just the dark in the wagon, the rasp of Jason's breathing, the thumping of her own heart. Outside, the wind hurled itself up and down the valley. Here, in the Korash, summer had not yet been thought of. Even spring was a starveling urchin of a thing, barely enough to set the grass growing. Tiryn's Juthan slave, Ushdun, had run off along with the rest of her fellows in the aftermath of the battle. Somehow they had known about the Juthan betrayal, and somehow they had known the perfect moment to escape, when all was in chaos and the fighting just ended. Tiryn had brought Jason back to her wagon to find it ransacked. The Macht walking wounded who had been set to look over the Juthan had instead joined the fight against the Asurians. There were no more slaves with the army. She was, Tiryn realised, the only Kufr in the camp. The thought startled her.

No matter. She drew Jason closer to her. His flesh was hot to the touch, and sweat was streaming down his face, but he was shivering convulsively.

I do not know why it is so, she thought, but I esteem this man, this Macht, this barbarian. It may even be that I love him. Rictus knew that. It may be he saw it before I did.

They had gathered in an open space between the fires of the centons, and there had piled up the carcass of a broken wagon and set it on fire. Around this blaze there now gathered several thousand men. The evening was setting in, and the firelight grew brighter as the light fell. The

Macht had come to debate on their predicament, to thrash out things in Assembly, as their race had been wont to do since the end of the Kings, far back in the mythical past. Most of the Kerusia were present, wrapped in their scarlet cloaks like the rest of the men, but wearing the Curse of God beneath as a kind of badge. Their numbers were fewer. Jason was wounded and Grast had died at Irunshahr, close by him in the line. Mynon had been kicked by a horse and now wore his broken arm in a sling, but his black eyes were bright as ever. Old Mochran, the last of the elder leaders, stood a little apart from the rest, wrapped in his cloak, his peppery beard sunk on his chest. He had saved the day, wheeling the right-hand morai inwards on his own initiative, trusting that the Juthan desertion was not a ruse. Had it not been for him, the army would most likely have been destroyed at Irunshahr. The knowledge made a little space around him at the bonfire. He stared into the flames, perhaps remembering the pyres on which they had burned the bodies of two thousand comrades. They had been three days at it, and the reek had soiled the air for pasangs around.

The men stood in silent crowds, ready to listen. They were tired and disheartened as they had not been after Kunaksa. They realised now that the thing was almost done. Fourteen thousand of them had taken ship with Phiron the year before. Of those, almost half were gone. They had marched more than three thousand pasangs, and had beaten every army brought against them, but now they felt that their luck was running out. They had had enough. Now all of them wanted to get home by the quickest route, to get over the mountains and march to the shores of the sea. They did not care if they were paupers when they got there; all that they valued now were the lives they lived.

Haukos has left us, Rictus realised, as he stood with the other generals amid the currents of talk. *Hope has gone. We are no longer unbeatable.*

And he bowed his head. *Gasca, you are well out of this.*

"We should have stayed at Irunshahr," big Gominos was saying, as truculent as he was ugly. He reminded Rictus a little of Orsos, but Orsos had been a fine leader of men as well as a rapacious boor. "We could have taken our ease there, had slaves, refitted and rested—"

"We cleared that city out of every bean and husk it had," Mynon said. "If we'd stayed there, we'd be starving in a week."

"Starving with a roof over our heads," Gominos retorted.

"The Great King has more than one army," Mochran growled. "We stop moving and we die, simple as that. At least here in the mountains we're less easy to find."

"So we're running headlong now after beating his best? Is that it?"

Rictus's voice, though quiet, cut through the rising quarrel. "Mynon, how do we stand?"

A bird with a broken wing, Mynon set his head on one side. Jason had done the same on occasion; it warranted a kind of detachment. "One week, at full ration. But that's for the men alone. Fodder for the draught animals is not to be had, not up here. They'll start dying soon, and then we'll be pulling the wagons ourselves."

"We've done that before. We'll hitch the mules to the wagons, and eat the oxen." Rictus paused. "There are fewer of us now, anyway. Fewer mouths."

Silence fell. The bonfire crackled and rushed, a soft roar in the blue gathering dark. Around the light of the flames the crowds of men drew closer, as if they could hear what was being said better in the light. Rictus saw Whistler there, and old Demotes from the Dogsheads. How many of them were left now, he wondered. Those nights in the Marshalling Yards of Machran seemed like a different world, and the boy he had been back then was someone else. Rictus raised his hand and touched two things which hung at his throat: Zori's coral pendant and the tooth of a wolf, clicking together under his fingers. Small things, to hold such a cache of memories.

Aristos stepped forward to warm his hands at the flames. "We're fewer now, it's been said. I would go farther. I would say we are not an army any more. We have not been since Kunaksa. Phiron knew how to lead us, and he did it well. When he died, Jason took his place, and he was an obvious choice. He was a good man. But he did not have the skills of Phiron. That is why at Irunshahr, so many of us died."

Rictus stepped forward, eyes blazing. "Is that why? Search your heart, Aristos. Is that really why?"

"Let me speak, Rictus." Aristos held up a hand, as regretful and reasonable as one could wish. Out of the assembled men, voices cried: "Let him speak!" The chorus grew. "Let him have a say. Fair's fair, strawhead."

Rictus stepped back. He was unarmed, as were they all, but one did not need weapons in the Assembly to fight one's battles. Words were better and he was not good with them, never had been. Jason was the man for that.

"I have seen a map of the Empire. Brothers, we are in the Korash Mountains. They are not so high as the Magron, but they are further north, and much colder. This valley we have been marching in, it runs all the way through them to the open lands of Askanon and Gansakr beyond. The mountains are some two hundred pasangs from east to west. Once we are through them the way is open to the sea, good marching country with cities on every side. And not the fortress cities of the Middle Empire, but smaller, many of them unwalled. Brothers, once we are beyond the mountains, it is a two week march to the sea. Two weeks."

A ragged shout went up at this, and men turned to their neighbours, grinning and striking one another on the bicep. They had not dreamed it could be so close, the end of the illimitable Empire. Aristos looked at Rictus, and their eyes met. He knew exactly what he was doing. He raised a hand to still the hubbub.

"Brothers, hear me out. For months now, we have been marching at the pace of the Kufr, held back first by their troops, our so-called allies, and then by the whole impedimenta of warfare as they fight it. These wagons we haul along in our midst—when we fought as centons in the

Harukush, which of us had a wagon to carry his baggage for him? Perhaps it made sense in the heat of the lowlands, but we are marching back into our own kind of country now, back to where the seasons are things we know. A cart for the centos, mules for the field-forge—what else did we need? We have been trained by the Kufr to walk at their pace. Brothers, we must strike out again at our own. We must leave all this behind and become again the men we once were. We must strike out at that pace. If we do, I promise you, we shall look once again on the shores of the sea within a month. What say you?"

"I say he talks too fucking much," Mochran said to Rictus out of the corner of his mouth. But it was no matter. The men were cheering Aristos to the echo. He was offering them hope, a way ahead, something to batten onto, and their cheers were an outpouring of relief.

"I will not serve under him," Rictus said.

"You must, lad. I believe he's about to call an election. With Jason out of the way, he'll swing the vote in the Kerusia. If you want to make the thing go otherwise, you'd best get up on your hind legs and do a little talking yourself."

"You'll vote for me?"

"So will Phinero and Mynon, I'm sure. Talk, Rictus. These men at the front of the crowd have been planted here; I see scores from Aristos's own mora. Start flapping your fucking mouth, or this son of a bitch is going to be leading us."

"I might not be any better,"

"Horse's shit. From what I hear, you're one of the best men in the fucking army."

That brought Rictus up short. He had not expected it; he even felt a kind of resentment. I didn't set out to do this, he thought. All I wanted—

All I wanted was to die facing an enemy. To have a good death.

And here he was, when so many better than him were burnt to ashes. He bent his head a second, remembering them, the dead whom he had loved. Of its own volition, his hand came up and touched the talismans which hung at his neck.

"Rictus—" Mochran said.

"He's going to take the fleetest and leave the rest. He's out for himself." And he's the reason Gasca died, Rictus added to himself. It might not be true, but it felt right to think it.

He stepped back into the light of the blazing wagon-carcass, a big man with a shock of straw-coloured hair and eyes that caught the light like some reflection of Phobos's moon.

"I am Rictus. The map which Aristos here is talking of belongs to Jason of Ferai, who commands this army. He came into possession of it after the death of Phiron. Phiron commanded us once, as you may remember. He took us to victory at Kunaksa. When he was murdered, Jason brought us through it. He led us all the way across the Middle Empire, to a place where home does not seem so far away. He brought us here together, and behind us we left only our dead.

"Aristos is right about the distance to the sea, but he is wrong about the time it will take to get there. We have wounded in the wagons who cannot be left behind. If we must travel faster than a wagon, then we must abandon our wounded. We are Macht. This is not something we do, or have ever done. I will not do it. Phiron would not have done it. If the army must have a leader while Jason heals, then I shall be that man. And I say that this decision will not be taken by the Kerusia alone, but by the whole army. Let us vote, here and now, every one of us who can lift a stone. Here in these mountains, decide, and let us be done with it."

Mochran took off his cloak and spread it on the ground. "I stand here for Rictus," he cried. There was a moment's pause, and then Gominos did the same, spreading out the fabric of his cloak and tossing a single stone upon it as he straightened. "This, here, is for Aristos."

The crowds of men about the bonfire stood silent for a moment. Beyond the light of the flames they could hear the more ardent souls running through the camp, shouting out the news. Mochran bent, and with careful intent, placed a stone on the faded scarlet fabric of his cloak. "Brothers," he said, "Let us vote on it."

Rictus and Aristos stood with their arms folded, as tradition dictated, while about them the gathered crowds of men pushed closer. The stones tossed onto one cloak and then the other began to clink against each other, and then to pile up. All through the scattered camp the news was spread, and more and more men began to congregate round the dying fire of the burnt wagon, some bringing more timber to keep it alight, some eddying in and out of the firelight, some standing fast once they had cast their stone to watch over the fast-buried scarlet of the two cloaks.

It took until the middle part of the night for the last stone to click down atop the cloaks. Those who were too injured to walk to the piles were carried there. Last of all, there came walking through the assembled crowds of men a tall, veiled shape. Tiryn strode through the firelight in a black robe, only her eyes showing above the veil, and set down a single stone atop Rictus's pile.

"And who are you to be voting here?" Aristos demanded.

"I set this here for Jason," she said calmly. Aristos seemed about to say more, but Gominos and Hephr drew him back. "Enough, Aristos; look at her."

The Macht stood as if thunderstruck by the sight of Tiryn standing all in veiled black before the bonfire, the hem of her robe flapping in the wind. "*Antimone*," someone murmured, and the name went through the assembled men swifter than rumour. Those nearest to her backed away a little. Some made the warding sign against bad luck, joining thumb and forefinger before spitting through it.

"Let's count these things before the sun catches us at it," Mochran said, weary and old-looking. "Gominos, you count for Rictus and I'll count for Aristos. You know the drill."

The click and clatter of the stones through the hands of the two men. Once the pebbles were counted they were tossed into the darkness beyond the firelight. Every time a hundred was reached, both Gominos and Mochran kept that stone and set it aside. It was cold, standing outside the light of the fire, but the Macht wrapped themselves in their scarlet cloaks and remained there, quiet, watching, many following the count with their lips moving.

At last the two cloaks were empty again. Mochran and Gominos lifted them from the ground and raised them up to show there were no more stones upon them, then donned them, shivering. Mynon stepped forward. "Well?"

"Three thousand, six hundred and seventeen," Gominos said, frowning.

Mochran grinned. "Four thousand, two hundred and sixty-three. Brothers, we have a new warleader, Rictus of Isca."

The Macht seemed little interested. It was the middle of the night, and the fires were burning low. The morai began to disperse to their bivouacs. Aristos smiled at Rictus, a bitterness twisting his mouth. "Who'd have thought a strawhead would prove so popular?" Rictus looked at him, but said nothing. He felt nothing but weary, and the realisation of what had just happened was sinking in.

"Come to my wagon," Tiryn said, touching him on the arm. "Jason would be glad of it."

Rictus shook his head. "Tonight I must be here. Some will want to talk to me, and others I must talk to. I will come see him tomorrow."

Tiryn walked away without another word. Tall beyond humanity, clad in black, she did indeed seem a visitation from another world.

"Get some sleep," Mochran said. "The dark hours are not a time to be making decisions. Best left for the morning." He paused, then added,

"Rictus, sleep tonight among your own mora, among men you trust."

"Have we fallen that far, Mochran?"

"Aristos was right; we're not an army any more, not right now. It may be you can change that, but in any case, be careful. Aristos does not take this kind of defeat well. He may try something before morning."

TWENTY-FOUR
THINNING RANKS

The sun rose, a grey light behind the mountains, no more. Snow was drifting down in shifts and shreds, whirling in flecks and flocks about the encampments, settling on men's eyelashes and in their beards as they lay shivering in half-sleep beside the butt-end of smouldering logs. In the baggage lines, the oxen and mules stood apathetic and head-down.

"How much of a head start does he have?" Rictus asked, rubbing grime out of his eyes.

"They were in at the baggage well before dawn," Mynon told him. "So I hear at any rate. They took a dozen mule-carts, no more."

"Travelling light," Mochran said, then bent over to cough and hawk and spit a green gobbet out onto the ground. "He's had two turns' march perhaps, and no wagons or wounded to slow him down."

"Why did no one tell me?" Rictus was bright-eyed with anger now.

"The men let him go. What were they going to do, start fighting in the camp, kill their own?"

"Just him and Gominos, then."

"Yes, and we're well rid of them," Mochran snapped. "They left the gold, which is something—too heavy for them, I suppose. But they took more than enough supplies to get them through the mountains."

"They left the rest of us short, then."

Mynon sighed, cradling his injured arm under his cloak. "Yes, they did."

Rictus peered west, along the winding valleys and looming white-tipped mountains. Two whole morai, some seventeen hundred men, had left camp in the middle of the night and no one had seen fit to wake the new warleader, that young fool who had thought he could lead them.

"If we're not an army, then what are we?" he said. Mynon and Mochran looked at him glumly.

"All right. Pack up. We'd best get on the road ourselves and make some distance today."

"You think the Kufr are still after us?" Mochran asked. He looked back east, but the air was a veil of blowing snow and there was nothing to see.

"I think they are."

"If the Juthan are up in arms against them, maybe they've enough in their pot to go around," Mynon said, rasping his fingers through his beard. It was coming out black and silver.

"Maybe. We'll keep a rearguard all the same, and march like soldiers."

Mynon walked away with something like a sneer on his face. Mochran stood a moment longer, looking up at the blank sky, the first gleam of the sun vanishing as he watched, swallowed up.

"It's not the Kufr we have to worry about now, Rictus. It's these mountains."

They made only a few pasangs before the snow thickened and the wind picked up to howl about the surrounding peaks. Phinero's mora, at the front of the column, broke track for the rest, stamping through the deepening snow using their spears as staffs and sending the more swift-footed among them forward to make sure of the way ahead. Now and then they came across evidence of Aristos's passage before them: a discarded pair of sandals, turds by the wayside. But soon the snow covered these and any other signs there might have been, and the main column of the army marched in a world of its own, a world defined by the whirling snow, the grey-glimpsed flanks of the rocky valley ahead, the labouring back of the man in front, muffled to the eyes.

The men fell out in the middle of the day to eat hard bread and stale cheese. Many of them cut strips off the hems of their cloaks and bound up their numb feet with them, others using emptied grain sacks from the baggage train. They were not equipped for cold weather, but they were Macht and were used to the mountains, familiar with the sleep of a man who was overtaken by the cold, and with the white hardness of frozen flesh that must be thawed before it turned black.

It had been a long time, however, since they had felt the bite of frost on their faces, or marched through snow; it seemed like a re-education in a past life to them. The deserts of Artaka, the steaming lowlands of Pleninash, seemed now like a brilliantly coloured dream half-remembered before waking. The snowstorms that raged about their faces, the half-felt loom of the encroaching mountains: these were reality. They were all that had ever been real.

That night, forage though they might across the lower slopes of the mountains and across the twisted valleys and re-entrants with their foaming white rivers, they could not gather up enough firewood to do more than heat their evening meal. The men gathered around the communal centoi with the snow plastering their backs, and took turns coming up to the heat to thaw out their feet and hands, the firelight playing on their peeling faces. They cupped the stew-bowls in their hands to savour the warmth before gulping down the thin broth within, clenching their teeth on their shivers and exchanging catcalls and insults with their comrades. Then they went to their bivouacs, laid their blankets on the snow, and lay belly to back in long rows with their heads covered, their frozen feet drawn up under the ragged hems of their cloaks.

Five days went by in this manner, the snow never quite thick enough to warrant a halt in their march, but never letting up enough to glimpse the sun. They climbed higher into the mountains and began to feel the air thinning about them as the earth under their feet rose to meet the sky. Only at night did the cloud clear somewhat, and the men lying there in the drifts could look up past the grey frame of their own breath to see the stars blaze out white and pitiless, as bright as they had ever been in the high places of the Harukush, Gaenion's Pointer showing the way home lay. In the morning they would have to break themselves out of their brittle blankets like men smashing glass, their beards frosted white so that they were an army of old men. When the first of the wounded died, they would have burned them with their dwindling store of firewood, but Rictus forbade it. The dead were buried under cairns of stone instead, the wood saved to keep life in the living.

Just over six thousand men laboured like this through the high passes of the Korash Mountains, in the eleventh year of the reign of the Great King Ashurnan, in the year of the Juthan Rebellion, the year after the death of the pretender Arkamenes at the Battle of Kunaksa. The Macht army, which had shaken the Asurian Empire to its foundation, disappeared into the rocky roof of the world as though it had never been. But its passage did not go unremarked; in the snow-covered hollows of the mountains, there were watchers who noted its progress.

Rictus brought a hot jar of army stew to Tiryn's wagon every night, usually accompanied by Whistler and one or two others from his old centon. Whistler had been a teamster in a former life, and now had taken it upon himself to see to Tiryn's wagon and the poor beasts that drew it, rubbing them down every evening and checking the vehicle for the day's wear and tear. When the wagons broke down, throwing a wheel or cracking an axle, they were at once hacked up for firewood, for there was no decent timber to repair them, and the field-forges could not be got hot enough to work the iron wheel-rims and yoke-fittings. The army's wake was a littered trail of abandoned gear, and many of the men had thrown away their shields to ease their travels.

Some oil yet remained to light Tiryn's sole lamp. Rictus produced the earthenware jar from under his cloak. Too hot to touch when he had first taken it, the clay was now only lukewarm. Tiryn spooned the stew into a pair of bowls. Jason was sitting up now, and though his face was white and wasted, his eyes were clear. The fever that had consumed him was broken at last, having feasted on his flesh since the Irunshahr battle. Rictus could have made thumb and fore-finger meet around his once brawny forearm. As Jason spooned stew into his mouth, the utensil shook in his hand as if even that were too much for his stripped muscles. He saw the look in Rictus's eyes and grinned, his face momentarily becoming a hairy skull.

"Don't you be wearing that long face for me. I'm alive, aren't I?"

"I thank the gods you are."

"Thank Tiryn. Without her I'd be buried under a pile of rocks in our rear." His free hand went out and clenched the Kufr woman's fingers. Tiryn smiled. She was beautiful. Rictus wondered why he had never noticed it before. For a second he envied Jason that look in her eyes. No woman had ever looked at him in such a way.

"You are a lucky man, Jason."

"I've been luckier," Jason told him, around a mouthful of stew. "Phobos! Are we down to mule already?"

"When the animals die, we carve them up at once. I'm trying to save the beans until there's nothing else."

"How goes our merry march, lad? Longer than expected, I take it."

"The weather has slowed us down, and there are so many westward-heading valleys that it takes time for the scouts to let us know which ones are not dead-ends. We're feeling our way forward pace by pace."

"And meanwhile, our old friend starvation marches alongside us. How are the stores?"

"Aristos took more than his share when he left. The army has been on half-rations for days now. As things go, we'll be all out in three more days. After that, it's just the pack animals, and whatever we can grub out of the ground. No one has seen a lick of game since we got high up, not so much as a bird. This is a desert, Jason."

"We'll march hungry," Jason said, shrugging his bony shoulders. "It's been done before."

"We'll march hungry," Rictus agreed, tonelessly.

Jason watched him by the low flicker of the lamplight, his bowl forgotten in his lap. "Not much fun, is it, Rictus, that lonely space above the snowline?"

"It's not something I've ever wanted."

"And yet I hear you are good at it. Mynon and Mochran have been to visit. Between them they've forty years on you, and yet they're happy as fresh fish to leave the decisions your way."

Rictus did not reply.

"I left you Aristos and his snot-nosed friends as morai commanders," Jason said. "That is on me. I should have looked harder for leaders."

"What's done is done."

"I hear your friend Gasca died."

"At Irunshahr, yes."

"That, too, was my fault."

"No! It was Aristos. He—"

"It was my fault, Rictus. I am not the strategist Phiron was. Give me a centon or a mora, and I am a happy man. But an army like this—I did not see it. I am sorry."

"These things happen," Rictus said.

"This is your army now. You will lead it home."

"And you?""

Jason stared at Tiryn, and she back at him. "I have what I want, right here. I am done with armies, done with war."

"I—I don't—"

"What was your father's name?"

The question threw Rictus completely. It was a moment before he could reply. "He was called Aritus."

"He must have been a good man, to raise such a son."

* * *

The next morning the snow grew thinner, hard flakes that struck exposed flesh with the heft of sand. The army staggered on through it, the morai bunched up around narrow-waisted gaps in the rocks, stringing out where the ground opened. The Imperial Road had long ago disappeared; the stone-paved companion that had led their feet all the way from Kunaksa had become a wide dirt track with stone waymarkers every pasang, then a mere half-guessed trail, and finally nothing more than a memory buried in snow.

A river crossed their path, a wide, wild, foaming wall of water racing down from the heights above and widening out as it crossed the valley floor. The men waded across it, shouting with the cold, leaning on their spears and manhandling the wagons and carts through the waist-deep torrent. One cart full of wounded hit an unseen stone and tilted over, the mule screaming in its harness as it went with it. Fifty men splashed and waded at once to right it again, but by the time they had done so the dozen wounded inside had been carried off by the roaring water, mere black dots hurtling downstream to be smashed to pieces against the rocks. The army went into camp that night shuddering and soaked, the water freezing their cloaks to the hardness of armour. They stripped off their clothes and rolled naked in the snow, pummelled each other until the blood showed pink under the skin, slapped life back into each other's flesh, and laughed while they did it, still able to see the absurd side of things.

Another morning, and with sunrise the men rising from their bivouacs found that some of their comrades did not rise with them, but lay in their midst stiffened and cold, their faces as peaceful as if they were asleep after a long day's journey. The centurions did a headcount and reported to Rictus, as they did every morning. He received their news with a grim face. Over three dozen men had frozen to death during the night, and many more had woken to find their feet mere useless frozen blocks.

The firewood was ended, and so the men chewed strips of raw mule and oxen. The hearts and livers of the animals were saved for those of the sick and wounded who remained alive, and Rictus authorised an issue of wine, the last of the barrels still remaining. There was enough to give every man a large mouthful, and then the barrels were broken up and the staves loaded onto the wagons to burn later in the day. The army built cairns over its dead, and marched on. Rictus thought that it had been easier to march into battle at Kunaksa.

Four more days passed, and then a shouting at the forefront of the column brought Rictus running up at a shambling lope, a ragged figure bound about with torn strips of cloth and blanketing, his feet wrapped in the scarlet remains of a dead man's cloak. Frostbite glowed in white patches upon the backs of his hands and on his face, but that was no matter. Every man in the army was now so afflicted, and many kept shuffling with the column though their flesh had rotted black upon their limbs.

Young Phinero joined Rictus, still fit and hale. The pair passed Mynon, head down and trudging, and Mochran, snow-blind, being led along by one of his centurions.

Gasping, they made their way to where Whistler and the last of Phiron's Hounds stood on a higher slope overlooking the meanderings of the valley floor. There had been an avalanche here at some time in the past, and all around boulders lay like a god's abandoned playthings, some as big as a good-sized house, split into leaning pieces by the violence of their fall. The wind was bitter here, winnowing the air and raising scuds of snow from the surfaces of the stone. Rictus fought for air. Hunger had stolen his stamina and now a half-pasang run left him panting like an old man. Even the Curse of God felt heavy on his back.

"What do you make of this, Rictus?" Whistler asked. He held up an iron aichme, snapped off the spear-shaft. Beside him, his men were rifling through the snow and exclaiming as they came upon other relics. One slipped and cursed as his feet skidded along the smooth convex face of a shield.

"This is new," Phinero said, tugging his cloak from around his face. "Look, Rictus, a sauroter. They make them like this in Machran. I see the maker's mark. Ferrious of Afteni."

"Keep looking," Rictus said. "Fan out. Whistler, run down and halt the column."

Their feet stumbled over a hoard of weapons and other equipment buried under the snow. Some of the aichmes had blood frozen upon them. They worked their way upslope, until they came upon a rocky knoll set upon the mountain-side, too rounded to be a thing of nature. Rictus began to pull away at the stones which surfaced it, wincing as they sliced into his cold hands.

And there, as he tugged away a rock the size of his head, a face staring out.

"Phobos! Phinero, look here!"

They tugged away more stones, and the men cried out as they discovered other bodies piled up beneath them.

"A burial cairn," Rictus said heavily.

"I know this face—I know this face!" one of the Hounds shouted. "This is Creanus of Gleyr, Gominos's mora."

Rictus and Phinero looked at one another. "There's been a fight here," Phinero said.

"But who were they fighting?"

"They got the best of it, or they wouldn't have stayed around to cover their dead." The bodies were stripped of all clothing, blue and naked save where the deep gashes and bruises of their wounds discoloured the skin. Their mound was taller than Rictus.

"He lost a lot of men," Rictus said. "This was no skirmish. There's two hundred dead in here, or more."

Phinero was staring up at the snow-wrapped heights of the mountains, the wind blowing white banners from their summits. Not so much as a bird stirred in that savage sky. "What in hell did this?"

Rictus began replacing the stones upon the cairn. "When we meet up with Aristos," he grunted, "I'll be sure to ask him."

* * *

That night the scattered bivouacs of the Macht drew together, and for the first time since entering the high mountains they camped like an army, with sentries set out every fifty paces and the baggage in the middle of the encampment. The big centoi were left on the wagons, for there was nothing to cook in them, nor anything to heat them with. The men lay close together in the darkness, chewing raw mule meat and speculating about the fate of Aristos and Gominos. Around them, the wind roared down the valleys of the Korash, picking up until it sounded like the howl of beasts lost somewhere out in the storm. On its white wings the snow began to come down harder, until a blizzard blanked out the world and the sentries were brought in lest they be lost within it. The snow raged and thrashed in the grip of the wind, fat, soft flakes that built up into drifts and began to bury the shivering men. When morning came there was no light, no dark, no east or west, only the empty shriek of the wind and the mounting snows, a world swallowed up by the fury of the endless mountains.

TWENTY-FIVE
THIS ANCIENT IDEA

When the sun was high, Vorus could stand up and see a single square of blue sky set in the vaulted brickwork of the roof. His cell was small, barely a spear-length to a side, but it soared up in blackened brick curves to come to this point. For a few, magical moments every day, the sun came down through this masoned hole like a ladder of light being lowered for him. He struggled to his feet every time, the shackles cutting into his wrists and ankles, his toes sliding in the sodden straw upon the floor. For that brief mote of time he looked up into the face of mighty Araian each day, and felt as light as the dust dancing in the sunbeam. Then the moment passed and he was in darkness again, awash in his own filth, the iron manacles cutting slivers from his flesh, the rats scuttling in the gloom around him. It seemed as though it had been a long time, this subterranean existence, but it had not been much more than seven days. Or eight—or ten. He was no longer sure. Perhaps it had been ten years. He was a patient man though, and his mind was clear. Since he had been here the only distractions he faced were the arrival of a bowl through the slot in the door every day and the coming of the sun. He had mused upon his condition with equanimity, knowing that things would come around to him again. He had only to wait, and fill in the blank hours with his thoughts.

After Irunshahr he had ridden south amid the mobs of his fleeing troops, not trying to halt them or bring any organisation out of that chaos. It was no longer his job. He had been four days travelling, subsisting on the scraps in his saddle-bag, following the Imperial Road south and east but remaining clear of it, watching the Empire slowly regain control of the army the Macht had broken. He had stayed one night with an elderly farmer, alone in his turf-walled house with his dog and his plot of corn. The old man had spoken of the end of the world, the fall of the Empire, and Mot coming back to haunt the face of Kuf to set the Great Bull free to trample all the works of the Kefren. Word of the Juthan mutiny had spread fast; now there were rumours of uprisings all over the Middle Empire, the slave-race turning on their ancient masters at last. The Bull let loose.

Word travelled fast along the Imperial Road. At Edom, Vorus had been arrested on the orders of Tessarnes, the Kefre to whom he had turned over the army. He had been thrown in here to contemplate a square foot of sky. After they had manacled him, he had lain down and had perhaps the longest and deepest sleep of his life. It had been a long time since last his mind had truly been at rest.

The lock turned in the door, a sound he had not heard since his arrival. He rose to his feet, naked, his beard matted, lice crawling in his hair, and awaited the new distraction.

Bent almost double, two Honai of the Imperial bodyguard entered the cell one after the other. So bright and bejewelled was their armour that it seemed a little of the sun had returned with them, even down to the golden sheen of their faces under the tall helms. They had naked swords in their hands, and took up station in the corners of the cell without a word.

A third Kefre entered, this one swathed in folds of midnight silk, komis pulled close about his face. Vorus knew the eyes, though. He bowed at once.

"Your majesty, you honour me."

The Great King straightened, and did the same thing Vorus had done upon entering the cell for the first time: he looked up at the square of sky high above. He met Vorus's eyes, his own almost black in the gloom. Nodding, he said, "Leave us," to the guards.

They hesitated, then dumbly did as they were told.

"And pull the door to after you."

The Great King and his general, alone together, stood in the stinking straw while the rats rustled heedless around their feet.

"I could not do otherwise, my friend," Ashurnan said. His voice was thick and raw.

"I know. You are a king, after all."

"You let Proxis go. You knew what he was about."

"I had an idea, yes."

"Why, Vorus—*why*?"

The Macht sank to his haunches in the straw. "Forgive me," he said. "I am getting old, I think." He smiled at the veiled figure which towered over him, as baleful and threatening as could be imagined, except for the real grief in the eyes.

"I wanted to let him choose for himself. I had not the right to compel him."

"You were his superior, his friend. You had every right."

"My lord, I owed Proxis a life. Now I have repaid that debt."

"He has shattered the Empire."

With great gentleness, Vorus said, "He has freed his people."

"He has bought his people a generation of war. The moment I heard, I set the army on the road. Jutha will be subjugated once more. The Empire will be reunited. It will endure."

"It will endure, yes; but perhaps in a different form. My lord, here at the end of my life, I have come to understand that an entire race cannot be enslaved forever."

"Is it only your friend's fate which has brought this thought to your mind, or has the pursuit of your own people changed you? The Vorus my father knew would not say things like this."

"I was younger then. I had not seen quite so much death. And yes, seeing my own people again has changed me. If Proxis had not deserted at Irunshahr, I would have destroyed the Ten

Thousand, and now I am glad that I did not, glad that Proxis took his people home, glad that my people escaped."

"I thought you were loyal. I thought you were my friend."

"I am your friend, Great King. But you and the Empire are not the same."

"They are; they must be. My race, my blood conjured up this ancient idea out of nothing. They ordered the world, quelled all wars, made it safe for the farmer to till his land. They brought peace to millions. What have your Macht done to make them so mighty?"

"They believe in freedom," Vorus said. "And that will never be taken out of them, not by you or any other king who ever wears a crown."

"Freedom! Was that what they were teaching the people of Ab-Mirza? They are barbarians. They have brought war throughout the Empire, and just when you had it in your power to crush them, you failed."

"Yes, I did. And yes, they are barbarians. But they are my people, when all is said and done. I shall die one of them."

There was a pause. Then Ashurnan asked, "Your black armour, where is it? You were not wearing it when you were taken."

"I buried it."

"So no Kufr would ever find it."

"So no Kufr would ever find it."

The Great King's eyes flashed. "A traitor, at the end."

"No lord. A loyal servant, come to the end of his usefulness."

"They want me to burn you alive, here on the battlements of Edom like a common criminal."

Vorus's face stiffened slightly. "So be it."

Ashurnan watched him for a long moment. "I do not think my father would do such a thing, not to his friend."

"Your father would have done whatever he thought necessary, and he would have regretted the necessity later, in private. But he would have done it."

Ashurnan reached under his robe and produced a long-bladed knife. He tossed it onto the floor before Vorus with a dull clang. "I am not my father," he said simply.

Vorus stared at the knife. Tears welled up in his eyes. He looked at Ashurnan and smiled. "Thank you, my lord," he whispered.

The Great King bowed deep before his servant, then snapped, "Guards!"

The door scraped open again behind him.

"Goodbye, Vorus."

The Macht general bowed wordlessly and Ashurnan left the cell, the door grating shut behind him, the key turning in the lock.

Vorus picked up the knife, tested the edge. He looked up one last time at the square of blue sky high above his head.

"Proxis," he said, "I wish you well."

Then he thrust the keen point of the weapon deep, deep into his heart.

TWENTY-SIX
GRAPES AND APPLES

Tiryn raised her head, listening. The wind had dropped a little, she thought. After three days of hearing it shriek in the same monotonous note, she was sure of it. Something else, though—something different over the wind.

Jason grasped her hand. She saw his eyes glitter, awake at once. "You hear that?" he asked.

A man screamed, quite close by, and there was a great animal bellow.

"Phobos!" Jason exclaimed. "Help me up."

"No—stay down. You're not fit to go outside."

"Shut up, woman, and help me."

Shouting all around them now, men casting orders into the storm, metal clashing. Tiryn unloosed the end-flap of the canopy and at once it flew up and flapped madly, scattering snow, beating against the frame. Freezing, snow-thick air struck her face, a physical blow. The blizzard was still upon them, snowflakes hard as gravel, the drifts halfway up the wheels of the wagon. She dropped down into them. Before her men were charging, black against the snow, disappearing and reappearing as the blizzard blasted about them. A line of white mounds close by; those were the mules.

She helped Jason down into the snow. He reached back into the wagon-bed and slid out his spear, leaned on it like an old man. Tiryn took his other arm. "What in hell is going on?" he wondered. "An attack?"

Something huge reared up out of the snow, barely twenty paces from them. It was taller than the spear Jason held. Two lights burned in its head, bright as frost. It opened a red maw and roared at them. They had a brief impression of a huge bulk, white-furred, and then it bowled away through the snow, man-like, bipedal, but using its great arms to gather speed, chopping through the drifts like a wind-driven boat.

"Qaf," Tiryn said. "It is the Qaf. Oh, Bel, be merciful. We must hide, Jason."

"What—and miss all the fun?"

"You can scarcely stand."

The camp was in chaos. In the gaps between curtains of driven snow they saw men coming together in knots and crowds, spears facing outwards. The Qaf came up to these and launched themselves on the spearpoints, white and unreal as ghosts, bellowing like maddened bulls. Tiryn saw one of the Macht picked up and flung thirty feet through the air, another lifted and torn to pieces between two of the giant creatures. Centurions were shouting orders, half heard in the storm. Throngs of men waded through the snow to the wagons to fetch their shields and armour. The Qaf launched into these and scattered them. A wagon was overturned, crashing onto its side. The wheels were ripped off and flung through the air. The roaring of the Qaf hurt the ears.

"Let's find a hole to hide in," Jason said. "These bastards are too big for me."

"Back in the wagon."

"No—out in the snow. Come on, Tiryn." With surprising strength he struggled through the drifts, out from the camp. Tiryn bore half his weight, his spear the other.

"Down—down," he hissed, and they collapsed into the snow. Half a dozen of the great beasts chopped past them. Their eyes were blue, and lit up like winter stars, deep-set in massively built skulls. Wide nostrils in the middle of their faces, not much more than holes, and fanged mouths from which the hot breath issued in smoking clouds. Their white fur was caked in rime and ice, as though this were part of their physiology. They were mere beasts, but they walked upright for the most part, and they had hands like those of men, pink-skinned, black-nailed, and as wide as shovels.

Tiryn and Jason lay in the drift, half-buried, the cold sinking through their layered clothing, smarting the exposed flesh of their faces.

"Are they just beasts, or do they have minds?" Jason asked, shivering.

"They can speak, after a fashion. They keep to themselves, in the high mountains. I heard tell there were some brought all the way to Ashur, but they did not do well in the heat."

The sounds of battle now carried clearly over the wind. Men had congregated together and were fighting back with the long spears. The smaller groups were overwhelmed, but where the Macht could present a united front of bristling aichmes they held their ground, stabbing out at the Qaf with the courage of desperation. The great creatures coursed throughout the camp, killing men who were floundering through the snow to join their comrades, tossing them up into the air as a dog would fling a rat. They killed the surviving draught animals with great blows of their fists, smashed the wagons to matchwood, and stamped the life out of the sick and wounded as they lay helpless in the snow.

Jason and Tiryn crawled into a snowdrift, tunnelling into it like moles and excavating a white cave for themselves. There they lay, spent, their noses touching. Jason smiled at her. "I did not think it would end like this, buried in a snowdrift." His lips were blue.

"It has not yet ended," she said.

"Wake me up when it does," Jason said. He was drifting off. He had stopped shivering. Tiryn drew him close to her, wrapped her limbs around him. The flesh of his face felt like cold wax. "Do not sleep," she said brokenly. "Stay with me, Jason." But there was no reply.

"Hold fast!" Rictus shouted. "Spears up. Forget about the damn shields. Skewer these bastards!"

Hundreds of men had come together now and were fighting in a great circular bristling mass, four and five men deep. About them the Qaf raged like some manifestation of the storm, charging into the spears in ones and twos, sometimes penetrating far enough to grab a man off his feet, more often pierced through and through, bellowing in rage as they died with the spear-points thrust in their eyes. They had no discipline, no fighting system, just the raw fury of animals, and they failed to combine their attacks. Had they done so, the line of Macht would have quickly been overwhelmed. Rictus stood back from the front ranks and watched the Qaf range through the camp beyond. There were not so many of them as he had thought. A few hundred, perhaps. Out in the shifting snow, he could see other formations of the Macht fighting as these were, gathering together shoulder to shoulder and setting their heels in the ground.

Whistler joined him. "They're backing off a little. They're not much more than animals, after all."

"Who's here—any centurions?"

"Dinon, and Navarnus of the Owls."

"All right—you hold here with them. I'm taking a centon forward."

"Rictus—"

"Do as I say."

Rictus gathered up perhaps a hundred men, and these he led forward into the caterwauling fury of the Qaf. They advanced step by step, spears out on all sides, stabbing like men possessed at the monsters that towered over them. One of the Qaf launched itself into their midst, its great weight bowling half a dozen men through the air. The men of the inner ranks drew their knives and swords and fell upon it like vultures, hacking the beast to pieces even as it struggled to regain its feet again.

The Qaf fell back. Across the gutted wreck of the camp, other formations of Macht were following Rictus's example, and moving forward to engage the largest crowds of the enemy. The Macht made of themselves bigger monsters than those they faced, monsters with a hundred heads and a hundred keen spearpoints all in a body, all moving as one. As the Qaf split up, so they became easier to kill, one by one, until some kind of tipping point was reached. A collective howl went up from the beasts. They backed away from the thick formations of spearmen, roaring and spitting hatred. The Macht were able to look up and see them streaming back up the mountainsides, scrabbling up the rock-strewn heights at incredible speed, quadrupeds now, their long arms hauling them forward.

They took the storm with them, it seemed. As the last of them disappeared into the folds and rock-fields of the summits above, so the wind fell, and soon after the snow drifted down in a heavy silence, the thick flakes intent now, it seemed, on burying the dead.

"It's quiet," Jason said. "Am I dead, then?"

"If you are, you're in bad company," Rictus told him.

Jason opened his eyes. Tiryn, as always, Rictus, and Mynon—all looking at him as though he were some form of freak. He was warm. He could smell woodsmoke, feel the heat of flames. He had almost forgotten what it was like.

Then the pain came, flooding his extremities, an exquisite rush of returning sensation. His lips drew back from his teeth. "I heard tell hell was a warm place," he said.

"We'll get you to it, soon enough," Mynon said, grinning.

"You look old, Mynon. Is that grey I see in your beard?"

"No more than is in your own, Jason."

"What happened?" The pictures trickled back into place now. He was alive—he was alive. And the wind had dropped.

"I thought it was time we got out of these mountains," Rictus said. "We're on the road again, making good time, or as good as you can get in this fucking place."

"Ah, Rictus, wake me up when we get to where there are grapes on the vine and apples on the tree."

"I will, Jason, you have my word on that. And it will not be so long now." Rictus tried to smile, but the gesture did not take. He had dried blood on his face, a great brown splash of it. His eyes seemed to look beyond Jason, into some unseeable distance. Mynon's eyes were the same.

When they left, Tiryn propped Jason up beside the fire so that he could look upon its wondrous heat and beyond it, the blinding white mantle of the world, dotted with the black, insignificant dots of moving men, pasangs away.

"What are they up to, so far from camp?" he asked Tiryn irritably.

"They're scouting a way out of the mountains. When the snow lifted, some of those furthest up the hills swore they could see green lands beyond, out to the west."

"How bad was it, Tiryn?"

"I thought you were dead," she said, touching his face.

"No, no, damn it—the army."

"Bad. I saw men weep. The sick, the wounded, they were all slaughtered, and hundreds more died in their blankets, or unarmed. Rictus brought them together. They stood with him and fought the Qaf to a standstill."

"So, another victory, I take it," Jason said, his mouth a bitter line.

"Another cairn. They built it yesterday, and then Rictus moved us on, up the valley. It's warmer—can't you feel it? Even here, spring has come, Jason. I can smell it. In the lowlands, it is full summer. When we leave these mountains, it will not be long before you have your grapes and your apples. I too promise you that."

"I love you," Jason said, not looking at her.

"What?"

"Help me up; don't just stare at me like a pole-axed calf. I want to stand up, to smell this new air of yours."

He was stronger—he felt it in his bones. He was over the worst of it now. His breathing would never be what it was, but he was alive. And he had this woman standing beside him, this fine woman who was not even human. And he did not care a damn.

"When we get clear of the mountains we'll find somewhere, you and I," he said to Tiryn. "Somewhere there is no snow, and there are no armies. A quiet place."

"Grapes and apples," Tiryn said, her arm about his shoulders.

"Hearth and home."

They came down out of the high places at last, a meandering column of ragged, limping men, their beards long and tangled, their faces blackened by wind and cold. They drew in their midst thirty or forty battered carts, taking turns to haul and push them bumping over the rocks. In these were piled shields and helms and the cooking pots they had not cooked with for many days, and in the beds of the carts lay the gold of Tanis, or as much of it as had survived. Knowing it was within the vehicles, the men manhandled them along without complaint. Now that it seemed they might survive after all, it had taken on a new importance.

They marched with their spears in hand. Their armour they had abandoned up in the mountains, except for those among them who wore the Curse of God. As they descended the air grew warm about them, and they cast off the rags they had bound about their bodies, unstrapped the filthy bindings from their feet and marched barefoot, feeling the new grass between their toes. Their eyes glittered, sunken in fleshless faces. Some wept silently as they marched, not believing what they saw.

The land swelled out before them, a green and blue immensity running up to the horizon. Here and there the gleam of a river caught the sun, and there were trees, crops, orchards, and pasture-land with animals moving across it in herds. Nearer at hand a large town or city sprawled in the foothills below, the smoke rising from it in a thousand threads of grey. It was unwalled, the houses built of pale stone, roofed with clay tiles such as the Macht used themselves in the Harukush.

"That is Kumir," Rictus said, pointing. "We'll form up before the city and send an embassy, ask for supplies. This is rich country here, and it's easy going all the way to the sea."

"How much farther to the sea?" Whistler asked, scratching his scarred pate.

"A man marching light could make it in two weeks, I reckon."

"Aristos must be close, by now," Whistler said. "If he's still alive."

"I think he is," Rictus told him. "His kind always are."

He had been here before them, him and Gominos. The town elders came out to talk to Tiryn and Jason and Rictus with several hundred of their young men armed at their backs. They saw on the hill above their settlement a fearsome army, five thousand men or more, all standing in rank with faces lean and hungry as wolves, a rancid smell about them, and filth crusting every facet of their appearance except their spearpoints. These glittered painfully bright in the early summer sun. It was an army of vagabonds, but vagabonds who knew discipline, and were the more frightening for it.

The town's Headman was an old Kefre, his golden skin faded, but his eyes still the startling violet of the Kefren high castes. He came forward leaning on a black staff and flanked by two others scarcely less infirm than he.

"You are Macht," he said in Asurian.

"We are."

"We have seen the likes of you before. Nine days ago your people came through here, a thousand of them. They stole our cattle and looted our farms and slew our folk out of hand. Are you here now to finish what they began?"

"Aristos," Rictus said through clenched teeth.

It was Jason who spoke up in the Headman's own language. "We need food, draught animals, and wagons. Give us those, and I swear we shall harm none of you."

"How can I believe you?"

Tiryn stepped forward, dropping her veil. "You may believe him. These are not like the ones who came before. They are men of honour."

The old Kefre stared at her, both startled and scandalised. "What do you do here, with these animals?" he demanded in Kefren, the language of the kings.

"I am guiding them home. The faster you provide them with what they need, the sooner they shall be gone. They are starving. If you do not give it to them, they will take it."

The Kefre nodded slowly. "So it has always been. The spearpoint cannot be denied. Very well." He paused. "I have heard stories from the south. These then are the Macht who fought the Great King?"

"They are."

"Then we will feed them. But we will curse their names, and rue the very footsteps they must take across our world."

Tiryn nodded. "I know," she said.

* * *

They marched across the green hills and open farmland of Askanon, and upon meeting the Sardask River, they consulted Jason's map and decided to cross it before it broadened in the flatter plains below. The army splashed through it thigh deep, and on the far side they pitched camp and sent out foraging parties. They drew water from the river and set it to boil in the centoi, whilst the herd of livestock that now travelled with them was picked through for the day's meat. The citizens of Kumir had handed over all their draught animals to Aristos, and what was left over in their grain stores after the winter. There had been little enough to spare for the main body of the Macht, but for hungry men it had been enough. For a while at least.

Rictus and Jason stood at the riverbank, watching the water pass by and tossing stones into it like bored children. Both wore the Curse of God. Both were as lean as a man can be and still live. They looked almost of an age now; Rictus had lost the last rags of his youth in the Korash. His face was lined and he had the makings of a beard on his chin, for all his light colouring.

"In the mountains, we passed the line at which rivers choose where to flow," Jason said. "In all our march thus far, they have been flowing from the west to the east, into the lowlands of the Middle Empire. Here, on this side of the high country, they flow east to west. This river ends in the sea, Rictus." He shook his head slightly, and chuckled.

"I was born by the sea," Rictus said. A moment later he added, "I like the sound of it, the smell. I shall be glad to look on it again."

"Ah, it's something to look at, I suppose. But I'll not set sail upon it again, not if I can help it."

Rictus turned, surprised. "You'll have to, if you want to make the crossing to the Harukush."

"There you have me. I've been meaning to say it, and now seems the time. I'll be leaving you very soon, you and the army." Rictus stared at him, mute.

"I've had enough of soldiering, Rictus. I've seen enough death. I've tramped halfway across the world, killing and watching others kill. Most of my friends are dead. I—" He stumbled a little. "I have no sons to carry on my name. I have nothing but this black armour on my back, and the spear-calluses on my hands. It is not much to show for a life."

"You have a name among us whom you have led, and one day soon you will have one among all the Macht. You go home, and you'll be a hero. There's not a city in the Harukush would not empty its treasury to hire the man who led the Ten Thousand back from Kunaksa."

"I am no longer that man."

Rictus looked away. "Is it the woman? Is it Tiryn?"

"It's her, as much as anything else."

"You think you can live here, in the Empire, in peace—a Macht and a Kufr together?"

"The Empire is a big place. I intend that we shall lose ourselves in it. I want that peace, Rictus. I want soil to till, grapes to grow, an old hound to lie scratching itself at my feet."

Rictus shook his head. For a second there flashed through his mind a picture of his father's glen, the farm buildings, the quiet river. "The Great King will hunt you down," he said, not without bitterness.

"I think he may have other things on his mind. From what we've heard, a good portion of the Empire is in chaos. Let him chew his way through that for a while, and he'll forget us."

"You're wrong, Jason. You should stay with us. Come back to the Harukush."

"And you think I could settle there in peace, with a Kufr woman for a wife? I'd sooner take my chances with the Great King's wrath. My mind is made up. Tiryn and I leave the army in the morning. I'm sorry, Rictus."

The Iscan moved away, stared out into the west and the blue distance there with the sun going down behind it. "I wish you luck, then."

Jason set a hand on his shoulder. "You have come a long way from the strawhead I hired in Machran. You were born to lead, Rictus. Your time in the colour is only beginning. You, too, have a name among the Macht now."

"Stay with us a little longer. Look upon the sea with me, Jason, and then take your leave. We'll have a feast to mark your going. I'd not have you leave like a thief in the night." Rictus's voice was thick and raw. He remained staring at the western horizon. Jason shook him slightly.

"Very well. I suppose a new life can wait a few more days."

TWENTY-SEVEN
THE SEA, THE SEA

Past the city of Ashdod the army marched, the Imperial Road unwinding beneath their feet like a carpet spread to speed them home. This was the province of Askanon, which once in the semi-legendary past had been conquered by their forefathers. They had landed in their black galleys at the mouth of the Haneikos River and had issued forth across the Great Continent with an arrogance the world had not seen since. Those ancient armies had marched east to the Korash Mountains, and there the black tide of the Macht had been foiled, beaten back by the overwhelming numbers and valour of the Kufr armies. That defeat had set the fate of the world for millennia, giving rise to an empire and an unbroken line of Kings. Now a Macht army was marching west in the footsteps of their ancestors. They were a mere remnant of what they had been: ill-equipped, half-starved, and ragged as tramps. But they were unbeaten, and word of their deeds had spread out across half the world.

Talking to frightened Kufr peasants in the farms they passed, Tiryn learned that the Juthan had set up a king for themselves, a soldier named Proxis. There were rumours of great battles with the Imperial armies along the Jurid River. And Ancient Artaka was still in revolt, shielded from reprisal by the bulwark of Jutha. All over the Empire, it was said, slaves were rising up against their masters, and chaos was threatening the line of Asur. Perhaps what men whispered around their night-time fires was true: the Empire's day had come and gone. The world was being crafted anew according to some unknown whim of the gods above and below. Mot had destroyed the harvest of Pleninash, and there was hunger in the Land of the Rivers, the most fertile provinces in the entire world. The march of the Ten Thousand had been ordained by God, the Macht the instrument with which he had visited his wrath upon the earth.

"Imaginative fellows," Jason said when Tiryn apprised him of the peasants' stories. "I never thought I would be an instrument of God. Still, it's something to know we've shaken the foundations of a world, the Juthan and us. I always thought those yellow-eyed folk were too quiet."

"It's why they were made slaves, far back in the past. They loved their freedom too much," Tiryn said.

"Then I wish them luck. May they be a thorn in the Empire's side forever."

"You dismiss a world you know little about," Tiryn said quietly.

"I do. I am an ignorant fool. I have walked half the earth with nothing in my heart but the craft of killing. I am changing, though. Be patient, Tiryn. Speak to me now, and tell me new words."

"The word for a plough is *kinshir*. The word for a hoe is *atak*." She paused. "The word for a child is *oba*."

Jason looked at her, and smiled. "Good words. I shall have need of them all one day."

The days passed, and the army came upon signs of Aristos's passage ahead of them. Burnt-out villages, looted farmsteads, smoke on the far horizon. Every time they came to a large town, Tiryn had to speak with the inhabitants and assure them that the main body of the Macht would not behave as these forerunners had done. The men were in no mood for looting at any rate. They took what the folk of the country gave them and moved on, intent now on the way ahead, the end of the road. There were some five and a half thousand of them left alive. The wounded, the sick had all died in the mountains, and those who were left were the hardiest or the luckiest of the fourteen thousand that had taken ship with Phiron the year before. They moved in a compact column not two pasangs long, the single-axled carts hauled along in their midst and clattering on the stones of the Imperial Road. They had no armour left worth speaking of, their shields were piled in the mule-carts, and they marched with their spears to hand like nothing so much as a procession of staff-bearing pilgrims pursuing some crack-brained vision. Most still had their scarlet cloaks; the only badge they bore now. Centons had been amalgamated from half-strength remnants, and the Kerusia had more or less ceased to function. They followed Rictus and Jason, obeying their orders without question—for there were not many orders left to obey. They had only to march, to put one foot in front of the other, to keep their ranks and eat up the pasangs day after day with their eyes fixed on the west.

Whistler commanded the light troops now and took them ahead every morning at dawn to sniff out the way ahead. Seventeen days out from Kumir the army found itself marching up a long incline, a line of high ground dotted with woods and cropland, the earth rising up to bring close the horizon. Rictus and Jason, at the front of the column, saw some of Whistler's men come running back down this hill, sprinting like men who carry news. As they drew closer, it could be seen that these were the youngest and fleetest among the Hounds, mere boys most of them, with hard eyes now wide and bright. They were shouting as they ran, waving their arms as though afraid they would not be seen.

"What is it?" Rictus demanded as one collapsed at his feet, chest heaving. "Geron, isn't it? Take your time."

"The sea!" the boy cried, gulping for air as though the words would choke him. "The sea!"

The words went down the column more quickly than a racing horse. They were repeated. The entire army took them up. Rictus bent over the gasping, grinning, hiccupping boy. "Geron, are you saying—"

The column broke up. Men began running up the long slope ahead. At its top, more of the Lights could be seen now, waving their spears in the air, hallooing down at their comrades. The Macht became a crowd of running men, hundreds, thousands leaving the road to begin running westwards towards the men on the hill ahead. The mule-carts were abandoned. Men tripped up and were knocked aside. Jason and Rictus and Tiryn stood together over the boy Geron as he climbed to his feet. "General, up ahead, you can see it from the hilltop, I swear. You can even smell it on the air."

Mochran and Mynon joined them, jostled and bumped by the tide of men running past. "Is it true?" Mochran demanded. "Boy, I'll brain you if it's not."

"Just a few pasangs, General, I swear by the mother that bore me. Go up the hill and see for yourself."

They looked at one another and finally Jason said, "Well, brothers," and led the way.

At the top of the hill fully two thirds of the army now stood and knelt and embraced each other and wept and shouted thanks to the gods. Rictus felt his heart rising in his throat, beating as fast as if he were going into battle. Beside him, Jason and Tiryn strode hand in hand. The Kufr woman had torn the komis from her head and her dark hair was blowing out like a flag in the wind.

And Rictus smelled it, that salt in that air, that slake of earth. He pushed his way through the raucous crowds on the hilltop and stood at their fore, his knuckles white on the shaft of his spear. So dazzled was he by his tears and the sunlight that for a moment all he could see was a bright blur, a blueness. He blinked his eyes clear, and there it was, all the way to the horizon.

"The sea, the sea," he whispered, the tears streaming down his cheeks. The immensity of it, and on the edge of that vast blueness, the darker shapes of the Harukush Mountains, a mere guess at the end of sight. He bent his head, and the hammering of his heart began to ease. He was thinking of Gasca, of Phiron and Pasion and a dozen others. The faces of the dead filled his heart until he thought it would burst.

Jason set an arm about his shoulders. "I wish you joy of the sight, brother," he said quietly. "I wish you joy."

They camped that night within sound of the breakers, and men left the campfires to splash in the shallows like children and throw up cascades of moonlit spray at one other, laughing. Phobos cast a long glittering path of broken light below him, so that men said he was making a road for them across the waters to the Harukush beyond. He had forgiven them their failings; his brother and his mother had softened his heart. He would let them see home again after all.

Rictus sat by a driftwood fire at the shoreline, his toes buried in sand. He rested his elbows on his knees and stared out at the waters, the vast panoply of the stars above them, the white foam of the waves catching the moonlight. All around him, the Macht had lit their fires up and down the coast and men were talking around the flames as they had not done in a long time. They talked of home, of ships, of Sinon. Some even broached the topic of employment. They talked of the future. It was something they had not cared to raise since Kunaksa. Something in them had come alive again, if only for tonight.

Mynon, Jason, and Mochran joined Rictus at his fire. All of them had left off their armour and reclined in the sand with just their filthy chitons on their backs.

"I never liked the sea, until now," Mynon said, poking at the fire with a wave-worn stick. "I believe I could sit up all night just to stare at it." Unconsciously, he clenched and unclenched the fist of his once-broken arm as he lay there.

"Sinon is up the coast a ways from here, at the end of the Imperial Road," Mochran said gruffly. He rubbed at his eyes; they had been troubling him ever since the mountains.

"Two days' march," Jason told him, "across the Haneikos River."

"At Sinon, we will use the gold to hire ships to take us home, and then whatever is left, we will share out among the men," Rictus said. "Agreed?" They all nodded.

"You think Aristos will be waiting for us there?" Mynon asked. "He's not got the coin to hire ships. His men may well be stranded."

"He can be sitting in hell for all I care," Jason snorted. "What is he to us, now? He can't loot Sinon as he has been these Kufr villages. May he rot there."

"He deserted the colour," Rictus said in a low voice. "The penalty for that is death."

The others stared at him. "You won't keep to that now, not now?" Mynon asked.

"When he left he took food out of our mouths when we needed it most. He could have warned us of the Qaf had he chose, and perhaps saved hundreds of lives. He betrayed us. He must die for it."

The cold, even tone of these words silenced them all. The fire cracked and spat, blue salt-flames hissing out of the driftwood.

"Let it go, Rictus," Jason said at last. "We've come too far to end it by killing our own."

"One man, Jason—it is just one man. When it is done it will be over for me, and not before." Rictus rose and walked away from the firelight, down to the breaking waves of the sea.

TWENTY-EIGHT
THE OTHER SIDE OF THE VEIL

They came upon Sinon in the late afternoon, after tramping through the shallows of the Haneikos River as it foamed and flashed in its broad bed. On the southern bank of the river the Imperial Road ended and on the far side a dirt track took its place, rutted by the wagons of those who carried on the trade between Sinon and the Empire. As the army set its feet on the bare earth of that road, so they left the Asurian Empire at last, and were back in the lands of the Macht. Before them the walls of Sinon reared up mustard-pale in the sunlight, and out from them the great encircling arms of the harbour projected, cradling within them the docks and wharves at which were moored the masts of half a thousand ships, their spars like a forest of spears against the shining water. Built on a hill, the fortress-port reminded them of the cities of the Middle Empire, each perched on its ancient tell.

Before the city walls the army grounded spears and set out its camp for the last time, whilst a steady stream of curious folk trickled out of the city to look at them, and the more enterprising of the traders clustered on the fringes of the camp, setting up makeshift stalls, hawking food, drink, clothing, and the services of women. Here, the Macht looked once more on their own people, not soldiers, but ordinary folk, and women. They had nothing to barter with save the weapons in their hands, and Rictus had to quickly ban the traders from the camp, lest their goods be taken from them by force. After living off the land for so long, the remnants of the Ten Thousand found old habits hard to break. They would have scattered into the city at once, were it not for the gold in the beds of the mule-carts.

This, the generals who were left to the army counted out coin by coin that night, in the midst of the assembled men. It was put to them that some should be held back to hire ships for their return to the Harukush, but this suggestion was howled down. They wanted it all in their hands, now, to do with as they pleased.

So there would be no ships. They would not sail back to the Harukush en masse. The army was no more. They had come back to their own people and were now disbanding, the centons breaking up, some disintegrating entirely, others being formed anew by friendships of the road. They wanted no more to do with generals, or a Kerusia. They wanted the old ways of their mercenary life, where battle was a struggle of a few hundreds here and there, and was fought among their own kind, according to rules they knew and understood. They wanted no more orders from on high. They respected the generals, especially Rictus and Jason. They wished them well, and would be glad to have them lead a centon if they had a mind to, but they would have no more truck with big marching armies, with great campaigns. All this became clear as the men crowded round in their thousands for assembly. Their last assembly.

"They want to go back to their little dunghills and crow upon them," Jason said, standing to one side of the cloaks whereon the gold had been piled. Centurions were now calling the men forward one by one and putting coin in their hands, the men grinning like fools.

Rictus was thinking of the stones that had been piled up on cloaks such as these in the mountains. They had voted for him then in their thousands. Now the process was in reverse. As soon as a man took coin from the cloaks he was free to go, and most that had been paid were already on their way into the city, their pitiful belongings bundled up in their cloaks, the gold like an ember in their hands.

"It's over," he said.

"Did you expect something different?"

"I don't know. Yes, I suppose I did. Something more than this."

"They're the scum of this earth," Jason said with great affection. "They're at their best when times are hard, but give them something to spend, and they'll squander it with all the wisdom of half-witted children. Most of these will be destitute in a month, and ready to try their hand at soldiering again, you mark my words. It's a tale as old as man himself."

Rictus clinked the coins in his palm. They were heavy, stamped on one side with the face of the Great King, and on the other the Kufr god Bel was killing the Great Bull.

"One of those will buy a farm and the tools to farm it, if you have a mind," Jason said lightly.

"That's what you'll do now?"

"That's what I'll do. In my free hours I shall learn how the Kufr speak. I shall perhaps sit down in the evenings and try to write out some of my memories. And I shall try and make children."

"What will they be like, I wonder, those children?" Rictus mused.

"Let us hope they take after their mother in stature, at least," Jason grinned. "I must say goodbye now, Rictus. Tiryn waits for me outside the camp. She's found us a mule from somewhere, and the poor beast is like to fold under the load it's carrying."

"Drink with me, just once," Rictus said quickly. "Come into the city with me, for an hour, no more. Please, Jason."

Jason looked at him, lips pursed. There, just there, was the boy still in him, the earnest look in the eyes, the fear of abandonment.

"All right, then. One drink, to seal our farewells. That's if our comrades have left the city with any to spare."

Sinon was a running hive of humanity, the streets clogged with paid-off mercenaries and those who were trying to relieve them of their pay. The men were running riot through the city, their gold allowing them to satisfy every appetite they had nurtured in the long months of marching and fighting. A scarlet night, lamps lit at every window and doorway, wine running in the gutters, mobs of Macht howling out greetings to one another. They shouted tearful protestations of friendship, bade lugubrious farewell to old comrades, and indulged in not a few brawls as long-held grievances were finally aired. Brightly painted whores helped their drunken clients through the crowds. Men robbed each other at knifepoint, or rifled through the bundles of the incapacitated. They gorged themselves on wine, on the food of the eating houses, on the charms of the prostitutes. They were making up for the hardships, the wounds, the friends buried under cold stone in the mountains or burned on pyres in the heat of the lowlands. They were, as one of them cried, guzzling at Antimone's tits while they could.

"And who's to blame them?" Jason asked. He and Rictus stood at a streetside wine-shop and lifted the deep bowls the owner had filled. "No cheap shit," Jason had told him. "We are Macht generals, leaders of an army. Bring out your best and nothing less."

They clinked the earthenware bowls together. Jason was about to volunteer a toast when Rictus said, "To a new life."

Jason smiled. "To a new life." They drank deep, savouring the taste, the warmth of the good wine as it touched their throats. They emptied the bowls and called for more. The drink brimmed red as blood in the flickering lamplight, whilst up and down the street beside them the pantomime of the night went on. Rictus cocked his head to one side, listening. "It sounds almost like the city is being sacked."

"Na," Jason said equably. "She's not being raped; she's just getting it a little rough, is all. The good city fathers are pissing in their beds, I'll bet, but they'll be glad enough of the gold once their teeth have stopped chattering. The men will spend a city's ransom in the streets tonight. If they want to break some crockery along the way, well, they'll have paid for it, fleeced like sheep by every hard-hearted whore and sharp trader in the place. It's the easiest thing in the world, to part a drunken soldier from his money."

"Perhaps we should do something."

"Like what—make a speech? There's nothing we could do would make them see sense. It's their money. Let them have a night where they don't have to count it, or collect every crumb that falls."

"There is that," Rictus said. The wine was sliding into place behind his eyes; he felt he could speak more easily, make more sense than he had before.

"What will you do now, Rictus? Will you keep to the colour, or have you hefted a spear long enough already?"

Rictus shrugged. "There's nothing for me in the Harukush. My city is gone, my family all dead. You are the closest thing to a brother I have in the world, and you're about to disappear too. I suppose I'll carry a spear. It's all I know."

"Then take my advice. Stay here for now. If you remain in Sinon you'll be able to have the pick of a centon in a matter of days. Right now, there are more mercenaries in this city than in half the Harukush put together, and the best of them at that."

Rictus smiled. "Well, it's something to think on."

They clinked their bowls again, as if they had made a bargain. Used to short commons and plain water, Rictus was quickly becoming drunk. "You know—" he said, leaning closer to Jason.

"Here he is, brothers. The strawhead general. Well, Rictus, how does the night find you?"

It was Aristos, standing hands on hips in the Curse of God. Gominos bulked large beside him, and a group of their men straddled the street to their rear.

"Speak up boy—or are you too drunk?"

Rictus straightened up from the streetside bar. In one moment, all the wine in him burned away, seared to nothing by a white-cold rush through his limbs. His fist fastened on the knife at his belt. Neither he nor Jason were wearing their cuirasses. Rictus had left his with Whistler, and Tiryn had Jason's strapped to her mule.

"Ah, hell," Jason said. "Aristos, the fighting is done with. Have a drink and pluck that spear-shaft from up your arse."

Aristos stepped forward. His face was flushed, his eyes bright; he, too, had been drinking. "I heard tell young Rictus here was going to see me dead," he said. "Did I hear wrong, or was he just yapping?"

Rictus stepped forward but Jason held him back, moved in front of him. "What's on your mind, Aristos?"

"I want my money, Jason. We all do. I brought over a thousand men out of the mountains and they haven't so much as smelled the gold that's due to them. Pay us, and we'll leave you be. We'll call it settled, no hard feelings."

"Pay you for what?" Rictus hissed. "For desertion, for stealing our food, for running away? Come here and I'll pay you myself, in coin you'll understand."

"Shut up," Jason snapped. "Aristos, the money is all gone—we shared it out already. If you want gold, you can talk to any drunk soldier in the city, for they're the ones who have it now. They're paid off, Aristos. The thing is over."

Aristos seemed taken aback. He hesitated a second, the men behind him murmuring. Then he smiled, and drew his sword. "I'll have yours, then."

"Come take mine," Rictus snarled, drawing his knife. "Come and try, you piece of shit." He shoved Jason aside and lunged forward. Aristos did the same. They came together like two stags clashing antlers, each searching for the other's sword-arm with his free hand. The iron of their weapons snicked together and they slashed and side-stepped, then stepped in again, breast to breast. A flurry of blows, clicked aside or dodged. Blood sprang out like a badge along Rictus's collarbone, a long slice. He dashed aside another blow with his knife, the metal screeching. He stabbed, and the point careered harmlessly off Aristos's armour.

"Enough!" Jason bellowed. He elbowed into the fight, thumping Rictus aside, and kicking Aristos in the chest. Both younger men went down on their backs, breathing like sprinters. Jason stood between them. "Enough of this," he said. "Gominos—take your friend here and—"

Up sprang Rictus and Aristos again, their faces flooded with fury, all reasoning gone. They charged each other once more. Jason got between them. For a second he had them at arm's length one on each side of him, and then they had come together again. Jason was knocked sideways. He fell heavily to the beaten earth of the street, and lay there with the lees of the wine running about his legs. He opened his mouth to speak, and then coughed. His feet scrabbled uselessly along the ground. He pulled his hand away from his side and saw the dark shine there. It was spewing out of him. "You've killed me," he said, wide eyed and incredulous, and fell back.

Aristos's men streamed forward, Gominos at their head. Rictus and Aristos stood looking first at each other, and then at Jason, appalled. Rictus tossed his knife to the ground and knelt down beside the prone man. "Jason, *Jason.*"

They stood around him. Rictus clamped his hand to the deep hole in Jason's side. His face was as white as marble.

"Damn you," Jason whispered. "I had a life. Ah, Phobos. Antimone, keep me." His voice trailed away.

"*Tiryn,*" he breathed, almost inaudible. And then he died.

All around them, the clamour of the city went on, the night bright and gaudy and tattered with the celebrations of the Ten Thousand. Aristos and Gominos and their men stood mute, frozen, staring. Rictus closed Jason's eyes, then bent and kissed his forehead.

"You were the best of us," he whispered.

Of its own accord, his hand went out and found the hilt of his knife. He stood up, and when he turned to face the Macht in the street they backed away from the light in his eyes, as men will give space to a mad dog. Three strides he took, the movement a swift flash, and the blade gleamed in the air as he swept it out before him. Aristos dropped his own weapon, startled. His hands scrabbled for his throat, to the great, gouting hole that had opened there. He gargled words through the blood, staggered, went down on his knees. One scarlet hand grasped Rictus's thigh. Then he fell to his side in the street, struggling to stillness in the steaming puddle of blood which was both Jason's and his own. Rictus watched him, and finally tossed the knife onto his body. He looked up at Gominos, at the rest of Aristos's men who stood silent and still before him.

"Now, it's over," he said.

EPILOGUE
THE DEBT

The flames of the pyre were nearly out; that which had burned in the midst of them was now no more than blackened ash. A wind came off the sea and lifted the ash into the air, sending it scattered about the heads of the assembled men like a flock of dark birds.

On the beach stood several hundred spearmen, shields on their shoulders, scarlet cloaks on their backs. Some wore the Curse of God. All had torn their chitons in the grief-mark. As the flames sank, so they began to sing the Paean, the death-song of the Macht, the hymn that had accompanied them into battle so many times. Standing at a slight distance from them were a tall, fair-headed young man and a veiled Kufr woman.

"What will you do now?" Rictus asked.

Tiryn did not look at him. "I don't know. All my thoughts were bent on him. All my hopes. There is nothing else."

"You could go home."

"I have no home. I am between two worlds now." One long-fingered hand came out from under the black robe and touched her belly. "In here, a child is growing whose father was Macht. In which world should he be born: in mine, or in his father's?"

Rictus stared at her. "Jason's child? Did he know?"

"I think perhaps he did. He had talked of a farm, a quiet life." She laughed, and the sound dropped into something like a sob. "Jason, a farmer."

Rictus stared out to sea, to where the dark guess of the mountains loomed at the edge of the world. That was home, that far place. It was home with nothing familiar in it, no man he called a friend, no blood his own.

"Stay with me," he said to Tiryn. "I will look after you."

"You! If it were not for you he would be alive yet!"

"I know. I owe you a debt of blood. I will repay it. Stay by me and I shall be a father to this child of yours and Jason's. He was my friend. He would not want it to come into the world without one." When she said nothing, he added. "Please, let me do this thing."

"What—so you can sleep at night without his ghost to haunt you?"

Rictus hesitated. His jaw worked. "I have no one. I have no family to go back to, no reason to go home. If you would let me, I would have you stay with me, to repay my friend for his death, and to make a new family. To have a new life."

Tiryn looked at him now. They were almost the same height, and he was as fair as she was dark. "A new life?" she said. She touched her stomach again. "This, in here, is a new life. I will bear Jason's child somewhere in the world where there are no Macht, no soldiers, where we can live in peace. I shall tell my child his father was a good man, who travelled with barbarians. Leave me be, Rictus. Go back to your soldiers. It is the only life you will ever know. It is the only thing you are fit for." She walked away.

Rictus watched her go, the files of Macht spearmen making a lane for her to pass. Her mule was hobbled on the hill behind, and upon it Jason's black armour glittered cold in the sun.

GLOSSARY

Aichme: A spearhead, generally of iron but sometimes of bronze. The spearhead is usually some nine inches in length, of which four inches is the blade.

Antimone: The veiled goddess, protector and guardian of the Macht. Exiled from heaven for creating the black Macht armour, she is the goddess of pity, of mercy, and of sadness. Her veil separates life from death.

Antimone's Gift / the Curse of God: Black, indestructible armour given to the Macht in the legendary past by the goddess Antimone, created by the smith-god himself out of woven darkness. There are some five to six thousand sets of this armour extant upon the world of Kuf, and the Macht will fight to the death to prevent it falling into the hands of the Kufr.

Apsos: God of beasts. A shadowy figure in the Macht pantheon, reputed to be a goat-like creature who will avenge the ill-treatment of animals and sometimes transform men into beasts in revenge or as a jest.

Araian: The Sun, wife of Gaenion the Smith.

Archon: A Kufr term for a military officer of high rank, a general of a wing or corps.

Bel: The all-powerful and creative god who looks over the Kufr world. Roughly equivalent to the Macht "God," but gentler and less vindictive.

Carnifex: An army physician.

Centon: Traditionally the number of men who could be fed from a single centos, the large black cauldron mercenaries eat from. It approximates one hundred men.

Chiton: A short-sleeved tunic, open at the throat, reaching to the knee.

Gaenion: The smith-god of the Macht, who created the Curse of God for Antimone, who wrought the stars and much of the fabric of Kuf itself. He is married to Araian, the sun, and his forges are reputed to be upon the summit of Mount Panjaeos in the Harukush.

Goatherder tribes: Less sophisticated Macht who do not dwell in cities but are nomadic hill-people.

They possess no written language, but have a large hoard of oral culture.

Goatmen: Degenerate savages who belong to no city, and live in a state of brutish filth. They wear goatskins by and large, and keep to the higher mountain-country of the Macht lands.

Hell: The far side of the Veil. Not hell in the Christian sense, but an afterlife whose nature is wholly unknowable.

Honai: Traditionally, a Kefren word meaning *finest*. It is a term used to describe the best troops in a King's entourage, not only his bodyguards, but the well-drilled professional soldiers of the Great King's household guard.

Hufsan / Hufsa: Male and female terms for the lower-caste inhabitants of the Empire, traditionally mountain-folk of the Magron, the Adranos, and the Korash. They are smaller and darker than the Kefren, but hardier, more primitive, and less cultured, preferring to preserve their records through storytelling rather than script.

Isca: A Macht city, destroyed by a combination of her neighbours in the year before the Battle of Kunaksa. The men of Isca were semi-professional warriors who trained incessantly for war and had a habit of attacking their neighbours. Legend has it the founder of Isca, Isarion, was a protégé of the god Phobos.

Juthan: The squat, grey-skinned slave-race of the Asurian Empire. They are a stubborn, secretive and hardy folk, and were one of the last peoples to be conquered by the Great Kings.

Kefren: The peoples of the Asurian heartland, who led the resistance to the Macht in the semi-legendary past, and then established an Empire on the back of that achievement. Throughout the Empire they are a favoured race, and have become a caste of rulers and administrators.

Kerusia: In Machtic, the word denotes a council, and is used to designate the leaders of a community. In mercenary circles it can also refer to a gathering of generals, sometimes but not always elected by common consent.

Komis: The linen head-dress worn by the nobility of the Asurian Empire. It can be pulled up around the head so that only the eyes are visible, or can be loosed to reveal the entire face.

Kuf: The world, the earth, the place of life set amid the stars under the gaze of God and his minions.

Kufr: A derogatory Macht term for all the inhabitants of Kuf who are not of their own race.

Mora: A formation of ten centons, or approximately one thousand men.

Mot: The Kufr god of barren soil, and thus of death.

Niseian: A breed of horse from the plains of Niseia, reputedly the best warhorses in the world, and certainly the greatest in stature. Mostly black or bay, and over sixteen hands in height, they are the mounts of Kings and Kefren nobility, and are rarely seen outside the Asurian heartland.

Obol: A coin of small value, made of bronze.

Ostrakr: The tem used for those unfortunates who have no city as their own, either because they have been exiled, their city has been destroyed, or they have taken up with mercenaries.

Othismos: The name given to the heart of hand-to-hand battle, when two bodies of heavy infantry meet.

Paean: A hymn, usually sung upon the occasion of a death. The Macht sing their Paean going into battle, to prepare themselves for their own demise.

Panoply: The name given for a full set of heavy infantry accoutrements, including a helm, a cuirass, a shield, and a spear.

Pasang: One thousand single paces. Historically, one mile is a thousand double-paces of a Roman Legionary, thus a pasang is half a mile.

Phobos and Haukos: The two moons of Kuf. Phobos is the larger and is pale in colour. Haukos is smaller and pink or pale red in colour. Also, the two sons of the goddess Antimone. Phobos is the god of fear, and Haukos the god of hope.

Qaf: A mysterious race native to the mountains of the Korash. They are very tall and broad and seem to be a strange kind of amalgam of Kufr and ape. They are reputed to have their own language, but appear as immensely powerful beasts that haunt the snows of the high passes.

Rimarch: An archaic term for a file-closer, the last man in the eight-man file of a phalanx, and second-in-command of the file itself.

Sauroter: The lizard-sticker. The counterweight to the aichme, at the butt of the spear, generally a four-sided spike somewhat heavier than the spearhead so the spear can be grasped past the middle and still retain its balance. It is used to stick the spear upright in the ground, and also to finish off prone enemies. If the aichme is broken off in combat, the sauroter is often used as a substitute.

Sigils: The letters of the Macht alphabet. Usually, each city adopts one as its badge and has it painted upon the shields of its warriors.

Silverfin, Horrin: Silverfin roughly correspond to a kind of ocean bass, and horrin to mackerel.

Strawhead: A derogatory term used among the Macht for those who hail from the high mountain settlements. These folk tend to be taller and fairer in colouring than the Macht from the lowlands, hence the name.

Taenon: The amount of land required for one man to live and raise a family. It varies according to the country and the soil quality, a taenon in the hills being larger than in the lowlands, but in general it equates to about five acres.

Vorine: A canine predator, midway between a wolf and a jackal in size.

ABOUT THE AUTHOR

Paul Kearney studied at Lincoln College, Oxford where he read Anglo-Saxon, Old Norse, and Middle English and was a keen member of the Mountaineering Society and the Officer Training Corps. He has published several titles including the Sea Beggars series to critical acclaim, being long-listed for the British Fantasy Award.

www.solarisbooks.com UK ISBN: 978-1-84416-651-0 US ISBN: 978-1-84416-588-9

Arch Wizard is the second thrilling adventure in The Falconfar Saga. Having been drawn into a fantasy world of his own creation, Rod Everlar continues his quest to defeat the corruption he has discovered within. He sets off in pursuit of the dark wizard Malraun, only to find that he has raised an army of monsters and mercenaries in order to conquer the world...

SOLARIS FANTASY

JAMES MAXEY
DRAGONFORGE
A NOVEL OF THE DRAGON AGE
"Maxey's world is stunningly imaginative." – Publishers Weekly

SOLARIS FANTASY